*"Stu Phillips' incredibly varied career
has included writing the music for Russ Meyer's
'Beyond the Valley of the Dolls.' I wrote the
screenplay. The story of that movie alone is
worth the price of admission to this book."*

—ROGER EBERT

"Stu Who?"

Forty Years of Navigating the Minefields of the Music Business

by **Stu Phillips**
[Record producer / TV and film composer]

cisum press
A DIVISION OF WRIGHTVIEW PRODUCTIONS, INC.
STUDIO CITY, CALIFORNIA

NOTE: The names Ann (chapter 1), Jane and Cheryl (chapter 2), and Karen O'Hara (chapter 3), are fictitious. The events depicted in the book concerning them, however, are true. S.P.

First printing 2003

ISBN 0-9720363-3-4
LCCN 2002105414

For Dori—my wife, lover and best friend

And to my daughters Toni and Julie

(Now you get to know the real me...)

ACKNOWLEDGEMENTS

To all of the music editors I have ever worked with,
God bless you all.
I still have my sanity thanks to each and every one of you.

To all the music librarians and copyists: I would like to offer my apologies for any rudeness on my part, that might have unfortunately occurred when I was under the pressure of impossible deadlines.

My deep appreciation to Alex Patterson for his encouragement and editing efforts in helping to make this book readable; and to Siouxzan Perry for her able assistance with the photographs. Also a sincere thank-you to Brian Gari for his helpful support.

My gratitude to the following people, who through the years were there for me when I needed their expert help: Judie Castano; Bob Levinson; Al Litrov; Harvey Geller; Jim Barrow; Sid Feller; Ami Hadani; Jean Young; Jan Walner; Joe Polito; Al Schmidt; Randi; Roger Carras; Irwin Pincus; Kathy Rubbicco; Phil, Todd and Stephanie Rodgers; Bud Stone; Gary Winters; David Abell; Don Boyle; Sidney Goldstein; Harker Wade; Ricki; Keith Pierce; Drew Mirisch; Ruth Schaeffer; Van Alexander.

Music was originally discreet, seemly,
simple, masculine and of good morals.
Have not the moderns rendered it
lascivious beyond measure?
—JACOB OF LEIGE 14TH CENTURY

The state of music is quite different from
what it was.
Taste has changed astonishingly,
and accordingly the former style of music
no longer seems to please our ears.
—J.S. BACH 1730

It is better to invent reality, than to copy it.
—G. VERDI, 19TH CENTURY

My advice to those disposed to pursue a career
in the music business
can be summed up in eight little words…

Get **in**…

    Get **lucky**…

        Get **smart**…

            Get **out**.
—S.W. PHILLIPS, 2001

TABLE OF CONTENTS

FOREWORD

IT SEEMS THAT EVERY TIME I give a lecture or an interview, people are so enthralled by many of my experiences in the music and entertainment business and the anecdotes that I recount, that I am often prompted by the question, "Why don't you write a book?" I'm certain that many other people in my position are asked the same question. In my particular case, I have a notion that it's how *eclectic* my career has been that appeals to some of these people.

I don't believe that there are a great number of professionals who have been as equally involved career wise in recordings, film, television and nightclubs as I have. I was very fortunate to attain a small measure of success in each field. Although I do not presume to equate myself to these people, Quincy Jones, Dave Grusin and Nelson Riddle are among a few whose careers have been similarly multifaceted.

I usually try to humbly shrug off comments concerning the writing down of my experiences as polite gestures on behalf of my audience. That is until a few months ago, when I was interviewed extensively at an Internet web site office. I was introduced as *"the most unknown, well-known man in the business."* Hence—Stu Who?

After two hours of relating many, many tales involving my career, and how I managed to survive over 40 years in the music business, I found an eager group craving for more. Once again the phrase "You should write a book," was uttered.

So, fortified with the impression that there really might be some fans that would like to know more about my life and career, I will bravely and innocently charge ahead and reveal things you most likely never needed to know about the business of music. With notes and harmonies I am knowledgeable; words and sentences are a new field for me.

As much as I would like to keep this book of memories strictly to the events concerning my career in the music and entertainment fields, I feel that certain personal events (*amours*) may have inadvertently had an influence on the outcome of my career. To the extent that these are necessary to connect all the events, I will include them. I will, however, try to keep the personal parts of my life rated PG-13.

In the course of recounting and mentioning some of the moments in my life, and the people whose lives I may have touched, and whose lives may have touched me, some of what I write may sometimes sound a trifle self-serving. And describing some of the successes I've been fortunate to achieve may appear, at times, like bragging. Please bear with me, as it is a difficult task for anyone to draw the line between honesty and modesty.

With all of the above in mind, I will do my best to "tell it like it was," and trust that my recollections are reasonably accurate as I guide you through the labyrinth of the music business whereby, the *what, where* and *why*, will eventually reveal the *Who?*

I do sincerely hope that in the course of my ramblings, no persons mentioned would feel offended by what I write. If by chance, you are one of the offended persons, contact me, and I will personally apologize. (Don't bet on it.)

♫   ♫   ♫

THE MOUNT EVEREST OF MY CAREER was conducting the Los Angeles Philharmonic Orchestra in the recording of my musical score to *Battlestar Galactica*. So I will begin my story here, in 1978, then reflect back to the events that made this moment possible.

As I stood on the podium on the scoring stage of Twentieth Century-Fox, about to give the downbeat to between 90 and 100 musicians, I was suddenly overwhelmed with the realization that I was standing on the same spot that at various times had been occupied by Alfred and Lionel Newman, Franz Waxman, John Williams, Jerry Goldsmith and many other great film composers.

I also realized that I was about to conduct an orchestra that had been conducted by the likes of Zubin Mehta and Andre Previn. To further increase the magnitude of the moment, it was now beginning to dawn on me that I might have finally attained one of my long sought-after goals. My career had advanced from playing piano in cocktail bars in the Hollywood of 1951, to…*this*. This moment, I thought, certainly had to be "as good as it gets."

If you are an inquisitive person—which, for the sake of this book, I hope you are—you might wonder what exploits brought me to this personal pinnacle. Well, it was a journey of about 28 years and consisted of so many highs and lows and ups and downs that there were times when my life strongly resembled the route of an elevator.

Without the assistance, friendship and love of numerous people—and an unbelievable amount of *luck*—I could never have achieved this proud position in my career and life.

There are many people who made this moment possible. Wonderful people like my father, who supported me regardless of the obstacles I presented him with; and who always provided for me financially and otherwise; and my brother Lee, who was there for me when I needed him.

There were Sammy Fain's feeble attempts at helping me, which nevertheless did have an impact on my career. There was a short but inspiring meeting early in my career with Morton Gould. And I will be eternally grateful for the guidance and compassion of my clarinet teacher Abram Klotzman, the friendship of Jonie Taps, Tony Owen, Igo Kantor, Glen Larson and last, and without a doubt the *most* important person responsible for any success I've been fortunate to experience, my wife Dori.

My career was at times quite exciting and at other times humorous. It was occasionally ironic, but it could never, ever, be referred to as boring. There were many smart decisions and many not-so-smart decisions. The enormous amount of fortuitous circumstances and little twists of Fate that entered into the equation are staggering.

The following pages of narrative, however, come with a *warning*. You will not find reference to any currently-fashionable topics in entertainment-business biographies. There are no chapters devoted to drug or alcohol rehab. Not a word about mental breakdowns. No wife-abusing or child-beating incidents. No infidelity. No multiple divorces: Just one wife for 44 years. *Can you handle such morality?*

If I have managed to stimulate your interest a bit, then I cordially invite you to read on…

♫   ♫   ♫

From Birth to Twenty

The Ripening Process

EVEN THOUGH THE INITIAL BEGINNINGS of my musical career began in the dark, medieval ages of the late 1940s, I will nevertheless set the story up with some brief—very brief—early childhood remembrances.

My mother passed away two years ago. Though it was a sad day for the family, it was fortunately not a tragedy, as she was 96 years old and left this world with a minimum of suffering. There was no pain from cancer or other debilitating diseases, and she passed away almost in her sleep in 1999. We should all be as fortunate.

The aftermath of an unhappy occurrence like this can quite often trigger many happy and cherished remembrances. As my wife Dori, my brother Lee, my sister in-law Marla and me were cleaning out my mother's apartment, there were many, many old photos and documents that triggered numerous pleasurable memories.

Several weeks later while I was preparing some albums of my mother's old letters and photos—she seemed to have saved everything she ever owned except my baseball cards, which currently could be worth a small fortune—I came across several items that got me reminiscing about some events very early on in my life.

I don't truly remember a great deal of anything about my existence before I was nine. My first distinct recollection, that I can truthfully say is crystal clear in my mind, is the year 1938 when our family moved to Chicago. My brother was a year

Me, my mother and baby brother Lee

old, I was nine and I vividly remember the over-night train-ride from New York City to Chicago.

My father was not traveling with us, for he had left earlier to find an apartment in Chicago, so when my mother became train-sick, it became my responsibility to take care of my baby brother. That necessitated my changing his diapers as well as cleaning up my mother's vomit. Is it any wonder why I remember that trip so well?

Chicago proved to be an ill-advised move for the Phillips' family. My father was not happy with his position there and the family moved back to New York a year later. During the brief time that we lived in Chicago, I remember earning some money selling The Saturday Evening Post and Liberty Magazine at the train station.

On our return to New York City, we settled in a hotel on West End Ave. in mid-town Manhattan. My father's business was not going particularly well and finances were tight. Fortunately, during the next two years his business improved and we moved nearby to an apartment on Broadway.

At the age of twelve, I took my first step towards music. Up to then, my main artistic aptitude seemed to be in the direction of art. My mother used to tell me that I could draw long before I could write my name. Currently, I can still draw better than I can write and modestly say that many people admire my artwork.

To set the following scenario up properly, I must give you a truthful evaluation of myself, by those who knew me. Even though I was 13, everyone concurred that I looked about nine. I had not as yet sprouted height-wise, and was extremely shy. Saying hello to anyone was a major feat for me. But I was cute. (So I was told.)

On this particular occasion, in my last class of the day, a cute girl with long hair—I don't remember the color, or her name, just that her hair was long—was sitting in front of me. I wanted so desperately to become her friend, but was embarrassed to approach her in front of all the other kids. I really was that shy. (To think that it took a 13-year-old female to jump-start my career. There would be others, along the way.)

Near the end of the period, a woman came into the classroom and said that she was going to give piano lessons to any children who might be interested. She said the classes would take place after the last regular school class. The cost of each lesson was 50 cents. When the girl of my dreams raised her hand, instinctively, I immediately raised mine. So did three other kids. This made me a little unhappy as I had hoped that maybe it would be only the two of us.

After two classes all of the students dropped out, including my dream girl—all except me. I peculiarly found myself becoming seriously interested in music and wanted to continue with my piano lessons. The piano teacher offered to teach me at my home (we did have a piano), since the school was not happy about her using the classroom for only one student.

When I informed my parents of my desire to continue taking piano lessons, they were very pleased, but expressed amusement at the lesson fee of 50 cents. My father assured me that we could afford more, and suggested we look for a different teacher. However, I insisted on my teacher, whatever her name was.

(A brief note: My mother had begged me to take piano lessons since I was ten, but I was not the least bit interested. So she locked the piano, supposedly, to keep the dust off.)

After a few months of piano lessons my progress, was at best, average. My ability was nothing too spectacular and it was quite obvious that I didn't possess Horowitz's fingers, or even Eddy Duchin's. But music still captivated me.

The joys of youth.   Vermont 1942

Farmer Stu and
a dog named Duke. 1943

I spent that summer vacationing on a farm in Randolph Center, Vermont. There was a piano in the parlor and that summer I took it upon myself to learn a new piece of music. I had heard a particular piece on the radio, fell in love with it, and decided that I would somehow learn to play it. The fact that the piece was far beyond my mediocre ability didn't seem to faze me one iota. The composition was the *Rachmaninoff C# minor Prelude*, and I proceeded to teach it to myself one bar a day. By the end of the summer I was able to play it—but very badly.

‖: 3 :‖

Still, even playing that difficult piece badly was some sort of an accomplishment.

When the summer was over and I returned to school, I discovered that the High School of Music & Art was holding auditions for the January semester and decided to take the test. My parents thought that I would be taking the audition for art, since, as I mentioned previously, I had always showed a talent in that direction. I surprised them when I said I was going to take the *music* exam.

(Note: The High School of Music & Art was created by Mayor Fiorello LaGuardia in 1936. It's purpose was to give opportunities to students wishing to pursue careers in either music or art, while still receiving the same complete academic training as all the other high schools. Classes at Music & Art ran from 8:30 A.M. to 3:30 P.M. It merged with the High School of Performing Arts about 25 years ago and is now known as The LaGuardia School of Performing Arts, currently located behind Lincoln Center.)

Music & Art High School 1940's

For my audition I played the *Rachmaninoff Prelude*. I could not execute a C major scale of four octaves with two hands, or any other scale for that matter, nor could I properly execute arpeggios, but I could play the *Prelude*.

To make a long story short, I passed the exam and got into Music & Art because of my audacity at even attempting to play this piece. And the fact that the teacher, Mr. Weber, who supervised my audition, felt that with my tenacity and determined dedication to music, I deserved an adequate chance to prove myself.

At Music and Art, I established and did prove myself. I also finally grew to a proper height for my age and became a little less shy, but I still looked nine or ten. In school I studied clarinet and became much more proficient at playing that instrument, then I ever was playing piano. My hands are a trifle too small and my fingers too short to ever be an accomplished pianist. However, they were just the right size for a clarinetist. After almost 59 years, I still do not play the piano as well as I'd like to.

During my time at Music & Art, it was my good fortune to have a wonderful clarinet teacher named Abram Klotzman, who saw much more potential in me than being a pianist or clarinetist. He diligently answered all my musical questions, whether sensible or stupid, with enormous patience, and encouraged me to become proficient in all areas of music. I owe whatever I have accomplished musically in my lifetime to him. He was a wonderful human being, and I feel badly that I never took the opportunity to express to him how much his friendship meant to my career.

The Music Department
YOUNG MEN'S HEBREW ASSOCIATION
Presents

The Centre Symphony Society Orchestra

Angelo A. Consoli
Conductor

Guest Soloist
Stuart Phillips
Clarinetist

Thursday, Nov. 29th, 1945, 8:30 P.M.
KAUFMANN AUDITORIUM, Y.M.H.A.
92d Street and Lexington Avenue, N. Y. City

In 1945, on a cold and snowy Friday evening, I was the featured clarinet soloist with The Centre Symphony Orchestra. I performed the *Mozart Concerto for Clarinet*. It was considered quite an achievement since I had only been studying the clarinet for two years. I received a favorable review from the critics, which greatly pleased Mr. Klotzman and myself.

My parents had always appreciated classical music but were not active in attending concerts. With *my* interest in music growing on a daily basis, their enthusiasm grew right along with mine. My father's fascination increased to such an extent that he decided to sponsor a small symphony orchestra consisting of music students from the New York City area.

My dad at that period of his life was not a wealthy man. You could describe him as financially well off, but he did not have a great deal of extra cash lying around. This was definitely a financial sacrifice on his behalf. The orchestra rehearsed four or five times, with James Yannatos (a classmate), conducting. The *Schubert Unfinished Symphony* was the only piece that we ever rehearsed.

The results were far from encouraging, as it was difficult to round up a full complement of musicians. Nevertheless, we set a goal for ourselves. Our goal was to perform a concert at The New York Times Hall. My father put a $100 deposit down for the rental of the hall, the date of the concert to be determined later. Unfortunately, the orchestra never was able to meet expectations and it eventually was disbanded. I still have the original rental agreement with The Times Hall in my album of memories

I would like to take a moment to tell you about some of my illustrious classmates at Music & Art. Call it bragging if you must, but in reflecting back to those days I now feel honored to have shared my High School days with them.

First there was Cy Coleman. (Known as Seymour Kaufman in his high school days). He of course is famous for having written the musical play *Sweet Charity* and the song "Witchcraft," as well as many other hit musicals and songs.

Also in my class for two terms (until he was unceremoniously kicked out of school for cutting classes and practicing in the bath room), was Stanley Drucker. He is currently the first clarinetist of the New York Philharmonic, and has been for at least 45 years. There was the previously mentioned James Yannatos, who at various times was the conductor of several American Symphony Orchestras. He is currently a professor of music at Radcliffe. Eugene Becker was principal violist with the Metropolitan Opera Orchestra and also played for a time with the New York Philharmonic. Freyda Rothstein (Freyda Simon at that time) was a bassoonist who became a producer of movies for television. We have met several times during the last ten years. Sadly, she passed away in 2001. Roy Eaton, though one class ahead of me, became a good friend. Ten years down the road, he was to hire me to write some commercials.

During my senior year at Music & Art, I was the first-chair clarinetist in the orchestra. Eagerly waiting for me to graduate was my assistant, Harold Lipshitz who would then take over the first chair. You might be more familiar with Harold under his current name, Hal Linden. (He was the star of the TV show *Barney Miller*, and frequently appears on the theatrical stage.)

My summers for the next two years were spent on the Cooley farm in Randolph Center, Vermont. The second and third year I spent there I worked and was actually paid. It was a wonderful time in my early life and I find myself remembering more events that happened to me in Vermont than at many other times in my life. But since these events have nothing to do with my career, I won't bore you with them.

In the early 1980s my wife and I traveled to the farm and I made contact with the Cooley family again. It was for me, personally, a very rewarding trip. There will be more about that trip later on.

At Music & Art during the time that I was first clarinetist in the senior orchestra, we were visited by Leonard Bernstein. It was shortly after his triumphal debut conducting the New York Philharmonic. He led our orchestra at an open rehearsal with an audience present. After putting me through the wringer—making me play the same passage about five or six times—he turned to the audience (standing room only) and said, "You should be proud of him, he's doing a wonderful job." This definitely was a moment that I was to treasure for a long time.

Towards the end of my high school education I applied to The Eastman School Conservatory of Music in Rochester, New York and felt very fortunate when they accepted me. When I was asked by people why I didn't choose The Juilliard School of Music instead of Eastman, my reply was concise and to the point. After 4 years of riding the subway five days a week to Music and Art in upper Manhattan, I was not about to ride the same damn subway five days a week to Juilliard, also located in upper Manhattan. I desperately needed a change.

Unfortunately, graduating from high school in January left me with seven free months before the beginning of the fall semester at Eastman. Through Sammy Fain, a very close family friend, I managed to get an appointment to see Morton Gould, who at that time was my musical idol.

♫   ♫   ♫

Sammy Fain and Morton Gould

SAMMY FAIN WAS ONE OF Tin Pan Alley's greatest songwriters. Among some of his most memorable standards are "I'll Be Seeing You," "Love is a Many–Splendored Thing," "That Old Feeling," "Secret Love" and "April Love." He had multiple Academy Award nominations, and two of his songs won him Oscars.

Sammy Fain and my mother
in the Catskills. 1916

Here they are in 1989. Notice how the pose
hasn't changed in 73 years.

Sammy's name will come up many times in my life, sometimes as a benefactor—sometimes dubiously. Sammy, his brother Harry and my mother spent a great deal of their childhood growing up together. Sammy and Harry Fain were closer to me than most of my relatives, and remained so throughout my life.

Morton Gould[1] was one of the most respected 20th Century composers of classical music, as well as a successful recording artist of popular music. At the time of our meeting he was the conductor and arranger of a radio

---

[1] Morton Gould is best known for his compositions Latin-American Symphonette, Cowboy Rhapsody and Pavanne from his Second Symphonette.

Morton Gould

show called *The Cresta-Blanca Hour*. Morton Gould was one of my musical heroes, along with Dave Rose[2].

Because of Morton Gould's great respect for Sammy Fain, Morton was considerate enough to grant me an audience. It turned out that the only time that he was available to meet with me, was on the day of my graduation from Music & Art. Graduation was at 11 A.M. My appointment with Morton was at nine A.M.

It was cold and gloomy that January day— and to make matters even worse, it was raining. After meeting with Mr. Gould in midtown Manhattan (42nd. St.), I took a cab to Music & Art (upper Manhattan, 137th. St.), arriving about ten minutes after the graduation exercises had begun. With my pants still rolled up to prevent them from getting wet in the rain, I sneaked into my position on the stage and graduated. I'm sure that my mother and father sitting in the audience breathed a sigh of relief when they saw me arrive on the stage.

My interview with Mr. Gould did not go as I had anticipated. I had hoped to take arranging lessons from him. Teaching, it turned out, was not a part of Morton's agenda. He suggested that I go to Eastman as planned and learn all that I could about music. Morton believed that to be a successful arranger a vast general knowledge of all styles of music would be a great asset. He was so right.

Morton then offered to make available to me his entire library of arrangements, for me to examine whenever I wanted. It was a wonderful opportunity, except that I had to study the scores in the library, and could not remove them. However, I took advantage of his generous offer, and for the next five months visited his office several times a week.

When I took up studying the clarinet, Benny Goodman joined Morton Gould and Dave Rose as one of my new musical heroes. I admired his ability to juggle both the jazz and classical music idioms equally: A feat that I also someday hoped to accomplish.

Goodman was appearing at some downtown venue in New York with his jazz sextet. I begged my mother and father to take me to see him, and

---

[2] David Rose was the composer of "Holiday for Strings," "The Stripper" and the music to "Little House on the Prairie."

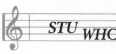

they did. For some reason, that I cannot recall, I had my clarinet with me. When Benny was finished with his first set, I somehow persuaded the guard backstage to allow me in to see Goodman. Maybe I was allowed backstage because I was carrying a clarinet case?

When I shook Mr. Goodman's hand he was less than friendly. Obviously, he disliked greeting fans and patrons. I quickly took a clarinet reed out of my case and asked him to autograph it. He reluctantly signed it and then quickly turned away from me. The encounter was over. I felt a bit embarrassed, but was happy that I got the reed signed so that I could proudly show it to my teacher Mr. Klotzman and the other clarinet players at school.

From January to September was, and still is, a long time. I decided to get a job and earn some college spending money. With Eastman being in Rochester, New York—about a seven-hour drive from New York City—I felt a little extra money might come in handy, so I went to Macy's department store and applied for a job. I was given a choice of stringing tennis racquets (in those days, they were strung by hand) or working in fur storage.

One day of stringing racquets proved to be bad for my fingers and hands. This job was definitely not for pianists or clarinetists. I transferred to fur storage and worked at Macy's until June. Twice a week I would take a long lunch, go to Morton Gould's office and study his scores. I also continued my clarinet lessons, as I had made the decision that clarinet was going to be my major at Eastman.

That summer (I was 17) I worked as a junior counselor at Camp Tioga, in Pennsylvania, and earned some more money for my college fun. My brother was a camper at the same camp.

It was that wonderful summer, at Camp Tioga, that I was introduced to some of the more profound reasons as to why boys dated girls. Up to now, a kiss and a little squeeze seemed to satisfy my teenage urges. At Tioga, I went about as far as a guy can go without actually engaging in sex. I also became a bit less shy, and by now I could almost pass for 14. Hallelujah!

♪   ♪   ♪

Eastman School of Music

I WILL BRIEFLY SLIDE OVER my experience in college, for scholastically it was rather uneventful. Succinctly, my two plus years at Eastman was a bit of a disappointment musically, but a revelation socially. I found myself becoming an expert bridge player and also became part of a weekly poker game: It was only nickel and dime, but to some of the students in school on the GI Bill, that was big money.

There was no dorm for the men at Eastman so each male student had to make his own private living arrangements. Many members of the Rochester Philharmonic were willing to lease out rooms in their homes to students, and I was fortunate in my first year to rent a room at the home of Robert Lurie, a violist in the Philharmonic. His son David, an oboist, was also a freshman at Eastman, which made it nice for the two of us.

Similar to many other universities and their *traditions*, the freshman class at The Eastman School of Music was subject to an initiation, or hazing if you prefer: Nothing violent or over the top, but something designed to possibly cause we freshman sheep to become a bit embarrassed. You could cop out if you wanted, but a small heroic (or foolish) group of us went along with the ritual.

We were all taken surreptitiously, both male and female students, to the local burlesque show in town and ushered to the front seats while the theater lights were still on. Every pervert, drunk and… I think you get the picture, watched as we young "innocents" took our seats. We were seated boy-girl-boy-girl to further add to our discomfort. When the theater lights went down, the first stripper on stage loudly introduced "the freshman class of the Eastman School of Music" to the audience, as the spotlight swept across and illuminated the rows we were seated in. As the show progressed, I truthfully think that the males were more embarrassed by the antics on stage than the females were. It all seemed to be a big kick for the girls, watching other women seductively undressing while all the men in the audience cheered them on. Even the raunchy humor of the comics seemed to score with the girls.

With a female classmate seated on either side, I held my breath hoping that the events taking place on stage would not sexually arouse me to a condition that could prove to be awkward. I'm not quite sure how this still-shy guy might have reacted in the company of two girls, with his pants bulging a bit at the crotch.

Considering the eroticism that currently takes place on movie screens, rock concerts, and even occasionally at the ballet and on the legitimate stage, what I saw occurring on stage back in 1948 was, by today's standards, really rather tame.

P.S. I did not embarrass myself. Little "dickie" remained his normal size. During the entire show, to avoid feeling ill at ease, I never glanced at the young ladies seated on either side of me. But after the show, as the group walked up the aisle, I must be honest and confess that I couldn't help but fantasize what each one of the girls might look like wearing nothing but a G-string.

In my freshman year at Eastman I met Ann, who played the violin and hailed from Richmond, Indiana. We became very close during my time at Eastman. Very, very, close. In fact, she was my first steady girlfriend, and my first lover. My virgin status had become despoiled.

The following year I rented a room directly across the street from the women's dorm where Ann lived. Living close to the dorm made life a bit easier for me to visit her. Winter in Rochester is almost too cold to imagine, so if you decide to walk anywhere, it's smart to keep the distances as short as possible.

It was at the previously mentioned poker games that I met Jim Buffington, Ray Shiner and Jim Fogelsong, who were to become involved in my career in later years.

Jim Buffington played French horn and Ray Shiner played all the woodwinds. They were both classically trained and also very proficient at playing jazz. Playing jazz on French horn was rather rare at the time, and still is, as is playing jazz on the English horn. Both men were extraordinary musicians and could play either style with equal virtuosity. Sometimes at the end of the day we would meet in a practice room and *jam*.

The third man, Jim Fogelsong and I played basketball together on an intra-mural team. He was a voice major and chorus singer, and our paths would cross again some 20 years later in Hollywood.

In my freshman year I flunked my piano classes with several different piano teachers and eventually, out of desperation, ended up with a pedagogue piano teacher. (She taught young children, ages seven through 12). She and I hit it off great. Although I was 18, she treated me like 12 and we got along famously.

I was, modestly I state, an expert clarinetist—but then so were about 20 other students. I found myself lost and drowning in a sea of talented people.

I transferred my minor from piano to composition, and added conducting to my schedule.

One of the pluses at Eastman was the opportunity to play in the Symphonic Band under the baton Frederick Fennel. (In later years, he became one of the top conductors in America). It was also my good fortune to get the opportunity to write four concert arrangements of pop songs for the Rochester Pops Orchestra, conducted at that time by Guy Fraser Harrison. This was my first chance to write the Morton Gould style arrangements that I was so enamored with. To add to my good fortune, the reviews of the concerts were positive and I felt I had found my future niche in the music business.

I managed to find the time to write several concert arrangements that were played at Music & Art when I would make an alumni visit. I even got to conduct my score at one of the symphonic band concerts, which became my first public performance as a conductor.

To earn some extra money, I answered an ad on the school bulletin board asking for someone to copy the parts to a one-act opera. The opera was written by some Italian composer (whose name escapes me), and who was in residence at The Juilliard School of Music. I copied the entire opera for $125.

At the end of my second year at Eastman I was unhappy with the progress I was making musically and I decided to seek some advice from Howard Hanson, President of the Eastman School of Music. Upon hearing of my ambition to be the next Morton Gould or Dave Rose—and after checking my mediocre grades and reading my newspaper reviews of the Rochester Civic concerts—he earnestly suggested that perhaps Eastman was not the right school for me.

After another half semester I left school for the real world. But before leaving, I proposed to Ann, my college sweetheart of two years. She said "no." What a bummer, for it was with her, on a memorable weekend in New York, that I had lost my virginity. I guess I believed that, at the very least, I owed her a proposal for helping me discover the wonderful world of sexual gratification. (I think that deep down inside, I was relieved when she said *no.*) Oh well. *C'est la vie.* It was June and I eagerly headed back to New York City to pursue my dream of following in the footsteps of Morton Gould and Dave Rose.

A Job… A Real Job

WELL THERE I WAS. June 1949 in New York, the center of the music industry and I was ready to become the world's greatest, okay, *third* greatest arranger. (Morton Gould was still number one in my mind.) But first came summer camp, once again at Camp Tioga. This time around I was a full-fledged counselor.

Most of my spare time in camp was spent trying to *make time* with the girls. Remember, I was no longer a virgin. Now I *knew* what I wanted from a girl. Unfortunately, I didn't get it, but it certainly wasn't for lack of trying. (Remember flirting? Nowadays you could end up in court, for what used to be a bit of hanky-panky.)

I managed to make use of my musical ability and helped to produce the summer ending big show, a decidedly very amateur staging of *Best Foot Forward*. I also accompanied singers on several of the weekend talent shows. Soon summer fun was over and it was back to New York and time to dive headlong into the music business.

So, how does one get started in the music business? I've been asked this question at least 100 times in the last 40 years and my answer is always the same: I haven't the foggiest notion. It's really a crapshoot. Vegas and the lottery give better odds.

My first legitimate paying job in the music business was about to come my way. I had never been paid for the Rochester Civic arrangements, which obviously might have been one of the main reasons why I got the job. And $125 to copy an entire opera can hardly be considered reasonable compensation.

Sammy Fain, after being continually pestered by my mother and father to do something for me, had somehow managed to get my name put on the copyist list at the *Milton Berle Texaco Hour Show*. As fate would have it, on Yom Kippur, the holiest of Jewish holy days, at four o'clock in the afternoon, I received a phone call from the Milton Berle copyist office. They inquired as to my availability to work for them that evening from 7:00 P.M. through the night, or as long as it would take to finish.

It appeared obvious that they called me because my name was Phillips, and Phillips is not a particularly Jewish-sounding name. (Racial profiling in 1949.) All the Cohens, Levys, Rosenbergs etc. who were on the roster were more than likely in Temple. It seemed that on the Milton Berle show, most of the copyists were Jewish. Why? I have no reasonable explanation. The arrangers, however, were Gentile.

I looked at my father and then asked him for his advice. Without hesitating, he told me to take the job. "God would understand," he said, "and there would be many other Yom Kippurs." I eagerly accepted. (Thank Heaven I had joined the New York Musician's Union, Local 802, the previous year, or there would have been no job.)

I worked from 7:00 P.M. until 8:00 A.M. the following morning—and made more money in that short period of time than ever before! There was all that overtime and penalty money for working through the night. Since no more deadlines fell on Jewish holidays, I was never called again.

Enter Sammy Fain, one more time. Sammy was now busy writing a Broadway musical. Being helpful and putting himself out on a limb for anyone was not one of Sammy's strong points. With my parents constantly bugging him to try and help me, he hemmed and hawed before he eventually suggested that I hang out at the Brill Building.

(For the uninitiated, the Brill Building, located at 1619 Broadway about seven blocks from Times Square, and another building at 1650 Broadway were the center of the music publishing and record business from the early thirties to perhaps the late seventies. Most of the important music publishers and independent record companies were located in those two buildings.)

To help me get started, Sammy gave me some names of a few people he knew with whom I might be able to make appointments. He didn't call them: he just gave me their names. What a guy. Every day I would leave my home at about ten A.M. and take a bus down to Broadway and 50th. St. I would hang around the offices, pester people, eat lunch in the local hangouts, and then at about three P.M., I would go to the movies. I usually got home about six o'clock.

For many months the only thing that I accomplished with this routine was to become a movie buff, having seen almost every film on Broadway, quite often more than once. I was also beginning to find great pleasure in listening to the films' scores. Of course my parents had no idea that I was spending my afternoons at the movies. Movies in those days were supposed to be only a Saturday-night affair.

Eventually all my hanging out at the Brill building finally paid off. I cannot recall the circumstances surrounding the event, as the brain cell containing that info has recently died.

Anyway, I was hired by the owners of a small record company to write two arrangements for a singer named Johnny Crawford. The record was

released on Rialto Records, and there on the label, at the bottom, in small print, was my name. It read "Arranged by Stuey Phillips," and was my first professional credit. The record was a flop. The name Stuey was also a flop. By the way, if anyone is interested, I have one copy available for sale.

When the predictable freezing New York winter arrived, it was no longer comfortable hanging out in front of the Brill Building. It was just too damn cold. If anything of any great importance happened during that time I cannot recall. So let's just assume that nothing happened. It was during this miserable cold winter that I began to entertain the adventurous concept of trying my luck in California.

Sammy Fain had left New York for California, as he had acquired several film assignments, which now made it necessary for him to temporarily move to Hollywood. The thought of Sammy in sunny California and me standing outside the Brill building freezing my ass was taking over my psyche. Up to now the only paying work I had gotten was due somewhat to Sammy's efforts, so I rationalized that maybe he could get me some work, if I also was in California.

At about this time my Uncle Archie passed away and left a $1,000 to each of his nieces and nephews, which was a tidy sum back in 1949. Combined with what I had been able to earn and save (I was living with my parents and they were nice enough not to charge me room and board), I had about $1,700.

There was little doubt that I would have to devise some devious and underhanded scheme to get my parents to sanction my going to Hollywood. Even though I was 20 years old, and didn't really need their permission, I still felt close to my family and wanted to leave only with their blessings and not in anger. So I kept telling myself.

The scheme I hatched was so simple that I amazed myself. I said that I needed to go to Hollywood in order to establish a six-week residency, which was necessary in order for me to get my Musicians Union card in California. After all, I said, I wouldn't want to lose a possible job in the future because of the lack of a Local 47 (Los Angeles) Union card.

I explained that, instead of going to camp that summer, I would take my inheritance and spend two months in Hollywood. My father was understanding and supportive. My mother on the other hand, was devastated. I decided to go regardless of her opposition. After the initial shock, she relented and supported my trip to Hollywood. My short eight-week excursion ended up lasting almost three years: Years of worldly and philosophical maturation.

Hollywood—1950

Where I Discover La-La Land

WITH MY $1,700 WORTH OF SAVINGS I boarded a train in New York City and traveled to the West Coast to begin the Hollywood period of my career. Age: 20. Looks: 14. I had taken up smoking when I was 18, and was constantly being asked to show proof of age whenever I would buy cigarettes. I looked that young.

Before I left New York City for Hollywood, my father contacted a distant cousin he probably had met about twice in his entire life, and asked him if he would please look after me when I arrived in LA. My father's cousin, Harry Stone, was married with several children but was gracious enough to offer me lodging in his home until I was able to get my act together. My cousin owned a women's shoe store on Fairfax Ave., a few doors north of Cantor's Deli. His home was on Orange St. just off Fairfax and within walking distance of the store.

In the first few days after my arrival I set out to accomplish my first goal, which was to establish my residency with the Musician's Union. The Union was, and still is, on Vine Street near Melrose Ave. My cousin gave me the simple directions from the house to the Union which were; WALK to Santa Monica Blvd., get on the streetcar, and get off at Vine Street and then WALK to the Union. This was easily accomplished for a kid brought up in New York City who was used to walking and riding buses and trolleys. Eventually,

LOS ANGELES RED CAR/TROLLEY 1950

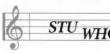

however, the word WALK became a dirty four-letter word. Hollywood, I was to soon realize, was not a WALKIN' town.

The Musician's Union had an entertainment room with three pool tables and I did a bit of hanging-out at the Union and soon became a pretty damn good pool player. My meager savings account however, prompted that I stay away from the poker games. They were not penny-ante as they had been at Eastman.

Hollywood in 1950 was truly a remarkable and exciting place. Almost every waitress was blonde and blue eyed and looked like they came from Kansas, Nebraska or Iowa. (Which they probably did.) They all dreamed of being movie stars and were very friendly to everyone. After all, these girls had no way of knowing whether or not the person they were serving was a talent agent, producer, director or studio mogul. So they took no chances and made sure that they were always at their best. It was pleasant having a bite to eat and ogling all the *pretty young maids*, who would always ogle back.

Even the police were something special. Every cop looked like he had just stepped out of central casting. They all appeared to be about 35 years old and were well built and handsome. It was a big change from the over-weight old cop who walked a beat in New York City. The cops in Hollywood cruised around on motorcycles and in squad cars, just like in the movies.

A common expression in those days was to refer to Los Angeles as a *group of towns in search of a city*. Each major motion picture studio seemed to have a town of its own: Warner Bros. and Disney in Burbank; MGM in Culver City; 20th Century Fox in West LA (now called Century City); Republic Pictures in Studio City; Paramount and Columbia in Hollywood.

The time had finally come for me to try and contact Sammy Fain. Sammy specifically had left New York City for Hollywood to prepare for a writing assignment at Disney Studios. He was soon to start work on composing songs for the movie *Alice in Wonderland*. After many unanswered calls I eventually reached him. (Remember, there were no answering machines back in those days.)

Sammy as usual, tried his best to somehow brush me off, but I was insistent, and he did not want to incur the wrath of my grandmother who was soon to come to Hollywood to look after he and his brother Harry. So he made arrangements to take me to the Warner Bros. studio and meet with Ray Heindorf, the musical director of the studio. Sammy asked me to meet him at his apartment near Ciros, on Sunset Blvd.

By now I was becoming familiar with the area and decided to WALK there. Bad idea. It was one hell of a trek. Sammy shared the apartment with

Jackie Barnett, one of Jimmie Durante's writers, and the apartment looked exactly like you would imagine a bachelor's Hollywood pad might look like. Clothes were strewn all over the place and when the phone rang Sammy had trouble locating it since it was buried under a pile of messy clothes.

Sammy, a divorced man at this time, had only three major interests in life. Writing songs, screwing young chorus girls and spending time at the racetrack—where he usually got screwed. His love of the horses was so strong that he eventually bought a thoroughbred racehorse.

After waiting about an hour for Sammy to get dressed, he and I finally took off in his chartreuse Ford convertible, with the top down of course, and headed for Burbank. As we drove through the canyon I imagined that someday I might own a car like that.

At the studio, Sammy introduced me to Ray Heindorf, who at that time was the Musical Director of Warner Bros., as the son of a distant relation. Ray Heindorf promptly informed me that with my lack of any experience as an arranger or orchestrator it would be difficult for him to justify hiring me. But since I had some experience doing copying work (the Milton Berle show and the opera at Eastman), he would put my name on the list of on-call copyists. It's presently the year 2002. So figuratively speaking, I have been on-call for 52 years, and have yet to receive a work call.

When we left Ray's office Sammy asked his secretary if she could spare the time to show me around the studio, claiming that he had some important meetings to attend. Ray's secretary was very pleasant and gave me an excellent guided tour of the studio.

She took me to the scoring stage and the dubbing stage where I was fortunate to observe a mix-down taking place. Upon seeing first hand the process of making movies, I was hooked. I began to realize that the movie business might just be what I *really* was searching for all along. Specifically, writing music for films. (It was to be 10 years before I would compose my first film score.)

Sammy became very involved with his co-writer (most likely some racehorse at Santa Anita) and said he was sorry, but he just couldn't spare the time to drive me home. Having absolutely no idea of how to get home from where I was, I invested some of my precious savings on an expensive taxicab ride.

I had been sponging off my cousins for more than a week and I felt that sensibly it might be time for me to leave. But first I felt that I needed some kind of a job to help offset my rent and make my savings survive as long as possible.

My cousin contacted a friend of his in Santa Monica who, coincidentally, also owned a women's shoe store. It turned out that he needed some extra help, so I boarded a Wilshire Blvd. bus and made the trip to Santa Monica. I got the job and it lasted one whole week. I do believe that I did more damage to that poor man's business in one week than he deserved. For sure, selling women's shoes was not in my future, and the owner was overcome with joy when I left. However, I did learn what an open-toed sling back was.

That four-letter word WALK was beginning to get to me and I could see it was imperative that my future life in Hollywood would require a car.

Note: I use the name Hollywood, not LA, since no self-respecting person in the entertainment business in 1950 would ever admit to living in Los Angeles. It was Hollywood, Beverly Hills, Bel Air or Malibu.

I checked the used-car pages and found what sounded to me like a reasonable deal. It was a 1939 Ford two-door for (are you ready?) $90. The address where the car was located was on Cahuenga Blvd. Once again I boarded the Santa Monica streetcar and got off at Vine St.

It was only May in Hollywood but a hot spell of temperatures in the mid-90s was blanketing the city. Being a proper New York City boy, I of course was wearing a sport jacket. Unfortunately, it was a jacket from back east, made for cold New York City winter weather. I started to briskly walk to Cahuenga Blvd.

It didn't take long before I began to get hot and sweaty. Within a few blocks my brisk walk had turned into a sluggish plod and my jacket was off. The location I was looking for turned out to be all the way up Cahuenga Blvd. about three houses from the current freeway. By the time I made the uphill climb to my destination I was soaking wet and exhausted.

I examined my prospective car with care, as I had been warned to be a cautious buyer and not get taken. Upon scrupulous examination of the car I found the following: One door was held closed with twine; the glove compartment was kept closed with a piece of wire; under the hood several of the hoses had electrical tape wrapped around them to stop any leaks; the paint was so old I can't even tell you what color the car was. All in all, it was a mess, but it ran, and it was only $90.

It was a far cry from Sammy Fain's Ford convertible but at least I had wheels. With my pink slip in hand I proudly drove away in my second car. My first was also a Ford that I had purchased in Rochester, for $75. Inflation, it seems, had run rampant during the last two years.

My Hollywood Abode

I SCANNED THE PAPERS WITH ANTICIPATION looking for my new home, and considered myself fortunate to find a room for rent just south of Santa Monica Blvd. on West Knoll Dr. If I remember correctly, I believe that the rent was around $80 a month. The room was in the back of the house and had its own entrance, which was a big plus for me, since I had visions of entertaining many girls in my room in the near future. Up until now I had experienced sex twice in my life. I was a young man who badly needed to get laid.

I thanked my cousins for their hospitality, packed my gear and drove my little Ford to my new home. My new home also gave me the use of part of the garage. My beautiful car would now be protected from the weather. That's a laugh. I notified the Union of my change of address and felt a sense of fulfillment at having succeeded in getting myself a home and a car.

Something still seemed to be missing from the scenario. A phone! Yes, of course, I had to have a phone. What if Ray Heindorf tried to reach me? Or Sammy? Within a few days my phone was installed and I now felt confident being on my own and ready for anything. Hopefully, sex and work—in that order.

So far Hollywood turned out to be everything I had envisioned it would be, and I had only spent about $200. (My father had graciously paid for my train ticket to Hollywood. He was that kind of man). It was at this time when I decided that to live in Hollywood full time was to be one of my lifetime goals. I just had to make it here. The weather was great and there was no snow, followed by slush, followed by ice, to contend with. This was my kind of town. Frank Sinatra can keep Chicago.

Numerous calls to Sammy Fain netted me nothing tangible except an outing to 20th Century Fox to meet with Lionel Newman. Sammy at that time had been engaged by Fox to write a song for the film, *Call Me Mister* starring Betty Grable and Dan Dailey.

Lionel and his brother Alfred were the Music Directors at Fox. Emil Newman another brother was a composer's agent. Alfred was considered one of the greatest of all film composers buy those whose opinions count. The Brothers Newman practically owned the town musically. Lionel was

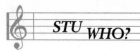

also a racetrack fanatic and he and Sammy often visited their money at the track together.

Almost the same scenario that previously had taken place at Warner Bros. with Ray Heindorf took place again. Lionel explained that without any previous experience as an arranger or orchestrator in the movie business, it would be difficult for him to justify hiring me. With Lionel, I didn't even make the copyists' list.

Like before, I received another studio tour and, little by little, was being sucked even deeper into the film business. There was something so glamorous about a motion picture studio to this relocated New Yorker.

(Note: In 1970 I was fortunate to work at Fox. However, Lionel Newman had nothing to do with my employment there. In 1981 I spent six years working at Fox, and once again, Lionel Newman had nothing to do with it. I eventually did become a friend of Lionel's, but at no time did he ever procure for me a working assignment at Fox.)

I now had a car, my own room and a phone. What I didn't have was a job, and some friends. I badly needed some friends, or at least, a friend. I was beginning to talk to myself in order to hear the sound of my voice. Loneliness was setting in big time. At least when I was staying at my cousins I had them to talk to. I took to cruising the Sunset Strip trying to meet people. Cruising the strip was the *in* thing to do in 1950, and it appears that it is still the *in* thing to do 52 years later in 2002.

Once again, the brain cell containing the events leading up to my meeting Gil Turner must have died last year, so let's just say that somewhere, somehow, I met Gil Turner. Gil's father was the owner of two drug stores on Sunset Blvd. One was at Doheny and the other at Larabee. The one at Doheny is still there, and to my knowledge is owned by Gil Turner. The one at Larabee is now called Terner's. (for some reason Turner is now spelled differently at that location) I've tried several times to reach Gil but I've never been able to make contact with him for the last 40 years. (Note: In July of 2001, I discovered that Gil Turner had passed away in 1997.)

Gil owned a black 1950 Studebaker convertible that he drove, rain or shine, with the top down. It was the coolest car on the Strip, and Gil was also one of the most popular guys on the Strip. We were close in age and despite having little in common, we somehow became buddies. I had neither Gil's money, nor his looks, nor his slick dialogue, but he liked me. Go figure. This next diversion from my career to my personal life is necessary to set up one of the most traumatic experiences of my entire life.

Gil knew about every party going on around the Strip, where he was usually a welcome guest. As a result of Gil's popularity I also got to attend these parties. I met a few nice girls, but had little success at dating any of them. I was still a bit shy and furthermore, still looked four or five years younger than I actually was.

At one party I spent a good portion of the evening talking with a very pretty and, to me, a very desirable girl. We seemed to hit it off, so I asked for her phone number and was overjoyed when she gave it to me. This was a real live possibility, and I felt aroused with the success of the moment.

During the next two weeks I called her several times but seemed to always just miss her. My 21st birthday was a week away. I tried one last time to contact her and finally succeeded. I invited her to be a part of my birthday celebration, with dinner, a movie and any bar of her choice where she would like to finish the evening. I was going to be 21 and of legal drinking age in California, and couldn't wait to show my I.D. She said yes to my invitation and I was elated.

On the night of my 21st Birthday I arrived at her home promptly at seven. Her mother answered the door and informed me that she was not yet home. I was a little puzzled but I said I'd be back at seven-thirty. Seven-thirty and she was still not home. Eight and eight-thirty came and went. It was evident that I had been stood up, and on my birthday yet. Talk about downers, this one was the worst one so far in my entire life. Completely dejected I went to a drive-in to have a bite to eat and self-commiserate.

(Note: I feel a need to explain what a drive-in was back in 1950. It was basically a hamburger joint where you drove into a parking space and were served while you sat in your car. A tray would be attached to your door and usually some very attractive young girl, waiting to be discovered for the movies, would bring you your order. Sometimes on roller-skates.)

In the car parked next to me, a middle-aged man and woman were also having a bite to eat. (Middle-aged to me at that time was 35 to 40.) The woman was seated in the passenger seat which put her about three feet from me. My dejected attitude was quite evident and she leaned out her window and asked me what the problem was. I was, at that moment, eager to spill my guts to anybody, so I related my entire sorrowful story to this stranger. She was a good listener and empathetically said she felt sorry for me.

About ten minutes went by when she again leaned towards my car and asked if I would like to join her and her friend at a party. Perhaps, she said, it might help to add a little cheer into my birthday evening. I eagerly accepted her invitation. She said I should follow them and that they were headed towards Melrose and Vermont.

When we reached our destination they parked their car and I parked mine. Then the three of us walked towards a cocktail lounge. It was a little after ten o'clock. The lady was, for sure, over thirty—but by how much I was not sure. She was very attractive and dressed quite fashionably. The man was older and dressed in a business suit and tie. His hair was thinning and he was a little paunchy. Forty at least, I thought.

As we entered the club I was overwhelmed by the darkness. It appeared to be very crowded and everything was veiled in a smoky haze. It was so dimly lit that it made it difficult to distinguish the patrons. I lit a cigarette and tried my utmost to look 21. In my case, the cigarette really didn't help much to hide my 16-year-old baby-face. The man guided me to two empty stools at the bar. The woman continued walking to the back of the room, and pulling apart a curtain, she disappeared into another room. The juke-box blared out one record after the other, mostly jazz.

After several minutes when my eyes grew more accustomed to the light, I noticed that, curiously, all the people in the bar were men. It did not hit me right away. In fact it took my naive little mind about five minutes to realize that I was in a *queer* bar. (I use the vernacular of the time period in describing the situation. Political Correctness was still some 40 years in the future. I apologize to all gays.)

To tell the truth, I was a little scared, since gay bashing by the police was definitely not uncommon in those days. Again I point out that this was 1950. "Fag bars," as the police referred to them, were not one of the cops' favorite places.

My curiosity as to what happened to the woman who was with us, was now completely aroused, so I excused myself on the pretext of going to the men's room (now there's a paradox) and headed toward the curtains in the back. As I looked through the curtains my adult education reached fulfillment. Only women occupied the room.

This was becoming a weird birthday celebration. I was celebrating with a lesbian and a homosexual. Until now, these were people I had only read about in dirty magazines. To me this was an unfamiliar world and certainly had not been included in my growing-up years. The subject was not readily discussed at home, in school, or even on the street during my adolescence. The story, unfortunately, doesn't end here.

I had a beer and planned to leave as discreetly, and as quick as I could. The man, let's call him Jim, since I don't remember his name, asked if I would care to join him at his apartment for another beer. He said that he lived close by, actually right around the corner. To this very day I don't know why I did what I did, but I left with him and we proceeded to his apartment. Maybe it was because I was feeling so rejected and dejected, and wondered out of curiosity just what *would* happen next, that made me accompany him. Maybe, I was just a stupid and juvenile 21-year-old.

In his second-floor apartment, which by the way was neatly furnished, he took his jacket off, removed his tie and brought out two beers. We sat on the couch together, and he made some idle conversation while I politely listened. I also began to sweat a bit. Soon he put his hand on my thigh. I instinctively moved away. He said he knew that I wasn't *queer*, but if I relaxed a bit I might actually enjoy the experience of being with a man. He promised that I wouldn't have to do anything. He said that he would *"do it all."*

His last statement *"do it all"* was the last straw. The thought of him doing anything to me became revolting. At this point in my life it was hard enough for me to be at ease with a girl, *but with a man… f— this shit*. As politely as I could I said, "No thanks." (With that remark I must have really sounded stupid.) I grabbed my jacket and left as fast as I could. Halfway down the stairs I suddenly realized that I had an erection. Now I was really disgusted.

This little escapade stayed with me for years. As I drove home it suddenly occurred to me that his friend, the lesbian, was most likely his pimp. It was the thought that this older woman might actually want *me* that made me go with them in the first place. Obviously, it was one of the ways that he got his *tricks*. I continued to mull over what he meant by *"he would do it all."* I had figured out the oral sex routine and the kissing, but *what else* was there?

When lightning struck this immature and inexperienced brain of mine, *what else*, finally hit me. I felt revolted and thanked my lucky stars that I had left when I did. As I drove home, I gingerly adjusted my backside on the seat.

♫   ♫   ♫

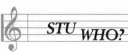

Things look promising

OCTOBER AND NOVEMBER OF THAT YEAR saw little progress in the pursuit of my career goals. Sammy Fain paid me to make a few lead sheets for him—and like a fool I kept thinking that I might actually receive a call from Ray Heindorf's or Lionel Newman's offices. To make things even harder for my slowly evolving career, I discovered that I had some serious competition in Hollywood. Specifically, a budding young genius about the same age as me, was taking Hollywood by storm. His name was André Previn, and he was the *Wunderkind* of MGM Studios. He was living the life that I wanted to live, even after being drafted into the Army in 1950.

Since the age of 16, while he was still in high school, André had a job at MGM as an arranger, orchestrator and composer, and I was told, had all the girls that he fancied. (Incidentally, I am a great fan of Previn, both in the jazz and classical fields, but I have never been fortunate enough to meet him. André, if you ever read this, I would love to meet you. It would be an honor. Call me. We'll do lunch.)

My grandmother and Sammy's brother Harry arrived from New York City and moved in with Sammy. He had by now moved to Hollywood Blvd. just West of La Brea, and Jackie Barnett was no longer his roommate. I began hanging out a little less with Gil Turner, as I decided I needed to cut down on my spending, since my bankroll was almost down to $1,000.

Still a California virgin, and continually searching for that elusive sexual encounter I had been anticipating, it was about this time that I discovered the sleazy world of "B-Girls." Specifically, they were a type of hostesses at some of the downtown LA bars. When you entered the bar and sat down it took only a few magical seconds before you were joined by a very attractive young lady attired in clothes that emphasized her sexual attributes. She would inquire as to whether or not you would like to buy her a drink. Her demeanor strongly suggested that she might be easy to pick up, so naturally one was eager to satisfy her. (Innocence like mine should have been bottled.)

Regardless of what drink you ordered, *she* would always order a champagne cocktail at five dollars a pop. Considering that a vodka and tonic at that time was about a dollar, five bucks was a very steep price. The girls were simply shills for the bar business, and would receive a percentage of the action at the end of the night.

The chance of anybody scoring with one of these lovely young ladies was slim and none. If they gave you a phone number it was always a phony.

If, perhaps, one said that they would meet you after they finished work, it was just a ruse. They always seemed to leave surreptitiously by the back exit. I was suckered twice before I realized that I had been had, and crossed B-Girls off my list of potential sexual partners.

There's a wonderful song called "California Dreamin'," that can whet one's appetite for the Southern California scene. Years before this song was written, this relocated New Yorker—while waiting for my big career break to manifest itself—was overwhelmed with the variety of exciting pleasures LA had to offer. Aside from girl watching, stargazing (the human kind), sun, sand and surf, there were the surrounding recreational areas. I decided to be adventurous one day and conceived and executed what I thought to be the perfect California experience.

At 6:00 A.M. one morning, I arose and drove to Big Bear Lake, located high in the mountains, roughly 100 miles from LA. There was still some snow scattered about and the air was brisk and cold. It was close to nine o'clock when I arrived. I found a sandwich shop and ordered breakfast. Then at about 10:30 I started down the mountain towards Palm Springs. When I arrived in Palm Springs, the temperature was in the high 80s. It was lunchtime, and after cruising up and down Palm Canyon Drive eyeing the pretty young bikini-clad girls, I stopped and had lunch.

By 4:00 P.M. I had started on my way back to LA, arriving at the pier in Santa Monica close to 8:00 P.M. (I remind you that there were no freeways from Palm Springs to LA in those days.) Though the water was cold, I forced myself to take a quick dip in the Pacific so I could complete my one-day odyssey. I had dinner on the pier and returned to my apartment and into my bed by 11:00. Where else could you have three seasons in so short a time—without jet planes?

Breakfast in the snow... followed by lunch in the desert... finishing with dinner by the Pacific Ocean, and all in under 17 hours. Today, 2002, with all the freeways now currently available, I'm not so sure it can be done any quicker, taking into consideration—today's travesty-of-traffic.

When December and Christmas rolled around, that dejected feeling came over me again, and I decided I needed to give myself a lift. All that wonderful sex that I dreamed I was going to experience in Hollywood, with all those beautiful *starlets*, had not come to fruition. Plus, I was out of work and horny, and that makes for a really bad combination. I decided that moving to a new place might be the perfect pick-me up.

I found a one-room apartment on Melrose Ave. just west of La Brea. Five steps up from the sidewalk was the door to the apartment. The apartment had a picture window facing the street and anytime that someone over five feet tall walked by I could see the top of their head. I guess they could also see into my apartment if they stood on their tiptoes. Fortunately, it came furnished—which of course was a necessity for me, since I didn't own one stick of furniture. If I remember correctly I believe the rent was $125 a month. I figured I had about four months to get a job or I was in deep shit.

The reason my apartment was on the ground floor, street level, was that I had told the landlord that I planned to have a piano. He said this was the apartment where I would be least likely to disturb anybody. I rented a studio upright from a piano-rental place and settled into my new pad.

My pad on Melrose Ave. in 2001. When I lived there from 1951-1952, half a century ago, there were no bars on the window. Life was a lot safer in those days.

Let me take a moment to describe the apartment for you. As you entered the room, the piano was about six inches to the right of the door. To the left of the door was an easy chair, an end table, another easy chair, the door to the bathroom, a blank wall of about five feet that housed an electric wall heater, and then the door to the kitchen. (The kitchen was very, very small.) Then there was another three feet of wall, a built-out wardrobe with drawers on the bottom and then a *day-bed*. During the day it was my sofa, but at night you took the pillows off and it became a bed. (Weird— it should have been called a *night-bed* or a *day-couch*.) To the right of the bed was a table-height cabinet with drawers and then the picture window with a desk in front of it. That was my palace: all 400 or so square feet! Strange as it may seem, this building still exists. Over the last 50 years it has been a store, a beauty salon and currently is part of a restaurant.

On one of my last girl-searching nights with Gil Turner, he took me to a bar that we had never previously been to. I had often passed by this intriguing place but had never gone in. Gil had been told that it might be a good place to pick up "broads." It was called The Garden of Allah, and was on the corner of Crescent Heights and Sunset Blvd. (That corner now houses a taco joint, a bank and some other fast-food places.)

I soon discovered that the Garden was a very *in* and exclusive place. I have read that it was originally built and owned by Alla(h) Nazimova circa 1927, and in the golden days of Hollywood, from 1935 to 1946, it was frequented by the likes of Robert Benchley, Errol Flynn, F.S. Fitzgerald, Hemingway, Bogey Bacall. and Dorothy Parker. It was a hotel, restaurant and bar much in the style of the current Bel-Air Hotel. Very often it was referred to as a prison and a playground, a sanctuary and a glorified whorehouse, where the greats of Hollywood could play unobserved. By 1951 The Garden had declined and had

The Garden of Allah

(Top) View of the Garden of Allah from Sunset Blvd. circa 1930s. (Below) A view of the inner courtyard.

lost much of its glamour. The most famous resident from 1951 until it was torn down in 1959 was Patricia Medina (Mrs. Joseph Cotton).

As Gil and I sat at the somewhat deserted bar (obviously Gil had either chosen a bad night or he was misinformed about it being a good pick up place), I noticed a piano situated behind the bar. It was on an oversized pedes-

tal. I asked the bartender if he would mind if I played it. The bartender shrugged and said, "Enjoy yourself." I sat down and proceeded to play my flashy version of "I Get a Kick out of You." I noticed that my technique was a little rusty from not having touched a keyboard since I arrived in Hollywood. I was glad that when I moved, I had also rented a piano. Practicing piano was definitely going to be a large part of my future plans.

Gil was somewhat surprised at my musical ability. No one in the restaurant, which adjoined the bar so that they were almost one, seemed to be paying any attention to my playing. I next charged into a performance of the last classical piano piece I had learned, which was "Malaguena." I ripped it off with a flourish. Confidentially, I was disgusted with the way I played it. I finished my little concert with the Boogie version of "The Flight of the Bumble Bee" (called "Bumble Boogie" in those days). I barely made all the notes, but at least my two hands finished together. One person politely applauded.

With no women in sight, Gil had had enough of the place and wanted to leave. Before we left, I asked the bartender if any one regularly played piano here. He said no, but that the manager was interested in hiring someone. He asked if I was interested. I quickly said yes. He made eye contact with the *maître d'*, who just happened to be the manager, and he came over to me.

We sat down at a table in the bar and he made me an offer. (He, obviously, had been listening when I played.) One hundred and twenty-five dollars a week for five days a week, Tuesday through Saturday, 5:30 until 11:00. I proudly informed him that I was a union member. He said that $125 was union scale. However, I would have to swing with him on the hours. Four hours a night, but he picked the hours. I was to play whenever customers were in the place and I could keep all my tips. If the place was empty I could loaf. Also as a bonus, I would get 50% off on food. That meant a five-dollar steak would cost me two-fifty.

It all sounded too good to be true, and I accepted the job. Hell, I *seized* it. My job at The Garden of Allah lasted about three months. That evening was the last time I ever saw Gil Turner.

Playing piano at the Garden of Allah was a very pleasant experience. It was never very crowded since it was basically a place for *show biz* people to have secret trysts. The film crowd, after a day of shooting at Columbia, Paramount or Fox, would drop by for drinks. On any given night you might find Robert Mitchum, Jane Russell, Nick Ray (the director) and others indulging in some idle conversation and booze.

Since the piano was behind the bar and not accessible to the patrons, I was rarely left any cash tips. Most people would say to the bartender, "Buy the piano player a drink." This I didn't need. I was, and have always been a very limited drinker. The effect of more than one drink had a profound effect on my pianistic ability. I would get sloppy, or should I say, *sloppier*. However, the bartender wanted the revenue and the more booze he sold, the bigger his tip. I suggested that he serve me water. He said that if he got caught charging the customers for booze when he was giving me water, that he could lose his license. We tried many combinations of drinks but they all failed. I finally wound up drinking straight vodka. I would acknowledge the drink with a little sip, and then put the glass down behind a stack of music, out of sight of the customer. Then when I would take a break, I would discreetly pour the contents into the sink without anyone noticing. Occasionally, I felt like one of those B-Girls in downtown LA, shilling for the bartender.

However, there was one woman who regularly tipped me with cash. Whenever she came in she would sit at the far end of the bar and I would segue right into her favorite medley. She indulged herself by drinking vodka and milk. When she left she would give the bartender a five-dollar bill for me. I later found out that her name was Kay Spreckles, the sugar heir.

♫   ♫   ♫

1951 — A January Surprise

DURING JANUARY OF 1951, COMFORTABLE IN my new apartment and delirious to finally have a taxable income, my second slightly traumatic personal experience was to befall me. Only this time the experience turned into an extremely pleasurable one.

Three blocks from my apartment was a little sandwich joint, which stayed open until midnight. I often would grab a late bite there around ten o'clock. A very pleasant and attractive waitress, with long, natural red hair (trust me, it was natural) and beautiful white skin was usually working behind the counter at that time.

The place was never too crowded and we seemed to have plenty of time to toss about some frivolous conversation. I liked talking to her, but never made a pass or even suggested we might go on a date. There was

something sad about her that kept me from sexually or romantically approaching her. She rarely smiled and at times I felt like I was intruding into her thoughts.

Once or twice I spied a wedding band on her finger. It seemed strange to me that the ring was not *always* on her finger. Anyway, that ring and her sadness were enough to keep me from asking for a date, even though I was still a California virgin.

On a rather cold evening at the end of January, I stopped in for a burger and she was on duty. (For the sake of discretion, we'll refer to her as Jane). The place was deserted except for me, and we talked extensively that evening. Then she began to tell me some of her personal problems. That began to annoy me. Her problems I didn't need, for without a doubt I had enough of my own.

Nevertheless, in spite of my trying to appear disinterested, she continued with her tale of woe. She said that her husband was in the Navy and currently stationed in Northern California. She was living with her mother, who was an ex-stripper. I kid you not. Jane's presence, it seems, was crimping her mother's love life. This was much more than I needed or wanted to know.

I quickly finished my coffee and paid my check on the run. The one thing I didn't need now, with success (I kept telling myself) just around the corner, was any complications. I walked briskly to my apartment and settled in for the night.

As I lay in bed trying to fall asleep I heard a soft knock on my door. I ignored it. It was 1:30 in the morning and I wasn't expecting company. However, as the knocks got louder I finally was forced to open the door. I usually slept in my under-shorts so that's how I went to the door. I opened it, keeping my body out of view. There stood Jane, and in her arms she was holding a *baby*.

I guessed that the infant was about a year old. It was cold outside and the only human thing to do was to have her come in. I told her to wait a second, grabbed my pants from the chair and put them on. She came in with the baby in one arm and a small piece of luggage in the other. She had not said a word yet, but I could see in her eyes that she had cried many tears in the last hour or so.

I looked at her in disbelief. "How did you know where I lived?" I asked. She said I had mentioned that my apartment was three blocks away and that I had this big picture window. And also, one afternoon on the way to work, she had noticed me in the window from across the street. I now asked the obvious. What do want from me? She then told me more of her tale of woe.

Her mother threw her out because she and the baby were interfering with her mother's sex life. It was getting too difficult to have men stay overnight with a baby crying some of the time. It just wasn't conducive to good sex. Her mother then took Jane's clothes, playpen and all of her belongings, and put them in the hall. Jane then took her baby and came here. That was her yarn.

I am not by nature an insensitive person, and could not find the words to say, "Take the baby and leave." But neither am I a complete *schmuck*, so I decided to check her story out. I asked her where she lived and she gave me the address. It was only six blocks away so I decided to walk it. I trusted her in my apartment alone since there was nothing of value for her to steal except my clothes and a piano.

Jane wasn't lying. There in the hallway were all her worldly possessions scattered about. I took the baby's folded-up playpen and headed back to my apartment. As I entered my place, I found her giving the baby his bottle. Thank God she wasn't breast-feeding. I don't think I could have handled it at that moment.

After a little profound thinking, I gave her my decision. The baby could stay until the morning, as I wouldn't throw an infant out into the cold, but there was no room in the apartment for her. The bed was only big enough for one, and I was going to be the one sleeping in it. She begged me to let her sleep in a chair. I finally relented and said yes.

It was difficult for me to fall asleep. In the center of the room was a playpen with a sleeping one-year-old and in a chair was Jane. Even though my back was turned to the whole situation, I still kept seeing her face in my mind.

I don't know how long it was, nor does it really make any difference, when I felt the covers move. It was obvious that she was getting into bed with me. This bed, a converted day-bed, was like an oversized single. It was not designed to comfortably sleep two. In the small confines of the bed it was nearly impossible for her body not to touch mine. It didn't take a wizard to quickly realize that she was completely nude. Not a stitch on. I however, still had my under-shorts on.

Nothing sexual happened that night, and the baby slept soundly and did not cry the entire night. But as the morning light began to come through the venetian blinds and the traffic noise on Melrose began to increase, Jane touched me. Not with her body, but with her hand. I drew my body away from her. Why? I haven't a clue. This moment seemed to be everything that this sex-seeking young man could ever wish for: My own apartment and a girl sharing my bed—who appeared eager to have sex with me. *A baby! A husband!* Well, let's skip that part.

I kept thinking about the wedding band. I tried to remember if she was wearing it the previous night when she first arrived. Again she touched me. I figured that sex was her way of saying "Thank you." I was now eager to say, "You're welcome."

We had sex—and *what* sex! Any intercourse that I had experienced before this was kindergarten. It was obvious that to me, this girl knew all there was to know about sex. When it was over she walked to the bathroom completely nude, and completely at ease. It was at that moment that I realized what a beautiful body she had. In the months that followed she taught *me* all I thought I would ever need to know about sex, but never had any intention of asking.

The next day she placed the baby in a foster home (so she said), and moved in with me. She explained that she and her husband were separated, and showed me the separation papers. I decided to believe what she was telling me, because for sure I did not want her to leave. I wanted desperately to believe her, even if she was lying. My life was now too glorious to believe: A job, my apartment and a girl all my own.

♫   ♫   ♫

My Career Heats Up

WITH MY LIVE-IN GIRLFRIEND, and my job at The Garden of Allah things were *cool*. (A 1950s expression.) Jane quit her job at the sandwich place and took a job as an usher at the Pantages Theater. That way she would be working the same hours as I was.

I vaguely remember meeting a fellow named Don Carl Eugster in a music store on Cherokee in Hollywood. We struck up a conversation and discovered that we had a lot in common. We left the store as friends and, quite soon after, Carl invited me to become part of a vocal group that he was involved with. He was the arranger for a group called the Clef Clan. I tried my hand at singing with the group but failed miserably, and eventually ended up being the accompanist for the group.

Two members of the Clef Clan were Clark Burroughs and Gene Purling. Eventually, they became the core of the "Hi Lo's," one the greatest vocal groups ever assembled. Several times, about 20 years later, I hired Clark Burroughs to do some vocal work for me.

Sometime in February, if I remember correctly, my mother and father decided to take a little trip to California to see how their son was really getting along in Hollywood. And to boot, not only was I here, so was my grandmother. My little excursion to California that was going to last only six weeks was now into its tenth month. I'm positive that my mother's intentions for coming to Hollywood, was to get me to return to New York.

I picked my parents up at Union Station in my $90 Ford. By the look on my father's face, I don't think he was too happy as we drove through the gates of the Ambassador Hotel on Wilshire Blvd. in my dilapidated car. He said that the first thing tomorrow we were going car shopping for something better. I said that right now I couldn't afford a better car. Of course, I knew in advance what his answer would be. My father said, "Think of it as a belated 21st birthday present." That was my father. The best there ever was.

True to his word the next day the three of us went car shopping. I ended up buying a light blue Pontiac, circa 1947 or 1948. It cost $375, and was quite a step up from my first two cars. (I now own a Jaguar, price tag over $60,000—doesn't that boggle the mind?)

The next stop was for them to see my new apartment. I had not mentioned Jane in my letters home, and I said nothing about her as we drove to my place. I figured I would play it by ear and ad-lib. Fortunately, Jane was not there when we arrived, but some of her clothes were lying around. My father smiled. My mother said, "And whose are these?" My father, bless him, said, "I don't think it's any of our business." My mother however, kept nudging. She was an expert at nudging. I finally gave in and said I have a girlfriend and she sometimes stays over. That seemed to satisfy her for the moment, but she managed

My mother and father. From the look of my mother's hairstyle, I'd guess about mid 1940s.

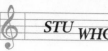
one more dig. "When can we meet her?" she asked. My father suggested dinner one night, and I agreed.

After dropping my parents off at the hotel, I returned home and waited for Jane. When she arrived I told her about the dinner invitation. She was not very enthusiastic about the situation, but reluctantly agreed to do it.

If you searched the whole world over you could not find a more *un-Jewish* looking girl than Jane, with her red hair, gray eyes and alabaster skin. Plus, I still looked sixteen, and Jane looked to be in her late twenties. (She was, in fact, two years older than I.) When my mother saw Jane she closed her eyes and gave the usual Jewish mother's sigh of displeasure. My father, always having a bit more tact than my mother, gave Jane a warm and sincere greeting.

Dinner was surprisingly quite pleasant. We left to go home under very comfortable conditions. Of course the next day the burning question on my mother's mind was "You're *not* going to marry her?" (Notice the negative connotation). I said that she shouldn't worry. I was much too busy at this time with my career to get married.

With all due respect to my mother, she did have a point. This was my second serious girlfriend—Ann at college having been the first—and neither one had been Jewish. Given a choice, my parents would definitely have preferred a Jewish daughter-in law. They went home after a week, and never did find out that Jane lived with me all the time. Of course, my father slipped five twenties into my pocket before they boarded the train. My father was like that.

At times during the week I would go to the Union to pay my taxes and kill some time shooting pool in the recreation room. There were rehearsal studios in the Union available for members to use. Several times I had played pool with a fellow who said he was forming a vocal group. He said if he got the right people he would need an accompanist and someone to perhaps write some vocal arrangements. (It seems he had met Carl Eugster, and Carl had recommended me). I had given up on him until this trip to the Union. He informed me that he finally had put together a vocal group. I invited him to bring the group to my apartment and they could rehearse there.

The group was called The Nightingales. It was composed of two men and two women. Alas, I only remember their first names. One of the girls was Laveda, who could pass for 25 or 35, and was very private about her personal life. The other girl, about my age, or possibly younger, was Lynn. The low voice was Les, who was married and, I guessed, about 30 years old.

Dick was the leader of the group and sang the high parts. They all had regular day-jobs, and we rehearsed only on the evenings when I had the night off. I wrote arrangements for the group and was their accompanist.

The group's leader showed up one night with an agent named Louis Diaz. Louis worked out of the Lita Grey Chaplin Office. (She was Charlie

The Nightingales (Les, Laveda, Lynn and Dick) performing at Travis Air Force Base in 1952. The young man at the piano is yours truly.

Chaplin's ex-wife.) The office was located at the corner of Holloway Dr. and Sunset, and was run by Lita and her son Sidney. Louis thought that he could book the group into a few clubs, but first he wanted us to get some experience. He suggested we do a handful of U.S.O. shows, and promised to keep them mainly in the Southern California area.

In 1951, with the Korean War in full swing, the VA hospitals were crowded with casualties. The soldiers were eager for any kind of entertainment, even us. We performed at quite a few places, even as far away as Fort Ord and Travis Air Force Base near San Francisco. There was no money involved, but a great deal of pleasure seeing the smiles on the soldiers' faces. We were well appreciated, and with each job we gained more confidence.

Louis also put me together with other solo entertainers as their accompanist. I remember one of the singers quite well. Her name was Patty Powers. She was tall with long dark hair and large breasts. The troops loved looking at her. I loved looking at her. Together we did several comedy routines that seemed to go over well with the troops. We worked well together but that's as far as our relationship went as she had an over-zealous stage mother, who kept her on a short leash.

I eventually became well known at the hospitals. Though this was not quite what I had in mind for my career, it turned out to be a definite plus in my personal character development. I was fortunately turning into a nice person.

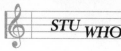

During this time Louis kept pestering me about starting a band. He suggested a society-type outfit of about eight musicians. I listened politely and then proceeded to ignore him. But when my tenure at the Garden of Allah was over, and I was replaced by someone who played and sang named Page Cavanaugh, I seriously considered the possibility of forming a band as Louis Diaz had suggested.

By the end of June I had assembled a seven-piece outfit including myself, and Louis Diaz booked us into the Chi Chi Club, which was the premier nightclub in Palm Springs. Unfortunately, the booking was in September, and that month is not the greatest time of the year to be in Palm Springs. It definitely is not the height of the season.

After leaving the Garden of Allah, while I was preparing my band for the Chi Chi, I managed to pick up a week here and there playing at different cocktail lounges. Because the word-of-mouth between the bar patrons about my playing had been positive, I found myself with a small following. For the time being, financially I was solvent.

I wrote arrangements for the band and twice a week we rehearsed at the musicians union. I should mention a little incident that happened during one of the rehearsals, as it will affect my life several years later in Japan.

While taking a break during one rehearsal, the band practicing next door was also on a break. The leader, whose name was Mark Gardiner, approached me and said he had listened to my band and thought that the arrangements were quite unusual. When I told him that I wrote them he was very impressed. He suggested that maybe when I had time I could write some arrangements for his band. My heart jumped a bit at his offer and I said, "anytime." Unfortunately, *anytime*, was not soon.

Louis Diaz called me one day and asked if I was interested in doing some work for the wives of two comedians. The comedians in question were Tom Noonan and Peter Marshall, who had just finished a very successful engagement at Ciros. It seemed their wives wanted to start their own little nightclub act. One of the wives was a ballet dancer and the other a comedian-singer.

I wrote a few arrangements and performed as their accompanist and cultivated a friendship with Noonan and Marshall. Tommy Noonan was to become a very popular character actor in the movies, and Peter Marshall emerged as one of the biggest game show hosts on TV. They were both *nice people*, especially Peter Marshall, who 25 years later, at a golf-driving range in LA, recognized me at first sight.

Alan Buckhantz is a name that I recall from that time period, but my memory cells seem to fail all attempts at remembering the events surrounding our working together. Carl Eugster informed me that it involved a charity show at the Shrine Auditorium featuring George Jessel. According to Carl, Nick Carras, whom I had done some work with, was conducting the orchestra. I was one of several copyists, and we were beneath the stage copying right up to the last minute. As each page was finished, we would pass the music to the musicians. It seems impossible that I cannot remember anything about this event. Nick Carras and Don Carl Eugster are still living in L.A. In fact I saw both of them in December of 2000, when they reminded me of this story.

Louis Diaz now thought that The Nightingales were ready for a real paying job. He booked the group and "The Wives" into the Zamboanga Club for a three-day weekend. The Zamboanga was somewhere near Florence and Vermont. It was utilized by a lot of comics and other acts to break in new material. The job went reasonably well, but the act was not particularly a hit. Louis talked about Vegas, but talk was all it turned out to be.

About this time one of those *God must have been watching over me* events took place. I answered a knock on my door to find two young girls standing there. They introduced themselves as my upstairs neighbors and said that they were going to have a party that evening, and rather than disturb me, they would like to invite me to the party. I don't recall why, but Jane was not going to be home that evening, so it sounded like a good idea and I graciously accepted.

That evening I went upstairs and was ushered into a larger version of my apartment. About six people were in the place. It reeked of a smell that wasn't familiar to me. Eventually, this naive schnook realized that what I smelled was pot or hash or whatever. Sitting cross-legged on the floor, in a yoga position, was a man whose face seemed very familiar. I didn't know him personally, but I sure knew who he was. The face belonged to Peter Ustinov, who was either a bit tipsy or a trifle high. I wasn't sure which.

I had avoided any drugs my entire life and saw no reason to start now. I politely had a drink, talked to a few not-yet-completely stoned people, and then went back to my apartment. Soon I decided to go out and grab a light bite.

When I returned to my apartment, three police cars were in front of the building. Within a few minutes, six handcuffed people were being led out to the street to the waiting police cars. I watched as my neighbors were

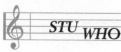

arrested—along with Peter Ustinov. The papers the next day made no mention of Ustinov. (He must have had a great public relations person.) I had luckily missed being arrested by about 45 minutes. Thank you Lord.

One day while visiting my grandmother at Sammy's place, I was fortunate to actually speak to Sammy. He was working with Jackie Barnett again. They had written two songs together and needed a demo. I begged Sammy to let me write the two arrangements and have The Nightingales record the demo. He agreed and the group learned the songs and we recorded them. Sammy and Jackie were pleased with the recordings and paid us. Not very much, but it was better than nothing.

As the summer approached, I discovered that all those rides home that Les was giving Laveda after rehearsals, were more than just rides. Seems they were having an affair. This didn't sit well with the boss, and little by little the group broke up. I threw myself into my arrangements for my band, as the big opening at the Chi Chi was only a couple of weeks away.

Life and love with Jane was still on track, although there were many sob stories about her baby, and whenever I asked her how the divorce was going she always tried to dodge the question. I never pushed it, as I had become pathetically selfish and didn't want to possibly jeopardize losing this great sex life I was having. (Today, as I reflect on my relationship with Jane, I'm ashamed at how insensitive I was.)

One afternoon, returning from a rehearsal at the union, I entered my apartment to find Jane with a visitor. Her guest, a woman, was a striking blonde (dyed, for sure) dressed in the latest fashions, as though she had just come from lunch at the Brown Derby—which she probably had. There was an air of *rich* about her.

Jane introduced her to me as Cheryl, and explained that she was her son's godmother. If I had to guess Cheryl's age I would say about 30. We all talked for a while and then she left. I intently watched her through the window as she got into her new brown Lincoln sedan. I said to Jane "That's one hell of a friend you have." Jane just smiled. It was a slightly devious smile, and in the very near future I was to find out why.

♫   ♫   ♫

We Open in Palm Springs

SEPTEMBER FINALLY ARRIVED AND the band, all seven of us, drove to Palm Springs. The Chi Chi was located on the main drag in Palm Springs only a block or two from Charlie Farrell's Racquet Club. The Racquet Club was an exclusive hangout for the rich and famous. It still exists, but is no longer the exclusive tennis-club it used to be.

It was cool for September on the night we opened… only 105 in the shade. One of the reasons for the band being hired was its ability to sight-read music. There were to be one or two acts a night that we would have to accompany. In between shows we would play for dancing. My arrangements were written featuring a lot of woodwind sounds instead of the usual saxes. It was pleasant music, but not particularly electrifying. The booking was for three weeks with subsequent weekly options.

The Stu Phillips Band at the Chi Chi in Palm Springs.
Once again I'm doing my impersonation of a piano player. 1951

On opening night Louis Diaz showed up and said that Mr. Schuman, the owner, was pleased. The crowd—that's a hoot, let's say the handful that showed up—seemed to enjoy the band. Schuman was a rather curious man who always wore either white pants and a blue shirt, or blue pants and a white shirt. We later found out that he was color-blind and that was his way of avoiding any embarrassing mistakes in choosing his wardrobe.

The billboard at the Chi Chi. 1951

On the second week the featured singing act was one of the Chaplin agency clients. Her name was Marilyn James. (She later changed it to Jesse James.) The third week was a pleasant surprise. The featured act was Lili St. Cyr. Yes, she's the one. A legend of striptease, and one of the first to be known as an "Ex-

otic Dancer." The band was moved to the back of the stage so that Lili could perform in front of us. All we ever saw of her act was her backside, and as I recall, it was a pretty ass. To my dismay, I never did get to spend any time with her—or see her *front*.

On one of my days off, I drove up to Hollywood to pay the Union taxes and see Jane. I decided to sleep over and went to my apartment. Jane was not there. I went to bed expecting her to come in at any moment. Morning came and when I awoke I was in bed by myself. I checked the closet and found that most of her clothes were still there, so I didn't dwell on the subject and returned to Palm Springs. When I arrived, the temperature had dipped to a frosty 100.

The band had been paid for two weeks, and we were eagerly anticipating being held over for a few weeks more. Everybody seemed pleased, so it seemed a cinch that we would have our option extended.

The front of Lili St. Cyr

One night Lou Diaz showed up and said he was working on getting the band a booking in Las Vegas following our engagement at The Chi Chi. The band was excited about the news, as several members were married and had children to support. And with the large amount of rehearsal time they had invested in the band, they had hoped to reap more than just three weeks' work in Palm Springs.

Four days after Lou left we were informed that we were *not* having our option picked up. It seems that the head chef's nephew had a band, and he had convinced the owner to give them a chance. Schuman, it appeared, did not want make his head chef unhappy so he let us go and hired the chef's nephew. The group was The Frankie Ortega Orchestra, which in time became one of the most sought-after Southern California dance bands.

Things now went from bad to worse. Not only were we through at the club, but also Louis Diaz had somehow convinced Schuman to give him—and not me—the check for the band's final week's salary. On pay-day, I couldn't pay the band and, needless to say, they were pissed. I promised that I would go to the Union and file a complaint, since this had been a legal Union job with contracts.

My attempts at collecting the money were futile. Nobody could find Louis Diaz. The Chaplin Agency apologized, but that did little to console me. I gave the band members what I could afford and the group broke up.

I managed to convince the bass and drummer to stay with me and suggested that we should try to get some work as a trio. Unfortunately, I couldn't find a booking, and soon the drummer left and it was just the bass player and I. I managed to get a few weekend gigs for us but that was just about it. It was a quick up and a quicker down for me, but I had managed to get a little taste of what success felt like.

Jane was still my live-in companion, but she seemed to be growing a lot cooler towards me. Plus, when I asked about her divorce, she would get a trifle hostile and refuse to discuss it. A few weeks later, Jane's clothes were no longer in the closet. Our affair was over. Eventually, I found out that Jane had gone back to her husband whose stint in the navy had ended.

Again, like the previous year, September and my birthday sucked. My job at the Chi Chi had ended badly, and to boot, Jane was gone.

♫　　♫　　♫

Moving, But Going Nowhere

IT WAS NOW OCTOBER, AND I decided to try the Garden of Allah once again. When I went in, I noticed that there was no one playing the piano. I found the manager and he seemed glad to see me. I told him of my experience with Lou Diaz and he sympathized with me. He told me that he lost Page Cavanaugh when Page decided to become a trio. There was no room in the bar for a trio. He offered me my job back and I eagerly accepted. I also got a raise to $150 a week.

Once again, I began to get that feeling that my life was due for a little uplifting. My small apartment was beginning to crowd me and it had too many bad vibes. I still felt Jane's presence in the room. I guess my feelings towards her might have been a trifle more than *fondness*.

I located one of those typical Hollywood single-story unattached cottages with Spanish architecture. The kind of place that was featured in all those B detective movies about Hollywood. The place had a central grassy-patio area surrounded by cottages in a horseshoe configuration. It was a definite step up from my previous place.

My new home had a large living room, a bedroom, a kitchen with a back door and a little breakfast nook. It also had a large walk-in closet. The only drawback to the closet was that from the bedroom to the bathroom you had to walk through the closet.

The place was located on Hollywood Blvd. two blocks east of Western, and the rent was $175. I upgraded my rented piano from an upright to a baby grand. I decided to splurge a little since I had fortunately managed to stay well ahead of my savings.

One evening while playing at the Garden of Allah, a familiar face took a seat at the bar. The face—and the body—belonged to Cheryl, Jane's rich-blonde friend. Cheryl stayed at the bar the entire evening until I was finished, which was at about ten. She remarked that she was very impressed with my playing, and said that she would like to try and help me further my career. Cheryl told me that she had many influential friends in the industry and was going get in touch with them. (She was the one who told me about Jane going back to her husband.) Her remarks lit a small spark under my sagging career expectations.

We left the Garden of Allah together and went to a bar near Sunset and Larabee. After a couple of drinks, Cheryl said she was hungry. Since I had only eaten a small sandwich at six o'clock, a meal sounded good to me. I put my hand in my pocket and tried to guess how much money I had with me. I seem to remember that it was about $11. I was almost certain that $11 was not going to be enough to pay the check.

We ordered and when we finished eating, the check came and I closed my eyes and prayed for a miracle. The miracle came. I suddenly felt Cheryl's hand touch mine and I could sense her put something between my fingers. I glanced down at my hand. What I was holding was a $20 bill. I paid the check and left a tip. Then Cheryl said I should keep the balance, that if she were going to help me, she might as well start now. Believe it or not, I was such a whore in those days that I kept the two bucks.

At 22, I had reached the next plateau of social decadence. For seven months I had kept a woman, and now I was about to be a kept man. My friendship with Cheryl progressed very quickly. Whenever we ate out she gave me money to pay the check, and I would keep the change. In retrospect, what a *putz* I was.

As the *coup de grace*, Cheryl then offered me the use of her beautiful Lincoln car five days a week. I was beginning to feel like I had just made a deal with the devil and, pathetically, loved every moment of my digression into Hell. It didn't take long before I found out all I *never* needed to know about Cheryl.

A very wealthy man (who, of course, was married) was keeping her. Every Thursday was his night with her, so naturally the car had to be in her driveway on Thursday evenings and Friday mornings. Oh, did I forget to mention that *he* had given her the car? This man also paid her bills at several of the best department stores, and was even paying the rent on her duplex apartment on Holloway Drive. What a fantastic sugar daddy he was!

This was an incredible scenario. Cheryl was being kept—and, in turn, was keeping me. So it was actually her sugar daddy's money that I was spending. Depravity was now my middle name.

After a couple of weeks of this insanity, I decided there had to be more than my mediocre talent that was persuading Cheryl to keep me. I wasn't *that* talented. My answer came one night when Cheryl called me to say she was on her way over to drop off the car.

The way the car routine usually worked was that she would drive the car over, we'd have dinner, and then I would drive her home. I always wondered how she got around on the days I had the Lincoln. I didn't dwell on that thought too long. Who cared?

Cheryl showed up at my apartment, took off her coat, and made herself comfortable on the couch. I sat down next to her. Since this is basically the story of my music career, and I have promised not to get too involved with my personal life, let's omit the erotic description of what happened next, and just say that she made Jane look like a beginner—sexually. Cheryl stayed the entire night and, no, we never did have dinner. At least *I* didn't. I now understood what that devious look on Jane's face was all about.

I knew that Cheryl was quite a bit older than I was—but *by how much* I didn't know. My curiosity got the better of me and I managed to steal a peek at her drivers' license. It said 26 but I was sure that she was a lot more than 26. Much later on I discovered that she was *36*, and had two ex-husbands. Off and on she would stay at my place, or I would stay at hers.

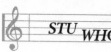

However, there were instances when Cheryl behaved in some strange, inexplicable ways.

Career-wise, she did try to make some contacts for me, but generally her attempts were unsuccessful. When I once again was let go by the Garden of Allah, she managed to get me a job playing at The Black Watch, a cocktail lounge next to Greenblat's Deli on Sunset Blvd. (and, coincidentally, just across the street from The Garden of Allah).

I was so captivated with the idea of being kept that one night I foolishly invited my grandmother and Harry (Sammy Fain's brother) to have dinner at Cheryl's place. I don't know what I was thinking. However, they both enjoyed the evening and Cheryl was the perfect host. She was very personable and easy to like and a hell of a good cook, but she did tend to drink a bit too much: Her only vice?

At various times I thought that I might be falling in love with this woman. I hated myself for even thinking this way, for there were many occasions when she actually felt more like a mother to me than a girlfriend or lover. Cheryl became number three on the girlfriend list—and, once again, not Jewish.

One night, having not heard from Cheryl for a few days, I tried calling her several times. There was no answer. With nothing better to do, I drove over to her place in her car. I parked across the street, and figured that eventually she would return home.

After an hour of waiting, at about nine o'clock, she and another woman came out of her apartment. They had obviously returned home while I was driving over. I suddenly felt self-conscious and slouched down in my seat hoping that she wouldn't notice the car or me. They proceeded to walk down Holloway Dr. to Santa Monica Blvd. where they boarded a streetcar headed for downtown Los Angeles.

My curiosity was aroused. I felt like Sam Spade as I followed the trolley all the way downtown. They got off and walked quickly to the Biltmore Hotel. The two of them entered the hotel and I lost sight of them.

It was close to ten o'clock, and I decided to wait for them to come out. I found a parking space that allowed me to see the hotel entrance, and settled in for the duration. A little past midnight, they exited the hotel and had the doorman get them a cab. The cab left going in the opposite direction from where I was facing. It was useless for me to try and follow them.

Let's quickly get to the bottom line without all the superfluous happenings. It turns out that Cheryl was a high-priced *call girl*. I don't believe that even her Thursday sugar daddy knew about her secret profession. I personally was flattered when I realized that this woman, who was getting $100 a night, was having sex with me for nothing. What a stud I was? No! Actually, what a lamebrain. This woman had had so many dicks stuck in her that heaven only knows what wonderful diseases she might be sharing with me. Drinking it appears, was not her only vice. Fortunately, I contracted nothing. Thanks again, Lord, I owe you big!

When I tried convincing myself that I should give up this affair right away, I couldn't do it. I was either in love or being a stupid, young and immature fool once again, who was overwhelmed by the entire situation and *in* slightly over his impetuous head. Either way, it was a bad scene.

God must be watching out for me number three, was about to take place. When Cheryl was aware that I knew all about her other life, she became quite distant. I no longer got the use of the car, and our time together grew less and less. It appeared that the end of our relationship was close at hand.

About a week later, early in the morning, Cheryl arrived at my door. She proclaimed that she had dumped her married sugar daddy, that she no longer had a car, and that she had taken a cab to my place. It was then that I received the shock of all shocks. Cheryl said that she thought it might be a good idea if we were to get married.

I was stunned, bewildered, but emphatically said "No." I quickly asked the obvious question, "Are you pregnant?" She replied "No," but with a bit of a smirk. I felt at that moment that my infatuation with her was definitely over.

She seemed devastated by my negative reply. To me, her attitude made no sense at all. Cheryl had never, at any time, avowed any love for me. I thought there must be some underlying reason for her demeanor. She left my apartment in a foul and angry mood.

Several days later I began to feel bad about my actions of that previous night, and I decided to apologize for my unsympathetic behavior. I drove over to her place and knocked on the door. There was no answer, so I assumed that she was not home. Once again, like before, I parked across the street and waited for her to return.

I didn't have to wait too long before a car pulled up and two men, along with Cheryl and Cheryl's girlfriend from the other night, got out and went to her apartment. This did not seem like a good time for me to make my apology. I drove off and went home.

The next morning I got out of bed, dressed, and went to the corner drugstore to have some breakfast. As I passed a newsstand, I stopped in disbelief at what I saw. There on the front page was a picture of Cheryl, her girlfriend and the two men. The headline read **"Four Arrested in Midnight Drug Raid."**

Once again, Dame Fortune had smiled on me, and I had escaped arrest by a quirk of fate. I would later find out that Cheryl had been an innocent dupe. She had only been helping out an old friend and was not a part of the "gang," and as a result, was not convicted of anything. Enough about Cheryl—let's get back to my floundering music career, since this is supposed to be a book about the music business.

♫　　　♫　　　♫

In a Rut

NINETEEN FIFTY-TWO ARRIVED AND I was sadly no closer to finding my special niche in the music business. I kept myself busy playing cocktail piano on weekends, and picking up an occasional arranging job. I soon found myself having to finally dip into my dwindling savings. At Christmas, my ever-wonderful father and mother sent me a gift of $150. It couldn't have come at a more opportune time.

I had gotten down on myself for having wasted so much time with my two idiotic and useless affairs. They were great learning experiences, and Lord knows I matured during those months. But they left me completely empty inside. I devoted a great deal of time to practicing piano and made up my mind to become a really good pianist. (It never happened.)

I became involved in several projects that didn't get off the ground, including a film, and another try with a band, but I did manage to get a few weeks work in a cocktail lounge in Westwood. I occasionally went to the Chaplin office to see if they had ever located Lou Diaz. They said that they hadn't, and advised me to drop the whole matter.

One day a letter arrived from my mother, saying that my brother wanted to spend part of his summer vacation in California. Lee arrived at the end of June and spent a few weeks with me. I managed to get him onto the Fox movie lot on my own. It seems Lionel Newman's secretary remembered me, which was somewhat encouraging.

There was a bowling alley a few blocks from my apartment where we bowled a few times. I was once again playing piano at the Garden of Allah for a few weeks and Lee spent several evenings with me while I worked.

After my brother left to go home, I received another letter from my mother. This time there was a second letter enclosed. It was my draft notice. I was shocked! Since my 18th birthday, I had been deferred with a 3C classification because of a head injury suffered when I was 13. It was not serious, but I was taken to the emergency room where X-rays were taken.

Head injuries were something that the Army didn't want any part of, regardless of their seriousness. But with the Korean War now raging in earnest, the Army needed soldiers, any soldiers. Uncle Sam wanted *me*. This, unfortunately, was not the part of André Previn's life that I wanted so desperately to share. Now, I'm *in*! He's *out*! And back to capturing the musical-movie industry *and* the women.

This was, to say the least, very unexpected and unwelcome news, and a real drag. My draft board was in New York City, and changing draft boards at this late date could cause complications (I was in the New York City quota), so I decided to return home. After all, it appeared that my conquest of Hollywood was not progressing as I had hoped. All I seemed to have conquered were two women—*or maybe it was they who conquered me?*

My draft notice called for me to report for enlistment in April of 1953, so I had the better part of a year to kill. By staying longer in Hollywood, all I truthfully accomplished was killing time. Feeling quite a bit deflated I tried to cure the blues by treating myself to a new car.

I fell in love with a yellow 1949 Olds convertible. Buying it depleted my savings, but I really didn't care anymore. I worked a few more cocktail lounges and did some accompanying for a few singers, but I seemed to have lost my drive to succeed. I was no longer that starry-eyed eager beaver of 1950. I felt worn out and depressed.

I managed to pick up a few days work playing a return engagement at The Black Watch. One night, a tired, old looking, washed-out blonde entered the club and sat down at the piano bar. It was Cheryl, although I barely recognized her.

A friend had mentioned to her that I was playing at the club, and she decided, for old times sake, to pay me a visit. We talked a bit and she told me that she was living on Laurel Canyon, just north of Ventura Blvd. In those days, the Valley was the boondocks, and quite a comedown from the glamour and excitement of Holloway Drive and Sunset Blvd.

Cheryl said that she moved there to get away from the influence of the Sunset Strip. It was quite obvious by her demeanor that she was again drinking quite heavily. After about an hour, she left. It was a very sad moment for me, for at one time we had been very close. I couldn't figure out why, but she left me her phone number, so I decided to try and do what I could to help her and gave her a call. Unpredictably, she begged me to stay away, so I did. I will never understand why she gave me her number.

In August I found myself playing piano at Edna Earl's Fog Cutters Restaurant, a steakhouse on La Brea. It didn't take long before a young lady became one of my steady customers. I sensed that it wouldn't take much to generate a little romantic fling between us. With my 23rd birthday soon to arrive on September 9, the last thing I needed was the possibility of another downer birthday in Hollywood. I dumped any romantic notions I might have had, and at the end of August quit my job at Fog Cutters.

I packed all of my worldly possessions into my convertible and with the top down (like Sammy Fain and Gil Turner), proceeded to begin my 15-day cross-country pilgrimage to New York. Ray Heindorf had never called, neither had Lionel Newman. Louis Diaz had completely vanished. Hollywood was living up to its nickname of "Holly*wierd*."

During my drive across the country, I stopped and visited some friends from Eastman School of Music. Since my adventures on this trip have absolutely nothing whatsoever to do with my career, I will skip the details and pick up my life and career in September of 1952, New York City. I was back home living in my parents' apartment. As Jimmie Durante and more recently, William Bendix (*The Life of Riley*) was famous for saying, "What a revoltin' development."

♪   ♪   ♪

3/3 Preparing for Uncle Sam

Into Each Life, a Little Dissonance Occurs

FROM MY OWN TWO-ROOM HOME in Hollywood back to sharing my old bedroom with my brother was a major drag. It appeared that a lot of overnight visits to hotel rooms with dates were going to be in my future. That is, if I could find any women to join me. You might ask why I moved back in with my parents? Unfortunately, I was close to being broke after my odyssey across the country to New York, and what meager savings I still had, I wanted to try and hold onto. I told you I was a bit of a whore in those days.

In an attempt to get my fading career back on track, I proceeded to the Brill Building and tried contacting my old acquaintances. Unfortunately, my *old acquaintances were all forgot*. Things were looking a bit bleak, which was in keeping with the weather.

I can't recall how or when I met Joe Reisman, possibly through an old contact at the Brill Building. Reisman was a successful arranger in the music industry and he mentioned to me that he was writing a nightclub act for a singer named Karen O'Hara. She was going on the road, and hadn't as yet, found an accompanist/musical director to travel with her. I told Joe that I was definitely interested and, a few days later, I met Karen at Joe's Manhattan apartment.

If there was a plus about my meager piano expertise, it was my ability to sight-read and *fake it*. After sight-reading through a few of Joe's arrangements, Karen was impressed and I was hired. She informed me that our first job was going to be in San Juan, Puerto Rico, at the Hilton Hotel. The thought of playing at the Hilton in San Juan energized me and I looked forward to the experience of travel out of the States. Thus far, one day in Tijuana and Rosarita Beach, Mexico, were my only out-of-country experiences.

Puerto Rico, and the two weeks we spent working there were outstanding. Karen was the featured act and a Spanish dancer (from Spain) was the

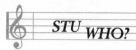

opening act. The shows went well, though Karen occasionally complained about my tempos. She was a trifle temperamental and, at times, could behave a bit *bitchy*. But overall, we seemed to get along fine. In fact, wherever she went, she insisted I be with her, and hung on my arm quite lovingly. This job I was really beginning to enjoy.

My personal contact with Karen never progressed any further than her holding my arm and occasionally my hand. This of course puzzled me a bit. Was this an invitation for me to make a pass—or not? I didn't want to be wrong and jeopardize my job with her. I had jumped much too blindly into sexual affairs in Hollywood, and now I intended to be just a bit more cautious.

The Hilton was filled with single businessmen looking for a little action, and single women seemed to be at a premium. Karen was quite a striking looking redhead (with an Irish temperament to go with it), and every night she was on display wearing a low-cut evening gown as she performed on stage. Plenty of men bought her drinks between shows, but that's always as far as her socializing went.

When the situation between us remained status quo, I soon figured out why she behaved with me the way she did. By appearing to show an interest in me, she was able to keep the men from making passes at her. Every man figured she had a *thing* going with her musical director. It seemed apparent that Karen was not eager to meet any men. I was, to put it bluntly, her decoy.

One of the highlights, or lowlights of the engagement, depending on your political views, was spending an afternoon at the hotel pool basking in the warm Puerto Rican sun next to Senator Joseph McCarthy. He at first spoke mostly to Karen telling her how much he had enjoyed her singing the night before. Then as the day progressed we all three conversed. This was 1952 and the Senator was taking a short rest from the House Un-American Activities Committee hearings in Washington. Despite his questionable politics, he was nevertheless a very charming man to talk with.

After the Hilton, we played a few more clubs back in the States. Karen wanted some new material and she now had confidence in my ability to write the arrangements. Joe Reisman became yesterday's news.

One day, after rehearsing at my parent's apartment, Karen asked if I could possibly drive her home. She said that she wasn't up to taking the train back to Long Beach. On the drive home she started telling me some personal things about herself. I listened with deaf ears. I had had enough of other people's troubles in Hollywood, and didn't need for our relationship to get any more personal than it already was.

To be completely truthful, I *did* find Karen very desirable. Who wouldn't? With her natural-red hair, a handsomely shaped figure and, as they say, an ample bosom, I'd have to have been blind to ignore all this. Nevertheless, I fought any urge that I might have had to once again become involved with another older woman, who was also technically—my boss. I wanted to keep my job more than I wanted sex with Karen.

One of the things Karen mentioned to me was her roommate, who was an airline stewardess. With her reference about a roommate, I suddenly got a slightly different image of why she might have been hanging on to my arm in Puerto Rico and avoiding the men.

At this point in my life, I was still somewhat traumatized by my experience with the gay gentleman and lesbian from my 21st birthday, and I was becoming slightly paranoid about the entire homosexual issue. On a need-to-know basis, I didn't *need* to know if Karen and her roommate were lesbians.

Karen said that her roommate was away at the moment and invited me up to her apartment for a drink. (Well, there went the lesbian scenario.) I said thanks but no thanks, and proceeded to leave. She seemed a little dejected at my answer, and on my drive home I began to reconsider my hasty conclusion about her sexual mores. I then decided that Karen was definitely straight, just a little weird.

♫   ♫   ♫

Sammy Davis Jr.

OUR NEXT JOB WAS IN TORONTO, Canada with two weeks at The King Edward Hotel. We were the opening act to the Will Mastin Trio, featuring Sammy Davis, Jr. What a blast these two weeks turned out to be. Being the opening act meant performing only four songs, so Karen and I were on and off the stage in a flash.

Davis and the trio had already hit it big-time, and this booking was an old commitment that they had to fulfill. Sammy was a bundle of energy on and off the stage. He loved having people around him at all times, and I became a constant companion of his. The last show ended at about 11:30 and Sammy and I, and whoever else was around (Huntz Hall and Gabe

Dell of The Dead End Kids were in town and were often part of the group), would party until about four in the morning.

Sammy liked to fence and carried two fencing foils with him. I had some slight knowledge of fencing, which I had picked up in Hollywood, so Sammy and I would fence on the mezzanine-floor, which was just above the lobby floor. To the guests in the lobby who were watching us at one o'clock in the morning, we must have looked like two of the biggest idiots in the world. Sammy, always the ham, would make a show out of it, and we would duel up and down the grand staircase mimicking Errol Flynn and Basil Rathbone. To this day I still have a half-inch scar on my left thumb from my duels with Sammy.

Partying in Sammy Davis' hotel room. I'm on the left. The guy above me is Huntz Hall, and at the top/center is Gabe Dell. Both were stars of the "Dead End Kids." Have no idea who the others were. Sammy Davis is taking the picture. I kid you not.

Needless to say, my friendship with Sammy did not sit well with Karen. She no longer had me on her arm to keep the men away. I was having too much fun to be concerned about Karen's problems with men. She became angry and took it out on me by constantly criticizing everything I did, and retreated into her *bitchy* routine.

I made up my mind I had had enough of her moods, and I would leave when we got back to New York. Up until now, I had not mentioned anything to her about my going into the Army in March, so the Army became the perfect "out."

All the way home on the plane, Karen's benevolent side returned and she was as sweet to me as she could possibly be. As long as she had me to herself, Karen was a doll. When I told her that I had been drafted she was very sympathetic. (She thought I had just found out.)

When we arrived back in New York, it was the end of January. We played one more weekend together in February, and with no more bookings on the horizon before March, we bid each other farewell.

Between my jobs playing for Karen, I worked a few Friday and Saturday nights accompanying a singer named Gayle Andrews in some classy East-side clubs. Someone had recommended me to her after hearing me play for Karen. Whereas O'Hara was one hell of a good singer, Gayle was just—okay. But she was a beautiful blonde, tall and slender and very easy on the eyes. In the dark bistros with her sultry low voice, she was sensational: A typical B movie chanteuse. All she had to do was stand poised near the piano and the crowd listened, or watched, or whatever. Unlike her sensual image while performing, Gayle was a very sweet, caring and a delightful person to be with.

Well that's how I prepared for Uncle Sam. Actually, my career, monetarily at least, was going a lot better in New York than it ever did in Hollywood. Maybe, I should have stayed home instead of going to California?

♫   ♫   ♫

Draft Day and the Army

IT WAS TOWARDS THE END of March 1953 at Camp Kilmer, New Jersey, where I spent my first full day in the Army. It was devastating. I no longer was my own person. I now belonged to someone, body and soul. The only difference between this and slavery, I thought, was that at least I got paid. After several seemingly endless days of carrying rocks from one side of a field to the other with absolutely no logical purpose, I was assigned to basic training at Fort Dix, also in New Jersey.

My entire squad consisted of nothing but misfits. All of us had been either deferred or overlooked for years. Some of the soldiers were 25 or older. We were the dregs of the basic training groups, and to make matters worse, our drill sergeant was a full-blown psychopath.

He had just come from front-line fighting at the Yalu River in North Korea, and was battle-hardened and battle-fatigued. We endured three weeks of his sadism before he was finally found out, relieved of his command and sent to a mental hospital. But in the three weeks he was training us we suffered. Oh boy did we suffer. Try the Manual of Arms at three in the morning with footlockers instead of rifles.

When the eight weeks of basic training finished, I was assigned to Radio and Communication School. The police action in Korea (as it was commonly called) had come to an end and negotiations for a peace treaty was in progress. (It's 49 years later, and they are *still* negotiating.) The threat of my having to fight in a war was over, and that of course took a large load off of my mind. And I'm sure that my parents were also relieved.

I was not happy when I read my name on the roster for radio school, as I had requested to be assigned to the band or special services. I had shown my commanding officer many letters complimenting me on my efforts with the USO in California, but it was all to no avail. However, my father, bless his heart, decided that I was going to be assigned to the band.

Somehow, he knew somebody, who knew somebody, who knew a retired General. My father reached the General and explained the situation to him. Within two weeks I was transferred to the Fort Dix Band. My father was that kind of man. Oh! Have I mentioned that before?

An odd thing happened to me at this time. A recruiting officer approached me and made me an offer. If I would enlist for three years, he would have me transferred to the Military Academy at West Point, where I would spend all of my time writing arrangements for the West Point Army Band. The West Point Army Band was at that time, a very prestigious outfit. He said that at the end of three years, I would also become an officer. I thought about it for about five seconds and then turned the offer down. The thought of more than two years in the Army was repulsive. However, a few days after our conversation while doing KP duty and scrubbing out some putrid-smelling garbage cans, I had some second thoughts about my hasty decision.

The Fort Dix band was fortunate at this time to be a part of the Arlene Francis[1] television show called *Talent Patrol*. The show featured talented Army performers in a variety format. It was supposed to be a morale booster and Army enlistment commercial. Once a week, the band (about 16 men) would be bused to New York City to the ABC television station for rehearsal. The show was at 7:00 or 7:30. I'm not quite sure which.

The leader was a fellow named Dick Castiglione, who was also one of the trumpet players. Dick was required to be in New York for three days during the show's auditions. When I joined the band they were, fortunately for me, in need of an Army pianist, and I immediately became part of the TV show band.

---

[1] Arlene Francis was best known as a regular panelist on *What's My Line.*

The Arlene Francis Talent Patrol Orchestra in 1953. As usual, I'm on the left. The trumpet player fronting the band is Dick Castiglione . . . the Judas.

ABC was happy not to have to use their own pianist for auditions and rehearsals before the whole band arrived, and asked for me to join Dick in New York for the three days of auditions. With the three days in New York, and a day off after, plus the usual weekend pass, I only had to be at Fort Dix for about a day-and-a-half each week. As a plus, we were given per diem money, since we were on temporary assignment off the post. This, is the Army?

The best part of this unbelievable arrangement was that I was able to sleep at home and pocket the per diem money. I also invited Dick to crash at my parent's apartment. He slept on the couch in the living room and of course my father would not think of taking money from him. So Dick had a free ride, pocketed the per diem allowance, and also joined us for dinner each night. He had it made.

I wrote some big-band arrangements of classical pieces like, *The Nut-cracker Suite*, *Lieutenant Kije Suite* and others, as a part of the audience warm-up. Eventually, with the band's popularity on the television show, the band was asked to perform at some of the Saturday-night dances at Fort Dix and Camp Kilmer. Also, four of us formed a jazz quartet, The Pete Compo Quartet, which played at the officers' club on weekends. This Army thing seemed to be a lot more fulfilling than my three years in Hollywood—except, of course, the sex in Hollywood was better.

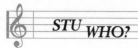

At this juncture, I would like to relate a story that happened during one of our performances at a Saturday-night dance. A busload of lovely young girls from the Philadelphia/Camden area would arrive on the night of the dance. After all, the soldiers needed someone other than each other to dance with. Pressing your body against some other guy was not the *in* thing, especially in those years.

On this one particular evening, I found a young fan (female, naturally) hanging out close to my piano. The band was on a stage and she stood near me watching me play for almost the entire evening. She wasn't beautiful, but she was attractive enough to get my attention. (Whom am I kidding? She was a female—I was a male. Close enough).

She certainly looked to me like an easy score, and I hadn't scored since California. At the end of the evening I looked for her but she was nowhere in sight. As the girls were escorted to the bus by their chaperones and some of the soldiers, I continued looking but still couldn't find her. I finally gave up and went back to the piano to collect my music. As I started to leave the empty hall, I spotted her coming out of the ladies' room. It was evident that she had conveniently missed the bus back to Philly.

I smiled and felt like the wolf in Little Red Riding hood. I was almost licking my chops. Of course, being a gentleman, as well as a horny bastard, I offered her a ride home to Philly (in my *Olds* convertible). It was quite obvious that that was her intention all along. As we drove to Philly, I began to realize that she was a lot younger than I had thought. Probably, just 18, if even that. My thoughts of sex lessened a bit when I realized how close to jailbait she might be.

As we approached Philly there was a big billboard advertising "At The Latin Casino... Sammy Davis, Jr. and The Will Mastin Trio." (By now Sammy was the hottest nightclub act in show business.) Suddenly, my ego grabbed hold of me and I asked her if she would like to see Sammy Davis. It was no surprise to me when she enthusiastically squealed, "Yes!"

We drove to the Latin Casino, I parked the car and we walked to the entrance. I was in my ill-fitting soldier's uniform sporting the rank of PFC. She was in her Saturday-night party dress. I asked the captain if we were in time for the last show. He said yes, but asked if we had a reservation? Of course we didn't. I asked him for a pencil and paper and wrote a note to Sammy.

Dear Sammy, Would you like to fence with me after the show? Remember Toronto and the King Edward? Stu Phillips.

I asked the captain if he would please have this note delivered to Sammy. He gave it to a waiter and I held my breath waiting for the answer. Depending on Sammy's reply, I was either going to feel like the world's biggest ass, or a magnificent hero.

Five minutes later, the waiter returned, whispered something to the captain and the captain said, "Follow me." He walked us to ringside and we watched as two waiters carried in a table and two chairs and placed them down. I sat there with my date feeling like the king of the mountain. Sammy's performance, as usual, was brilliant. When he looked in my direction, I thought that he seemed to actually recognize me.

After the show we were led backstage to his dressing room, where Sammy greeted me with a big hug. What a triumphant moment it was for me. Sammy had actually remembered me, I thought—or if he didn't, he sure knew the right way to treat a member of the Armed Forces. There also was no check for me to pay. He truly was *Mr. Wonderful* that night.

I tipped the captain and proceeded to drive whatever her name was home. When we entered her house it was close to 2:00 AM and her mother was waiting up for her. She definitely was not smiling or too happy about the hour of the morning that I was bringing her daughter home. I quickly said goodnight to her and we politely shook hands. She then gave me the most grateful, and sensual, look anybody could give, and blew me a kiss. I looked for her at subsequent dances but she never showed up. I guess her mother was really pissed.

It was getting close to a year since I had entered the Army. Dick Castiglione's tour of duty was coming to an end. It had always been assumed by my Commanding Officer, and the staff at ABC, that I would take over the musical direction of the band when Dick left. However, we were all unaware that during the two years that Dick was in charge of the band he had become exceedingly friendly with a high-ranking executive at ABC.

Without anyone's knowledge, Dick had convinced the exec that with anyone else in charge, the quality of the band would suffer. He persuaded the exec that he should be retained as a civilian in charge of the band after his stint in the service was over. The ABC execs contacted higher-ups at Fort Dix and, *voila*, one dismal day in March 1954, my name showed up on the overseas shipping list to Japan. I had received the proverbial *finger*, and my ass was burning.

After sponging off of my parents for almost a year and pocketing all that per diem money, this was how Dick said thank you. What a pricky-dicky he turned out to be. For years I planned on finding him and getting even. Fortunately, a little voice inside kept saying, "Drop it, it isn't worth your effort." I listened to the voice and dropped it.

I was scheduled to leave for Japan in two weeks, and in spite of all my pleas—to whomever I could find —my entreaties fell on deaf ears. It appeared that no one wanted to defy the higher-ups. For me it was, *Sayonara, USA… Kohnichiwah*, Japan.

♫   ♫   ♫

Welcome to Hokkaido and Japan

MY TRIP TO SEATTLE FOR EMBARKATION to Japan was not to be believed. I was to travel to Chicago by train on my own, where I was met and ordered to report to a nearby Army base and await the next part of my journey. For some reason, which I can't recall, the Army could not find a commercial flight with available seating for the 20 of us who were on our way to Seattle. So the Army chartered a plane that seated about 25 and we took off.

The food we were served was egg-salad sandwiches, which had obviously not been refrigerated properly. Several of the soldiers got sick and threw up, and the smell in the small plane became nauseating. I had not eaten my sandwich. Thankfully, I hated egg salad sandwiches in those days.

Somewhere in Montana, at around two o'clock in the morning, we landed at a small airstrip to refuel. We all got out of the plane and found ourselves standing in the middle of nowhere. As far as we could see in any direction there was nothing. The wind blew and it was cold, and what you might laughingly call a terminal was closed. We couldn't wait to get back on board the plane, even with the foul smell.

All the way to Seattle the small plane would bounce, bank, dip and dive. The flight was about the roughest I have encountered in my entire life. Eventually, we miraculously got to Seattle alive.

At Fort Lewis in Washington State, we all waited for *The Lists* to be published. The Lists, as I sadly found out, told those of us who were to be shipped overseas, the mode of transportation we would be assigned. There were two lists, and you were chosen kind of *eeny, meeny, miney, moe*. The lucky ones would get to fly and arrive in Japan the same day. The unlucky ones would go by troop ship and arrive about two weeks later. Guess how

I went. You got it. An ocean cruise by way of the Aleutian Islands on a World War II troop transport.

I shared a large dormitory-style hold with about 75 other soldiers. It was so cold on deck that it was almost impossible to stay there for more than ten minutes at a time. The "head" consisted of only a handful of urinals and a few stalls, so there was a constant line to the "john" all day long. The odor from normal bodily functions, coupled with the smell from the soldiers who were throwing up, made a visit to the bathroom a living nightmare. This definitely was not a Carnival Cruise, but in spite of the miserable conditions we all managed to survive the voyage.

It was May when I finally arrived in Hokkaido—specifically, the city of Sapporo. This city had to be the place where, if God were going to give the world an enema, he would stick the plunger. It was, in my opinion, the asshole of the world. I've been told that it's a much nicer place nowadays.

From the age of 10 to 17, I grew up with a daily diet of newspaper headlines dealing with war, death and cruelty. After the Japanese bombing of Pearl Harbor, I remember I felt a constant hate of anything Japanese. Reading about the Bataan Death March and the Rape of Nanking fed my growing hatred. Most Americans shared the same feelings.

Finding myself here in Japan about eight years after the war was not easy for me to cope with. I constantly felt that the Japanese people were sharing the same animosity towards me as I felt towards them. It was difficult to erase the images of tortured soldiers and civilians that I had been exposed to through the newsreels and movies for five years. During my ten-or-so months in Japan, I managed to handle the situation without any adverse incidents.

After leaving Japan in 1955, I have never felt any inclination to return. But I have managed to accept the Japanese people and currently hold no animosity towards them. One of my dearest friends, Sol Schwartz, was a prisoner of war in various Japanese prison camps for four years. After surviving torture, starvation and hard labor, his brave attitude of acceptance was a prime factor in my change of heart. I suffered nothing, compared to him. If he can forgive—so can I.

I spent about a month in Sapporo doing absolutely zero. I ventured into town a couple of times and encountered only prostitutes, hustlers and thieves. The smell of the city was unbearable, and I stayed on the Army base most of the time. (I later discovered that the horrible smell was caused by the human waste—shit to you and me—that they used as fertilizer on their crops.)

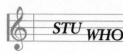
I eventually was assigned to a band unit at Camp Schimmelpfennig (named by the Japanese after a German General who had visited the area) in Sendai, which is about 150 miles north of Tokyo on the East Coast of Honshu. To get from the island of Hokkaido to the island of Honshu, it is necessary to take a ferry from the port of Hakodate. The waters in the Tsugaru Strait between the two islands are considered quite dangerous. The trip was rough but fortunately without incident.

We proceeded south to Sendai by train. Halfway there, the train stopped and we got off to stretch our legs. Several Japanese who were gathered on the platform were reading a paper and reacting very excitedly to the head-line. When we finally found someone who spoke some English, and asked them what the excitement was all about, he explained that a ferry crossing the strait between Hokkaido and Honshu had sunk, and many lives had been lost.

Once again, the Lord was looking over me, as that particular ferry was the next one to leave Hokkaido after us—a mere six hours later.

At Camp Schimmelpfennig I discovered that the division stationed there was the First Cavalry Division, 7th Regiment. (For you movie buffs, that's John Wayne's Division and Regiment featured in all those John Ford west-erns.) I proudly sewed on my insignia, a yellow patch with a black horse's head. It was kind of a kick being in John Wayne's outfit.

Up to this point in the army, I managed to handle most of the *loss-of-individualism* that was thrust upon me. That is, all but one little thing—communal bathrooms, where you "took a crap," as we commonly used to say, in the company of anyone and everyone. This I really abhorred. So the first thing I did upon my arrival at Camp Schimmelpfennig was to reconnoiter some of the isolated emergency toilets around the camp. These were usually single-stall affairs where one could lock the door and have a modicum of privacy. I managed to find two. I adjusted my bowel move-ments to coincide with times of the day when I had enough free time to leave the band area. To enjoy a few moments of privacy was bliss.

The advantageous part of being in this particular band unit, was that the director and commanding CWO (Adam Shpakowsky), was on the U.S. Far East Army bowling team, and spent a great deal of his time traveling with them. That left me, PFC Stuart Phillips, as the only qualified conduc-tor in the outfit. With several sergeants in the band outranking me, there was a lot of resentment towards me whenever I would take command for a musical formation. To help alleviate the situation, I was promoted to

Corporal, even though I did not have enough "time in grade." My new rank seemed to appease "the two Sergeants" for the time being.

I wish that I could complain about my experience in Japan, but I would be dishonest if I did. I took full advantage of my favorable situation and began organizing extracurricular activities for the musicians. I formed a quartet that played the officers club on weekends and also organized a Sauter-Finnegan-type band, which toured the island of Honshu giving concerts at many of the other military installations.

I vividly remember a little flying trip across the mountains to an Army base on the West Coast of the island. If I thought that the flight from Chicago to Seattle was bad, than this flight could only be described as horrific.

I was asked to travel in advance of my outfit to this base and oversee the setting up of the stage and sound system for our band's performance three days hence. Since it was winter, the mountain roads would be very slow and possibly closed, so base transportation looked for an alternative method of transit for me. As luck would have it, the Commanding General was away from the base and his personal plane was available. It was arranged for me to fly in his plane to my destination.

The pilot was a hotshot Lieutenant who loved playing "top gun." (I use this simile, even though *Top Gun*, the movie, was still some 35 years in the future). Flying the General gave this pilot little chance for any fancy maneuvers. However, with me as the passenger—just a poor insignificant Corporal—he was free to play his aerodynamic games.

The plane was a single-engine four-seater. The trip became his personal

1st Cavalry Division Camp Schimmelpfennig show-band. I'm the one in the gray suit.

contest of seeing just how close to the mountains he could fly—without hitting them. I had only flown in a plane about six or seven times but I considered myself a reasonably good traveler. This lunatic went up and down, side to side, banking quickly left, and then right. I grabbed on to the seat and held on for dear life as this future Tom Cruise got his jollies off. When we finally landed, I looked at my hands and saw for real, the derivation of the expression "white knuckles." I decided to stay at the base overnight and not fly back with *the flying jockey*. After the concert, two days later, I was happy to return to Sendai with the rest of the band in an Army truck via the snowy, icy, mountain roads. It seemed a whole lot safer.

The *coup de grace* of my endeavors was to march the entire band to the Commanding General's headquarters at eight in the morning and, while in formation beneath his window, play "Happy Birthday" for him. This surprise so touched the General—and the General, knowing that the commanding officer of the band was not on the post at this time—assumed that it was my doing. He honored me by promoting me immediately to Sergeant. I had only been a Corporal for three months. This really pissed off "the two old Sergeants."

Receiving my Sergeant's stripes and commendation from General Vander Heide. 1954

One of the members of the quartet that played the officers' club, and an integral part of the touring band, was Emilio Raddochia. Later he would be known professionally as Emil Richards. Emil

The jazz ensemble. For a change, I'm on the right side.
Emil Richards is playing the vibes.

and I became close friends and we have worked together on and off for 45 years.

All this hard work finally took a toll on me, and I awoke one morning with an excruciating pain in my stomach. The pain was so intense that I was unable to straighten up. After being examined by the doctor, he gave me a shot of Sodium Amytal to relieve the muscle spasm that I seemed to be suffering from. The shot put me out for almost a day-and-a-half, and when I woke up I was in a sort of stupefied state. My buddies told me that I appeared to be *dead drunk*.

What happened next is what I was told happened, as I do not remember any part of it. It seems that when I awoke, I put on my boots and my hat and proceeded to the Commanding Officer's office to report. There I stood in his office—dressed only in under-shorts, boots and a hat—saluting and proclaiming, "Sergeant Phillips reporting for duty, Sir!" I was told that the Commanding Officer laughed and saluted back. I was not punished for my un-military behavior but my comrades teased me unmercifully about this incident.

On my next visit to the doctor, he prescribed a shot of something or other, and two weeks of R & R (Rest and Recuperation) in Tokyo. I had been diagnosed as having a viral infection in my prostate. (It sounds a lot worse than it actually was.)

I informed my father by phone that I was going to Tokyo on leave, and asked if he had any connections there. Of course he had some, he said, and would immediately proceed to contact them. I told him that I would be staying at the Nikkatsu Hotel.

It turned out that another member of the band, who was a friend of mine, had also gotten two weeks leave in Tokyo. The two of us traveled together and shared the room at the hotel. My father, true to his word, had several people contact me at the hotel. One was an American gentleman who had opened a manufacturing plant in Tokyo; the other was a Japanese businessman that my father occasionally did business with.

A day after we arrived at the hotel, a package with a Diners Club card and a letter allowing me to sign my father's name arrived. My father was that kind of man. (I seemed to have mentioned that many times before.)

I remember in particular the dinner given by the Japanese man. For the first time in my life, I sat at a table Japanese style and was served by smiling and giggling *geishas*. I must admit that my hatred of the Japanese people softened quite a bit during my Tokyo hiatus. They really seemed to be charming people.

The morning following my Japanese dinner, two of the *geishas* who had served me the previous evening came unannounced to my hotel room to give me a massage and bath: An unexpected gift from my host. Unfortunately, a bath and a massage was all I got.

My traveling companion was the kind of fellow you might refer to as a B.T.O. (Big Time Operator). He enjoyed living close to the edge, and was always on the lookout for adventurous things to do. One evening he told

My friend and I taking in the Tokyo sights.

me that he had discovered an underground LIVE SEX SHOW. Still being a bit on the naive side, I thought he was talking about some nude strippers. When he explained to me that there was going to be couples having sex while we watched, I wasn't sure I actually wanted to go. However, I did. (More youthful curiosity?)

We went to what appeared to be a small, warehouse-type of structure, and after paying an exorbitant entrance fee, we were escorted to a large room. There were no chairs, and about 15 to 20 men stood against the wall and watched as a man and woman had sex—first on a cot bed, and then on a chair. Their little performance was followed by two women doing things I never, *ever* imagined.

Very often my eyes wandered away from the action and stared at the men standing against the opposite wall. There seemed to be many large bulges just below the belt area in a majority of the men. All in all, I did not find the show an enjoyable experience, nor did I become sexually aroused. Actually, I found it rather pitiful. However, my adventurous friend ate up every single moment. On the way out, I learned that the man and woman were married. Unfortunately, this little bit of information didn't make what I had just viewed any less disturbing. What a way to make a buck. (Excuse me... *Yen.*)

My hiatus in Tokyo was indeed the cure for what ailed me. My pain disappeared, and I seemed to have found renewed vigor. Unfortunately, good things must come to an end, and soon it was back to Sendai and the military.

♫   ♫   ♫

Homeward Bound

AS 1955 ROLLED AROUND, I started counting the days until my discharge. I figured that I would be sent home sometime in March. Although I still hated being in Japan—instead of conducting the band on Talent Patrol back in New York—I now look back fondly on my Japanese experiences, and wouldn't trade them for anything.

In February, a voice from the past contacted me. If you search your memory, you might recall my meeting a man at the Hollywood Musician's Union named Mark Gardiner, now also stationed in Japan. (He was the bandleader who had liked my arrangements.) My reputation in Japan had grown to such an extent that many people knew of me. When Mark Gardiner heard my name mentioned, he tracked me down at the base and called me.

Mark was now an Air Force Captain stationed at a base a few miles from Sendai. He was in charge of the entertainment at the officers' club, which had a reputation for presenting many fine shows. Mark said he would like me to write special arrangements for his band. I informed him that, within a month, I was due to be shipped home. Mark said a month would be plenty of time for me to write what he needed. He indicated that he would have me put on special assignment to the base, and would get me transferred there immediately.

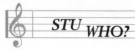

My commanding officer at the band was sorry to see me go, but realizing that I was soon to leave for home anyway, he had started to make plans to have me replaced. I don't remember the name of the Air Force Base I was transferred to, but it turned out to be one cushy job. I was given a private room, with a bathroom (which was the greatest gift of all, after a year of publicly-observed bowel movements), and my only military obligation was to appear at the morning lineup. The rest of the day was all mine.

I was given a key to the officers' club, so that I could use the piano, and took my meals whenever it pleased me. God bless Capt. Mark Gardiner. Of course, Mark was getting several thousand dollars' worth of arrangements for free, which I'm sure he took home with him and used later with his civilian band. For me, the sacrifice was well worth it. Having a private bathroom again was Shangri-La.

When my time came to be shipped home, once again there were the two Lists. One was for flying to Seattle; the other was an ocean voyage. It was, like before, basically a blind draw. Guess which list I turned up on? Of course—it was to be another beautiful ocean cruise for me. Mark tried his best to get me switched but, alas, he failed.

But he did do one last favor for me. He procured some Infantry brass for me to wear home on my lapels instead of the band insignia. As a Sergeant in the 1st Cavalry Division, Infantry, it was assumed by most people that I had fought at the Yalu river—which therefore, made me sort of a hero and one of the untouchables on the troop ship. I was assigned to work in the library and spent the trip sharing a stateroom with one other soldier (instead of sleeping with 75 other men as I had done on the voyage over). And, joy of joys, the stateroom had a toilet! Utopia! (I seem obsessed with the toilet issue. This, I swear, will be the last time it is mentioned.)

Two weeks later, I arrived at Fort Lewis, Seattle, and, after spending a few days being processed, was soon on my way to Camp Kilmer, New Jersey, for my final discharge. Uncle Sam had been good to me: I was still alive.

A Rejuvenated Career

I Meet the Magnificent Dori

SO THERE I WAS: 25 YEARS old; back home with my family; an honorable discharge in hand; many letters of commendation from several Generals—and absolutely nothing on the horizon for my future. I had managed to save most of the money I had earned in the Army and, combined with what I had saved before I entered the service, I was reasonably financially solvent.

But I was in a bit of a quandary. I had not lived in Hollywood for two-and-a-half years, and had only spent five months out of the last five years living in New York City. Plus, a great deal of those months in New York was spent on the road with Karen O'Hara. I found myself without any real roots, and now had to decide exactly where I intended to pursue my stagnant career.

Even though "I had left my heart in Hollywood," my decision was to set up shop in New York City, since living at home would allow me to save money. This time I had my old room mostly to myself, as my brother Lee was now a student at Cornell University.

My brother, who is eight years younger, had followed closely in my footsteps through his teen years. He studied piano and clarinet, and also attended Music & Art High School as I had. But now his career choice was law. With such a big age difference between us, there was little we had in common during our younger years. In 1957, we finally got to know each other on an extended trip to Europe.

Between 1955 and 1957, I remember most of what took place but unfortunately, try, as I will, I cannot remember the proper sequence of all of the events. So in typical musician fashion, I'll fake it.

I immediately had to get my act together and proceed towards my ultimate goal of being the "third-best arranger in the world." (By the way, André Previn, career-wise, was catapulting way ahead of me.)

I called everybody I ever worked with in New York. Of course I called Karen O'Hara. She was excited to hear from me, but explained that things were a little slow at this time. However, she would love once again to have me as her accompanist—if and when she got some bookings.

I also located a soldier buddy I had met at Fort Dix. His name was Al Ganci, and he played about the worst tenor sax you have ever heard. His entire repertoire consisted of two songs, "Night Train" and "The Stripper." Al lived a few blocks from me and said he had a carload full of "broads" available for a good time. This sounded fantastic to me, as my life in the Army had been quite chaste and sex-free. There were way too many diseases floating around Japan to make sex with prostitutes enjoyable. And *nice* girls were impossible to meet. It had been a long time since my last sexual encounter.

Allow me to take a brief moment to describe Al Ganci to you. He was about six-foot-three and one of the best-looking Italian-American men I had ever met, with muscles on his muscles. Women had a habit of lifting their skirts and dropping their pants for him. He was a genuine stud. Think of a tall Sylvester Stallone. Al was also probably the stupidest person I had ever met. But he was willing to share his *excess* women with me. He was all heart. The fact that I had a car available for double-dating didn't hurt my cause either.

On one of our double dates Al got a suite at a neighborhood hotel for free, from a friend who worked at the hotel, and we took the girls there. Al went into the bedroom with his date while I stayed in the living room with mine. She was not my type, and I couldn't get myself motivated to make any serious sexual advances. We necked a little and, when Al came out of the bedroom with a look of complete satisfaction on his face, I was more than happy to call it a night. I made the mistake of giving the girl my phone number and two days later she called and asked if I could drive her to Yonkers (about a 30 minute drive north of the city) to pick up her dog. Lacking anything better to do, I reluctantly decided to give her a ride.

When we arrived back at her apartment in Manhattan she said that there was someone in the bedroom who would like to say hello to me. As I entered the bedroom, there, lying in the bed was an old friend. It was Cheryl, from my past and wicked Hollywood days.

She looked like hell—older than her years and to complicate matters, she had a cold. We reminisced about our time together in Hollywood and then she casually suggested that I join her in bed, for old times, but I said no thanks. I wasn't trying to be gallant, or anything like that; it's just that she did not seem that sensual to me anymore. Once again in the late 1960s her name will come up. I'm sorry about all these detours about my personal life, and I will now quickly return to my stumbling, bumbling career.

♫   ♫   ♫

Harry Revel

ENTER, HARRY REVEL. For those of you not familiar with his name, let me give you a brief introduction. He was a contract songwriter at the Fox and MGM studios in Hollywood. Among some of his big hits, written with Mack Gordon, were "Stay as Sweet as You Are," "With my Eyes Wide Open I'm Dreaming," and many more. He also had several hit albums on Capitol Records, which featured beautiful instrumental arrangements of his melodies. Among the albums were, *Perfume Set to Music* and *Music from Out of the Moon*. The conductor and arranger on these albums was Les Baxter, who became more famous from the success of these albums than Harry Revel did.

I still to this day don't recall how Harry got my name (probably from Sammy Fain), but in late 1955, he contacted me. He was residing in New York on West End Ave.—actually, only about eight blocks from where I was living. Harry informed me that he was trying to put together another one of his instrumental albums and thought I might be interested in working with him. Was he kidding? Interested! I would have jumped through a wall of fire to do his album, considering the fame that came to Les Baxter after collaborating on Harry's other albums.

Ah! But of course, there was a catch. Harry said that he didn't have a deal with any record company—so naturally Harry didn't have any financial backing to make the album. My dream began to go up in smoke. I needed a small miracle.

I told my tale of woe to my father and explained to him how Les Baxter had become famous from his collaboration with Harry and the success of their past recordings. My father responded in his usual way. "What can I do to help?" he asked. I explained that money was the problem.

My father, I reiterate, was not a rich man. He made a respectable living and kept his family in good stead. When I told him how much money was needed, he offered to finance the recording sessions. Once again I say with pride, "My father was that kind of man."

Needless to say, Harry Revel was thrilled when I told him the news. He met with my father, and they discussed the terms of an agreement. My father was a generous man, but not a *stupid* one. He made sure that he had a proper legal agreement with Harry.

Subsequently, my father managed to get us a meeting at MGM Records. It seemed my dad had done some business with the head of the record company; a man named Harry Meyerson, who was happy to put the album out—especially, since he didn't have to pay for the recording sessions, and MGM's only outlay of cash was the artwork and pressings.

The name of the album was *Music from Out of Space*. It featured an orchestra and chorus, with the chorus vocalizing only *ahs* and *oohs*, instead of words. Easy listening at its best. I now, finally, had the opportunity to write Morton Gould and Dave Rose style arrangements. My enthusiasm was uncontrollable as I prepared for the recording sessions.

I planned to feature several piano solos and called my high school buddy Cy Coleman, hoping he might be interested in playing piano on the ses-sions. Cy was now the darling of the East Side cocktail lounges; he and his trio were the talk of Manhattan. Cy was a brilliant pianist in both the jazz and clas-sical fields. He reluctantly said, yes. I couldn't blame him for being reluctant: he worked every night with his trio until 3:00 A.M. The sessions were to start at 9:00 A.M., and that gave Cy very little time for sleep.

My high school buddy Cy Coleman and Harry Revel. I'm explaining to Cy what all those black dots on the paper mean.

Someone had to make sure that Cy got to the sessions on time. It so happened that when we recorded in early January of 1956, my brother was on hiatus from Cornell. Each morning his assignment was to go to Cy's apartment, wake him up, and personally escort him to the session. He performed magnificently. (Cy, if you happen to read this, thanks again.)

I also called two old friends from Eastman School of Music—Jim Buffington (French horn) and Ray Shiner (woodwinds)—to play in the orchestra. They both were considered top recording musicians in New York,

Tom Phillips, my brother Lee, Harry Revel and me.
It appears as though my music needs a lot of explaining.

and I was fortunate to get them. The sessions went well, as far as I was concerned, and of prime importance, Harry Revel was pleased.

Unfortunately, the album was released with little fanfare and, as a result, died a horrible death. I felt so badly for my father. He was never to see that money back, and I'm sure that the expenditure left a small hole in my parents' savings. This was my first major "flop," and I felt devastated. Although the arrangements were acceptable, I was well aware that I still had a lot to learn. I was not up to Gould or Rose—yet!

The Music from Out of Space orchestra.

I think it was either through the arranger who worked at ABC on the *Arlene Francis Talent Patrol Show*—or that Raymond Scott the music director of *Your Hit Parade* heard my album of *Music from Out of Space*—that I was hired to do an arrangement for the TV show *Your Hit Parade*. The song that I arranged was "Wake the Town and Tell the People." I only did one other arrangement for the show. It was obvious that what I wrote did not particularly impress the people in charge, since they saw fit not to hire me again.

Early in 1956, after the *Music from Out of Space* fiasco, I received a call from Emilio Raddochia (my Army buddy in Japan), now known as Emil Richards. He had recently been discharged and had moved from Connecticut to New York to begin his professional musical career. Emil's call triggered an idea I had been kicking around since Eastman. I called Jim Buffington, Ray Shiner and Emil and suggested that we cut an album featuring Jazz French horn and English horn, and vibes. They agreed to the idea and it was now up to me to sell it to a record company.

Rehearsal for the album *A Touch of Modern*. 1956 From left to right: Me, Dick Romoff, Ray Shiner, Terry Snyder and Jim Buffington. Emil Richards is off camera.

Harry Meyerson at MGM records was my first call. It turned out that he thought very highly of the Harry Revel album, and was puzzled and disappointed by its lack of sales. He was eager to hear my idea. Since a sextet was not a very expensive project, Meyerson decided to okay the recording sessions.

I managed to get Terry Snyder (the best studio drummer in New York) to play the drums. Then I hired Dick Romoff, the bass player I had used on the Harry Revel album. I wrote arrangements for all the tunes with many jazz choruses featuring Jim, Ray and Emil. I only occasionally took a chorus, as jazz piano was not really my forte.

The album was called *A Touch of Modern*, and is available for sale at my home. It bombed worse than the Harry Revel album. It was my second consecutive *flop* and I was batting *zero* in the record business.

As a passing note, the album did wonders for Emil Richards. He went on to become an integral part of the George Shearing group and, upon moving to Hollywood, became one of the top studio percussionists in the world.

At this time I became friendly with Al Herman, an agent who felt that I had some potential. He managed to get me a week's booking on a radio show called *NBC Bandstand*. This was a daily morning radio show, which each week featured some band or singer and was usually hosted by Bert Parks and Skitch Henderson. I acquired the job based on the work I had done on the *Music From Out of Space* album. Evidentially, the arrangements were better than I thought.

I put together two different orchestras: one with strings and voices; the other more dance-band oriented. We played some standards as well as several tracks from *Music from Out of Space*. To the best of my recollection, the shows went well. Though this was a prestigious accomplishment, I somehow felt little gratification. I do believe I was becoming a bit jaded.

♪   ♪   ♪

Chris Connor

I CIRCULATED MY SEXTET ALBUM around the industry, as best I could, and a copy somehow got into the hands of jazz-vocalist Chris Connor's manager. Chris had been playing club dates with an accompanist who was completely jazz-oriented. Her management and record company (Atlantic Records at the time) felt that a change in her accompanist might just enhance her club appearances, so I was called in to audition for the job.

I wasn't sure that playing for Chris was how I really wanted to proceed with my career. Accompanying vocalists was not what I had pictured as my

future in the music business. On the other hand, Chris was somewhat famous having performed with the Stan Kenton and Claude Thornhill bands, and just recently had two hit records: "All About Ronnie" and "I Miss You So." She was considered one of the top jazz vocalists in the industry, and I personally had always admired her singing—so what the hell! Why not?

I passed the audition and got the job—but I somehow had the uneasy feeling that Chris was never completely happy with me as her manager's choice. However, she seemed willing to give me a chance. What her management liked most about my playing was that I was strictly an accompanist, with no agenda of my own to distract from Chris' vocals.

We played four club dates together, and I was the pianist on one of her recording sessions for Atlantic Records. For me, the two most important clubs I played with Chris, was the one in Camden, New Jersey, and the date in Boston. Although I received my best reviews as her accompanist at the two jobs in Washington, D.C. (Chris was brought back by popular demand), the other two play dates seem to remain more distinct in my memory.

At the club in Camden, I was joined by the Modern Jazz Quartet in backing Chris. What a thrill it was playing with these superior musicians. In the audience were two big fans of Chris'. They just happened to be burlesque strippers from Baltimore who, unsurprisingly, I became friendly with. I decided to spend my day off visiting them in Baltimore; where I learned all about the backstage escapades of burlesque and discovered that stripping was a job like any other—only without clothes. (As a freshman at Eastman, eight years earlier, I sat in the audience gawking. Now, here I was, buddy-buddy with the strippers and getting a close-up view.)

Chris Connor performing in Camden, New Jersey. 1956
As usual you can find me at the far left. The other musicians
are part of The Modern Jazz Quartet.

It appeared that our collaboration was a success, and I was beginning to enjoy my job with her. She was very sweet, but at times could be a bit moody and hated singing the same songs night after night the same way. Chris felt a need to do everything up one level from the previous performance. Her back phrasing got so far back, that at times she was singing to the wrong harmonies. She sometimes became difficult to follow and would occasionally blame me for her less-than-brilliant performances. Possibly— she was right.

Although in her big-band days, she was romantically involved with several men, it was sometimes rumored that she might be more inclined towards women. With her very close blonde, boyish haircut, she of course invited many inferences that she might be a lesbian. Although I never had any concrete reason to believe the rumors, I also had no tangible reason to doubt them.

The other engagement was in Boston, Mass. at Storyville, the most famous jazz club on the East Coast. It was during this engagement at Storyville that I met Dee Lawlor. (Here I go again with the personal stuff.)

After a casual meeting with Dee on opening night, she returned on several subsequent evenings to see the show again, each time accompanied with a girlfriend. After each show, I would join her at her table and we would talk until the next show. On her third visit, she either planned it, or it was accidental, but somehow found herself without a ride home. It was 2:00 A.M. (Shades of Fort Dix and my adoring underage fan. There seems to be something about piano players that attracts women.)

I had driven up to Boston from New York in my car, so I of course offered her a ride home. This, needless to say, was what she was hoping for. Dee was a lovely girl and taking her home was definitely what *I* secretly had been hoping for. We had a light bite at a diner, and then she suggested that we watch the sunrise from this very romantic spot she knew. This was too much like a movie to be actually happening. But—it was.

Being late October, it was cold. (Seems like Boston is always cold.) We parked and snuggled close, and watched the sun come up. It was very idyllic, for sure. Only a little tame necking took place, but I was definitely enamored.

In the weeks that followed we corresponded and spoke on the phone many times. I began to really believe that she was the right girl for me. I finally convinced her to come down to New York City and stay over for a weekend. She eagerly accepted my invitation. We spent three wonderful romantic days together. Nothing was consummated sexually, and I took

this to be a positive, rather than a negative sign in our relationship. When she left to return home, I said I would come up to Boston to visit at the first opportunity.

We wrote to each other several times. I got a little busy and didn't get to Boston as soon as I would have liked to. Little by little, the letters stopped. Eventually, so did the affair. I was really quite sad when our friendship ended. I had been so sure that she was Miss Right.

Not only did our affair end, but also so did my job with Chris Connor. At a weekend engagement soon after Boston, her manager told me that Chris wanted to make a change. She and I parted without any animosity and as good friends. In her dressing room as I said my final goodbye, she warmly embraced me. She was nice people.

I now decided that living at home was not conducive to entertaining female company—and I was sexually stagnant. I had some serious money saved up and I felt it was time for my own apartment. I had lived alone for almost three years in Hollywood; two-and-a-half years in Rochester; and two years in the Army. Living with my parents was getting to be a little claustrophobic, and I felt absolutely infantile.

When I announced my decision to my parents, my mother almost went into cardiac arrest. How could I even think of such a thing? Of course my father, as usual, was more understanding. When I explained to my mother my reasons for wanting my own place she got even angrier. I was 27 years old and my mother seemed oblivious to the things that grown men did sexually. However, I still only looked about 18. Maybe that's what she kept seeing.

Anyway, she made such a fuss and got my father so aggravated that I stayed at home. My father had been diagnosed with angina pectoris in 1947, and had been told to stop smoking and avoid stress as much as possible. His stress and his health were my main concern, as well as my mothers.

Karen O'Hara called soon after my split with Chris. Her call was very welcome as I was beginning to go bonkers from lack of work. Karen had a new agent, and he had gotten her a one-shot recording deal with MGM Records. Harry Meyerson was still there, and when Karen said that she was going to use Stu Phillips to write the arrangements and conduct, he was pleased with her choice.

We recorded two sides. One was a new song by Arthur Hamilton (of "Cry Me a River" fame), and the other was a standard. The recording was good, but sold *nada*. That made three flops at MGM. Three flops and you're out, I guess.

A very wealthy gentleman from Philadelphia named Leonard Tose (he of the Tose Trucking Company) invited Karen to spend a weekend at his estate outside of Philly. How Karen and Leonard knew each other I have no idea, but it was apparent that, for some reason, which Karen kept to herself, she wanted to be Leonard Tose's "friend."

Karen called me and asked if I would be her escort for the weekend. I of course assumed that we would be performing. She said that I had assumed wrong. She just wanted me to be her escort.

Once again, as in Puerto Rico and Toronto, it was obvious that Karen wanted Leonard Tose to think that she was involved romantically, so that he would not be tempted to make any sexual advances. And like before, *I* was being used. Only this time it was necessary for Karen to do more than just hang on my arm. Leonard Tose's intentions were not at all honorable. He had invited her to Philly for the weekend for one reason and one reason only: *sex.*

Karen realized that she was going to have to make our relationship look even more realistic. She did a great deal more hand holding and on occasion planted several rather warm kisses on my lips. Now *I* was getting a bit perturbed. I'm only human, and this little sham was going farther than I appreciated. I felt like I was one kiss away from *all-out sex* with her.

It was a long weekend, but it finally ended and neither Leonard Tose nor I scored with Karen. I thought about renewing my previous "lesbian" evaluation of her.

Soon after Philly, Karen got a booking in Chicago at the Drake Hotel. She asked me to go with her and I accepted. I did make sure that this time we were going to perform. Anyway, I was desperate to get away from my room at home, and any excuse sounded like a good one.

At the Drake Hotel, Karen was the featured act, and a young sister-team was the opening act. The sisters danced, sang, and did imitations plus a little comedy. The girls were a lot of fun to be around and, for two weeks between and after shows, the three of us hung out together—just friends.

Karen, who didn't particularly like me hanging-out, became very moody again, as she had previously. She grew difficult to work with and started to demand more of my time. I tried avoiding her as much as possible when we were off the stage. By the end of the engagement we barely spoke to each other. She was acting like a jealous lover, even though she had no reason to. I had never made a pass at her, and although we often embraced and kissed, as close friends often do, I still had the idea in the back of my mind that she just might have been gay, and so I kept my hands to myself. Anyhow, the

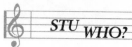

job in Chicago turned out to be the end of my association with her. To clear up any doubts, I finally did discover that she was definitely "straight." (Or maybe—a switch hitter?)

Once again, Sammy Fain inadvertently came through for me. When Benny Fields mentioned to Sammy that he and Blossom were going to record an album at Mercury records—and that they were looking for a young arranger to spice up some of their old arrangements—Sammy brought up my name. It turned out that Benny and Blossom had met my mother and father at some function and when Sammy mentioned me, they were aware of who I was. I was Minnie's son... the arranger.

Benny Fields and Blossom Seeley were two old vaudevillians who were attempting a bit of a rebirth. They were trying to make a comeback, and Hugo and Luigi (remember these names, as they would soon become two of the most important people in my life), were at the time A&R men with Mercury Records. They were the producers of Benny and Blossom's album.

Benny Fields and Blossom Seeley:
A couple of old vaudeville troupers.

Benny and Blossom requested that I conduct the orchestra and write several of the arrangements. The album was titled *Two a Day at the Palace*, and when it was released it caught the attention of Ed Sullivan, who booked them on his TV show. Benny and Blossom asked me to conduct for them on the show, and Ed Sullivan agreed. I conducted two Sullivan appearances for them. Working for Benny and Blossom was indeed a *vintage* experience.

I searched out Gayle Andrews (the sexy blonde with the sultry voice), and played a few weekend gigs with her. It was a nice change of pace from the large hotel rooms, to be working again in those small, dark, East-Side supper clubs.

If any other significant happenings took place during the period from 1955 to 1957, I have absolutely no recollection of them. But one event that was to take place in 1957 would become the most important chapter in my life. This event I will never forget. Now all the brain cells are alive and well and cooking. The magnificent Dori entered my life.

The Copa Gal

ENTER WITH FULL FANFARE, Dori Anne Gray, "The Copa Gal." Born Dorian Saundra Fogel, she has become my main reason for living. Dori became the inspiration for my moderately successful career, and the fulfillment of all those stupid romances that I believed was the real thing. She is, and will remain, my only *true* love.

Now, how did we meet? Remember Hugo and Luigi? Well they were Dori's A&R men, as well as Blossom and Benny's, at Mercury Records, where Dori was under contract. When Hugo (Perretti) and Luigi (Creatore) left Mercury records and moved to Roulette Records they took Dori Anne Gray with them. Dori, was a vivacious 19-year-old with a great big voice. Although only five feet tall, she sounded like six: Sort of

Have you ever seen a prettier face?
Is it any wonder that I married her?

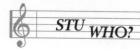

a smorgasbord of Theresa Brewer, Ethel Merman and Judy Garland.

She had made several singles at Mercury with moderate success, but through the recordings had become one of Alan Freed's favorites. Through Freed, Dori soon became the token *white* at Alan's rock and roll concerts—which featured mostly black acts—at the Brooklyn Paramount. (I know this is my biography, not hers, but to tell a bit of her story is important to me, so indulge me for a moment.)

Dori's whole life had been devoted to show business. She was a show-biz child through and through, and longed for stardom. While still in her teens, she sang in The Borscht Belt, at old age homes, anywhere people would listen. She danced and sang her way into people's hearts. She was that kind of performer, and is now that kind of woman. I have never heard even a rumor, that anyone ever disliked Dori. At the present time, nobody can say one evil word about her, because there is nothing bad to be said about her. She's not perfect—but close to it.

Dori had wanted to record an album for the longest time, and Hugo and Luigi—who where her managers as well as her A&R men—promised that at Roulette Records she would have the opportunity to record an album.

Enter...me. Having read in the trades of Hugo and Luigi's switch to Roulette Records, I seized upon the opportunity to see them—on the out-side chance that they might hire me after recalling the work I had previously done. I hoped that they would remember me from Blossom and Benny.

Hugo and Luigi's secretary, Cathy Favaro, did remember me, and let me hang out around the office. For days I sat there outside Hugo and Luigi's office hoping for any little job that they might throw my way. After awhile, Kathy recalled that Dori was looking for someone to do arrangements for her nightclub act (preferably *cheap*). Since Cathy knew that I was eager to do some arranging, she decided to introduce us. Dori and I played each other like a couple of con men. I wanted a job, any job; she wanted "cheap arrangements." And I was as cheap as you could get.

At that time, Dori was working at the famous Copacabana nightclub as the featured singer with the floorshow; and as a lounge act in the bar: hence the derivation of *Copa Gal* as the title of her album. For several months I dated her. When I found out that her album was soon to be recorded, I decided that I had to get the job of writing the arrangements. Dori, as it turned out, also wanted me to do the arrangements. (It's inter-esting to note, that after 44 years of sexual favors, I never did write her nightclub act.)

64   NIGHT CLUB REVIEWS

Copacabana, N. Y.
Frank Sinatra, Joey Bishop, The Petticoats (3), Ron Beattie, Dori Anne Gray, Michael Durso and Frank Marti Orchs; staged by Douglas Coudy; songs, Durso, Mel Mitchell & Marvin Kahn; costumes, Sal Anthony (Mme. Berthe); orchestrations, Deac Eberhard; $5 minimum.

As you can see in this newspaper column, Dori Anne Gray worked with the "crémé de la crémé."

We had obviously grown fond of each other during our conniving period. By now, aside from wanting to do the arrangements for her album, I also wanted Dori—wanted her *real bad*. But I kept my wits about me, kept my hands in my pockets, and remained a reasonably genteel young man. This turned out to be a wise move on my part.

During various times in 1957, I found myself rising at three in the morning; getting dressed; driving down to the Copa; waiting for Dori to finish her last set in the lounge (at about 3:55 A.M.); take her to breakfast; and then drive her home. At about six, I would go back to bed.

The plan was for the recording of the album to take place in either late September or early October. Meanwhile, my brother had just finished his fourth year at Cornell, and before he started law school, my father decided to give him a graduation present: a trip to Europe. My father felt that my brother was in need of a chaperone, so he came up with the following blueprint and made me an offer I found hard to refuse.

He said that he would foot the bill for my round trip to Europe on the *Ile de France*; the cost of a rental car; the hotel rooms—and all I would have to pay for was my food and extras. It sounded like a good deal to me. In August, after my brother's birthday the two of us left for a six-week tour of Europe.

I told Dori to wire me when the recording dates for her album were finally scheduled. I was excited about the excursion to Europe, but a little sad about leaving Dori for so long.

Since this trip has nothing to do with my

The brothers Phillips rushing to catch the United States. 1957

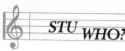

musical career, I will not devote any time to our adventures on the conti-nent. That little odyssey in itself is worthy of an entire book. Suffice it to say that my brother and I got to know each other a lot better. Our journey started in Paris and after touring many countries by car, we were to return there for about four days before proceeding home.

When we arrived in Paris in mid-September, there was a cable waiting for me. Dori's recording was to take place very soon, and if I did not return within the week, I would lose the job. We could not get on any flights to New York, as they were all booked. But we did manage to get on the *United States Steamship*, the fastest liner in the world at that time. It got us to New York in five days, and my job was secure.

Upon seeing Dori again after arriving home, I realized how much I had missed her. I had never before really missed any other woman like that. When my other romances had ended…that was it. I sometimes reflected for a while of what might have been, but the feeling never lasted very long.

We recorded the album together, and managed not to get on each other's nerves. Thank God for that. The album, of course, was called *Copa Gal*. Unfortunately, it also joined a long list of my flops. I was still batting zero in the record business. I felt badly for Dori, as she had wanted so much to have a successful album. I had a bad feeling in my gut that its failure might have been my fault, and I hoped that her disappointment wasn't going to have any effect on our personal relationship.

In a moment of either extreme flippancy or complete seriousness, I suggested to Dori that if I could find an apartment, perhaps we should get married. And in a moment of either flippancy or seriousness on her behalf, she calmly shrugged and said, "Why not?" Quite a proposal, don't you think? I fortunately found an apartment in the same building I had been living in with my parents (The Schwab House on Riverside Drive by the Hudson River), and we set a date in February for the wedding.

We were married at the Sheraton Hotel, in a small ceremony with only immediate family and close friends. Of course, Hugo and Luigi were there, as was Cathy Favaro. Hugo and Luigi were not happy with the entire affair, and prophesied that the marriage would never last. Forty-four years later, I say *phooey* to Hugo and Luigi.

The band (excuse me, trio) at our wedding consisted of Moe Weschler (sometimes known professionally as Knuckles O'Toole) on piano; Kenny Burrell on guitar; and Dick Romoff on bass. All three were musicians that either Dori or I had worked with. We walked down the aisle towards the

The newly-weds...1958...Love in bloom.

chuppah to the romantic strains of "You'll Never Know," our favorite song. No Wagnerian "Bridal March" for us.

We had no honeymoon, as Dori had a job the following morning appearing as a guest soloist on *NBC Bandstand*. (The same show where I had performed with my orchestra). The following weekend, her agent had booked her into a club on Long Island. She was no longer working at the Copa, and money became our first priority, so we both grabbed whatever work we could find. At that point in our marriage, Dori was the star and bread-winner.

Later on in the year she made several return appearances on *NBC Bandstand* with Bert Parks and Skitch Henderson, and performed magnificently. But then again, I'm just a teeny-bit prejudiced.

As Dori and I settled into married life, I was pleasantly surprised when I was contacted by Hugo and Luigi. Jimmie Rodgers ("Honeycomb," "Kisses Sweeter than Wine") was one of the hottest singers around at that time, and his agents wanted to see just how he might fare on the nightclub circuit. Jimmie was now in the market for a musical director.

Aware of my brief stint with Chris Connor as her accompanist and musical director, and the work I had done for Dori, Hugo and Luigi suggested me for the job to Jimmie's agents. When Rodgers agreed to hire me, I quickly accepted the offer. The money was reasonable and I would, once again, be working with a full-fledged recording star. The job started right away, and I left my lovely bride of only a few months to hit the road with Jimmie Rodgers.

♫   ♫   ♫

5/5 Rodgers to Light to Colpix

Not Quite What I had in Mind

JIMMIE RODGERS BELONGED TO A GROUP of performers that could best be described as the "good old boys." He was from the area around Camas, Washington State, and prided himself in his small-town roots.

Jimmie Rodgers

Rodgers was sort of an "aw shucks" John Denver type, and the public seemed to love his lack of show-business attitude. Jimmie's wife, Colleen, a very good-looking woman, was not quite as small town-ish as Jimmie, and her opinions seemed to sometimes have a large influence on many of his decisions.

Our first engagement in Washington, D.C. was, coincidentally, at the same club that Chris Connor and I had previously played. Jimmie's rustic charm pleased the audience, but the critics were not overly enthusiastic about his future as a nightclub act.

Early on in my association with Jimmie we played the Steel Pier in Atlantic City. Dori and I had only been married a few months, and we were still getting to know each other. Since Atlantic City was so close to New York, I decided to have Dori accompany me.

We stayed in a motel that was close to the pier. I awoke one morning feeling sick as a dog. I kept telling Dori I was running a high fever. She became very concerned and called a doctor. The doctor came, examined me, took my temperature and told Dori that I had a fever of only 91 degrees. His diagnosis was that I really wasn't very sick. Dori learned then, that with just a smidgen of fever, I fall apart. I still do. All my doctors seem to agree that I'm a lucky person to have that type of reaction.

At an outdoor concert at massive Soldier's Field, in Chicago, I discovered the pitfalls of trying to follow a singer when the audio speakers were incorrectly positioned. Jimmie's voice was arriving to me many milliseconds late. With the swirling Chicago wind added in, that concert was a bitch to conduct. Fortunately, in this day and age, technology has advanced and this type of audio problem is less frequent.

We played several other dates including one in Washington State near Jimmie's hometown of Camas, right across the river from Portland, Oregon. Needless to say, performing among his hometown crowd, he was a smash.

We also appeared in a club in Boston, but chose not to stay in the city. Instead, we found accommodations several miles north at an old hotel in Rye Beach, New Hampshire. The hotel was called The Farragut, and upon entering the lobby, we all felt that we had been transported back in time to 1900. Everyone in the lobby of the hotel was seated, and either reading the paper or playing cards. They were dressed as though they were about to leave for a fancy dinner—even though it was only noon. (It was very much like a scene out of the recent film *Gosford Park*.)

All eyes turned to look at the new arrivals. (Jimmie, Colleen, Dori, myself and Sid Gould and his wife Wanda.) Dressed in our very casual and sporty clothes, it was obvious that we did not fit in. First of all, four of us were Jewish, and I do believe these people might have thought that all Jews should be living in Israel. Secondly, since none of our ancestors had come over on the Mayflower—in their minds, I'm sure it must have branded us as second-rate Americans. A handful of these people appeared to have been old enough to have actually *been* on the Mayflower.

To compound the situation, Sid Gould was a comic with a very obvious Jewish accent. When he spoke, all heads, in unison, turned back to their papers and card games and tried to act as though they hadn't heard him. For days, Sid had a ball putting on the group in the lobby, by constantly calling out to his wife, in the loudest possible voice…"*Vanda, vere are you?*" It was rather a funny moment. Then again, maybe you had to be there to appreciate it.

After Boston, Jimmie's agents booked him into the big-time, and we were scheduled to perform at The Fairmont Hotel in San Francisco, where Ernie Heckscher led the in-house orchestra at that time.

It was July, and Jimmie and his wife Colleen were taking a short vacation at Lake Tahoe, where they were camping out in their station wagon. I called Dori in New York and asked her to grab a plane and meet us in San Francisco. Since the job required me to only work in the evenings, the rest of the day Dori and I were free to have a little vacation time in San Francisco.

Opening Thursday, July 3

ROULETTE RECORDING STAR

JIMMIE RODGERS

Stu Phillips, Musical Director

ERNIE HECKSCHER
and his Orchestra

Venetian Room Fairmont Hotel

When Jimmie and his wife pulled into the driveway of the Fairmont Hotel and opened the back of the station wagon, empty Coke bottles and milk cartons fell out onto the pavement. Then the valets unloaded sacks of dirty laundry. Jimmie—who hadn't shaved in a week—and his wife Colleen were both dressed in dirty blue jeans. When they entered the lobby of the hotel and walked to the registration desk, heads turned and it looked like a replay of the Farragut Hotel episode. In those days, the Fairmont still required men to wear jackets in the lobby, so Jimmie and Colleen looked quite out of place. Even though there was a big sign in the lobby with Jimmie's picture on it, he was not given the star-treatment.

Booking a country/folk singer into such a classy hotel was definitely a dangerous experiment by Jimmie's agents. However, Rodger's charm shone through, and despite his almost amateurish demeanor, the sophisticated San Franciscans liked him. In fact, probably what they liked most about him *was* his amateurism. An even bigger test for Jimmie was to be our next booking.

♫   ♫   ♫

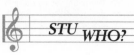

The Moulin Rouge, Hollywood
Liberace

AFTER ENJOYING OUR LITTLE WORKING vacation in San Francisco, Dori returned to New York, and Jimmie and I went south to Los Angeles. We were to appear next at The Moulin Rouge, a mammoth new nightclub on Sunset Blvd. in Hollywood, near Vine Street. Opening night was a lesson in "showmanship" that has forever remained with me

At the home table were Gabbe, Heller, Lutz and Loeb. They were Jimmie's agents and they all showed up with their wives. Jimmie's wife Colleen and I were also at the table. Gabbe, Heller, Lutz and Loeb were also Liberace's agents—and Liberace, big as life, with his patented smile, was seated with us. The following anecdote was a learning experience I have never forgotten and, in my opinion, a good lesson for everyone in show business.

Liberace. The dog's name is unknown.

The opening act was a female comic/singer. She was not very good, and after about five minutes the group at the table began quietly talking among themselves. Liberace and I sat watching the act, and did not join in the chit-chat. Little by little, the conversation between the agents and their wives grew louder. Liberace, quite annoyed at the behavior of the others, uttered a loud "shush." The group immediately shut up, and went back to watching the entertainer. Poor girl—she was bombing horribly! At the end of her routine, Liberace politely applauded and, of course, the rest of us at the table joined in.

Unable to contain himself, Sam Lutz turned to Liberace and asked, "Did you really think she was any good?" Liberace, acting as adamant as he could, replied, "She was horrible. But as long as I choose to come here, I will give her my undivided attention, because that's what I would expect from anyone who chooses to come to *my* show. It's the professional and respectful way to behave."

I will never forget Liberace's statement and, to this day, I watch movies and shows I don't particularly like right to the bitter end—as a courtesy to the people who worked on the project. It drives my wife crazy.

After Jimmie's performance, Liberace visited the dressing room to offer his congratulations. "Lee," as his friends affectionately called him, questioned Jimmie as to why he left out all the little vocal tricks that were a hallmark of his hit records. (The vocal trick or mannerism in question was his "Uh Oh.") Jimmie said that he was really tired of that corny little gimmick, and decided to dump it on his personal appearances.

Lee proceeded to soundly chastise Jimmie for that decision. He explained that the customers had paid to hear an entire performance of Jimmie Rodgers' hits, not a watered-down version. He then shocked both of us with his candor when he delivered the following bit. I loosely quote Liberace: "Do you think that I really enjoy smiling from ear-to-ear, and looking like a moron, for an entire show? But as long as the audience likes it, I'll keep smiling—all the way to the bank." Liberace was the personification of "a show-business professional."

This little bit of self-deprecation on Liberace's part took both of us by surprise. From that moment on, Jimmie went back to using his special identifiable vocal trick.

Moving on, Jimmie's show was passable, but it was not the hit that his agents had hoped for. It was evident that Jimmie was a *small folk-club* type of entertainer, not suited for the big rooms. However, a year later, Jimmie was to become the star of his own network television show. Go figure: So much for smart and knowledgeable agents.

♫   ♫   ♫

Enoch Light...I learn the record business

IN 1958, MY FATHER'S BUSINESS involved the purchasing of products for drug stores. They were generally referred to as sundry items. Some of these were low priced records, mostly in the $1.98 price range. Enoch Light was one of the largest producers of this type of product. The record labels he owned were called Grand Award and Waldorf (Grand Award Records being the high priced line at $3.98, and Waldorf Records the cheap one at $1.98). Before Enoch entered the record business he was a bandleader. Specifically, he fronted a society band called "The Light Brigade," playing only the best hotels up and down the East Coast.

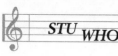

My father, indulging in a little fatherly bragging, casually mentioned to Enoch that his son had made several albums, and was currently Jimmie Rodgers' musical director. Enoch was evidentially impressed, and told my father that he would like to meet with me.

At my meeting with Enoch, he seemed to care little about my previous credits in music, explaining that what he currently really needed was someone to keep a check on *quality control*. Let me take a moment to explain quality control in the manufacturing of records in 1950s.

In those years a vinyl LP went through many stages in the course of production. These included numerous steps of separation, which was the main cause of clicks, pops, and surface noise on a record. Enoch Light prided himself on the lack of clicks and pops, and the superior sound quality of his records, which was his primary merchandising gimmick. Someone that Enoch could have confidence in had to oversee the pressing plant's quality-control staff, as he did not trust them.

Light asked if I might be interested in the job. This position was really not what I had expected—or the direction I wanted my career to take. The decision to leave Jimmie Rodgers was difficult to make. With Jimmie, I had a position of importance and often found my name in the newspapers. (Everyone's ego occasionally needs a little gratification.) With Enoch, I would be working behind the scenes, in complete anonymity.

Had I not been married with a wife to support, I probably would have said, "No thanks." I discussed it with Dori and she left the decision up to me. With Enoch, I realized that I would be home in New York and actually able to live with my wife. The thought of seeing Dori every day appealed to me, and I left Jimmie and accepted the job with Enoch Light. For the next year, I hated every day, every hour, and every minute and second that I worked for him. My disappointment became even more distressing when Rodgers was given his own TV show, and I realized that I most likely would have been the musical director.

Enoch was the type of boss that thought nothing of making you work on holidays—even New Year's Eve—which he actually did to me. He was as equally contemptuous to his daughter Julie, who worked for him, as he was to the rest of his employees. He was an equal-opportunity bastard who made Simon Legree look like a pussycat.

But the pay was good, so Dori and I were able to save a little and enjoy some financial security. Eventually, Enoch started a more expensive line called Command Records, devoted to furthering the current rage... *Stereo*! Enoch now found a use for my arranging ability.

Whenever he would produce a Command Record, utilizing a large orchestra, I would then be required to duplicate what he had done, but with a much smaller orchestra—and for a lot less money. My version would come out on Waldorf Records for $1.98. I made about 10 albums for him, and it made my job a little more palatable—plus I got paid extra for the arrangements. However, I *still* had to supervise quality control.

As much as I hated working for Enoch, I did gain some very valuable knowledge about the workings of a record company. I also became a friend of the staff at Fine Sound Recording, where Enoch did most of his recording. It was there that I had my first opportunity to learn about the intricacies and technical aspects of a recording studio, and gained much knowledge that was to benefit me later on in my career. I learned to do much of my own editing of quarter-inch tape and, at times, George Piros the engineer would allow me to assist him at the console.

At one point, Enoch bought some old tapes of Mahalia Jackson that had been stored in a warehouse for years. Mahalia Jackson, for those not familiar with her, was the Queen of Gospel in that era. The tapes, having been stored for years in a hot warehouse, were in horrible condition: very brittle; on hubs; and not on reels. It was a volatile situation with disaster just waiting to happen. Enoch gave me the task of picking out the best of the recordings and putting together an album. George Piros didn't want any part of handling these fragile tapes, and suggested that I do the editing myself. I went to work on the project and, of course, the *expected* happened. On a fast rewind, the tape tore into a hundred pieces and there on the floor of the editing room lie Mahalia Jackson—in shreds.

I took all the pieces, stuffed them into my attaché case, and brought them home. Dori and I laid the scraps out on the floor of our living room, then spent the weekend trying to match the torn ends and splice them together. It was like a giant jigsaw puzzle and, if we didn't fix it, I would probably be fired. With Dori's help, I saved my ass. We managed to get it back to its (*almost*) original state. I don't really know if Enoch was ever aware of what had happened, nor do I care.

♪   ♪   ♪

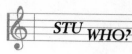

Commercials and Madison Ave.

AL HERMAN, THE AGENT, once again entered my life. He now specialized in the commercial field, and wanted to represent me. I signed a contract with Al, but was careful to exclude all other facets of my musical career, and limit it only to commercials. I was beginning to really believe in the possibility that I might actually reach some of my career goals, and I didn't want Al Herman to reap the benefits of my nine years of hard work.

It was in 1958, through Al Herman, that an old friend from my high school days, Roy Eaton, got in touch with me. At Music and Art, he had been a budding classical pianist. Now, surprisingly, he was working at Benton & Bowles—one of the biggest ad agencies in New York—as their musical director. (I say *surprisingly*, because Roy was *black*, and Madison Ave. was not particularly color-blind in those days.)

Roy asked if I might be interested in working with him on some arrangements. Commercials were a new field for me, and I was really enthused at getting the opportunity to expand my knowledge. For the next three years, even though I was to be employed in other areas of the business, I did many commercials for Benton & Bowles, as well as other ad agencies. Among some of the product commercials that I was fortunate to be involved in were; Jello Pudding and Pie Filling; General Tires; Yuban Coffee; Roi-Tan Cigars; Martini & Rossi and Conoco Gas.

As an illustration of the deceitful deal making that permeates all of the entertainment industry, I offer the following example. Al Herman called one day to give me some good news. He had procured an assignment for me at the Young & Rubicam agency. I was to write several pieces of music to be used under narration in the new Jello Pudding and Pie Filling commercial.

When Al, the ad-exec and myself met at the agency, I was briefed as to the style and amount of music I would be required to compose. In my mind, I quickly figured out how much the budget would be, including my fee. Let's, for argument's sake, say that the orchestra cost was 3X and my fee was X.

I quietly related to Al my calculations. He asked me to remain silent and let him do the bargaining. At the end of Al's presentation, the ad-exec agreed to the orchestra budget being 6X and my fee would be 4X. I was flabbergasted. This was more than three times the amount I had in mind, and I had been giving myself a good deal.

The bottom line is that Jello, at the beginning of the fiscal year, had prepaid the agency a predetermined amount of money to cover the music budget for one year. With the fiscal year about to close, the agency found that they had not spent as much as they thought—and therefore would have to either return a portion of the money (a horrible idea) or make sure that they spent it all.

Not only did I get a bigger orchestra and more money but Al and the ad-exec split about 4X between themselves! When the accounting office saw my fee, they informed the higher-ups, and the agency banished me from doing any future work for them. I later found out that the ad-exec left that agency—was probably fired—and Al Herman was also *persona non grata* with them.

While involved in the commercial field, I met Mort Kasman and his wife Lillian. Mort hired me to write several commercials as well as the themes to two radio shows. During these years they became close friends of Dori and myself. As recently as a few years ago, we had dinner in New York with Mort and his second wife, Sherrill.

Also in the early years of our marriage, Walter Hofer (a lawyer) and his wife Sandy joined our business and social life. They infected us with bridge-fever (the card game), and the four of us enjoyed playing together when our busy schedules permitted. It was with Walter and Sandy that Dori and I finally got to take our long-anticipated honeymoon. We went to the U.S. Virgin Islands and, despite a few minor problems with insects and lizards, we had a great time.

Socially, Dori and I also attended a weekly penny-ante poker game. Among some of the stellar participants were Bebe Bourne (daughter of Hal Bourne of Bourne Music); Charles Strouse (who would eventually write the musical *Bye, Bye Birdie*); Fred Tobias (Charley Tobias' son) and his wife Jo; Stanley Mills (of Mills Music); Clint Ballard; Aaron Schroeder; and others.

In October of that year, my father passed away, just a few months shy of his 59th birthday. He was born on January 1, New Year's Day. As I have previously mentioned, back in 1947 he had been warned, because of his heart, to take it easy and stop smoking. However, his business caused him far too much stress, and he never really did completely stop smoking. His death was sudden and not expected, as he had just that day come home from having a physical exam, and been pronounced in good shape by the doctor. That night he collapsed, and within minutes died of a heart attack.

Since Dori and I lived in the same building as my parents, we were there within minutes. But it was not soon enough to make contact with him. I thought I would be devastated by his passing, considering how much he had meant to me, but curiously, I found myself strangely unmoved. He had been the greatest father a son could ever want and I felt confused at not falling apart emotionally.

About fifteen years later, I started to have dreams about my father. In my fantasies he was usually returning from a long trip. Strangely, in each dream he somehow seemed to remain by himself, and was more of an observer than a participant in the dream. I now miss him very much, and feel the loss and sadness I thought I should have been experiencing at the time of his passing.

With the steady work I had experienced during the previous two years, Dori and I were able to move to a larger, four-room apartment in the same building. Our new next-door neighbors were Shirley and Larry Katzman. Larry Katzman was, and still is to a certain degree, the owner and President of Kaz vaporizers as well as a successful cartoonist. Some 40 years later we are still very close friends.

In 1960, I was to reach a goal I never even remotely dreamed of. It was one of those right-place at the right-time happen-stances. The kind of event that makes you speculate on just how your life might have turned out had this event not taken place.

I was at the RCA Recording studios waiting to do some editing with my favorite engineer, Mickey Crofford. While in the hallway outside the editing room, I was approached by a man who asked if I was, perchance, Stu Phillips. I replied yes, and asked how he knew of me? He explained that Mickey had remarked to him that he occasionally worked with a talented arranger and producer by that name—who was currently working for Enoch Light. Mickey had also mentioned to him that I was not particularly happy with my current position. The man, whose last name was Wexler (I have forgotten his first name), asked me if I might be interested in an A&R position at Colpix Records. He told me that his brother, Paul Wexler, the president of Colpix Records, was searching for someone to fill that position.

Somewhat surprised at his offer, since I had almost no track record in this field, I nevertheless said I would gladly meet with his brother. I subsequently met with Paul Wexler a few days later at 711 Fifth Ave., the Columbia Pictures building.

Paul Wexler had only recently become president of Colpix (a division of Columbia Pictures), and it was his intention to change the company headquarters from Hollywood to New York. At the time, Colpix was being supervised in Hollywood by Jonie Taps.

Wexler knew little about music or the producing of records, his expertise being sales and promotion. At well over six-feet tall, Paul was an imposing figure. He was the athletic type and talked a great deal about his football-playing days in college. His staff consisted of Howie Berk and Joe Snyder, neither of them having the faintest idea about the record business. They were FOP—Friends of Paul. Howie Berk eventually migrated to Hollywood and became a successful screenwriter.

Using my inexperience as a bargaining wedge, Paul proposed a month-to-month agreement. He would appraise my work monthly, and then decide whether to renew the deal—or let me go.

I cherished the idea of working for Columbia Pictures, even though I knew the job would be comparable to a crapshoot. Furthermore, the money was less than what I was earning at Enoch Light's, but it was obvious that I would be much happier working at Colpix than at my present job with Enoch. (Anything would have better). As an added incentive, Paul gave me a royalty on the sale of records, which of course, was to be applied against my salary.

I happily left Enoch Light and a job that I really despised and started at Colpix Records full of enthusiasm and optimism. But it would take until January of 1961 before I was to taste any real success—and reach one of the first high-points of my career.

♫   ♫   ♫

6/6 The Fantastic '60s… Part I
Colpix Records and "Blue Moon"

IN MY WILDEST DREAMS, I NEVER imagined that having an office at 711 Fifth Ave. (with a window overlooking the avenue) and a secretary named Ricki, could be exciting. But it was! As soon as the article in the trade papers announcing my hiring was printed, I was inundated with publishers plugging their latest songs. Even though at that time I was virtually unimportant and unknown, I nevertheless had access to several important recording artists on Colpix. Among those assigned to me were, Nina Simone; James Darren; the Chad Mitchell Trio, and several others.

Originally, Colpix Records was started as a promotional tool to help exploit Columbia Pictures' films. Movies like Picnic, From Here to Eternity, Gidget, Pepe, and others. Jonie Taps very informally supervised the music division, and carried the title Executive in Charge of Music—which meant absolutely nothing. Before his position at Columbia, Jonie had been a song-plugger for Shapiro-Bernstein Music Publishers, who were now the administrators of the Columbia Pictures Music catalogue.

Jonie Taps was a short, slightly pudgy man with gray stubble growing from his head. There was a sort of dictatorial air about him, and he generally avoided any detailed conversation dealing directly with his relationship with Harry Cohn—the head mogul of Columbia Pictures. (It was rumored around Hollywood, by those in the know, that Jonie at times pimped for Harry Cohn.)

On one of Jonie's trips to New York we had occasion to lunch together. We talked at length about my past endeavors, and what my future goals might be. Jonie enjoyed referring to anyone that was younger than he as Kid. So for the duration of our relationship, I was simply referred to as Kid. In answer to Jonie's question concerning my future, I mentioned to him that film scores always seemed to intrigue me, and I was thinking of someday pursuing a career composing music for films.

Jonie stored this little tidbit of information in his memory banks for later use, and then complimented my work and professional attitude toward my job at Colpix. Unexpectedly, from out of the blue, he informed me of his dislike of Paul Wexler. His remark definitely took me completely by surprise.

It seems that some top executive in New York went over Jonie's head when he hired Paul Wexler without Jonie's knowledge. This is something you don't do to Jonie Taps without suffering some dire consequences. Since Jonie could do nothing about the Schneiders (Abe, and his sons Stanley and Bert, who ran the East Coast division of Columbia Pictures, and were probably responsible for hiring Wexler), it had to be poor Paul Wexler who eventually was going to feel Jonie's wrath. It took about a year, but ultimately Jonie got his pound of flesh.

As I settled into my position at Colpix, I started to plan recording sessions for my artists. James Darren was in Greece filming The Guns of Navarone, and was not available to record for a while. He had just married Evy Norlund, who was a recent Miss Denmark, and currently a starlet at Columbia Pictures. With Darren not available, I turned my attention to Nina Simone.

♫   ♫   ♫

Nina Simone

I RECORDED NINA SIMONE and the Chad Mitchell Trio but, unfortunately, with little commercial success. Nina, in particular, was difficult to produce. She had a great deal of artistic temperament—some of it good and some of it questionable. Nina demanded input in every facet of the production, which naturally made things a little difficult for me—as I was still in a learning mode. But I respected her great talent, smiled a lot, and together we made some damn good records—unfortunately, no hits.

There was one incident involving Nina Simone that bears relating. Ray Charles was flying high with a big hit record titled "Hit the Road, Jack." A very enterprising and enthusiastic publisher (Knollwood Music) had two of their staff writers (Schuman and Carr) come up with an "answer song" to "Hit the Road, Jack"—called "Come on Back, Jack." They wrote it

A very svelte Nina Simone.

specifically for Nina Simone. The publisher showed me the song and I agreed whole-heartedly with him that this could be a great vehicle for Nina.

Since time was of the essence, I got the song to Nina as quickly as possible. She said that she liked the song, but would not record it unless Ray Charles personally said that he didn't mind her following up his record. Naturally, I asked Nina if she new Ray personally. She replied, no. I then explained to her that Ray's permission was not required and there was no legal reason why we couldn't record and release this song. However, Nina was adamant about having Ray's personal okay.

Her decision put me in the unenviable position of having to contact Ray Charles on my own. Ray was a West Coast artist and a trip to LA was not on my calendar. Dame Fortune smiled on me when I read in the paper that Ray was appearing in concert at Madison Square Garden within two days. I managed to contact Ray's agent and explained my predicament to him. He reinforced my original statement to Nina that Ray wouldn't particularly care one way or the other what Nina recorded.

When I explained that she was insistent, he left a pass for me at the back door so that I could meet with Ray before his concert. He said that the only reason that they would do this was because of the great respect that Ray had for Nina's talent.

When I met Ray, as he sat on a chair in a semi-lit dressing room, I was truly in awe of the man. He was certainly one of music's great performers and, when I shook his hand, I felt honored to be in his presence. I explained the situation to him concerning Nina's request. He answered quickly in language I would rather have not put in this book, that he "doesn't give a flying f— what the f— Nina records."

Later, when telling Nina of my meeting with Ray, I lied a bit, and told her that Ray was flattered that she wanted to record an answer to his song. I had now added diplomatic lying to my expertise. I was learning. The record we made got instant air-play as a novelty item, but never reached hit status as we had hoped.

One creative project that I produced with Nina was an album titled *Nina Sings Ellington*. It was inevitable that she would one day record an album of Ellington songs. Nina and the Duke were a natural. She conceived the arrangements, but I don't remember who actually did the work. I only remember that I didn't. The Malcolm Dodds Singers performed the backup vocals. We felt it was a rather good album, but once again, failed to meet sales expectations.

It was very fortunate for me that Paul Wexler liked most of the records I produced. He also admired the fact that I stayed within my budgets. At this time, Colpix was still not a profit-making enterprise. After my first couple of months, despite "no hits," Paul exercised my option.

One day a music rep from Shapiro-Bernstein, the publisher representing Columbia Pictures Music, came to my office and suggested to me that there just might be an opportunity to get a main title song onto the soundtrack of *The Guns of Navarone*. The film was soon to wrap up filming in Greece.

My first comment to the rep was that, to my understanding, Carl Foreman, the producer and director, had already assigned Dimitri Tiomkin to compose the film score. It was also a well-known fact that Mr. Tiomkin preferred writing his own songs. The publisher, however, felt that we had nothing to lose, and mentioned that the publishing company was willing to pick up the cost of the recording. With Colpix still operating in the red, this kind of news—where the company avoided having to pay for the product—always seemed to please Paul Wexler. So with enthusiasm, he gave the project a go.

The publisher put me in touch with my old friends Fred Tobias and Clint Ballard, and the three of us quickly came up with a song called "Six Men." It seemed a perfect vehicle for the Chad Mitchell Trio, and after hearing the song they were eager to record it.

Everything had to be done quickly, so that we could beat Dimitri Tiomkin to the punch. I wrote the arrangement in record time and we rushed into the studio with the Chad Mitchell Trio, and made one hell of a good record. Everyone was excited. Paul Wexler; the publisher; the brass upstairs; everyone. Everyone, that is, except Carl Foreman.

Mr. Foreman had no intention of stepping on Dimitri's toes. Foreman didn't even give us the courtesy of listening to the recording. *Quel dommage.*

Dimitri Tiomkin did eventually write a song and, in my—and everyone else's—opinion, it was only so-so.

Eventually, Colpix did release the Chad Mitchell Trio record, but without *The Guns of Navarone* as the title—and without the assistance of the film company's promotion department—the record didn't have a prayer. The picture, on the other hand, was a big hit.

Sometime in 1960, an old voice from the past called. It was Gayle

Gayle Andrews

Andrews. (Remember her from the early '50s?) Gayle had recently married a very rich gentleman named Lloyd C. Douglas (no relation to the famous writer), and he was going to finance an album for Gayle. She asked if I would do the arrangements and produce the album. I said yes, and we proceeded to select material.

The album, titled *Love's a Snap* was a great showcase for my arrangements. Although Gayle sang as well as I'd ever heard her sing, I must admit that I overestimated her vocal potential and, at times, over-powered her with some of the arrangements. It was another learning experience for me on my road to enlightenment. The album did not sell, and joined a long line of *Phillips' flops*.

During this same time period, Roy Eaton, my old Music & Art friend, called to say that Yuban Coffee was starting a new ad campaign. He had read in the trades that I was now at Colpix Records, and thought that I might have entrée to Nina Simone. Roy felt that a new jingle written by he and myself, and featuring Nina Simone singing, might be just what the client was looking for in their new ad campaign.

I met with Nina and her agent and, after a great deal of pleading, followed by some friendly persuasion, Nina agreed to meet with Roy Eaton. When Nina saw that Roy was black, she felt quite a bit better about the situation, and agreed to make the commercial. The jingle—"Deep, Dark, Delicious Yuban"—was recorded with Nina performing the vocals. The client unfortunately, hated the recording. They felt that Nina (with her very extreme low voice), sounded much too much like a man and definitely, "too Black." (I will remind you that this was 1961, and these little racist games were everyday occurrences.)

Roy was devastated by the news. He had hoped that this might be a major victory for he and the ad agency. Something had to be done quickly to remedy the situation, since the commercials were due to air within days. Fortunately, the client said that although he was not happy with Nina, he really did like our jingle.

Where to turn? Of course—who else but the magnificent Dori? Stepping up to the plate with complete professionalism, Dori saved the day. She recorded a demo of the jingle and sounded white and definitely female. The client was now happy; Benton & Bowles were happy; Roy was happy; I was happy. (Eventually, Darlene Zito recorded the final version that aired. In the future, Dori would come to the rescue in other very similar situations. What a gal. Excuse me—Copa Gal.)

During the years from 1961 to 1963, I wrote the scores for four ABC Television specials, as well as the theme to a new show on ABC called Sunday Night Movie, which ran for several years. The producer of the specials was John Secondari, who I met through my friendship with Mort Kasman. The shows were called Bell and Howell's "Close-up;" "Small World;" "Do Not Enter;" and "The John Glenn Special."

The "John Glenn Special" in particular has a cute little personal story attached. It was March, and Dori and I were in Los Angeles. Jonie Taps had graciously given us two tickets to the Academy Awards. We were excited about going—but at the last moment I received a call from the ABC Studios in New York telling me that they were ready to score the "John Glenn Special." This was an assignment that I did not want to lose, so I gave my tuxedo to my brother-in-law Wynn. He lived in Los Angeles, and had about the same build as I did. I went to New York and worked, while Wynn escorted my wife to the awards. To this day, I have never been to an Academy Awards presentation.

Around the same time as the Yuban Coffee event, James Darren returned from Greece with his pregnant new bride. It was difficult to tell if James was enthusiastic with the prospect of recording with me. I had, as yet, no successful track record to speak of, and James had already had a moderate hit with "Gidget," as well as several follow-up quasi-hit records. That was more than I had accomplished so far. However, the record company thought that Darren's vocal on "Gidget" was a bit too Frank Sinatra-ish. They wanted Jimmy's recordings to lean more towards rock and roll.

Darren was not completely happy with that decision. But contracts are contracts, and besides—if James was uncooperative with the record company—it might have an effect on the people in Hollywood who were guiding his acting career. And for sure, at that time, acting was Darren's main objective. So he cooperated with me and we began to make records.

Jimmy was from "South Philly" (Philadelphia), a really tough neighborhood. Darren's language was, to put it bluntly, peppered with more four-letter expletives than one could imagine. His beautiful bride, the aforementioned Evy Norlund, spoke just a little English. During their stay in Greece, Evy learned what English she spoke from Jimmy—including all his colorful words, which she evidently took for granted, were normal American slang.

To become better acquainted, I arranged for Dori and I to take James and Evy out to dinner. We chose the most exclusive and high-class French restaurant in New York. It was a weekday night, and the restaurant was not crowded. Of course, Darren was immediately recognized by the staff; he was at that time a real-live-Hollywood movie star. Dinner was pleasant and James managed to control his language. Evy was in the last month-or-so of her pregnancy and quite large and feeling very uncomfortable. She spoke only occasionally, being a bit hesitant about her inability to converse at length.

As we arrived at the dessert stage, the restaurant had emptied out and there were only one or two other tables occupied. When the waiter asked what we would like to order for dessert, Evy Darren finally spoke up. She pointed to a mouth-watering tray of delicacies and, in her loudest voice exclaimed to the waiter, "I'll have some of that fuckin' mousse." Needless to say, it was a very embarrassing moment for everybody—except Evy. She naively looked at us and, for a brief moment, could not fathom what she had done wrong.

During my association with Darren, we all became good friends, and I do believe that some 40 years later, Evy and James, as well as their two sons Christian and Anthony, are still our close friends. No hits came from our partnership during this time period, but we maintained a good working relationship.

Month three came and went, and I modestly say I think we produced some good product—but unfortunately no hits. And let's face it… hits are what record companies are primarily interested in. Good records are a dime a dozen, and without any hits, my job was tenuous. To complicate matters even more, there was an identity problem with James Darren that added to the difficulty of merchandising his records. Bobby Darin was his name, and he had big hits. Darren and Darin were continually being confused.

Fortunately for me, on the plus side, the opportunity to produce records was giving me another chance to accomplish one of my career goals—that of being an arranger—although I was still a long way from Morton Gould and Dave Rose.

For several months I had been receiving demo tapes from a group in Pittsburgh called the Marcels. Their manager was a bartender named Jules Kruspir. The group had a good sound, but all the songs on the demo tapes were other people's hits. The Marcels seemed to have no material of their own. Since they lived in Pittsburgh, and I had no money in my budget to bring them to New York, recording them appeared not to be a likely prospect.

But Jules Kruspir was persistent and, truthfully, his persistence was beginning to become quite annoying. To get Jules off my back, in a moment of reluctant resignation, I said, "If you and the group can get to New York on your own nickel, I'll record you." I was sure that with that statement, I would finally get Kruspir and the Marcels to give up. This was during December of 1960.

In the fall of that year, Paul Wexler had signed the Skyliners. This group had just come off a Number One hit titled "Since I Don't Have You." Paul spent some big bucks signing this group, and asked me to drop everything and devote my time exclusively to them and their lead singer Jimmie Beaumont.

Joe Rock, the manager of the group, and I listened to some of the best new material from the likes of Goffin, King, Mann, Weil, Greenfield and Sedaka. We believed that we had found several great songs for Jimmie. We did at least two or three sessions with him and the group, but somehow none of the records had the magic that was in their original hit.

By now Paul Wexler was sticking his neck way, way out every time he hired me for another month. I had made good records—which unfortunately had made no money.

Jonie Taps happened to be in New York at about this time, and he encouraged Paul to stay with me just a bit longer. For some reason, Jonie had faith in my ability. I was able to exhale a bit when I received a reprieve for one more month.

Taps was an active member of the Friar's Club in LA, and suggested that I join the New York chapter. He felt that it would give me a classy place to entertain important people. With Jonie's recommendation, I was enthusiastically welcomed into the Friar's Club.

During this time, as Stu Phillips and his Orchestra, I recorded several movie themes from Columbia films. There was "Strangers When We Meet"; "Black Stockings" (an original theme by John Barry, who was not yet a film composer); "Pepe"; "Song Without End"; and others—all, humbly he states, well produced and well arranged flops.

All of my records were released with much enthusiasm on the company's part, but somehow always seemed to fall a bit short in sales. Once again, the partial success of the records gave me a reprieve for yet another month. I was beginning to feel like a death-row inmate—living from month to month on reprieves.

♫   ♫   ♫

The Saga of Blue Moon

IN THE MIDDLE OF FEBRUARY 1961, one of the worst blizzards in the last 20 years was howling outside my office window. As I watched the snow swirl about in the wind, I had the feeling that this month was most likely going to be my last at Colpix. I began to sense that I had run out of reprieves. I entertained the thought of resigning rather than the stigma of being fired.

My secretary Ricki buzzed me to say that I had a phone call from Jules Kruspir, the Marcels' manager. A call from Jules was certainly not going to help make this day any better, but thinking, what the hell, I took his call. Jules said that he and the group had just arrived by bus from Pittsburgh and were in New York. When I asked where in New York they were, Jules replied, "Just outside the Lincoln Tunnel." He said that he and the group needed directions to my office. With all means of transportation stalled by the blizzard, he said that they would walk.

I couldn't believe it. The group had accepted my off-handed challenge and, was about to walk in a raging blizzard from the Lincoln Tunnel to my office. Like a fool, I had idiotically committed myself to recording them. To add to my dilemma, Paul had told me to spend all my time exclusively with the Skyliners. My day was definitely going down the tubes with this new development.

When the group arrived at the Colpix office, they were cold, wet and disheveled. I needed to keep them hidden from Paul Wexler, so I secreted

them into the rehearsal room. Then I had my secretary draw up the most basic recording contract we had, and got all of them to sign it. Next, I called Bert Keyes, a pianist and arranger I had used on a few occasions. Bert hurried up to my office and I put him in charge of keeping the group hidden in the rehearsal room and going over material with them.

The Marcels were an inter-racial group, composed of three "coloreds" (African-American was not yet in the vernacular of the day) and two whites. Even though this was New York City, a bastion of the Democratic Party and liberal ideologies, the three black members of the group were unable to stay at the same YMCA as the whites: So much for racial equality in the '60s in New York City.

The lead singer's name was Cornelius Harp (Nini for short). The bass voice belonged to Fred Johnson. Bingo (Ronald Mundy), Dick Knauss, and Gene Bricker rounded out the group.

When Paul Wexler left for the day, I went into the rehearsal room and had the group sing every song they knew. I gave them one new piece of material that I liked, and told them to learn it by the following morning. Then, after a long and tiring day, I sloshed my way home in the snow.

When I told Dori about my predicament, and let out my frustrations, she gave me some TLC—but just a little. After much discussion we came to the conclusion that I had only one out. I had to send the group home.

In the middle of the night I awoke and started thinking about this poor group of guys. They had taken all their savings and spent it on a trip to New York, hopefully to be recorded by Stu Phillips. My conscience began to bother me. As yet, I had not learned how to be a tough son-of-a-bitch kind of A&R man. Come to think of it—I don't think that I ever did reach that time-honored plateau.

After arguing the options with myself, I woke my wife up and declared, "I don't give a damn if I have to pay for the recording session myself, I can't send these poor kids home without making a record with them." I don't recall my wife's reaction to my emphatic declaration, but my mind was definitely made up.

The next day, February 15, 1961, I again played tag with the group and Paul. Fortunately, on this particular day, Paul spent a great deal of time out of the office. I was lucky to find recording time at RCA Studios that evening, with Mickey Crofford as my engineer.

The session was to start at 9:00 P.M. and end at 12:00 midnight. Since the charges would very likely end up being paid by me, I wanted no part of any overtime. Late that afternoon Bert and I were satisfied with three of the songs, but we needed to prepare one more. In those days it was considered a must, that you record four songs on each session.

One of the songs we discarded kept spinning around in my brain. I loved the intro but hated the song. The intro was obviously some standard type of Doo Wop riff. Some of the riff continued under the song. I realized that the chord changes to the song were very common, what we used to call "We want Cantor" changes. I mentioned "Heart and Soul" as a possible tune that would fit the harmonies. The group did not know the song. Next, I mentioned "Blue Moon."

Eureka! The lead singer Nini said that he knew the song. He told us that his mother used to sing it to him as a lullaby. The group rehearsed it—I added little touches here and there—and, voila, in an hour-and-a-half, we had "Blue Moon." There was however, one small problem: Nini kept singing the bridge wrong. No matter how much Bert and I tried, we could not get him to sing it correctly. Screw it, we thought, it wasn't going to be the A-side anyway.

That evening at the session, with a group of five musicians reading quickly jotted down lead sheets, we recorded. Of course Paul Wexler had no knowledge of this, and my friends at RCA were willing to hold back on the paper work for a few days so that I could either prepare Paul for the shock, or pay the bill myself. I must comment that the vocal group was professional and unflappable. They did a wonderful job.

With ten minutes left in the session we had three of the songs in the can. There was ten minutes left to record "Blue Moon." One rehearsal and we were recording. At four minutes to midnight I said "One more take, quick." The take was nowhere as good as the first. Midnight arrived and I bid the musicians goodnight.

In the booth, as we all listened to the mono playbacks, we were visited by Danny Winchell. Danny had been working for Colpix for only a day or so, as its new promotion man. Somehow, he had found out about my secret session at RCA. Being a real go-getter, Danny thought this might be an opportune time to get in tight with me. At the time that he arrived, we were listening to the last song we recorded—"Blue Moon."

When the playback was over, Danny literally flipped out. He said it was the greatest record he had ever heard. I figured he was just trying to flatter me so he could get on my good side. (Little did he know that I was on my last legs.) We all agreed that the record sure was catchy, and Danny's emphatic enthusiasm seemed to fuel ours. At one A.M. we called it a night and all went home. That is—everyone except Danny.

After we left, he somehow convinced the engineer to cut him a demo of "Blue Moon." With demo in hand, Danny went straight to WINS radio and Murray the "K" (Murray Kaufman). Murray was the King of the all-night disc-jockeys. He took one listen to the record and went ape. He played it on the air immediately. There was no license, no permission, and—of course—there were no records available for sale in any stores.

The next morning as I entered the office, my secretary said I had better go see Paul Wexler immediately. She emphasized that he was mad as hell. When I entered his office, he slammed the door and said, "What the f— is going on?" Paul had never before used this curse word in my presence, so I knew without any doubt that he was really angry. "I've got every station in New York City and some in New Jersey calling me wanting to know why Colpix gave WINS radio an exclusive on 'Blue Moon.'" I, of course, had no idea what he was talking about. "Also," he said, "all the local stores have already called wanting to know when they can expect to get shipments of the record."

When Paul noticed the stupid blank stare on my face, he realized that even I seemed to be as much in the dark as he was. Slowly, he calmed down, and explained that Murray the "K" had played the record 15 times between 2:00 A.M. and 6:00. Murray had introduced the group as The Marcels on Colpix Records. "Who the hell are the Marcels?" Paul demanded, and why in the world did I give the record to Murray the "K"? I said I had absolutely nothing to do with giving the record to him, but that I had a pretty good idea of who did. (It obviously had to have been Danny Winchell.)

I proceeded to explain the whole ugly mess to Paul, and reassured him that I would pay for the session. I figured I was about to be fired and decided I would walk away in grand style. Instead of firing me, Paul said, "Well you better quickly figure out some magic way to get a whole lot of records made in a hurry! And please—tell me we have a contract with them?"

When I explained that not only did we have a contract, and it was for the bare minimum, he started to smile for the first time. Colpix had its first big hit—and Stu Phillips had produced it. This of course made Paul a hero with the big brass upstairs for sticking with me against all odds.

Within a few days, every radio station in New York and the surrounding area was playing the record. It was impossible to find any mode of station—from rock to R&B to pop—without hearing it. Inside of a week, in New York City alone, we had received orders for 75,000 copies. Needless to say, Colpix decided to pay for the recording session.

With my royalty deal, I was about to make a great deal of money on a fortuitous record. It was my production, and now I felt that having paid my dues I had earned my moment of triumph. By April 1st the record was Number One in the USA and most of the rest of the world, and Colpix was in the black for the first time in its history. At the age of 32, I had finally accomplished something really important in my life: As well as making a pot-full of money.

An interesting story accompanies this episode. "Blue Moon" was written by Rodgers and Hart. It was not one of their greatest songs, even though it had previously been a hit several times—most recently by Elvis Presley and Mel Torme. I was told by the publisher's rep that when Richard Rodgers heard the Marcels' version of the song on the radio, he immediately called him and demanded that the record be taken off the air. Rodgers felt that the Marcels' performance of the song was injurious to the copyright. Since we had yet to be granted a license by the publisher, we were skating on thin ice.

Day by day, as the record grew in popularity, the publisher said that he would do his best to stall any action that Rodgers wanted to take. Within weeks, the record was so big that nothing could stop the inevitable. Months later, after the record had become Number One in the world, I was told that, at a cocktail party, when Richard Rodgers was questioned about the success of the record, he replied, "It's great to have Rodgers and Hart at the top of the charts again. And that record company had better spell my name right on all the checks."

"Blue Moon" was nominated for a Grammy award as Record of the Year—but, unhappily, it lost. Ironically, the record it lost to was "The Lion Sleeps Tonight" sung by the Tokens—and produced by Dori's old managers and A&R men, Hugo and Luigi. Life is full of strange twists, isn't it?

Murray the "K," the Marcels and yours truly display our Gold Record for "Blue Moon."

The Marcels did a handful of concert dates and eventually were featured in an Alan Freed rock-and-roll movie. As I recall, about three movies during the last 20 years have featured the Marcels' record of "Blue Moon" on their soundtracks. However, in the film Grease, a group called Sha-Na-Na copied the Marcels' record verbatim, and performed it in the film. For years now, Sha-Na-Na has been performing the song as though it was originally their hit. Sha-Shame on them.

Of course, Colpix Records now wanted to sign me to an ironclad contract. No more of this month-to-month crap. At this time, I called on my lawyer friend Walter Hofer. Walter was one of the top music attorneys in New York, and had handled a few of my commercial contracts, so I retained him to negotiate my contract with Colpix. Jonie Taps called to congratulate me on the record, and said he was personally going to see to it that I got a good deal with Colpix.

I would like to enlighten you to some policies concerning motion-picture companies that you may not be aware of. The last thing motion-picture companies ever want to part with is cold cash. They are more inclined to offer all kinds of perks in lieu of money: fancy dressing rooms; first-class air travel; secretaries; hookers; etc. Walter Hofer let them know that I wasn't going to come cheap. I was looking for big dollars.

This is where Jonie Taps jumped in. He recalled my past conversation with him about film-scoring that he had filed away in his memory, and made me the following offer. In lieu of some of the money we were demanding, Columbia would guarantee me the opportunity to score (compose music) three movies during the term of my contract. It would be pay or play—meaning that if they don't assign me the films to write, they would still have to pay me for them.

This was a pretty tricky move on Jonie's part. If I didn't do the films, then they were paying me the money I had originally asked for. But on the other hand, if I did do the movies, they were getting two jobs for the price of one. I discussed it with Walter and decided that, even though they benefited monetarily, I got a great opportunity to do three first-class Columbia movies. It was too good of an opportunity for me to pass on, so I took the deal. Hooray! I think I finally did something right.

I continued to receive a royalty on any records that I would produce, but I signed a separate contract as a recording artist. Then they appointed me the head of A&R for Colpix Records, East and West Coasts. This, of course, took the West Coast position away from George Duning and Morris Stoloff, which I'm sure made both of them very happy. (I'm serious.)

I had suddenly become the talk of the industry. Along with Snuff Garrett and Shelby Singleton, the three of us were described in one trade paper as "the young lions of the record business." For the remainder of the year, things occurred at such a dizzying pace that it is difficult to recall the actual sequence of events. Let's just say that 1961 was pure magic.

I had finally found my place in the music business and—even though it was not quite the area of music that I had envisioned—the feeling of achievement and recognition was exhilarating. I also seemed to have acquired a benefactor, who for no apparent reason—other than my being me—had faith in my abilities. Jonie Taps was the most unlikely person to fill that role. But he did.

Robert Blake in front of a photo of the Marcels.

FLASH! THIS JUST IN: Currently, Robert Blake has recently become a newsworthy item. Many years ago in a film titled *Electra Glide in Blue*, Robert Blake changed his clothes while listening to a recording of the Marcels. He had a picture of the group hanging on the wall of his room, and during the scene he moved in front of the picture, thereby becoming a part of the Marcel's history.

The photo after Blake has moved away.

$\frac{7}{7}$ The Fantastic '60s... Part 2

Eureka! The Hits Continue

AT ABOUT THE TIME THAT "Blue Moon" was sweeping the country, a film producer named Ed Schreiber was peddling a movie he had produced called *"Mad Dog" Coll.* Columbia Pictures had decided to pick up the negative rights, and since the film as yet had no musical score, they suggested to Ed that he proceed downstairs to Colpix Records and see if they could help in finding a composer. Ed Schreiber met with Paul Wexler, and Paul, knowing absolutely nothing about music in films, recommended that Ed "go down the hall and see Stu Phillips, Colpix's A&R man."

When Ed told me about the film, I had a feeling that this could possibly turn into an opportunity for me. (Jonie Taps had not yet made me his offer of three films.) I humbly suggested to Ed that I might just have time to personally write the score. Ed was delighted with the concept of having me compose the music for his film, and believed he was extremely lucky to have me working on the picture.

Cash Box—February 29, 1964

Examining the special trailer on "Mad-Dog Coll" are, left to right, Stu Phillips, composer of the original score; Edward L. Schreiber, producer of the Columbia release; and Robert S. Ferguson, Columbia's national director of advertising, publicity, and exploitation.

MOTION PICTURE EXHIBITOR

I must inform you that this was Ed's first movie. He had written the screenplay but was a little green about the inner workings of the movie business, since he was primarily in the real-estate game. Little did Ed know that this was also *my* first movie. It may have taken me a while, but I had finally

become a bit of a schemer. I guess a little taste of success can ruin anyone's character.

"Mad Dog" Coll was, as you might expect, a period film about the infamous 1930s gangster. The cast was really exemplary. Though unknown at the time, it co-starred Telly Savalas; Vincent Gardenia; Brooke Hayward (daughter of producer Leland Hayward); an unbilled Gene Hackman; and Jerry Orbach, currently, of TV's *Law and Order* fame. (Orbach, at that time, was the young star of *The Fantastiks*, a very successful off-Broadway show. After a run of more than 40 years, the show finally closed in January of 2002.) The lead in the film was John Davis Chandler who was never to be heard of again. But I do see him at Academy screenings every now and then, and wonder exactly how he got his Academy card.

Ed wrote a lyric that I set to music for the main title. At the time, Colpix had a young singer named Hal Waters under contract and we had him perform the song on the sound track.

Even though I knew very little about the finer points of film scoring, I forged ahead with reckless abandon. In the evenings, after spending all day toiling at Colpix, I would come home and work on the score until about 1:00 A.M. Then I would get a little sleep and go to work at Colpix the next day. I asked Roy Eaton if he would do me a favor: read scores for me in the booth and cue the engineer. Naturally, I was going to conduct.

I conducted the entire score without film, and with a hand-held stopwatch. This was not the usual or professional method of recording music to film. I had no clicks, no streamers, and no music editor to assist me. I was truly a-babe-in-the-woods, learning my profession while on the job and flying by the seat of my pants. By some miracle, the result was completely professional sounding. To this day, it compares favorably with anything I've ever done—notwithstanding all the computerized scoring aids that composers now have available to them.

Unfortunately, *"Mad Dog" Coll* the movie, was a flop. (There's that ugly word again… flop). Ed Schreiber tried his hand at movie making one more time with a little 25-minute dramatic short film called "Katie's Private Lot," which he asked me to score as cheaply as possible.

The film did not seem to call for a large ensemble, so I agreed to do it and I composed a score that utilized about six musicians. With myself at the piano and most of the old group from my 1956 jazz album, we performed the score. It was very Aaron Copland-ish, but it worked quite nicely with the picture. This picture was also a flop. I don't believe that Ed Schreiber ever made another movie.

The Ronettes

IN THE SPRING OF 1961, a very amiable gentleman named Phil Halikus came to my office and asked if I would audition a female trio that he was representing. It consisted of two sisters and their cousin. I agreed to meet them at a small practice room in the Wurlitzer Building, where the group performed for me. It was only necessary for them to sing one song to convince me that they were deserving of a shot at recording. They were fantastic and I couldn't wait to get them signed and under contract. Paul Wexler, after just looking at them, also agreed that they were something special and was excited to sign them.

The Ronettes: Colpix Records, 1961

The lead singer's name was Veronica (Ronnie), and the group was called The Ronettes. (The other two girls were Nedra and Estelle.) From June of '61 to August of '62 I recorded some singles and an album with them. Having no immediate success with their first single release, Colpix started a subsidiary record label called May Records and released the Ronettes on it in an effort to garner more R&B play. Somehow the magic of "Blue Moon" did not rub off on the group, and we couldn't seem to break into the top 50. (I quote a line from Ronnie's autobiography *Be My Baby*: "Stu Phillips just didn't know what rock and roll was.")

Obviously, Ronnie and the group were unhappy with the situation and, while still under contract to Colpix, they were secretly being serenaded by Phil Spector. The group eventually told Colpix that it was going to quit the business and become nurses and secretaries. Colpix bought this far-out fairy tale of theirs—even though I didn't, and begged them to keep the group—and released the group from its contract in early 1963. After a very short and phony retirement, the Ronettes magically appeared on Phillies Records with a monster hit called "Be My Baby." I must admit that Phil Spector out-produced me in this particular instance. (To this day, Spector persists in taking credit for having discovered the Ronettes. I hate to burst his bubble, but...) The Colpix album that I recorded with the group is currently valued as high as $150 on the collector's market.

Recently, the original Ronettes recordings that I produced were re-released on a CD by Rhino Records. No credit was given to me, or anyone else, as the producer of these records. I have been considering suing Rhino for the last ten years. Maybe, someday, I will. While we're on the subject of Rhino, I'd like to go on record and say that they have—for some reason that only they are privy to—omitted my name from *all* the old records I produced that they have recently re-released. Hey Rhino—give me a break!

♫   ♫   ♫

James Darren and "Goodbye Cruel World"

SOMETIME IN LATE SUMMER OF 1961, James Darren arrived in New York ready to cut some new singles. With my recent successes, I had become one of the favorites at Aldon Music. (Aldon Music was owned by Don Kirshner and Al Nevins, though Nevins would soon leave the company.) The publishing rep who did most of the legwork was Emile LaViola, one of a handful of *nice* guys in the music business. He started supplying me with the cream of the Aldon catalogue. I had first look at most of the Mann/Weil, Goffin/King and Sedaka/Greenfield songs.

The fact that I had entrée to these writers impressed James Darren, and gave him more confidence in me as his producer. I had been holding a piece of material from Aldon called "Goodbye Cruel World." I liked it from the first time I heard it. I told Emile LaViola that I would definitely record the song but had to make sure that I married it to the right artist. (In my humble opinion, the main ingredient in the success of a record is the chemistry between the artist and the material. Everything else is window dressing, which may or may not be of any consequence to it becoming a hit.)

The demo of "Goodbye Cruel World" was sung by a singer named Tony Orlando, and I thought that his rendition was perfect. I believed it was a master record in its own right. The song was written by Gloria Shayne, and the calliope effect on the demo and on the Darren record was done with her voice at double-speed.

When I played the song for Jimmy, he was only mildly enthusiastic. Truthfully, he was not at all impressed and stated that there was no way that he would record that song. I stuck my neck way out and promised him that this song could be a hit for him. All he had to do was sing it exactly like Tony Orlando on the demo. After a little gentle persuasion—and my telling him that if he didn't sing it, I was going to release the demo—he agreed to record it. Of course as we now know, Darren did a magnificent job.

When the record was released it was not readily accepted. In fact, its prospects looked rather dim. Good reviews managed to keep a handful of stations playing it. While strolling down Broadway one day, my wife spied an inexpensive little porcelain figure in a novelty shop of a man flushing himself down a toilet, while saying "Goodbye cruel world." The company bought about 100 of the figurines and sent them out to some disc jockeys in an attempt to entice them to play the record. It might have helped a little. Who knows?

We went to Tony Owen (of *The Donna Reed Show*) and asked if it might be possible to feature James Darren in one of the Donna Reed episodes singing "Goodbye Cruel World." Tony discussed it with the powers that be at Screen Gems and the song, with James singing, was featured in one of the Donna Reed episodes. One little change had to be made in the lyric for the TV show. Instead of it saying, "I'm off to join the circus," it was changed to, "I'm off to join the service," Darren also re-recorded the vocal singing it in Italian and German.

Jimmy Darren (Moon-doggie) 1961

I'm sure that the TV exposure was one of the keys to the success of the record. Also of great help was Bill Gavin's report of big airplay in Washington State. Eventually, very slowly, the record started selling and creeping up the charts. In December of 1961 it reached Number One or Number Two, depending on which trade paper you read. "Goodbye Cruel World" was nominated for a Grammy for best vocal performance. It lost to Jimmy Dean's "Big Bad John." (I was now…0 for 2 in Grammy awards.)

Darren's follow up to "Goodbye Cruel World" was "Her Royal Majesty," which found hit status; and thereafter, several lesser hits followed.

One of my favorite albums during my tenure at Colpix was an album that Jimmy and I recorded in New York, featuring some great standards, along the line of the Sinatra albums. Darren was and still is a really fine singer. He has great natural phrasing and interpretation. In this album I had a chance to express a little of myself in the arrangements, and was fortunate to have Doc Severinsen (of the Johnny Carson show) playing the trumpet solos. I still consider it one of the best records I have been involved with. The album was called *Love Among the Young*. A pity it didn't sell.

With Colpix's newfound success, Paul Wexler was riding high. The company now had hits in the pop field as well as the R&B area and Paul felt that he now wanted to expand Colpix into the country/western field. He contacted Wesley Rose of the Acuff-Rose Publishing Company and offered him a production deal with Colpix.

Wesley and his partner Roy Acuff (a very successful country recording artist) were big-time operators in Nashville. Wesley was very interested in Paul's offer, and Paul jumped at the opportunity. He asked me to accompany him to Nashville—having just appointed me head of A&R he felt that I should join him in representing the company. (I was also there to help cover Paul's ass, since he knew very little about the actual producing of records.) The major point of this story is to relate, what I considered, a profound statement made to me by Wesley.

For several months I had been offered a master record for Colpix to distribute. Twice I turned it down. I even played it for Paul, and he agreed that my decision was right. I also heard through the grapevine that every company in New York had turned this master down—that is, all but one. Dave Kapp (of Kapp Records) decided to give it chance. It became a monster hit. The record was called "Midnight in Moscow."

While chewing the fat with Wesley, I mentioned how dejected I was when "Midnight in Moscow" became a hit. "I had it in my hands and blew it," I said. Wesley then offered the following tale of woe in an attempt to console me.

He said that early in '50s he auditioned a young singer from Memphis. After hearing him sing a few songs, Wesley asked the singer what he did for a living. The singer said that he drove a truck. Wesley advised him to go back to truck driving and forget about a career as a singer. The young man's name was Elvis Presley.

A year or so later, he continued, two young boys (brothers) came to audition for him. They knocked him out, and he immediately signed them. They were the Everly Brothers. Wes finished his story with the old bromide: "You win some... you lose some." This was supposed to console me? I was still mad at myself for missing an easy opportunity to once again be involved with a Number One record.

(Through the years, I have heard many different versions of the Presley story attributed to people other than Wesley. I can only relate to you what I was told. Considering Wesley Rose's reputation, I tend to believe his version.)

After the success of "Blue Moon" and "Goodbye Cruel World," Jonie Taps suggested to Tony Owen, the producer of *The Donna Reed Show* and Donna's husband, that perhaps Stu Phillips should try and record Shelley Fabares and Paul Petersen, who were the two juvenile leads on Donna Reed's television show. Jonie had someone on the West Coast make a rough audition demo of Shelley and Paul singing. The demo was sent to Paul Wexler in New York—who upon hearing it said that there was no way that Colpix was going to pay for a session with these two non-singing actors. Paul felt that they were that bad.

When he informed Jonie Taps of his decision, Jonie asked if Stu Phillips had heard the demo. Paul replied that as yet I hadn't. Jonie insisted that Paul have me listen to the demo. I played the record and subsequently called Jonie. "Did I think I could cut a decent record with them," Jonie asked. I said that they were, in my opinion, no better, or no worse, than many of the singers currently having successful records. "We might get lucky," I said, "and then again, we might not."

Jonie decided to interpret my evasive answer as a *yes*, and informed Tony Owen that Stu Phillips said that he would like to record Shelley and Paul. However, despite my opinion and Jonie's enthusiasm, Paul Wexler still refused to spend Colpix's money on the recording. The company was obligated to release the record—since Colpix was a division of Screen Gems and Paul was low man on that totem pole—but Colpix did not have to record it.

Tony Owen, wanting the publicity for *The Donna Reed Show* that he felt they might get from a hit record, and recalling the success of "Goodbye Cruel World" after it aired on the show, offered to pay for the recording sessions himself. This meant that Colpix's share of the royalty would be less. Hence, so would my share, since my cut came out of Colpix's portion.

This turn of events did not sit well with me. Also, after the remarkable success of my last two records, I wasn't exactly sure that I wanted my next release to be one with these two artists. (As you can see, it didn't take me long for me to become a bit of a self-seeking jerk.) Shelley and Paul's chances of success were very minimal. Jonie Taps, in his distinctive and commanding way, put it to me very bluntly that this would be a good move for my career. Having convinced myself that it would be suicide to dissatisfy Jonie, I went about planning my trip to Hollywood.

Important people were now expecting me to come through for them. I reflected back to Hollywood 1951, and realized that I was exactly in the position I had always hoped to be in. However, producing teenybopper and doo-wop records was not quite what I had envisioned as my goal.

On the way out of my office, while waiting for the elevator, two songwriters, Lyn Duddy and Lee Pockriss, approached me. They grabbed me and insisted I look at their latest song. I said that I was on my way to the airport, and this was not the time or place to solicit a song. I urged them to make an appointment to see me when I got back from LA. All the way down to the ground floor, they kept insisting that I take the lead sheet and demo with me.

Soon we were standing in the street and I was trying frantically to hail a cab. In order to get them to leave me alone—at the last moment before entering the cab—I grabbed the damn song and shoved it into my attaché case. With several other pieces of new material in my possession, I hopped on a plane to LA.

♪ ♪ ♪

The Johnny Angel Story
Shelley Fabares and Paul Petersen

ONE OF THE SONGS I BROUGHT along for Shelley to record was called "I'd Do Anything for Him." I sincerely believed that this song had hit potential, and I figured it would be the perfect vehicle for her. However, to my dismay, all material had to first be approved by Tony Owen, whose task it was to protect the squeaky clean image of *The Donna Reed Show*. Nothing off-color was to ever take place on the show.

Before we continue, I believe a brief description of Tony Owen is essential. Tony had been a sports writer in Chicago before he married Donna Reed, which was hardly a qualification for being a TV producer. He was the most typical-looking Hollywood producer one could imagine, and often wore an open-collared shirt unbuttoned most of the way down, almost to his waist. He had a very hirsute chest, and usually wore a large medallion around his neck. His voice was quite raspy and deep, which added to the mystique, and his overall appearance as he sat behind his massive desk was, to say the least, overwhelming. But he could at times be a pussycat and very considerate.

Tony read the lyric to the song and immediately said "No way... not on *The Donna Reed Show*." He felt that the lyric was much too risqué. With this bit of unexpected news, I was now in a quandary. I had counted on that song for Shelley. A wave of frustration overwhelmed me. But then Dame Fortune saw fit to smile on me—once again.

With Tony Owen's rejection of the song that I had intended to record with Shelley, I was in that proverbial *shit house*. I grabbed the song that the writers had forced on me while I was on the way to the airport, and I gave it a quick sight-sing. It at first seemed completely wrong for Shelley. I felt that it was much too jazz- oriented, but I was desperate, so I showed the lyric to Tony.

He quickly approved of the lyric. "Johnny Angel..." he reflected. He thought that name had a nice ring to it, and the lyric seemed to prompt a good story line for a *Donna Reed* episode. He gave it his stamp of approval. I immediately went to a piano and fooled around with the song, trying my best to make it sound more "Teeny Bop." I guess I succeeded, considering what happened next.

In February of 1962, Shelley, Paul Petersen and I went into United Recording, and together we recorded four sides. "Johnny Angel" with Shelley, and "She Can't Find Her Keys" with Paul. The recording engineer on the session was the legendary Bones Howe. We also recorded a duet with Paul and Shelley. Again recalling what had happened when James Darren's record was performed on the show, Tony Owen immediately had the writers come up with a story line that featured Shelley singing "Johnny Angel." He also did the same for Paul's record of "She Can't Find Her Keys."

Shelley Fabares never had any aspirations of being a singer. She was well aware that singing was not her forte, and would rather have preferred dancing naked in the streets, to singing. However, what Tony Owen wants, Tony Owen gets. He wanted Shelley to make a record for the sake of the show and Shelley had little to say in the matter. To her credit, she cooperated with me 110%. She had to, or Tony might have fired her. No one but Donna was the star of *The Donna Reed Show*. Everyone else was—expendable!

I felt sorry for Shelley but I had my own little problem. It was vital for me to make Jonie's statement

The very adorable Shelley Fabares. 1961

to Tony Owen—that I could successfully record Shelley and Paul—come true. If I failed, then I would be responsible for Tony losing money, and that is definitely not a good way to make one's mark in Hollywood.

Paul Petersen was also a bit reluctant about singing, but unlike Shelley, he was confident that he could handle anything. And despite his untrained voice, he attacked singing with great confidence and bravura. I admired his attitude. With Paul it was *damn the torpedoes, full speed ahead*. His enthusiasm rubbed off on me and I closed my ears to his lack of vocal prowess and accepted what he had to give. In the future, both Shelley and Paul improved their vocal abilities to such a great extent that I treated them as any other accomplished vocalists.

Needless to say, having "Johnny Angel" sung on *The Donna Reed Show* was a tremendous help in the promotion of the record. Millions of people watched the show every week.

The director of the *Donna Reed* episode where Shelley performed her lip-sync of the "Johnny Angel" record was a complete control freak. During the filming of the song, he would walk between the camera and Shelley in order to ruin certain camera angles, so that in post-production, the editing could only be done one way—his way. He would never have tried that crap with Donna herself. She would have had his hide. But Shelley was only a co-star and was, at all times, under the complete control of the director.

I watched the scenario as it unfolded and thought about going to see Tony Owen (the executive producer), and make him aware of the situation. I quickly decided against this action. Why, I reasoned, make an enemy of one of the bright, new, up-and-coming TV directors who might seriously consider hiring me in the future? Oh well, to quote Gordon Gekko, "greed is good." Later that day, I regretted the gutless decision I had made. And by the way, I never did work directly with this director.

The record felt like it had a chance of being a hit, albeit a small chance. There was something so naive and simple about the song and Shelley's rendition of it.

The new promotion man at Colpix was Bruno Sardi, who had replaced Danny Winchell, the promotion man responsible for the success of "Blue Moon." Winchell had been fired soon after the record became a hit. It was discovered that he went around New York City claiming that he had helped produce the record. This didn't sit well with Paul Wexler, and unquestionably—not with me.

Bruno was a very charming young man who everybody liked. With the addition of his efforts, very soon after the broadcast of the *Donna Reed* episode that contained Shelley's performance of the song, the record began to take off. The possible *small* hit we had envisioned turned into a *monster* hit. Eventually, "Johnny Angel" became Number One.

I will never forget the moment when I walked onto the shooting stage at Columbia Pictures, where *The Donna Reed Show* was filming, and made the announcement to everyone that Shelley's record had just reached Number One on the charts. The response from the cast and crew was a standing ovation. Everybody was congratulating and applauding Shelley.

The Donna Reed Show family.
Paul, Shelley, Donna and Carl Betz.

I stood in the midst of the crowd watching Shelley receive her accolades. Donna Reed, who was standing next to me, turned and embraced me. It was a glorious moment, and suddenly memories of 1950 again flashed through my mind. I recalled Lionel Newman; Ray Heindorf; Sammy Fain; and all those other people I had

tried to impress without success. Now here I was—for the moment at least—on top of the heap in Hollywood, and it only took 12 years. As they quite often say in Hollywood, I was an overnight sensation.

During the period that I was working with Shelley on her first album, and acting as her vocal coach, an amusing little incident occurred. Since Shelley worked all day filming, it was sometimes necessary for me to rehearse with her after five P.M. One evening we worked until about seven. Both of us were quite hungry, and I suggested we go across the street to the Villa Capri restaurant, and the company would spring for dinner.

The Villa Capri had a notorious reputation as a place for a quiet and secret rendezvous. It was dimly lit and the owners were very discreet. Shelley I believe was 16 or 17 years old at the time, and as we sat in a dark corner of the restaurant I began to feel slightly uncomfortable. I might have been 33 years old—but I still looked about 25—and could easily appear to have been Shelley's date… or even worse, her *lover*. I began to panic when I realized that some Hollywood gossip columnist might just be in the restaurant observing us.

After all, Shelley was a star, and all stars are potentially prime material for gossip. And though not a movie star, I was not completely unknown in

Hollywood. Immediately after leaving Shelley, I immediately called my wife Dori in New York, and said that if she happened to read anything in the newspaper about Shelley and I being seen together, it was only dinner and nothing more. I felt quite relieved after making the call and cleansing my conscience.

Things began to get even better when Paul's recording of "She Can't Find Her Keys" also enjoyed some success. I was really flying high now. Two Number-One records within six months, plus several fringe hits.

Paul Petersen

Now, the cold fact that I was going to earn less money on Shelley and Paul's records was beginning to irritate me a bit. (Amazing how a bit of success can change your appreciation of what little you used to have.) I went to see Tony Owen and told him that I didn't think it was fair that I should suffer financially because of Paul Wexler's decision not to pay for the recording session. Tony agreed with me that it was unfair, but said that there was no way he was going to give me a better deal. When it came to business, Tony displayed little compassion.

However, to show that he really appreciated what I had done for Shelley and Paul, and to help make amends, Tony said he would offer me the opportunity to compose the music for the show. He felt this was the least he could do. Once again I would be doing two things and getting paid for one. The idea of being a composer was starting to excite me even more than ever, and I voiced a grateful thank-you. I now had *The Donna Reed Show*, three movies at Columbia, plus the two I had already done in New York as my composing credits. For the following years until *The Donna Reed Show* was canceled, I was its music director.

Paul Petersen eventually cut a Mann/Weil song called "My Dad," which after it appeared on *The Donna Reed Show* reached hit status. To this day, every Father's Day brings about its rebirth. Paul, like Shelley, had also improved as a singer and with some very personal experiences motivating him he poured his heart and soul into the vocal performance.

(Paul—who will reluctantly agree—was a bit wild in his youth. Currently he is the exact opposite. He founded and heads an organization called "A Minor Consideration," dedicated to preventing the exploitation of young stars by the film and TV industry. A most worthy endeavor, by one of the *good guys*.)

As a merchandising gimmick, we packaged Shelley, Paul and James into a *Teenage Triangle* concept and did two albums along that line. Both were mildly successful.

We also recorded an album of songs from the hit show and Columbia movie *Bye, Bye, Birdie* that showcased Shelley, Paul, The Marcels, James Darren and the Stu Phillips Orchestra. Shelley in particular knocked me out with her rendition of "How Lovely to be a Woman." James and Paul were their usual brilliant selves. I was flattered when I received a telegram from Charles Strouse and Lee Adams (the writers of "Birdie") expressing their delight with the album.

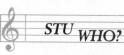

Darren, Fabares and Petersen during the recording of *Bye, Bye Birdie*.
Jimmy has obviously cracked Shelley up with some humorous story.

For the remainder of the year, and into the early part of 1963, I commuted between New York and LA, recording the Marcels, Shelley, Paul and James Darren. They were now my stable of artists.

The Marcels' follow up to "Blue Moon" was "Summertime," which unfortunately was not a big hit. It seemed that following up a worldwide smash like "Blue Moon" was not a simple matter. It took a little time, but we eventually had another hit with the Marcels called "Heartaches," which made the top-ten in the trade papers at the same time as "Goodbye Cruel World."

Shelley's follow up records never attained the hit status of "Johnny Angel," but Shelley herself became a fairly capable singer. In her album *The Things We Did Last Summer*, Shelley showed a great improvement in her vocal ability, and handled a large variety of songs with apparent ease. With Paul, we put together an album of old standards that "My Dad" might have listened to. Paul surprised the hell out of me with his wonderful vocal interpretations.

With the large amount of recording that I was doing on the West Coast, I was beginning to rely on certain studio musicians to play on my dates.

Among a few of my favorites were Earl Palmer, Ernie Freeman, Bill Pitman, Hal Blaine, Tommy Tedesco, Lincoln Mayorga, Carole Kaye and a wonderful guitarist who couldn't read a note of music. His name was Glen Campbell. It was always a kick when Glen was able to make my dates.

Manny and Dopey Klein were my orchestra contractors during those years. They were the in-house contractors at Columbia Pictures. Dori quite often contracted some of my recording sessions.

During the two-year period from 1961 to 1963, I recorded a large number of Stu Phillips and his Orchestra singles. The bulk of them were renditions of themes from the then current Columbia Pictures releases. I also was involved in putting together some of their soundtrack albums: *Pepe*; *Song Without End*; *Barrabas*; etc.

On *Song Without End* (*The Franz Liszt Story*), a concert pianist by the name of Jorge Bolet performed all the piano music on the film's soundtrack. To help exploit the soundtrack album, Colpix decided to have Bolet record a solo piano album of Liszt and Chopin music included in, or inspired by the film.

We arranged for the recording to be in the ballroom of the Great Northern Hotel in New York. Bob Fine, of Fine Sound Recording, was the engineer. The ballroom was chosen to help replicate the acoustics of a large concert hall. Sitting at the piano in this grand ballroom with crystal chandeliers

Jorge Bolet and I discussing the merits of Chopin and Liszt.

and mirrored walls, Jorge Bolet performed.

After the first day, Maestro Bolet discovered the wonderful science of tape editing. He then proceeded to record Chopin and Liszt in brief sections, relying on us to splice together the best takes. On 35-mag film this was a reasonably easy task. On four-track tape in the early '60s, it was a nightmare—especially with the natural reverb of the ballroom hanging across every splice. When he asked me to make a cut from the middle of one 32nd note scale to another

||:131:||

take, I considered walking out and telling him to do it himself, but diplomacy dictated that I stay and see it through. With the brilliant assistance of Bob Fine and George Piros, the job was, fortunately, satisfactorily completed.

It had been about 12 years since I last pestered Sammy Fain, asking—no, begging—him to help me make some connections in the music business. At this point, ironically, it was now I who could be of help to Sammy's career. I was in the envious position of saying yes or no to recording Sammy's songs. I must be honest and fair to him and mention that at no time during this period did he ever ask for my help, even though I knew he would have liked me to have recorded a few of his *new* songs. The old songs, everyone, including myself, recorded many, many times. He was after all, one of the 20th Century's greatest songwriters.

A precursor of things to come took place during my recording of two songs for the film *Gidget Goes to Rome*. James Darren was co-starring in the film and was to sing two songs, including the main title. The film company asked me to write the arrangements and produce the recording of the songs, since they were to be released as James' next single.

It happened that the musical layout of the main title, where one song was to be performed, segued from an instrumental cue, to the song, and then back to the cue. A relatively new composer, named Johnny Williams, had been hired to compose the score.

When I spoke to Johnny, he thought it might be beneficial for us to meet and coordinate our efforts, so that the instrumental cue and the song would have a smooth transition from one to the other. We met at Johnny's house in his little office, which was right off the kitchen and was most likely, originally, a housekeeper's room. Only a few minutes were needed for us to coordinate our efforts. It would be almost 16 years before our paths would once again cross. By then he would be known as John Williams—the dean of the modern-day film composers.

Every three or four weeks, I would spend several days composing music for *The Donna Reed Show*, and occasionally was fortunate to have a few other Screen Gem's projects fall my way. *Gidget* and *The Farmer's Daughter* joined my still modest—but slowly growing—résumé.

I was beginning to really believe that "life could not better be." Then Dori got pregnant—and life even did better get.

♫   ♫   ♫

VIII: The Fantastic '60s... Part 3

My First Major Film

Donna Reed

I WOULD LIKE TO TAKE A short detour from the account of my career to honor and praise a remarkable movie star—who was also an outstanding and thoughtful person, as well as an Oscar-winning actress. Donna Reed encompassed all of these traits. Though she was one tough lady when it came to business, as a person, she was all class.

Donna Reed

The first event involving Donna was sometime early in the 1960s. I had arrived in Hollywood to write some music for her show. On this trip Dori accompanied me. We stayed at the Sunset Towers Hotel on the Sunset Strip, and after we checked in I took a cab to Screen Gems to meet with Tony Owen, Donna's husband and the producer of the show. I had intentions of renting a car after meeting with Tony, as Dori and I were going to be in Hollywood for at least a week.

After meeting with Tony, I casually mentioned that I had to pick up a rental car. Owen told me to forget about it, and that he would lend me one of Donna's cars. Donna and Tony as a rule traveled together, usually in their Bentley. Tony gave me his home address and called and left instructions with the housekeeper to give me the keys to the car.

I took a cab to their house in Beverly Hills and was presented with the keys. There in the driveway waiting for me, was a classic 1956 T-Bird convertible, replete with opera portholes. For a week, Dori and I drove around Hollywood in opulent style in Donna Reed's car.

On another occasion, some of my wife's eastern relatives came to visit us. If I remember correctly there were four or five of them. They were of the star-struck variety, and since they knew that Dori's husband worked for Donna Reed, they of course expected me to arrange for them to meet her. I contacted Tony Owen and he graciously provided passes for them to get onto the shooting stage. I met them and my wife on the stage, and together we waited for Donna to emerge from her dressing-room trailer.

When she emerged, Donna spotted the group and immediately walked over to us. She asked everybody's name and spoke at length with each person. When the director called for "Miss Reed," she politely excused herself. After about a half-hour of filming, a break was called. Donna came back over to the group, spoke briefly again with everybody, and then respectfully pardoned herself explaining that she had some new lines to learn. She said goodbye to each person by name. Everybody was impressed with her graciousness and, fantastic memory.

The last incident occurred in 1966. My wife was pregnant with our second child, and her friends decided to give her a baby shower. As a gesture of proper protocol, and just for the hell of it, I suggested that they send an invitation to Donna Reed.

Donna RSVP'd *yes*, which was quite unexpected, considering her busy schedule. The party was at the home of Evy Darren (James Darren's wife)—and on the day of the party, there was Donna, on time and, as friendly as she could be with a group of people she hardly knew. Donna had found no phony excuses for not coming—as some Hollywood personalities are prone to do. Donna Reed... a magnificent lady.

My very pregnant wife Dori and Donna Reed.

Sorry for the detour. Now back to the nitty-gritty. In 1963, Jonie Taps finally attacked—and Paul Wexler became a casualty of war. And I became a reluctant hero. The details are unimportant. Paul Wexler it turned out had done a no-no: Enough said.

Meanwhile, Leo Jaffe, an executive who was very high up at Columbia Pictures, and a loyal friend of Jonie's, took a liking to me. With my success at Colpix and the work I was doing at Screen Gems, I was now quite the fair-haired kid around both organizations. (I was still a *kid* to everyone. And even though I was now 34 years old, I still looked about 25. Lucky me!)

With Paul Wexler no longer in charge, Jonie Taps toyed with the idea of having *me* run Colpix. With my being somewhat beholden to him, Jonie felt that he would be able to retain a solid hand in the running of the company through me. I thanked him for the offer and told him that I didn't want the best part of that job. All I really wanted to do was make records and do my film and TV composing. (Truthfully, what did I really know about running a record company? Perhaps in retrospect, it might have been a hasty decision on my part. Only time would tell if turning down being the headman at Colpix was an irrational move on my part.)

A man named Jerry Raker was hired to fill Paul's position. Right from the beginning, he and I did not get along well. I especially didn't like it when he hired Jack Lewis, another A&R man. Up to now, I had been the only producer at Colpix, and as head of A&R it should have been my job to hire someone else.

To further complicate the situation, the Schneiders were in the process of working out a deal with Don Kirshner for him to move all of his operations over to Screen Gems—and eventually take over Colpix Records and all of Columbia's affiliated music companies.

It was at about this time that I asked for a new contract. My brother was now out of law school and working for Robert Kennedy in the Department of Justice. Lee's eventual goal was to become an attorney in the music business, so it made sense for me to turn to him to help me negotiate my new contract. He did a skillful job, as I was to soon find out.

♪   ♪   ♪

Stu Phillips meets Danny Kaye

THE TIME HAD FINALLY ARRIVED for me to score my first film under the terms of my contract. I was told it was to be *The Man from the Diners' Club*. The film starred Danny Kaye—and sadly turned out to be the last picture in which Danny Kaye's would be the featured star. The movie also co-starred Telly Savalas (from *"Mad Dog" Coll*), Cara Williams, Martha Hyer, Everett Sloane, and introduced George Kennedy.

Up to now I had never scored a film to picture and I was about as green and inexperienced as one could be. (*"Mad Dog" Coll*, as you may recall, was scored to a stopwatch. Also, all the commercials, Donna Reed shows and ABC Specials I had worked on were done "wild.") However, with the help of some wonderful music editors—mainly Carole Knudsen, Irma Levin and Jim Hendrickson—I quickly learned about click tracks, streamers and punches. It also helped that I had spent many hours on the scoring stage observing Franz Waxman conducting *The Last Command*, and Johnny Green on *Bye, Bye, Birdie*.

Unfortunately, there was a little snag connected with this project. When I asked the producers if they were interested in having a song for the main title, they replied that a song had already been written and performed by Steve Lawrence. No one had informed me about this beforehand, and I felt quite stupid after I asked my question.

The plot of the film was about a man who worked at the Diner's Club office, and had problems operating the computer. The computer was about 20 feet wide, and eight feet tall. (I remind you that this was 1963, the dawn of the computer age.) In one of the early scenes Danny Kaye was supposed to react comically to the lights that were sporadically blinking on the computer. When he accidentally pushes the wrong button the lights begin to go crazy, flashing erratically. The director, Frank Tashlin, felt that it might be amusing if the music that was to accompany the scene was in tempo with the lights, and at the same time underscored the various wild gestures that Danny Kaye would be performing on the screen.

When I was presented with this problem, I suggested that perhaps the lights could be rigged up to a dummy piano keyboard, so that I could play them off camera as the scene was being filmed. I reasoned, that if I wrote down the rhythmic patterns I was playing, then at a later time I could write music that would fit what I had performed. My idea was agreed-to by the director, and the grip department rigged up the lights and keyboard.

That particular scene was scheduled for the first day of filming. I flew from New York to Hollywood and composed and played my first—and only—"Concerto for Computer Lights."

I had always been a fan of Danny Kaye's and the wonderful songs he had recorded. In fact, in my youth, I used to commit to memory some of his songs, like "Anatole of Paris," "The Russian Composers" etc. I had eagerly anticipated meeting him personally.

My encounter with Danny Kaye did not turn out as I had envisioned. Danny was quite upset with Columbia Pictures for deciding at the last moment to switch from color film to black and white. He was in a very lousy mood during the days that I spent on the stage and, although he was polite to me, he was in no mood to be overly friendly. He spent most of his spare time in his trailer listening to baseball games on the radio.

Bill Bloom, the producer, was a likeable man and we got along well. The fly in the ointment seemed to be that Danny Kaye was holding him personally responsible for the fiasco with Columbia over the cut in the budget—which resulted in the change from color to black and white. To my knowledge, Bill Bloom never produced another motion picture. (At least nothing that I'm aware of.)

When it was time to compose the music for the picture, Columbia provided me with an office on the lot. The room was large and smelled extremely musty. I doubt that it had been cleaned in the last five years. I continually had the premonition that the ghosts of previous film composers from the '30s, '40s, and '50s were rotting in the closet. But it was quite a thrill to be able to say that this *composer's shrine* was now my office—although, only temporarily. For a short time, I had the authority to call the front gate and have passes issued to allow people to come on the lot and visit me. (A major Hollywood ego trip and sign of importance.)

Realizing that this was my first significant film-scoring endeavor, Jonie Taps decided that I should definitely have an orchestrator to assist me with the score—whether I wanted one or not. He assigned Arthur Morton—who at the time was probably the finest orchestrator in Hollywood—to lend a hand. Up to now, I had always done my own orchestration and my sketches were written *for my eyes only*. They were a tad sloppy and very incomplete. Since I was always the orchestrator, I saw no reason to waste my time on neat and complete music sketches.

The first long cue I prepared for Arthur to orchestrate took me longer to sketch than I was used to, and I felt it was a big waste of valuable time. While Arthur was orchestrating the cue I gave him, I was busy orchestrating two others. After the first week, Arthur did not show up again, and I completed the remainder of the movie by myself. When I queried Jonie as to what had happened to Arthur, he replied that, after Arthur had checked over my orchestrations, he felt that they were completely professional and saw no reason why I would need his help. Obviously, Jonie had been a bit worried about my ability to handle the assignment, and had placed a *spy* in my office.

Four weeks into composing the music, I was attacked by a hoard of ghosts from the past. One morning, as I entered the office, an entire wall from ceiling to floor was covered with termites. Being from New York City, I had never seen termites before, and to me they looked like ants with wings. It took several days of extermination before the office was ready to be occupied again. For the next few weeks I kept a sharp eye out for any more uninvited guests. (I was told that rats were not uncommon around the studio.)

Of great help to me during this, my first really professional film composing assignment was Ross DiMaggio. Ross was the music librarian and one of the permanent fixtures at Columbia Pictures. During the years I knew him, he related many interesting stories to me about composers, including some about Morris Stoloff and Leonard Bernstein. (The movie *On the Waterfront* was scored on the Columbia stage.) Now that I have mentioned the scoring stage at Columbia, I feel it is necessary to give you some of my impressions of this monstrosity.

The scoring stage at Columbia Pictures belonged in the British Museum, or some other building housing ancient artifacts. I don't know exactly when it was built, probably about 1930 at the advent of sound, but I'm sure no improvements had been made since its creation. The recording engineer, one "Mac" McClaughlin, appeared to me to be as old as the stage. His major attribute was that he recorded Nelson Eddy and Jeanette MacDonald. On the negative side, Mac was hard of hearing and, had a heart condition. Perfect qualifications for a stressful job like recording engineer. (Mac was the result of unionism at its highest level of stupidity.)

The engineer's recording booth was up a flight of rickety wooden stairs. The mixing board contained about six large black rotary knobs and a few smaller ones. It was about as antiquated as the stage and the engineer. In order to hear a playback of a take, it was necessary for the engineer to walk down this flight of wooden stairs to the floor of the stage, and use the mixing console situated on the floor.

Up, down, up, down, up and down: As the day progressed, Mac's assent and descent of the stairs got slower and slower. Eventually, we would have to call a *timeout* for Mac. I have never ceased to be amazed at some of the wonderful scores that were recorded on that stage under such adverse conditions, by the likes of: Leonard Bernstein; Elmer Bernstein; George Duning; Johnny Green; and many others. They were and are truly geniuses.

The score I eventually composed and conducted for the film was good, not great, but very adequate and professional. I personally was proud of the writing I had done. I had no complaints from anyone, and the score even managed to garner some favorable mention in many newspaper reviews. I felt like I had reached a new plateau in my career, and I was eagerly looking forward to my next film.

♫ ♫ ♫

The California Resolution

IN EARLY 1963, WHILE MY brother was reviewing my new contract, he pointed out to me that the Columbia Pictures' lawyers had failed to notice that nowhere in the contract did it state the location where I was to physically perform the duties of head of A&R. This meant that I could be the head of A&R in Los Angeles (or for that matter, anywhere else in the world) if I so desired. It was a pleasant little oversight by Columbia's attorneys—in my favor. My brother had outfoxed the foxes.

Columbia's oversight, coupled with the contract's guaranteeing my employment for the next several years, seemed to present ideal conditions for a possible move to the West Coast. From the very beginning we both agreed that some day we would make the West Coast our home. With the birth of our first child only months away, I discussed relocating to Hollywood with Dori.

To help reinforce our decision, three of my most successful artists lived in Los Angeles, plus I was still composing music for *The Donna Reed Show* every three to four weeks. The Marcels, by now, were no longer a hot group, and their recording sessions were few. It seemed that more time was spent in LA than in New York, and when we would put the key in the door of our suite at the Sunset Towers, we were home. New York now felt like being on the road.

On one of my trips to Hollywood around that time, I informed Jonie Taps of my decision to go west. He was very amenable to the idea. Of course he was. After all, that would once again put him in close proximity to having some control of the record company.

When we mentioned to Jonie that we were looking to buy a house, he suggested that we should consider the area in the hills south of Universal Pictures. Mindful of Jonie's suggestion, Dori and I set out to go house shopping.

Searching for a house wasn't easy for us, as we both were brought up in New York City apartments, and had never experienced the extraordinary joys of home ownership. (Ha, ha, ha!) I was a Manhattan boy and Dori was a Bronx girl. With Dori's due date rapidly approaching, her doctor suggested that she return home immediately. Meanwhile, I stayed in LA and continued looking for our dream house.

One day, after looking at several properties—none of which I liked—the real-estate agent and I drove by one that I did like. I told her that this house was more in the line of what we were looking for. Unfortunately, it was not for sale.

When I got back to my hotel, there was a message waiting for me from the real-estate agent advising me that the house I liked was, indeed, available. I met her back at the house (on Wrightwood Drive), looked it over, and decided it was perfect. What I loved most about the house was the very large swimming pool, and the beautiful tranquil view of a mountainside covered with wild oak and eucalyptus trees.

I called Dori from the house and told her that I was considering buying it. She asked me some silly questions concerning insignificant things like a dining room, a maid's room, carpeting, etc., etc. I assured her she was going to love this house. What else could Dori do but say yes? She was in New York, and I was in California.

On March 6, 1963 in New York City, Toni Elizabeth Phillips entered this world. It was at about this time, that I informed the New York office of Colpix Records that I was moving to LA, and would head the A&R department from there. At first, they did not take me seriously and proceeded to remind me that I was under contract. I subsequently pointed out the clause in my contract that allowed me to perform my duties anywhere in the country. They became a bit hostile, but had no come-back.

Sometime in April, I left the New York office of Colpix for the last time. I had entered these offices in 1960 with uncertainty, but was leaving them with a sense of fulfillment and my head held high. In the last three years I had become wiser, more confident, and definitely, a lot wealthier.

In the elevator with me on my last descent was Don Kirshner. The deal that had been pending between he and Columbia had come to fruition. Kirshner was now in charge of all the music, record and publishing divisions at Columbia-Screen Gems.

Donnie said he heard the news about my relocating to the West Coast and thought the move might work out to everyone's benefit. He actually sounded excited about the possibilities that this arrangement might produce. His last words left me with an attitude of confidence and optimism about my decision to move to LA. I began to envision a prosperous relationship between Don Kirshner and myself.

♬   ♬   ♬

Donnie Kirshner

DONNIE KIRSHNER, ALONG WITH SEVERAL other publishers, was very influential in the successes of many of the important writers and artists during the period of 1957 to the late 1960s. His innate ability at recognizing raw writing talent was quite exemplary. He also possessed an incredible knack of ascertaining a potential hit song when it was played for him; and that talent is certainly of prime importance in the basic formula

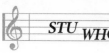

for making hit records. In the jargon of the industry, Kirshner had "good ears."

It was these aptitudes that made him an important figure in the pop music field of that time—an important and creative period in the music business that prospered, in part, due to men like Don Kirshner—even though the man himself possessed little or no actual musical talent. Without question, there were many others who contributed as much; but Donnie was, to borrow another phrase of that era, *The Big Kahuna*.

To know Kirshner, was for some, to love him. Others loathed and despised him for a myriad of reasons, which I will not elucidate on in this book. I shall remain—neutral.

As an individual, Donnie was an enigma. An intellectual giant he wasn't. He appeared to be mired in endless adolescence—which of course was the perfect attribute for making teenage bubble-gum pop records. Kirshner was able to guide and mold his writers into hit-making machines. There were Mann and Weil; Goffin and King; Neil Sedaka; Howie Greenfield; Jeff Barry; Gloria Shayne; and many, many others. One of the greatest stable of songwriters ever assembled.

I remember clearly one typically Kirshner-like experience. Shortly after Don and his wife Sheila had moved into their South Orange, New Jersey "mansion," Donnie called me at my office around three o'clock and invited Dori and myself to dinner at his house. Though I tried desperately to beg off, he would not take *no* for an answer, and explained that his limo would pick us up at six at my office and drive us to his house. I phoned Dori—who was quite pregnant at the time—and told her that His Majesty the Emperor Kirshner had requested our presence for dinner. Dori, being a bit self-conscious about her less-than-appealing appearance, would have preferred not going; but she was aware that it might be important for me career-wise. She took a cab to my office and, promptly at six, the limo picked us up and we were driven to Donnie's house.

Donnie and Sheila greeted us at the door. Talk about being casual, Don wasn't wearing shoes. But at least he was wearing socks. (At his office, he often sat around with his shoes off while conducting meetings.) Sheila was dressed as though she was about to do some gardening, or clean out the basement. I was wearing a suit and tie and Dori, of course, was properly dressed for a social dinner. We were led into the den where I quickly noticed that most of the reading matter strewn about was *Archie* comic books. (Kirshner in the late '60s was to produce several successful ventures associated with the Archies. Could it be we should all spend a little more time reading comic books?)

From the very casual attire of Don and Sheila it was quite evident that this was not going to be a sit-down dinner, and that Dori and I were quite over-dressed. When the doorbell rang, we became aware that dinner was to be… *pizza*. This was Kirshner's idea of entertaining an important A&R man? Not quite what Dori and I had expected. But if you knew Donnie, it figured.

At about ten P.M., after some lousy pizza and insipid conversation, I asked if his chauffeur could possibly drive us back to the city. Don insisted that we sleep over. We explained that we had not brought any personal items. Sheila said we could borrow anything we needed. I could see in Dori's eyes that she was set on going home, but there was no dissuading them. They insisted, for no apparent reason, that we stay the night. We felt *kidnapped*. With no means of getting home other than Donnie's limo, or a cab ride of about $60, since we were way out in the boondocks, we acquiesced. While I found the whole incident a bit amusing, Dori was seething inside. The next morning we skipped breakfast with the King and Queen, and the chauffeur finally delivered us home.

Being the first kid on the block with some new gadget or electronic toy was of prime importance to Kirshner. He loved toys. I recollect once when I was in Hollywood, it was probably around 1963, that I received a phone call from Donnie. The conversation went something like this.

Donnie: Hi Stu, guess where I'm calling you from.

Stu: Where, Donnie?

Donnie: Come on, guess!

Stu: I'm really busy, Donnie. Where are you?

Donnie: You'll flip when I tell you.

Stu: Okay… I'll bite. Where?

Donnie: I'm in my limo and I'm just crossing 53rd St. and Park Ave. Ask me how I can do that.

Stu: How can you do that?

Donnie: I'm talking on a phone *in my car*! Ain't that wild? Can you fuckin' believe it?

Stu: Fantastic. Anything else, Donnie?

Donnie: You don't sound too impressed. Talk to you later. I got to call some more people. They're never gonna believe this!

Obviously, Kirshner was one of an early group of people (we will assume that the President of the United States was probably first), to own a

car phone. In 1967, I got the bug and rented one for my car. It cost about $75 a month and around a dollar a minute. I managed to make use of it about nine or 10 times over a two-year period. It never seemed to fascinate me as much as it did Donnie.

Now that the big decision to "go west" had been resolved, Dori and I decided to have our new Olds Cutlass convertible driven to the coast, and then with all our worldly possessions on a moving van, the three of us took a plane to California.

Since escrow on the house had not as yet closed, we moved into the Sunset Towers until our new home was ready. Also sharing space in our apartment at the Towers was my brother Lee—who, coincidentally, had decided to move to LA at the same time as us.

My brother had been hired by the prestigious law firm of Mitchell, Silberburg & Knupf to start a music division for them. This move of my brother's and ours naturally upset my mother, who was now left in New York without either son, and was still mourning my father's passing. In a few years she also moved to LA.

Eventually, our house was ready, and the big day arrived. We moved in and became proud and *almost* happy homeowners. The property was on the top of a hill and, as I mentioned earlier, had a tranquil view of a tree-forested mountain across the canyon. When we finally moved into the house, the view was no longer what I had described to Dori. In a matter of two months, it had been transformed into a bare, dusty and desolate hill, soon to be known as Laurelwood East. For the five years we lived in that house, construction across the canyon took place almost every day. Our dream house was more of a *bad* dream.

Upon seeing the size of the swimming pool, the first thing Dori did was register our daughter Toni in swimming school: Before Toni could crawl or walk, she could swim. It was obvious at an early age that she was quite a natural athlete. She became a very strong swimmer, played on her high-school tennis team and currently has a room full of Karate trophies and a coveted black belt. She's a very determined young lady, who coinciden-tally, works for a law firm in competition with my brother's firm.

The fact that there was no formal dining room and no maids-quarters added to my wife's annoyance over my choice of house. To add to our disillusionment, during the first big rain, the hill below our house slid down and it cost quite a bit of money to put it back. Oh, the bliss, excuse me... the *miseries* of owning a home.

As my film and TV composing became more active, it became necessary to add a room to the house so that I could write in peace and quiet. Five years later we moved to our current home on Fryman Road. Dori wasn't particularly fond of this choice of house either—but unlike before, this time, she at least had some input in its purchase.

9/9 The Fantastic '60s... Part 4
The Move to Capitol Records

WHEN I ARRIVED AT COLUMBIA PICTURES on Gower Street eager to start working, Jonie escorted me into my new office. I would only be exaggerating slightly, if I said it was as large as about half of my new house. My secretary, who was a lovely elderly woman, and had most likely been at Columbia since its inception, had her own little office. I quickly got my act together and put out calls to all the music publishers in town, advising them that I was in the market for new material. I called my artists and said that I was preparing sessions as soon as possible. Needless to say, they were delighted at the news.

I then placed a call to Don Kirshner in New York, to discuss some studio options. His secretary said that Donnie would call me right back. However, she never said *when* right back was. The next day I called again. Don was still *unavailable*. When he didn't call back for a week, I decided to place one last call, but was still unable to make contact with him. He didn't call back, he didn't write, he didn't send flowers. I knew a brush-off when I got one, and this was definitely one major snub.

Several more days passed before I received a call from Lou Adler, who ran the Hollywood office of Donnie's publishing company and was Kirshner's West Coast liaison with Colpix Records. (In the very near future, Lou Adler would marry Shelley Fabares. Their marriage was short lived and a divorce followed soon afterward. Lou can currently can be seen seated next to Jack Nicholson at most of the Lakers' home basketball games. He's the one in the pork-pie hat.)

From the very beginning, Adler and I had a rather frigid relationship. When I was subsequently told that I would have to clear all my recording sessions through him—and that he would screen and have approval of all the material that I would select to record—I flipped out. This was not what

I had anticipated when I last saw Donnie, whose final words had been so encouraging. I was getting royally screwed and I wasn't even being kissed.

I went to Jonie Taps and explained the deplorable situation. Jonie was just as unhappy about this development as I was and said he would talk to Leo Jaffe (a vice president of Columbia Pictures) about it. Meanwhile, Jonie said I should do the best I could, under the circumstances.

Unable to get any approvals for my recording sessions, I was growing impatient and was also losing face with my artists—all of whom felt that I had lost control. (Which, in truth, I had.) As the weeks wore on, I suddenly felt that Dori and I might indeed have made an ill-advised decision in moving to LA.

Though I was being well paid every week for doing absolutely nothing, I was still disheartened and incensed over the current situation. In a state of utter frustration I searched for a solution to my dilemma. I remembered meeting Voyle Gilmore at a past recording-industry function and decided it was time to call him.

Voyle Gilmore was the head of A&R at Capitol Records. At that time Capitol Records was, in my opinion, the greatest record company in the business. (I have since drastically reversed my opinion.) It was the company of Frank Sinatra, Nelson Riddle, Billy May, Les Baxter, Peggy Lee, Stan Kenton and of course, The Beatles. When we first met, Voyle had said to me that if I ever got fed up with Colpix Records, he would love to talk a deal with me. I contacted Voyle, and told him I was in a quandary, and ready to listen to any arrangement that he might have in mind.

When we met, I explained to him that my Colpix contract allowed me to produce records at other companies while still working as A&R at Colpix. He was delighted at that news and said, "What can we work out?" I explained that money was the least of my concerns, since I was being well paid every month by Colpix. All I really wanted was the opportunity to produce records, an office, a secretary, a parking space, plus a royalty on the sale of any records that might sell a little. That's all. After a chuckle or two over my list of minimum requirements, Voyle agreed to the deal and I immediately went to work at Capitol Records.

Another one of my 1951 dreams had come to pass. I was a part of Capitol Records, the *Taj Mahal* of record companies. When informed of my decision to work at Capitol Records, Jonie Taps was not at all pleased. Who could blame him? He had helped to foster my career, and now felt that I was shafting him. However, there was little he could do about it. But it did put a dent in our relationship, which saddened me a bit. Naturally, I no longer had the use of that great executive office at Columbia. My new office at Capitol Records (the round building seen in most pictures of Hollywood) was quite small and unglamorous. The view from my window was only the parking lot, and I also had to share my secretary with another producer. Life's tough!

Capitol Records...The Four Preps

WHEN I STARTED WORKING AT Capitol Records, Voyle asked if I would do one small favor for him. The recording contract of The Four Preps, a somewhat successful vocal group that at the present was without a hit, was soon to expire, and Capitol still owed them one session. Voyle had been personally producing them, but now was too busy. He said that he would appreciate it if I would produce this last session with the Four Preps. Feeling somewhat beholden to him, I of course said yes.

The Four Preps had had several hit records during their Capitol years. "Down by the Station" and "Twenty-Six Miles" being two of them. The group was led by Glen Larson and Bruce Belland who also wrote most of their material. (Coincidently, The Four Preps and Glen Larson were featured in the film *Gidget*, which had made a star of James Darren.) When I met with them, they showed me a new song hot off the burner called, "A Letter to the Beatles." I fully agreed with them that this song definitely had *hit* potential. We promptly went into the studio and recorded the song, and two other sides. The session went smoothly, and we seemed to get along well with each other.

I must explain that up to now in my career as an A&R man, I did all my own dubbing-down, with just the engineer and myself. Dubbing was a fairly simple matter in those days; there was no 16 or 24 track recording in existence. As I dubbed down the Four Preps recording, Glen Larson came into the studio and asked if he could listen. I shrugged okay and proceeded with the dub-down. After a short period, Glen started making suggestions—some of which I thought were quite unnecessary. When he continued on, I asked, in a rather annoyed voice, if he wouldn't mind leaving. Reluctantly, he left, and I finished the dubbing. I didn't know whether or not Glen was angry when he left, and truthfully at that time, didn't really care. My work on this production was basically a favor to Voyle.

When the record was released in the summer of 1964, it made an immediate impact on the market and started to rapidly climb up the charts. It was without a doubt destined to be a monster hit. I now had renewed faith in my ability to produce and still recognize potential hits. It had been almost a year since my last chart record.

Suddenly, the beautiful balloon burst. The Beatles' management informed Capitol that they were not happy with The Four Preps' record. They felt it poked too much fun at the Beatles, and might be injurious to their image. The Beatles' lawyer and manager demanded that either Capitol recall The Four Preps record or Capitol might stand to lose distribution of The Beatles. Of course we know that The Beatles remained at Capitol and The Four Preps' record was recalled. Needless to say, Glen Larson and the group were furious. I didn't closely follow all the subsequent events, but I was told that The Four Preps tried to sue Capitol Records. I never did find out what the eventual outcome was.

♫   ♫   ♫

The Hollyridge Strings

EVEN THOUGH MY LATEST PRODUCING effort was technically no longer a hit, Capitol was encouraged by my efforts and their deal with me. One day I approached Karl Engemann at Capitol with a far-out idea of recording an album of Beatles songs in an orchestral setting geared toward easy listening. A sort of "Beatles for the older set." Karl liked the idea and said he would discuss it at the next A&R meeting. Ten minutes later he returned and said, "Do it! Voyle loves the idea." I then had to explain to Karl that, although I was free to produce records for someone other than Colpix, I was still under an artists' contract to Colpix as Stu Phillips and his Orchestra.

Karl said the problem was easily solved. He advised me that Capitol had an in-house orchestra called The Hollyridge Strings. I would record the album under that name and it would be produced and arranged by me. I immediately started writing the arrangements and rushed into the studio as soon as possible. We needed to stay abreast of the Beatles' popularity and try to ride in their wake.

The album, titled *The Beatles Song Book* was a big success and by August of 1964 it reached Number Seven on the *Cash Box* chart. The album was so successful that we rushed out a *Beach Boys Song Book* and a *Four Seasons Song Book*. On November 7, 1964 all three albums were simultaneously in the Top 100 Albums on the *Cash Box* chart.

Back at Columbia, when Jonie Taps saw the charts, he called and asked me to please meet him at Colpix. Jonie reluctantly congratulated me on my success at Capitol, and then asked me to do him a big favor. He suggested, rather emphatically, that I take an ad in the Hollywood trade papers, especially *Variety* and the *Hollywood Reporter*, ad-

"Sleeper" of the Year!
A great new instrumental album that's storming up the best-seller charts...

...conceived by one of Hollywood's most talented, young producer/arrangers

STU PHILLIPS

COMING SOON: "THE BEACH BOYS SONG BOOK" (ST-2156) ...more great instrumental arrangements of today's greatest teen hits, played by The Hollyridge Strings, arranged and produced by STU PHILLIPS!

vertising the success of the Hollyridge Strings. He felt that when Leo Jaffe and the Schneiders saw the ad, they would want to know why someone being paid a great deal of money by them was earning money for Capitol Records. Jonie hoped that this would seriously blemish Don Kirshner's image with the studio and, with Paul Wexler gone, Kirshner was now Jonie's new target. Although he tried to make light of the subject, down deep inside Jonie still wanted to wield some control over the record division. He always considered it his *baby*.

Since Taps had been responsible for so many of the positive things that had happened to advance my career, to say *no* to him would have definitely been a disastrous move on my part. I took the ads in the two trade papers and paid for them out of my own pocket. Immediately after they appeared,

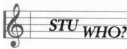

Leo Jaffe personally called me and said that there was no way that Columbia Pictures was going to allow this absurd situation to continue, and stated emphatically that I would be hearing immediately from Don Kirshner about renegotiating my contract.

True to form, Donnie didn't call. When I told Jonie that I had not as yet received a call from Kirshner, his eyes lit up and he immediately called Leo Jaffe. Once again, Leo reassured me that Donnie would call. A few days later, Kirshner finally did contact me. He explained that he thought we should make a fresh start and negotiate a brand-new contract—all the while making it sound as though this whole thing had been his idea. What an ego! I told him to have his lawyer call my lawyer, Lee Phillips, and let them hammer out a deal.

To make a rather long and frustrating story short, after much bickering between the legal-eagles, the entire deal was telegraphed to me—all 24 pages—for my approval. The telegram was my brother's idea since he didn't trust the Columbia attorneys or Don Kirshner's word. It was one sweetheart of a deal. I went to Capitol Records and showed the telegram to

Cash Box—November 28, 1964

Stu Phillips Inks Artist Pact With Capitol, Stays As Colpix A&R Man

Karl Engemann, left, and Tom Morgan, of the A&R and business affairs departments of Capitol Records, Inc., congratulate Stu Phillips after the arranger-conductor signed a long-term artist contract with CRI. Phillips is the originator of the songbook series of instrumental hits by The Hollyridge Strings.

Voyle Gilmore and asked him, "What would you do?" Voyle looked at the telegram and said, "If you don't take the deal, then by God *I* will." Then we shook hands and I bid farewell to Capitol. Or so I thought.

It now appeared that Columbia's less-than-brilliant lawyers had goofed once again. This time they forgot to renew my Colpix *artist* contract, which had recently expired and was no longer valid. My attorney certainly wasn't going to remind them.

I was now free to record for Capitol Records as an artist. Unfortunately for me, with five albums on the charts and the name Hollyridge Strings synonymous with the songbook concept, I had to continue taking second billing to the orchestra. If nothing else, at least my name now had the top position over the orchestra on the cover.

During the next few years I recorded a total of ten albums. One of the albums, *Feels Like Lovin'*, featured Stu Phillips and his Orchestra and Chorus. It was not a successful album, but it will always be one of my favorites. The arrangements featured a vocal group performing more as a section of the orchestra than as a conventional chorus. Ron Hicklin led these fabulous singers, and the job that they did was outstanding. Throughout the years from 1963 to well into the 1980s, Ron, Jackie Ward or Sally Stevens supplied me with the créme de la créme of studio vocalists.

It took 14 years, but I finally accomplished the first of my musical aspirations. With the Hollyridge Strings and the Stu Phillips albums, I at long last had the opportunity to write those Morton Gould-style arrangements (albeit with a rock-and-roll beat) I was so enamored with when I was young. And get paid! I was getting closer to Gould and Rose.

At this point I worked simultaneously for two record companies: With Colpix, as an A&R man; and with Capitol, as a recording artist. Once again the Columbia brass were not too enthralled with me. But it had been their legal department's sloppy and inefficient work that had caused the problem, not me. Nevertheless, the mere fact that it was their fault didn't help further my cause, and my popularity with Columbia was sinking to a new low point.

Colpix Records was at this time, in need of a West Coast president, and the New York office struck a deal with Bob York (who had just left his position as president at RCA Records). When Bob and I met, we seemed to get along famously. He went back to New York to prepare for his move to the West Coast, and left me with the job of finding office space. Bob decidedly did not want Colpix Records to any longer be located on the Columbia Pictures lot. He felt that it would be too close to Jonie Taps, and Don Kirshner had made it definitely clear to Bob that he did not want to have Jonie any longer involved with the record company. Jonie was *out*. Gone. *Sayonara. Kaput.* Even Leo Jaffe couldn't save him.

I located some office space on Cahuenga Blvd. in Hollywood just south of Sunset Blvd. and, when Bob York arrived, he approved of my choice, and the entire staff moved in. I was now officially head of the West Coast A&R department—which, as it turned out was actually a big joke. But unfortunately, the joke was to be on me.

Within a matter of weeks, Bob proceeded to sign acts without my knowledge or approval, and assigned independent producers to A&R the sessions—*also* without my approval. (My new contract stated that I was to

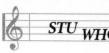

have approval of all releases.) I was having little success with my artists, and every record I produced was released with almost no promotion—as though I was being punished. My constant prying into Bob's very private deals was a major annoyance to him, even though protocol demanded that all contracts cross my desk. Bob and I quickly began to get on each other's nerves and barely communicated. This was not a situation or a climate ripe for creativity.

It also didn't help matters any when, during this time, I was nominated for a Grammy in the category of best instrumental arrangement. It was for *The Beatles Song Book* with the Hollyridge Strings; and was my third Grammy nomination. The fact that the album was on Capitol Records and not Colpix made Bob York even more hostile towards me. (By the way, I lost again—this time to Henry Mancini's *Pink Panther.* The awards count was now 0 for 3.

♪ ♪ ♪

Henry Mancini

MENTIONING HENRY MANCINI'S NAME brings to mind the first time I met him, so I will digress for a moment from my Colpix dilemma. After moving to California, I decided to have someone handle my small publishing company: Someone who could give it some attention, since I was really quite busy (Thank God). Larry Shayne was a publisher that I had occasionally seen regarding new material and we became friends. When I discovered that he represented Henry Mancini's publishing enterprise, I felt that my little company would be in good hands.

Mancini had office space at Larry Shayne's office in a building on the corner of Sunset and Vine. One day when I went to visit Larry, I was introduced to Henry. Before I continue, let me say that Henry Mancini was one of the truly great film composers, as well as an outstanding gentleman. Henry knew who I was, and invited me into his office. Then after a bit of superfluous conversation, he proceeded to give me some unsolicited professional advice.

He informed me that it had taken many years for the film composers to get the studios accustomed to paying extra for orchestration. A composer's fee, he informed me, did not necessarily include orchestration. If the composer did some of the orchestration, then he was to be paid extra. Henry had discovered that my package deal with Columbia included orchestration as well as conducting. By accepting this form of contract, he said I was partly responsible for helping to tear down the established agenda. He very politely said that since I was a member of The Composers and Lyricists Guild (which most Hollywood composers' were), I should try to respect the gains that my co-workers had made after many years of negotiations. After weighing his words of wisdom, I decided to continue doing my own orchestrations whenever possible and, eventually, so did quite a large number of other young composers.

Meanwhile, back to the Colpix Records dilemma. After about five months, Bob York and I barely spoke to each other and he wanted me out of his life. However, I had a three-year contract with options and, considering the amount of money I was being paid, I had no intention of leaving. Bob, however, had other ideas. He contacted Bert Schneider, now liaison between Screen Gems (who controlled Colpix) and the record company, and asked him to handle the unsavory job of getting rid of me.

Bert Schneider contacted me and offered to buy out my contract. I said, "No way!" He then threatened that I would no longer be writing *The Donna Reed Show*, or any more films for Columbia. (I still had two films to write under my original contract.) Also, he mentioned that I might find it difficult working anywhere else in Hollywood for a very long time. This was studio and show-biz blackmail in its ugliest form, but unfortunately, not unusual for most high-level Hollywood executives. For me—this was *war*.

I immediately called Tony Owen (producer of *The Donna Reed Show*), and told him of Bert's ultimatum. Tony said, "No one tells Tony Owen who to hire. Don't worry about it, kid. I'll take care of the whole thing."

Several days later Tony called me, and somewhat sheepishly announced that his hands were tied, and there was nothing he could do about my problem. My next S.O.S. went to Jonie Taps who also offered no support. After Bob York had made sure that he, Jonie, no longer had any input with Colpix, Taps now wanted nothing to do with the company—and that included me. Jonie also had no intention of taking on Bert Schneider *mano a mano*. Obviously, neither did Tony Owen. I seemed to have lost the battle *and* the war.

I called my brother and, after describing my dilemma, told him that I had decided to hang in at Colpix. I explained that I would come to work for the next two-and-a-half years and collect my salary. Screw Bob York, Bert Schneider, et al. My brother said that to continue on as I had just suggested doing was indisputably a bad idea. He reminded me that these people were powerful and merciless. He said that I might regret my decision for the rest of my life, and he convinced me to take the deal. "After all," he said, "If you take the buy-out, you'll have Capitol Records, and will again have *The Donna Reed Show* and the two movies to compose."

I hated the idea of giving in to these sons-of-bitches but, pragmatically, I realized that what my brother was saying made good sense. Reluctantly, I agreed and took the deal. The money owed to me was to be deferred and paid out over the course of about six years. That way the IRS wouldn't hit me quite as hard. It took until 1971 for me to collect all the money I was owed from the buy-out.

Ironically, two months after I left Colpix, Bob York was fired. It seems Screen Gems had uncovered all those under-the-table deals that Bob had been doing without my knowledge. All my suspicions about his shady transactions were now confirmed. I was no longer completely certain that I had made the right choice in accepting the buy-out. With Bob York gone, I would once again have been the logical choice to take over the company. I present to you… the music business—where everybody's your *fiend.*

It was a strange sensation for me, being fired from a job at which I had—for a short time—been so successful. I wasn't sure that I could handle this large a setback to my career. As usual, Dori was my Rock of Gibraltar and helped me keep things in focus.

♫   ♫   ♫

Vince Edwards

ONE OF MY LAST RECORDINGS before I left Colpix was with Vince Edwards, TV's Dr. Ben Casey. In spite of his reputation as being difficult to get along with as an actor, I found him easy to work

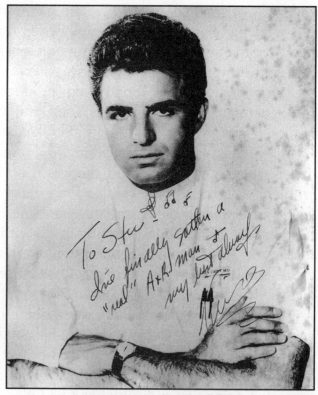

Vince Edwards (Dr. Ben Casey)

with, and we made a reasonably good record.

Edwards was not lacking in singing talent and had a pretty decent voice. The record, a revival of an old hit called "No Not Much," did not however go any farther than reaching the Top Ten in LA.

Vince was a racetrack aficionado on a par with Sammy Fain and Lionel Newman. In spite of the short time that I spent with Edwards, years later at a cocktail party he searched me out to say hello. I count Vince as one of the nice people I have met in the business. I'm sure that there are many who would argue with me.

Another project at Colpix that I remember enjoying, involved working with Bronislaw Kaper: One of the greats in the field of film scoring. I had the extreme pleasure of spending several days at United Recording Studios editing and re-mixing his magnificent score to the film *Lord Jim*.

Bronislaw was a very slight man in build, but he was deceptively strong. I spent many hours watching him do Tai Chi and Karate while we were editing. He was proud

Bronislaw Caper conversing with Charles Albertine and myself.
The pretty female face in the background is Dori.

of his conditioning and loved to show off his strength by doing endless pushups. He was not a young man at the time, and we were all amazed at his ability and dexterity. The industry lost a wonderful and talented composer when he recently passed away.

Also in 1965, before I left Colpix, I produced a record featuring Carol Connors and her sister Cheryl. They went under the name Carol and Cheryl, and later on as the Carmel Sisters. The two songs we recorded were "Sunny Winter" and "Go, Go, GTO." Carol Connors went on to become an award-winning lyricist. Recently, while browsing through a price guide of old 45's, I noticed a listing for that recording. The value of this record was listed as high as $150. For a single that was never a hit, the price really

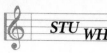

surprised me. After a more thorough search of the guide, I found quite a few of my *flops* that were now worth a great deal of money.

♫   ♫   ♫

Ride the Wild Surf

MY SECOND FILM FOR COLUMBIA turned out to be a movie called *Ride the Wild Surf*, starring Shelley Fabares, Fabian, Barbara Eden, Peter Brown, Tab Hunter and other teen idols. It was not a very good film and, to boot, the title song was assigned to Jan and Dean (a successful surf-music duo) for them to write and perform. Again, just like *Diner's Club*, I was unable to even get the opportunity to write a title song. However, the instrumental theme I composed for the film was recorded by a group and released as a single. This film was definitely *not* a high point of my career, and director Don Taylor and I never seemed to be on the same page. Oh hell, let's face it—he hated me.

Originally, *Ride the Wild Surf* came to being as a surfing-documentary project that was filmed by Art and Jo Napoleon. They shot some very exciting footage of surfing in Hawaii, and showed it to Columbia Pictures. Columbia decided to add a story line to the picture based on the surfing footage. They also chose to feature many of their teenage artists who were currently under contract.

After less than a week of filming in Hawaii, Columbia realized that the Napoleons had absolutely no idea of how to direct a *real* movie, so they were sent packing and replaced by Don Taylor. Taylor, of course, would have preferred his own choice of composer, but found that he was stuck with me. I presume that this is why he gave me such a hard time.

When I thought about trying to record a score of contemporary rock-and-roll music on the Columbia scoring stage, I shuddered. I had been recording most of my records at either Western or United Studios, which were right around the corner from the studio. I pleaded with Jonie Taps to let me record the score of *Ride the Wild Surf* at United Studios, and he agreed. United however, did not have any projection capabilities, so I still had to do some of the dramatic cues on the Columbia scoring stage.

It was at the film dubbing that Don Taylor and I really butted heads. The music mixer, Art Piantadosi, was considered the best in the business.

However, every time that Art raised the music level, Don Taylor made him turn it down. Art asked me to intercede with Don, but my attempts were brushed aside. I was very embarrassed to have no say in the music. To my knowledge, the picture was not a huge monetary success, but similar to several of my other films, has become a cult favorite.

Frank DeVol, one of the most affable music personalities in Hollywood, was a very active composer on the Columbia lot. Only Henry Mancini surpassed DeVol's adept handling of music for light comedy. Frank was also a part-time actor, excelling in extremely humorous and inventive characterizations.

One of the films that Frank had been assigned to score was *Good Neighbor Sam*, starring Jack Lemon, Mike Connors and Romy Schneider, and directed by David Swift. There was quite a great deal of music that had to be prepared during the pre-production of the film. Frank, unfortunately—but *fortunately* for me—was on a cruise around the world and not available to oversee the pre-production. When David Swift asked for a recommendation of someone to handle the job, DeVol recommended—me. Why me?

On a film titled *Under the Yum Yum Tree*, again starring Jack Lemon, James Darren had been given the assignment of singing the Sammy Cahn-James Van Heusen title song. As was the case previously, when Darren sang the songs for the *Gidget Goes to Rome* film, I was asked to produce and do the arrangement. Frank was obviously impressed enough with my work to suggest me to David Swift—and when Jonie Taps concurred, I got the assignment.

It was a cool job that entailed my going on location to San Francisco with the company, where I supervised belly-dance music for two days. I also composed several pieces of source music that were needed.

There was one extended comedy scene in the movie that involved the filming of a Hertz ("Let Hertz put you in the driver's seat") commercial. Even though it defied realism, the director wanted to have a *live* band on camera playing the Hertz jingle. Since the musicians were to actually play (a rarity in those days of filming), sideline musicians seemed a complete waste. I decided to gather some of the top studio men in the business, and they were thrilled to appear in the movie. The following picture (a still from the film) is a rare gathering of the *best of the best*. Yours truly is conducting.

Back row: Left to right: Zeke Zarchy/Manny Klein/Manny Stevens/Tommy Shepard/Lloyd Ulate/ George Roberts and a bass player yet to be identified. Front: Jack Nimitz/Ethner Roten/Ted Nash/Plas (*Pink Panther*) Johnson/Shelley Manne. That's me conducting.

Under the heading of "it's a small world," I'll close this little anecdote with the following postscript.

Late in the 1980s, my wife and I traveled to Scotland and spent two days in a lovely old manor north of Edinburgh called Cromlix House. When we entered the hallway we were warmly greeted by the staff and asked to sign the register. As I prepared to write my name, I noticed that the last name in the book was Frank DeVol. When I inquired as to whether Frank was still there, they said that he had just left, about 20 minutes earlier. Think about it: 8,000 miles from LA, Frank DeVol from Toluca Lake and Stu Phillips from Studio City, miss running into each other by 20 minutes. With that little diversion over with, the time has come to return to my slowly disintegrating record- business career.

By now my little dynasty of recording artists had passed into partial oblivion. The Marcels returned to Pittsburgh; while Shelley, Paul and James were being recorded by other producers—albeit with little success. I continued recording the Hollyridge Strings and some new artists at Capitol, none of which set the world on fire.

In May of 1965, The William Morris Agency, recognizing the success of *Stu Phillips and the Hollyridge Strings,* made Capitol an offer to represent the orchestra and myself for concert appearances. Since the orchestra's name belonged to Capitol Records, any deal had to include Capitol in the negotiations.

The first engagement we were booked on was a live TV broadcast from the Rainbow Room in New York City for NBC, which was sponsored by Seal-test. The orchestra was to accompany several acts, as well as perform on its own. The featured acts included Rosemary Clooney, Jack Carter and Chita Rivera. I decided to take Dori and Toni (now almost three years old) to New York with me. It was time for Toni to visit the city of her birth. The performance was successful, but not particularly noteworthy. However, it did impress the agency enough to make them want to continue booking the orchestra.

Back in LA, I met with the concert division of the Morris agency to devise plans for a Hollyridge Strings tour. Since the Hollyridge Strings was basically a studio orchestra of local musicians, it was decided that I would carry only three or four key players with me, and hire the rest at each individual concert. Our target audiences were the Pops Symphony Orchestras in the United States.

The main stumbling block seemed to be that I was expected to be personally responsible for all the preliminary expenditures. This didn't sit well with me. Capitol was already deducting the cost of recording sessions from my royalties and, now with the concerts giving them all this free promotion, they still wanted me to foot the bills. William Morris also showed no desire to come up with any front money. I decided that I was getting shafted by both sides, and this was not a first-rate deal. When everyone held their ground during the negotiations, I said, "the hell with it," and walked out. Conceivably, could this have been... one more Stu Phillips blunder?

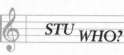

Above is a *gag* publicity photo of The Hollyridge Strings. All the people in the picture are executives, department heads or secretaries at Capitol Records. Why I'm holding on to a chair, I have no idea. Actually, why the chair? Period. This picture was never used.

There is a companion photo similar to the one above, except that I'm pretending to lead a group of four to ten year-olds. Unfortunately, it was a color photo and while hanging in my office has drastically faded.

♫ ♫ ♫

The Monkees

THE BIGGEST SURPRISE TOWARDS THE END of 1965 was receiving a phone call from Bert Schneider (the man who had fired me from Colpix Records). He spoke to me as though nothing negative had ever taken place between us, and asked me if I would be interested in composing the background music for a new TV show that he and Bob Rafelson were producing, called *The Monkees*. I couldn't believe what I was hearing. I thought that certainly Bert must have an aversion to me. Or, unquestionably, have some doubts about working with me. I categorically felt a slight distaste towards him. Stupidly I replied, "Are you sure you dialed the right number?"

Bert didn't laugh, and I knew then that he was dead serious. I said, "Just kidding Bert, I'd love to do it." I had now learned that in show business, business is business and not to take adverse situations *too personal*. I also rationalized, that after Bert had found out about Bob York's larceny, he felt that I had basically been given a raw deal.

I ended up composing music for the entire *Monkees* series, with the exception of three episodes and the pilot. Once again I was working with Don Kirshner, but *mercifully* did not have to deal with him directly. Mainly, I worked with Rafelson, Ward Sylvester and Lester Sill. Igo Kantor, who was later to become a great influence on my career, was the music editor and supervisor on the series.

The show's background music, which is what I was hired to compose, consisted of comedic cues written for small ensembles of between six and 10 musicians. Each episode would feature some unusual solo instrument—instruments like a tuba; or a harp; a solo cello; a harpsichord; and, in one episode, even a small chorus. Scoring the show required a rather twisted

and warped sense of humor. I quickly learned and mastered twisted and warped.

The average length of each music cue was in the neighborhood of 10 to 15 seconds. On some episodes there might be as many as 25 music cues, totaling a whopping six or seven minutes.

During the two seasons that I was with the show, I had only occasional personal contact with any of the Monkees. Davy Jones was the only one that I ever became somewhat friendly with and on several occasions worked directly with him. He was a pro, and knew how to handle himself with his associates. Mickey Dolenz was friendly, but Michael Nesmith and Peter Tork were in their own little worlds.

Davy Jones in full regalia with my four-year-old daughter Toni.

The show would probably have run for a good deal more than the two seasons it ran, were it not for the friction between the group and the producers. When Nesmith and Tork decided that they wanted to direct and write more shows—as well as compose more of the songs—Donnie, Bert and Bob tossed in the towel and called it quits.

About ten years ago, Rhino Records released a package of the entire *Monkees* TV series, with a booklet describing each episode. The original price was somewhere in the neighborhood of $350. When I picked up my copy at Rhino (which incidentally I had to pay $150 for), I noticed that my name was not to be found on the packaging. In the accompanying booklet—47 pages of every conceivable bit of noteworthy and a great deal of trivial information—my name appears... *nowhere*. The only credits for the background music on the packaging are given to the composers of the three episodes that I *did not* write. In fact, the only place that my name still exists is on the videotape, on the end-credits of each individual episode. What is it with Rhino? I reiterate that they have omitted my name from just about everything that I produced and arranged that they have re-released. I am taking it very personally. What did I ever do to you people?

For the rest of 1965, along with scoring *The Donna Reed Show*, I continued recording the Hollyridge Strings for Capitol, and did a few more independent-producing jobs. I was also fortunate to get assigned several more *Gidget* TV episodes, as well as a few other Screen Gems shows, and three pilots; *Rock-a-bye the Infantry*, starring William Bendix; *The Barbara Rush Show*; and the first of two versions of the TV adaptation of *From Here to Eternity*, starring William Devane. Regrettably, none of the above shows made it on the air, except a later version of *Eternity*.

On the whole, at this point in my career, I can truthfully say, in retrospect, that despite a few minor setbacks, it wasn't too shabby. Not great, mind you, but I could find no reason to complain. I had been blessed with a great deal of luck in a callous profession.

♪   ♪   ♪

10 The Fantastic '60's... Part 5

Epic Records and the Switch to Composing

AS 1966 CAME IN, IT did so with a bang. Dori and I made Walter Winchell's column. He announced that record producer Stu Phillips and his wife were expecting a new addition. In November, Dori gave birth to our second daughter, Julie Phillips.

Her birth was accompanied by many wonderful new career opportunities. In spite of *The Donna Reed Show* ending its long run, 1966 managed to be a fairly successful year for me. The *Monkees* show went on the air for its first season, and that was indeed good news. I also continued with The Hollyridge Strings, but unfortunately did not do any other A&R work for Capitol.

One day early in 1966, I received a call from Jim Fogelsong, my old basketball buddy from my Eastman School of Music days. Jim was now an A&R executive at Columbia Records. He and Bob Morgan (one of the vice-presidents) offered me a position at Epic Records as head of the West Coast A&R department. (Epic was and still is a division of Columbia Records.) Len Levy, the president of Epic Records was situated in New York, and he agreed with their choice. It seemed to be a step forward in my career and I eagerly accepted the position.

Two sales/promotion people and myself set up offices on Vine Street opposite Capitol Records. That particular location made it very convenient for me to hop across the street to Capitol and the Hollyridge Strings. From my office window, I could see the distinctive round tower of the Capitol Records building—my old stamping grounds.

Once again I reacquainted myself with all the publishers and agents, and began screening new material and searching out new artists. During the next two years at Epic, no hits were forthcoming. Even though I felt that a fair share of the recordings had some hit potential, they did not catch the fancy of the public like so many of my earlier endeavors had.

Among some of the artists I produced albums and singles for at Epic were Enzo Stuarti; The Doodletown Pipers; Nancy Ames; Don and The Goodtimes; Ian & Murray; Bob Crane as well as *The Monkees Songbook* with the Golden Gate Strings. (I was still a recording artist under contract to Capitol Records, hence The Golden Gate Strings, Epic's in-house orchestra.) I even signed Little Richard and Johnny "Guitar" Watson for a one-shot deal. Nothing big came from that effort, but I sure got a kick out of working with Little Richard. He's one of the few sincere screwballs in the record business, and I mean that as a compliment.

Not only did it appear as though my magic producing touch was on hiatus, but I was also, not on a lucky streak. To wit, the publisher at Irving/Almo Music, Chuck Kaye (one of Lester Sill's sons) brought me a demo of a new duo. He explained that every record company in town was eager to sign them, so I had better make a quick decision. When I heard the demo of their song "Sit Down, I Think I Love You," I agreed that they were something special.

Chuck advised me that the group wanted a $5,000 advance. That amount was way beyond my $25,000 signing budget and would require me to get an okay from the legal department in New York.

That evening, I went to the Troubadour, a rock-and-roll club on Santa Monica Blvd., where many new artists were showcased (and still are). The two musicians, Steve Stills and Richie Furay, performed their act for just about every important A&R man in Hollywood. I definitely wanted to sign them, and I'm fairly certain so did everyone else.

The next morning, I tried desperately to reach the lawyers in New York but couldn't seem to convince them to get off their butts. I left emergency messages, but still got no reply. A few days later I was informed that the duo had been signed to Atco Records. Eventually, they joined with Neil Young and evolved into The Buffalo Springfield. Lawyers! God love 'em. He better, because I don't think anyone else does.

♫   ♫   ♫

Bob Crane

BOB CRANE, RADIO DJ, but better known as Colonel Hogan of the TV show *Hogan's Heroes*, was a joy to work with. We had become friendly

Me and Bob (Colonel Hogan) Crane discussing his latest escape plan. 1968

when he joined the cast of *The Donna Reed Show* for two seasons He left his morning disc jockey show on CBS radio when he was offered the role on *Hogan's Heroes*. Bob also had aspirations of being a stand-up comic, and any time spent with him always included a lot of jokes and one-liners. He loved to entertain and was always "on."

Bob's ability as a drummer was professional enough to give us the idea of producing an album of TV themes, with him playing the drums. Bob suggested that he also add a few comedy routines to the overall conception. For three recording sessions, the musicians and I had a ball being entertained by Crane. He was, as far as I was concerned, a great guy. With his tragic, unexplained death in a motel room, maybe I didn't know Bob Crane as well as I thought I did. Neither did his two families.

At an upcoming Columbia/Epic records convention in Las Vegas, Bob Morgan asked me if I might consider conducting the orchestra for the stage show that was to take place. The show was to feature many of the Columbia and Epic recording artists. Bob thought that it might be a kick to have the West Coast A&R man conducting the orchestra. He hoped it might hark back to the old Mitch Miller days. I said sure, why not. What I hadn't counted on was Bobby Vinton. (He is probably best remembered for his hit recordings of "Blue Velvet" and "Roses are Red.")

Bobby was one of the most demanding singers I ever worked with. For Bobby on that particular day, nobody did anything right. The arrangements had mistakes. (What did he want from me? They were his arrangements.)

He felt that I got all the tempos wrong. The band was out of tune. Mention anything, and he found fault with it. Maybe he was just having a bad day. For a brief moment, I regretted that I had agreed to conduct the show.

Itching To Go—Stu Phillips, West Coast A&R head for Epic Records, was itching to go in the conductor's spot at Bobby Vinton's rehearsal for his performance at the Sands during the Epic Convention. Epic's Bob Morgan appears to be oblivious to Phillips' consternation. **Cashbox— Sept. 3, 1966**

During 1966, I finally fulfilled my film deal with Columbia Pictures and scored my third film. The movie was called *Dead Heat on a Merry-Go-Round*, and it starred an up-and-coming actor named James Coburn. It was also the first speaking role for Harrison Ford, who played a bellhop with two lines of dialogue. I wonder whatever happened to him?

I was never really secure in the feeling that the producers of this film were happy with the studio's choice of me as the composer. I do believe that they had their sights set on someone with a bit more prestige. But I had a contract and the studio wanted to make me work for my money. All the same, I did a professional job, though not particularly noteworthy. Once again, a handful of critics gave the music favorable mention.

(Many years later, the reverse situation happened to me. I was up for, and practically hired, to compose the music for a Kirk Douglas western at Paramount Pictures, but lost the assignment to Maurice Jarre. Seems that Maurice had a contract with Paramount that needed fulfilling, just as I had had years before with Columbia. I was quite unhappy at losing this picture, for I had hoped that it might be my ticket away from B-movies to first-class films and an "in" with another studio.)

In the West Magazine section of the August 13th, 1967 Sunday issue of the *LA Times*, Burt Prelutsky, who wrote a West-View column very week, did a profile of me. In the article he featured my association with the Hollyridge Strings and how I managed to make pretty music out of the

Beatles songs. He also wrote about my experience with an eight-year old, who questioned me as to whether I was the guy who made all of those pretty Beatles albums. When I proudly admitted that I was, the young man wanted to know... *Why in hell I had to go and ruin all that great music?*

It was while working at Columbia and Screen Gems (on *The Monkees*), that I became friendly with the aforementioned Igo Kantor, who at the time was part of Isidore Freidman's company, Edit-Rite, who supplied the music editing services for Screen Gems TV. Igo was about to have a very important influence on my career.

Early in 1967, Igo, who had formed his own post-production company with Jim Nelson called Synchro-Film, called me and said he might have a deal that would interest me. I met with him at his office on Highland Ave. and he told me that he was working closely with a producer named Joe Solomon, who had just made a motorcycle picture called *Hells Angels on Wheels*.

The deal, as Igo explained it, was that Joe Solomon was considering hiring a fellow named Mike Curb—who knew very little about composing, but had some ghostwriters doing the writing for him. (Yes, that's Mike Curb, the ex-Lt. Governor of California.) Joe was getting the entire score for $5,000, which was dirt-cheap even in those days. Igo said that if I would produce the score for the same price as Mike Curb, he could persuade Joe to engage me instead of Curb.

I said, "That's one hell of a lousy deal. I thought slavery went out with the Civil War." Igo convinced me that it would be worth my while to make this deal, since he knew that Joe had at least three or four other pictures lined up and ready to go. I agreed to the deal, as I was still earning a living at Epic, and also still being paid off by Colpix. Money, at least at that time, was not my most important consideration.

Joe Solomon was another of your typical Hollywood producer types. Short in both stature and temper, he was quite similar to Jonie Taps. Personally, I liked Joe because he would tell it like it is. There was no guessing about what was on his mind, and he let you know his desires in no uncertain terms. After all the bullshit artists I had been exposed to so far in the business, it was almost refreshing to deal with someone who screamed and yelled and let you know what he thought and what the hell he wanted—wrong or right.

The director of the movie, *Hells Angels on Wheels*, was Richard Rush, a son of a bitch if there ever was one, and very nearly a clone of Don Taylor. Rush was very unhappy with Joe's choice of composer. Rush wanted a composer of his choosing and didn't really care that Joe was getting the entire score for $5,000. Like most motion-picture directors, he wanted Joe to spend a great deal more than five grand on the score. As a result of their disagreement, Rush hated everything I wrote, but fortunately for me, Joe liked the score. That's really all that was important to me at that time.

In spite of Rush's attempts to throw in other music, the score appeared in the movie exactly as I wrote and recorded it. The sessions, musicians and studio ended up costing $4,950. I personally cleared a bountiful $50. We managed to get a soundtrack released on Smash Records and a recording by The Poor of a short song that appeared in the movie. The lyric to the song was writ-ten by Chuck Sedacca, who I will discuss later on.

The film co-starred a still somewhat unknown ac-tor named Jack Nicholson. I do believe you might have heard of him. As the title suggests, the film is about

Hells Angels on Wheels screen credit. I seem to be riding a "cycle-guitar."

Sonny Barger's Hells Angels, out of Oakland, California. It was quite raun-chy, but for the genre, a passable film. I've scored worse, and I've scored better. It, like several of my other movies, has turned into a cult item.

Close to the preview date I discovered that my contract with Fanfare Films (Joe's company) and myself had not been executed. I called my brother Lee to ask what the hang-up was; he explained that he and Joe's lawyer were not seeing eye-to-eye on some legal language. Lee said he didn't be-lieve that we should give in on the disputed points. Actually, my brother and Joe's attorney were playing a lawyer's game called telephone-tag. That's a game that lawyers like to play where each one waits for the other to call him, not wanting to be the one who is available. It's the epitome of the sport of "attorney power-moves." Fortunately, I was not on an hourly rate with my brother, but I'll bet you anything that Joe's lawyer was.

Since the contract had not been executed, I had not as yet been paid my $5,000. Also, part of my deal was to receive all the publishing rights since I was doing the score for such little money. On the day of the film's preview on Hollywood Blvd., Lee and I met in Joe's office with him and his attorney to try and straighten everything out. All did not go smoothly, and tempers began to flare up. We threatened not to grant any sync rights for the performance of the music. This meant that Joe could not hold the Hollywood Blvd. preview of the film he had planned for that evening. It was a form of blackmail on my part and, after Joe threw a few things around the room, a settlement was reached. The preview went ahead as scheduled. I was well tutored by Bert Schneider in the field of hard-nosed business tactics.

I figured that with this little fracas, my association with Joe Solomon was probably over. To the contrary, I ended up doing seven more films for Joe, and the two of us became very good personal friends. It seemed that he admired people who stood up for their point of view. Similar to the Bert Schneider and Tony Owen incidents, *business is business*, and *nothing personal*.

Considering how little the picture cost to make, it was a big moneymaker. I was pleased when many reviews mentioned the good score. I'm sure this completely pissed off Richard Rush. In fact, at a party at his house celebrating either the opening of the picture or Christmas (I don't remember which), Rush hardly acknowledged my presence.

Igo Kantor had been accurate about this being a smart move for me. During the next couple of years I scored: *Angels From Hell*; *The Curious Female*; *The Gay Deceivers*; *The Name of the Game is Kill*; *Simon, King of the Witches*; *The Losers* and *Run, Angel, Run* for Joe Solomon. Not a stellar list of films, but it was a living.

There is a story about *Run, Angel, Run* that always seems to be of interest to people when I recount it. During a discussion of the score to the film, Joe said he would love to have a main-title song that he might be able to utilize in merchandising the film. I agreed that this was a good idea, and went back to my office and placed a call to the Nashville office of Epic Records. The A&R man at Epic was Billy Sherrill, and was probably, at that time, the hottest producer of country music in America and a successful songwriter.

Tammy Wynette and Billy Sherrill

BILLY AND I HAD CROSSED PATHS at an Epic Records gathering in New York, where we shared a hotel suite. One night over dinner Billy mentioned how jealous he was of the opportunities I had to compose music for the movies. He declared that he'd give anything for an opportunity to write a song for a film. (Conversely, I would have given anything to have produced Billy's hits. Funny at times, how discontented we all can sometimes be.)

I remembered Billy's words, and those statements are what triggered my call to him. Billy was the producer and writer for Tammy Wynette, who was known as "The First Lady of Country Music." Billy gave me a big friendly hello, and I explained that I might have an assignment for him to collaborate with me in writing a song for a Hollywood movie. "Shit, yeah, I'll do it," he exclaimed, without even knowing what the movie was all about. I cautioned him that there might be a major stumbling block. We wanted Tammy Wynette to sing the song on the soundtrack. Without hesitation, Billy agreed. I was elated and, when I explained to Joe who Tammy Wynette was, he was overjoyed with what I had accomplished. For the first time, Joe was going to have a record star singing in one of his movies.

A few weeks later, I arrived in Nashville. It was about noon when I walked into Billy's office. I sat down and explained the plot of the picture to him. Within 30 minutes, he had written the lyric to the first verse and the chorus. With myself at the piano and Billy on his guitar, we had a melody in a matter of minutes. At two o'clock we went to lunch. After returning to the office, by about four o'clock, we had finished the song. I caught a late plane back to LA feeling very good about what we had written, and anxious to fill Joe in.

As I composed the score to the film, I made sure that I integrated the theme of the song into the dramatic score. I knew that would please Billy, and at that time I wanted to please him and keep him happy. I recorded the score and Joe scheduled the mix-down of the film as quickly as he could. The whole deal was beginning to seem a little too perfect: Though I had as yet not received a tape of Tammy Wynette's recording of the song from Billy.

Joe was getting antsy, and I couldn't blame him. I called Billy and explained the urgency of the situation and Joe's consternation. He promised that he wouldn't disappoint us. The time to the dubbing grew shorter, and there was still no tape from Billy. Again I called and explained that we were to start dubbing the film in two days. Billy assured me that he was going into the studio that evening, and that I would have the tape on time. He now, of all times, wanted to know what we were going to pay Tammy for singing the song. Joe said he couldn't afford more than $500. Billy said that he'd make that figure work.

Then Billy hit with me with a brick. He told me that he wanted to have 100% of the publishing on the song. I explained that Joe and I were splitting the publishing 50/50, but that I'd be happy to give him my 50%. Billy said that he wanted it all. The perfect deal was now beginning to acquire a few snags. By the way, Billy eventually did get 100% of the publishing.

The tape from Nashville arrived barely in time. Tammy's recording of the song was great. Joe loved it so much that he could hardly contain his enthusiasm. He immediately sent out flyers to his distributors telling them that they could advertise Tammy Wynette in conjunction with the movie. Joe gave me some opening dates of the film around the country to relay to Billy to help him coordinate the release of the record.

That's when brick number two hit me. Billy said that there would be no single release of the record. Tammy's next record was to be a song she and Billy had written, and our *Run, Angel, Run* song was too strong to put on the B-side, as he wanted to avoid any split airplay. When I informed Joe of this new development, he hit the ceiling. So did anything within his reach.

Solomon, however, did eventually get a small amount of revenge. In many southern cities, the picture was advertised as *starring* Tammy Wynette. The film's cast was basically unknown, and the theater owners felt that they could entice more customers into the theater with Tammy's name out front. Billy got hell from Tammy's managers when they were told about the situation. Billy also took a lot of flak about the $500 recording fee—$5,000, or better yet, *$50,000* would have been

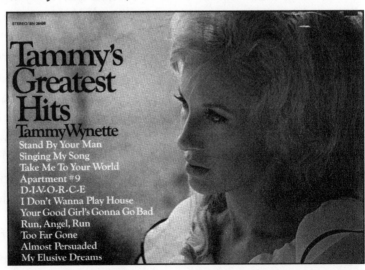

Tammy Wynette's album. The eighth title down is "Run, Angel, Run."

more likely what her managers would have preferred.

About a year later, Billy called me to say how sorry he was about the whole *Run, Angel, Run* incident. He knew it must have been tough on me dealing with Joe Solomon and, as a gesture of good will to me he would put the song "Run, Angel, Run" into *Tammy's Greatest Hits* album. Talk about a nice gesture—to this day the album has sold over several million copies, and Billy has never missed a payment to me in 34 years. I earned a nice piece of change from that song. Thank you, Billy.

The soundtrack album came out on Epic Records, with the Tammy Wynette vocal as the first track. Thank God she was on the same label as the soundtrack album, or Joe might have killed somebody—most likely me.

♫   ♫   ♫

Goodbye records… Hello movies

I WOULD LIKE TO TAKE A moment and give credit to a band who for quite a few years was my "jack-of-all-trades" group. Whenever I needed something performed or written they were ready to oblige. The group was The Peanut Butter Conspiracy, and consisted primarily of Allan Brackett, John Merrill and Barbara Robison. As a group or as soloists they appeared in at least seven of the films I worked on. They never let me down and, though I knew that they indulged in a little drug usage now and then, they were always cool and *with it* on my dates, and respected my *rules* of recording. They worked fast and never caused me any problems. I still keep in touch with John Merrill.

Things at Epic were not half as good as my film career at this particular juncture. With no big hits, I was beginning to think that I might have completely lost that magic producing touch. To make matters even worse, Len Levy, the president of Epic, had been replaced by the manager of Sly and the Family Stone; one Dave Kapralik. The record business, like the Vietnam War, was slowly plummeting into a drug-addled, psychedelic world and this was, for sure, not my cup of tea.

Throughout my career in nightclubs, records, TV and films, I had managed to stay clear of the drug scene, and had no intention of ever joining it. But these were the Vietnam and Woodstock years, and drugs it appeared were here to stay. LSD and booze was not a part of my approach to the process of making records. I guess you could say I was—and still am—a bit of a square. But at least I'm a living, breathing square.

Most of the new groups wouldn't even dream of entering a studio to record before eight or nine in the evening. All-night recording sessions seemed to be the new trend. Instead of an album being recorded in a week or sometimes two, groups now retired to a retreat where they would spend months or even a year making an album. The cost of recording was getting out of control. (It's even worse now.)

At a company meeting in New York, Billy Sherrill and I were introduced to Kapralik's new staff. One stoned person after another was introduced to us. Billy—who liked his beers but stayed relatively clean drug-wise, as far as I knew—agreed with me that perhaps Epic was not the company for us anymore.

Soon after I returned to LA, I resigned from the company. They were not particularly *unhappy* to see me leave, as I had produced no big hits for them, and I definitely didn't fit into their new scene. Billy, I was told, tried to quit—but since he was the hottest producer in Nashville, with one hit after the other, they were not about to let him go. Instead, they gave him *carte blanche* and freedom from any interference by the New York office. He recently retired as one of the most successful country-music producers in Nashville's history.

The fantastic '60s, it seemed, were not drawing to a fantastic close. My record career was on the wane. *The Monkees* TV show had ended. There were no more films due at Columbia—and the three films that I had written obviously had not impressed the brass enough for them to assign me any more. All the films that I now scored were low-budget B-movies. I still managed to do some TV composing and, with a few commercials thrown in, things were actually not all that bad. Though in my mind I felt that my career was on a downhill slide.

What concerned me the most, was that the recognition factor I had become accustomed to in the record industry was gone. I had been reasonably well known and respected in that industry, but unfortunately, just another *hack* in the film-composing business. All those B-movies I did for Joe Solomon were not exactly doing anything positive for my reputation. Plus, I really didn't get paid a lot of money up front for my services. The publishing royalties and BMI composing monies that were to come in the future would take at least ten years to materialize. Our cash flow was taking a bit of a hit.

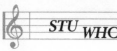

One evening while having dinner with my mother and Sammy Fain, I mentioned that it would sure be great to be a member of the Motion Picture Academy. My mother pointed out to Sammy that, since he was a member, maybe he could do something about getting her son in. Sammy, always reluctant to put himself on the line, stammered a bit, but finally said he would check into it. Sammy had my mother to deal with, and as I mentioned earlier, she could *nudge* with the best.

To get into the Academy at that time, you needed to be sponsored by two members and then approved by the Board of Directors. Sammy was one sponsor and, needing another, he went to his racetrack buddy Lionel Newman and asked him to be the other sponsor. Suddenly, after 16 years, Lionel Newman was back in my life. I still don't know how, with all my crummy film credits, I got accepted—but I did. I've been a member since 1968.

The happy and positive event of that year was moving into our new house on Fryman Rd. The house on Wrightview (the city had changed the name of the street from Wrightwood to Wrightview after we moved in) was beginning to get a little crowded. For a couple of years on occasional Sundays, Dori and I would drive through the Fryman Rd. area admiring the homes.

One in particular always seemed to get our attention. It was a corner house with an adjoining orchard that contained apple, orange, plum and peach trees. One Sunday, a FOR SALE sign appeared out front. We went directly to Art's Deli on Ventura Blvd. (a studio hangout in those days), and immediately called the real-estate agent. It took months and months of negotiating, but eventually we were the proud owners of a… *wreck*.

For me, the major attraction of the property was the guesthouse out in the orchard. Since I was no longer attached to a record company, I now had no office in town, and I needed someplace convenient to meet with publishers and artists. I fully intended to try and do some independent record production, if any came my way. As a bonus, the guesthouse had two rooms and I would be able to use one room for work and the other for meetings.

Unfortunately, the house itself needed quite a bit of fixing-up, and 33 years later we are still fixing it. The roof leaked, Dori hated the carpets; the kitchen was an abomination, and so on and so forth. The fact that the house had a dining room and a maid's room gave Dori some small solace. The rest of the house she would have liked to burn down. In fact she has mentioned many times over the last 30 years that a *fire* might not be all that bad. All visitors meanwhile, appear to admire our house, so I presume it must be our great taste in furnishing the monster that compensates.

We immediately cut down some of the trees in the orchard, built a swimming pool, and began the lifelong job of putting the house in living condition. (The orchard was replaced about 15 years ago with a tennis court. The pool was dug up, for the tennis court, and rebuilt in another area several years later.) Dori got her new kitchen about 14 years ago and, since we now completely own this place, I think we are here to stay. We have lived in this house for 33 years and I do believe that Dori finally likes the house. (Uh-oh… she just mentioned the "R" word… *remodel*.)

Every year during the '60s and into the '70s, there was a golf tournament (and later on a golf-and-tennis tournament) sponsored by the music-industry and managed ably by Dave Pell and Morris Diamond. I joined the group in 1963 when I first moved to LA. Originally, it took place at Desi Arnaz's Indian Wells Hotel. Then it moved to The Canyon in Palm Springs. Later on, it relocated to San Vincente near San Diego. It was known as The Music Industry Golf Tournament, and encompassed a three, or four-day weekend. Almost everybody who attended was either in the record industry or the music-publishing business. Occasionally, some peripheral occupations were invited, such as music-industry lawyers and agents. My brother Lee, a music-business lawyer, was a regular at these events.

Initially, it was supposed to be "family free." But many of the men brought along their secretaries, lady-friends or significant others, and when I decided to participate, I saw no reason to leave Dori back in LA. My wife was *my* lady-friend. It wasn't long before a large group of men started bringing their families. I guess Dori and I were responsible for screwing up a lot of extra-marital affairs.

I remember one year in the late 1960s, when a publisher I knew casually said his new wife wanted to send me her regards. I said, "That's nice. What's her name?" He answered, "Her name is Cheryl, and she said she knew you in Hollywood back in the '50s." I was so shocked when he mentioned her name that I didn't quite know how to react, or what to say to him. I had no idea how much she had told him about our relationship some 17 years prior, or her previous *profession*, so I replied as indifferently as possible, "Oh yes, I do remember her. Please say hello for me," and left it at that.

♫   ♫   ♫

A Period of Transition

I FIND THE YEARS BETWEEN 1968 and 1972 difficult to put into any chronological order. All the films, commercials and independent recording sessions seem to have blended into one big mass of confusion. So in no particular order, I'll write about a few of them that have might have some relative interest.

I did a film called *2000 Years Later* for which I had to write five songs. (The film starred Terry-Thomas, Pat Harrington, Casey Kasem, Murray Roman and Edward Everett Horton.) It failed terribly at the box office and disappeared into oblivion. On that film, I worked with a wonderful writer whose name was Chuck Sedacca. (He had worked with me previously on *Hells Angels on Wheels*.) Tragically, very soon after working with him on this film, he and his entire family of four were wiped out in a crash on the 405 Freeway. It was a very catastrophic event.

Through Igo Kantor, I was hired to compose the score for a semi-documentary film about surfing. It was called *Follow Me*, and was a production of The Robert E. Petersen magazine company. The film, which was originally titled *Surfers Three*, filmed three surfers traveling around the world surfing in many exotic locations. Places like North Africa, Portugal, Spain, India, Ceylon and eventually Hawaii. For me it was an exciting musical challenge, and I believe that some of my best writing is contained in that score.

Follow Me presented me the opportunity to work with David Gates (of the hit group Bread), a writer that I greatly admired. The main-title song "Through Spray Colored Glasses" was sung in the film by Dino, Desi and Billy (Dino Martin, Dean Martin's son, Desi Arnaz, Jr., Billy Hinsche). The movie also provided me with my first opportunity to record outside the United States. We chose London and proceeded to hire a studio and book the musicians.

When the time came for me to leave for London, I had not completely finished composing the score, and still needed several days to complete the writing. The production company arranged for me to stay at The Dorchester Hotel. The company rented a piano and the hotel placed it in my room close to a window, which looked out on a side street. They insisted that I occupy this particular room on the first floor (second floor in the USA). This location, they deemed, was where I was least likely to disturb other guests in the hotel with my playing.

I'm sure you must be aware of the fact that most buses in London were of the double-decker variety. That made them approximately one story high, which happened to match very closely the level of my hotel window. The bus stop was right below my window, and when I sat at the piano working, people would wave hello, and I would wave back. If I had opened the window and extended my hand, and they extended theirs, we probably were close enough to shake hands. It was amusing the first few times. Then the whole situation became slightly annoying.

When we returned to the States we did some sweetening, and I dubbed down the multi-track. The soundtrack album to this film remains my own personal favorite. The picture, unfortunately, was a bomb at the box office. For years I have been trying to get a video of the film from Robert E. Petersen, but to no avail.

A movie called *The Appointment* has an interesting little side story. An MGM picture, it starred Omar Sharif and Anouk Aimée. It was shot completely on location in Rome and Milan, Italy and directed by Sidney Lumet. The original score was composed by Michel Legrand and recorded by the Paris Opera Orchestra and Chorus. The studio, unhappy with the length of the picture, ordered some editing done and the music re-scored. MGM threw out the Legrand score and hired John Barry and Don Walker to compose a new score to replace the original. *Still* not satisfied with either the picture or the score, they wanted yet another score and more editing.

The music publisher at MGM, who knew me from my days in the record business, recommended me for the third score. I met with Bob Justman, the president of MGM's Television Division, (who greeted me wearing sock-less loafers, blue jeans and a tee shirt), and he personally hired me on the spot. I had been assigned to replace the music of both Legrand and Barry: Now there's a challenge calling for the utmost *chutzpah*.

The film editor in charge of overseeing the new post-production was a wonderful woman named Margaret Booth. She was one of the deans of film editors, her career dating back to the very early studio days. When I viewed the film with Margaret, she discussed with me the possibility of making the score a bit more contemporary than the previous two had been. *The Appointment* was shot in such a manner that a contemporary score would have sounded ludicrous. I did my best at compromising old and new in the music that I wrote, but it wasn't easy.

I recorded the score (which included two songs, with lyrics by Bob Stone), dubbed it, and waited for the film to be released. I thought it just might be my first "class-A" film.

Unfortunately, the film has never been officially released in theaters, being mired in a legal quagmire between the producers and MGM for 30 years. It did appear on television a few times. At least two or three times, that I'm aware of, it was aired with my score.

This film and the television show *Chicago Story* (in the early '80s) gave me the opportunity to conduct on the same stage as Andre Previn. I do believe that many changes had probably been made to the stage since the 1940s and 1950s but, nevertheless, I was finally at MGM studios, where Andre Previn had once been. It took me a hell of a long time to get there, more than 20 years!

♪   ♪   ♪

Max Baer, Jr.

MACON COUNTY LINE WAS WRITTEN and produced by Max Baer, Jr. (Jethro of *Beverly Hillbillies* fame). Max and his partner Roger Camras tried to hustle me on the Brentwood Country Club golf course where they wanted

to play me double-or-nothing for my composing fee. Since I was well aware that Roger was an ex-golf pro and Max was a scratch golfer, I adroitly turned them down. After our round of golf, we spent some time at the bar. Max said that I was chicken not to have accepted his and Roger's challenge. Then they confessed to having raised the bulk of the financing on *Macon County Line* from hustling some of the club members on the golf course. Max said that they raised over $50,000 in a little over a year from gambling on the golf course. They made their investment back and quite a bit more when *Macon County Line* became a big money maker.

Max Baer Jr. (Jethro on the *Beverly Hillbillies*), with an unidentified bloodhound.

Max used to like to tell stories of when he and the cast of *The Beverly Hillbillies* went on tour promoting the TV show. Max is well over six feet tall and, as you're probably aware, very muscular. The character he played on the show was of an extremely strong, ignorant hillbilly, who supposedly could lick anyone in a fight. Considering the fact that Max's father, Max Baer Sr., was once heavyweight champion of the world, the combination of fact and fiction could be volatile.

Max said that on almost every trip, anytime he and Buddy Ebsen would go into a bar, a few overly intoxicated patrons would decide to challenge Max to see just how tough he really was. Max would exclaim, "Hey guys... it's only a TV show." That sometimes was not enough to appease the antagonists, and blows would be struck. Since Max had a very explosive temper, and I'm sure that the endings of these little escapades were slightly different than the ones he told us. I always wondered why he bothered to go into those bars in the first place. I think I might have just answered my own question.

In 1971, the last film for Joe Solomon that I was involved in was *Evel Kneivel*, starring George Hamilton. Joe asked me to write a song for the movie long before the picture was finished shooting. I worked with my favorite co-writer Bob Stone on this project and we came up with a song that Joe loved.

Unfortunately, things did not go as smoothly as we would have liked. On this film, Joe was spending big bucks and had hired John Milius to write the screenplay and Marvin Chomsky, a well-known TV director, to direct the film. Chomsky had no intention of using any of Joe's usual people on the film, including the composer. The catch was that he had never told Joe of his intentions.

At a screening of the first cut after the picture had completed filming, Joe asked me to bring the demo of the Evel Kneivel song we had recorded, so that the director could listen to it. After the screening, Joe said to the director that he would like him to hear this great song that Stu Phillips and Bob Stone had written. Chomsky then informed Joe, in front of everyone present, that he wasn't the least bit interested in hearing the song. This was very embarrassing to Joe and myself, but with all the money Solomon had tied up in the film he didn't want to risk a blow-up with the director—at least not until the Chomsky had turned over his final cut. So Joe backed down from any confrontation.

The picture was eventually scored by Pat Williams; and he also wrote a song for it. Joe wasn't particularly excited about Pat's song, but neverthe-

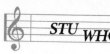

less released the film just as it was delivered to him by the director. A week or so later I went to see Joe about some other matter and, when I walked into his office, casually sitting on the couch, was George Hamilton, tan and all.

♫ ♫ ♫

George Hamilton and London

JOE INTRODUCED US, AND THEN said to George that he should hear the wonderful song that Stu had written for the picture. George was eager to hear it—and I, always prepared for any occurrence, just happened to have a copy of the tape in my attaché case. I played it for George and he flipped out. "I love it! Why isn't this song in the movie?" he inquired. Joe proceeded to tell him the whole story. George decided that he wanted to sing the song in the film, and asked Solomon to consider re-editing and re-dubbing the necessary reels. Joe said it was out of the question, since the film was over budget and he was out of money. He said that the picture was going to be released, as is.

George wasn't especially happy with Joe's decision. He then turned to me and said that he would like to record the song even if it wasn't going to be in the movie. When Joe heard us planning the recording session he decided that he didn't want to be left out and wanted in on the project. He eagerly offered to finance the recording. For this, he seemed to have money.

George asked me to meet him at his house in Beverly Hills and told me to bring along some additional material. (Actually, the house belonged to a wealthy friend of his, Bernie Kornfeld, who was nice enough to let George have the use of a few rooms.) The place could better be described as a *mansion.*

Naturally, I bought along several songs that Bob Stone and I had recently written. George must have been in a good mood that day, for he liked everything I played him. He gave me a tape with six songs he had previously recorded, and said that we would cut an album using these existing recordings and five or six more that we would record together.

Next we had to decide on a place and time to record. When I mentioned that I was going to be in London scoring a film in the very near future, he jumped up and said, "That's perfect. I'm going to be in Switzerland at about the same time getting my injections of sheep urine. I'll meet you in London when I'm done, and we can record there." He then asked me to set the whole thing up, which I happily did, since he was about to record three Stu Phillips/Bob Stone songs in the album.

On this trip to London Dori decided to keep me company. The film I was recording there was *A Time for Every Purpose*. (Eventually renamed, *Pick-up on 101*). It had a wonderful cast that featured Martin Sheen, Lesley Warren[1] and Jack Albertson. When I arrived in London, I hired an arranger and copyist to work on George's music and booked the studio and musicians for his recording session. Then I went about recording my film score.

The dapper, dashing and glib... George Hamilton.

George arrived precisely on the day he said he would, with his latest companion, Alana. This was a good omen, since people who knew George well had advised me in advance, that he was not always completely reliable. He introduced Alana to Dori in the hope that together they might keep each other company, and do bit of shopping while George and I worked. However, Alana's shopping haunts (at Dior, Chanel, and Gucci), were a little beyond our financial means. They were probably also beyond George's, but minor details like that never seemed to faze him. Dori quite suddenly acquired a few convenient headaches over the next several days.

One evening as Dori and I were getting ready for bed, we received a call from George asking us what we were up to. George said that he had a yen for an ice-cream soda or a sundae, and since Alana had gone to Paris for an overnight shopping spree he wondered if we would like to join him. It was a little after 11 P.M. Now I ask you, seriously, do you turn down a major movie star when he asks for your company—especially when he is about to record three of your songs? Of course not. So we agreed to meet him in

---

[1] Lesley Warren soon became known as Lesley Ann Warren.

front of The Grovsenor House—where his good buddy Laurence Harvey had graciously allowed him the use of his apartment.

Dori remembered that a few days earlier, she and I had found this quaint little ice-cream parlor somewhere behind our hotel in the *mews*—exactly where, we couldn't quite remember. George insisted we go look for it. The idea that it might be closed at this time of night did not seem to worry George one iota. So at a little before midnight, we three idiots went aimlessly wandering through the back alleys and mews of London, looking for an ice-cream parlor.

To say the least, at that time of night the back streets of London are not the safest place to go wandering. I do believe that Dori and I rationalized that, being in the company of George Hamilton, no mugger in his right mind would attack us. (We prayed!)

Somewhere approaching one A.M., we found the place. Of course, it was closed. We managed to track our way back to George's hotel, where we discovered, to our amazement, that the coffee shop was still open. George finally got to have his ice-cream soda, and we were all lucky enough to escape being mugged.

At the recording session, it became obvious that—even though he had played Hank Williams in a movie—Hank's vocal ability did not rub off on George. But in his individual, irresistible way, George did a very commendable and professional job. If there is one thing that can be said about George Hamilton, it's that he can charm the pants, or skirt, off of anyone. He also, very often, seems to find himself a little short of cash. Every cab ride we took together ended up being paid by me. I don't plan to try and collect.

When we arrived back in LA, I went to Russ Regan at Uni Records, and played the album for him. He liked it, and said that he was interested in making a deal for the master. To my knowledge, the album has never been released, but a single of the "Evel Kneivel" song *was* released. The song was also recorded by a group called Rawhide, produced by Bill Trout out of Chicago. Neither recording of the song ever became a hit.

I have seen George several times since our London escapade, and he always remembers me and has a warm hello to offer. A very nice man with a great sense of humor and *joie de vivre*.

Sometime during 1969, I was contacted by Lester Sill of Colgems Music. (The new name for Screen Gems Music.) I had previously met Lester during the two years that I worked with the Monkees. He said he had a job for me if I was interested. A teenage star from India was appearing in a TV show called *Maya*, and there was interest in making him a recording star.

The main stumbling block was that he couldn't sing very well. Lester remembered the work I had done with Shelley Fabares and Paul Petersen who also did not sing particularly well, and thought that I might be the perfect producer for him. His name was Sajid Khan and Lester was right: he couldn't sing a lick.

Sajid Khan and I listening to a playback. 1969

His sponsor and guardian was Alan Courtney, who was an executive at Four-Star Television. Alan was a wonderful person and working with him was a pleasant experience. Despite all the publicity the album and Sajid Khan received in the teen magazines, it was not a big seller. And though I later recorded some additional sides with him, I don't believe they were ever released.

Alan Courtney of Four-Star was impressed with the work I had done with Sajid, and was also aware of my track record in the music business. He said that his company was in the process of trying to make some changes to its music division, and offered me the opportunity to take over the operation. Besides the record company, there was also a music publishing company.

Though I had some basic knowledge of the music-publishing business, it was in no way my strong point. I contacted Roger Gordon (son of songwriter Mack Gordon), whom I had dealt with many times during my record days, and asked if he would be interested in partnering with me on this project. Roger was experienced in the publishing business, and I felt that together we might make a good team. He jumped at the opportunity and together we proceeded to set the organizing process in motion.

But problems arose when some infighting among the executives at Four-Star, concerning the expansion of the music division, began to put a damper on the project. Soon the whole idea was scrapped: So much for my very brief sojourn into the business end of music.

Lester Sill also teamed me with Rich Little, the voice impersonator, and I produced an album of Rich's vocal impressions. He was fun to work with, and had a multitude of show-biz stories that he shared with me during the sessions.

♫   ♫   ♫

Nancy Sinatra

NANCY SINATRA AND PAUL PETERSEN were devoted fans of my *Feels Like Lovin'* album on Capitol Records. They each played the record so often that they had worn out several copies, and I had to keep refurbishing them with fresh ones.

Nancy liked my arrangements on the *Feels Like Lovin'* album so much, that when she was ready to put together her television show, she called me and asked if I would join her staff and do some arranging for her. I spent several days at pre-production meetings but nothing ever came out of them. Just recently Nancy reminded me that the show never made it on the air.

I originally met Nancy Sinatra back in 1962, when she was married to Tommy Sands. She and Tommy came to visit Jimmy Darren at one of our recording sessions. In fact, I have a tape of Jimmy, Tommy and Nancy

Those "Boots Were Made for Walkin'" gal. (Nancy Sinatra)

fooling around with the song we were in the process of recording. It's quite funny, but not particularly flattering, and definitely not politically correct. (If you get my gist.) I swore to them that I would never play it for anyone. Just recently, I saw Tommy Sands (who is, unfortunately, not in good health) at a Hollywood Collector's Show, and gave him a copy of the tape. He never called to say whether or not he had listened to it.

In the summer of 1970, Dori and I received an invitation from Frank Sinatra to attend the opening of his daughter Nancy's nightclub act at

Caesar's Palace in Las Vegas. The invitation was on black paper and appeared to be hand written in gold calligraphy. All expenses were to be paid by Frank including air transportation, lodging and food. What a daddy. We felt quite honored to have been included on Nancy and Frank's "A" list.

Though I don't see Nancy that often, when we do meet or speak on the phone, she is pleasant, warm and friendly. I hope she always remains that way, for it's refreshing in this business of show-people jerks, to find someone who does not fit into that category.

♫　　♫　　♫

The Russ Meyer Connection

SOMETIME IN 1969, IGO KANTOR had another one of his brilliant ideas. He had been working with Bill Loose on some of Russ Meyer's little soft-core skin flicks, and was trying to convince the maverick director to perhaps inject some songs into his films. Russ's next movie was called *Cherry, Harry and Raquel.* Bill Loose had already been hired to supply the score—but on this film, Russ decided to include a main-title song. Igo convinced me that it would be a good move on my part if I would undertake the assignment. This was precisely what was missing from my career: porno movies! They would certainly fit right in with all the B-pictures I had done. But recalling how well Igo's last brainstorm had paid off, I reluctantly said, Yes!

After seeing the film I was truly inspired. Inspired perhaps, to get laid, but certainly not to write a great song. I needed raunch—and I knew exactly where to go for it. I called Allan Brackett and John Merrill of the Peanut Butter Conspiracy and said, "I've got a great big 42 D-cup-job for you." They laughed a bit, but after I explained the film to them they couldn't wait to get started. Fools, they thought that they were actually going to get to see the whole movie.

Anyway, out of our collaboration came a nifty little ditty called "The Toys of Our Time." Not wanting to have the name Peanut Butter Conspiracy connected with the picture, they decided to use phony names as writers and call the group The Jacks & Balls on the credits. I, however, had to use my real name on the song, as Igo didn't want Russ to feel that this job was beneath me.

Once again, Igo had hit the bulls-eye. A short time later he called to tell me that Russ Meyer had just made a deal with 20th Century Fox to produce and direct *Beyond the Valley of the Dolls*. Russ wanted me to score the picture, as well as write all the new songs. I became really excited about this project. What made it even more attractive was that Russ did not have to record the music at Fox. This meant that I would not be under the supervision of Lionel Newman—which also meant that I would be my own boss. (A little amusing side note: Andre Previn and Dory Previn had written a song, and Andre had done some un-credited scoring work on the original *Valley of the Dolls* three years earlier.)

I contacted Bob Stone, and gave him the fantastic news. We met with Russ to go over the screenplay (which incidentally, was written by Roger Ebert, the film critic). Russ pretty much left us on our own, and said that he would work with whatever ideas we might come up with. A short time later, we played four songs for Russ. He loved them all and told us to forge ahead.

The next step was to find a singer to record the vocals for the actresses to lip sync to. Bob Fitzpatrick and Bob Stigwood, who managed the Strawberry Alarm Clock (who appeared in the film), turned us on to a singer they handled named Lynn Carey (daughter of actor Macdonald Carey.) She also recorded under the name of C.K. Strong, and years later as Mama Lion. We listened to her recordings, and Bob and I both agreed that her voice was perfect for our songs.

When I finally met Lynn, all I could focus on were her very large breasts. Russ

Lynn Carey looking a bit "evil."

was a *big breast man*, and all his films featured women with over-sized bosoms, as that was his trademark. Lynn was perfect for Russ in every possible way. He even considered using her in the film, but she declined.

There were many rumors about Lynn that were circulating around town labeling her as a stoned '60s rock-and-roll singer. After working with Lynn and getting to know her, I quickly found out otherwise. What I did discover was that she was a fantastic musician. A pro of the highest caliber, with great pitch, a vocal range not to be believed, and the ability to change styles from rock to jazz to pop at the blink of an eye. And she did them all equally well. To my mind, Lynn Carey remains one of the greatest vocal talents I have ever encountered in the business.

Unfortunately, portions of the rumors were true, and with nothing but bad relationships and bad management, Lynn has floundered in the business and, to this day, has never made it to the top. There's still time, however, and I hope that someday she does reach her goal. (By the way, we are very close friends.)

During the pre-production, it became evident that one or two more songs would be needed. Lynn asked if she could take a shot at co-writing, and together we wrote two songs. She had a way with words, a gift no doubt from her father, an aspiring poet, and wrote two excellent songs.

Since the Carrie Nations (the name of the group in the movie), were all females, we decided to add Barbara Robison of the Peanut Butter Conspiracy as a back-up singer.

This helped to spice up the vocals with a little variety.

Dolly Read   Cynthia Myers   Marcia McBroom

Once the pre-recording was done, it became my job to teach the songs to the three actresses who were the leads in the film. Two of them had been *Playboy* Centerfolds (Cynthia Myers and Dolly Read). For the next few weeks while they were filming, the girls would spend all of their off-camera time in my office at Fox working on the lip-sync with me. They also had to learn to play instruments, so I became an instrumental coach. Talk about jobs with perks. This one beat them all. How many composers get to spend two to three weeks in such close proximity to two *Playboy* Centerfolds? Unfortunately, it was *look, but don't touch*. What a bummer!

"What a bummer" very nearly—I repeat, *nearly*—turned into something unforgettable. After completing the pre-recording of the songs for the film,

I decided to deliver Cynthia Meyer's tape cassette copy to her house, since it happened to be on my way home. I arrived at her place, just off of Laurel Canyon, at around 7:00 PM. After ringing the bell I heard her sexy voice say, "It's open… come on in." As I entered the dark room, lit only by a solitary lamp, she again called out from an adjoining room, "Make yourself comfortable." I sat down on the sofa, made myself comfy and waited for her.

After a few minutes, Cynthia entered from another room. She was dressed in skin-tight blue jeans and a flimsy top that left nothing to the imagination. It was obvious she was not wearing a bra and, with Playboy Centerfold measurements emphasizing her very large breasts, she exuded more than enough sexuality to tantalize any mortal man.

She walked directly to me and stopped only a few inches away from where I was seated. With her standing, and me seated, her hips and my eyes were at the same level. Without warning, she proceeded to unzip her jeans and pull them down low enough for me to see the cheeks of her derriere. (She was not wearing any panties.) "Look what happened to me on the set today," she exclaimed. I stared at her rear and saw the ugly bruise at her lower hip and backside. "Gee, that's awful," I stammered. I wondered if this was her way of getting me aroused enough to make some kind of sexual advance? Or, did she simply want me to see her injury?

I immediately thought of my beautiful wife, no more than five minutes away, patiently waiting for me to arrive home. There she would lovingly greet me with "Hi honey… how was your day?" After what seemed like the longest six or seven seconds of my life, Cynthia finally pulled her pants up and zipped her fly. We talked about the songs for several minutes, and I soon became convinced that sex was definitely not on her mind.

As we said goodnight at the door, her smile was sensual and still inviting. However, I assumed that this was simply her behavior when around men. In her profession, as a model and actress, Cynthia was so used to being stared at in the nude, that it hardly ever occurred to her what revealing a sensuous part of her body could do to a man. Or maybe—*she did*. I briskly walked to my car, my momentary sexual fantasy having come to an abrupt end. Minutes later, as I opened the door to my house, my wife called out, "Hi honey… how was your day?" Little did she know. Well, she does now.

There was one other perk that fell into my lap… literally. At the end of filming, Russ wanted to do a publicity photo layout with one of the male leads and an exotic dancer named Angel Ray, who had a bit part in the film.

The actor was so fed up and disgusted with the picture, that on the last day of filming, he rushed off the set and left the lot.

Russ spied me hanging around for the wrap party, and noticed that I was approximately the same build as the actor. He asked me if I would like to do a photo layout with Angel. After meeting Angel, I enthusiastically said yes, and changed into the actor's wardrobe. As you can readily see, I was having the time of my life. But like before, it was look but don't touch.

Angel Ray *does* Stu. I'll bet there isn't another composer in Hollywood
who worked a photo-shoot with Russ Meyer.

The main title song to the movie was recorded by The Sandpipers on A&M Records, but never had any commercial success. To close out this episode about *Dolls*, let me add that the picture was a critical flop, and went into obscurity for several decades despite the fact that it made money. Recently, it has acquired cult status, and is now in great demand. Yet Fox, for unknown reasons, won't promote the film. Considering the *slime* movies and television that Fox is involved in these days, it's really weird that they won't work on re-releasing this movie. It appears as though they would like to completely disassociate themselves from the film.

Fox's contract with Russ Meyer was for three movies, so even with the apparent failure of *Dolls*, Russ started on another film for them almost immediately. It was *The Seven Minutes* and Russ again wanted me to do the score. I really did not want to do another Russ Meyer film, for it was not

going to help me get out of the B-movie syndrome that I had fallen into. This time, the score was going to be under the jurisdiction of Lionel Newman's music department. I did a complete 360 and now rationalized that working under Lionel might present me with the opportunity I had been looking for to finally establish myself with him. I hoped that maybe after all these years, he might find *his way* to throwing a crumb *my way*.

Lynn Carey and her boyfriend at that time, Neil Merryweather, wrote a song for the film that I played for Lionel who immediately turned it down as being too suggestive to be in a Fox picture. This from a man who had trouble saying three words in a row without dropping in some four-letter expletives!

So Bob Stone and I composed a replacement song that Lionel and Russ approved of. We also wrote two other featured songs. We hired Lynn and Neil and their group to perform one of the songs in the film. We felt that was the least we could do after their song had been rejected.

To our surprise, the music publisher convinced B.B. King to record the title song. It definitely wasn't the right marriage of material and artist and we weren't surprised when the record bombed—just like the picture. This film is without a doubt, the worst movie I have ever been involved with, and I've been associated with some real stinkers.

On a personal level, Russ and I were not *close buddies*, but Dori and I were invited to his wedding. His marriage to *Beyond the Valley of the Dolls* starlet Edy Williams took place at the very fashionable Bel-Air Hotel. Can you picture this: Edy Williams walking down the aisle— which was bordered by a fishpond with white swans gliding on the surface—dressed in a white mini-skirted wedding dress that barely made it below her crotch and scarcely covered her breasts. The dress was almost as high as it was low. It was definitely a *Playboy* or possibly even a *Hustler* wedding.

Russ Meyer... The Big Breast King.

Shortly after the wedding I had occasion to visit Russ and Edy at their new home, just off Mulholland Drive. I seem to recall that the house was once owned by Lizabeth Scott, a famous B movie star of the 1940s.

The living room was enormous and featured an oversized fireplace with a hearth big enough to walk on. The fireplace itself could easily accommodate four or five standing people. It reminded me of similar fireplaces I'd seen in movies like *Ivanhoe* or *Camelot*. Unfortunately, this magnificent structure was not being used for warm crackling fires, but as a garbage can. It was littered with empty beer cans—not to mention candy wrappers and discarded cereal boxes. The rest of the room had newspapers and magazines strewn about on the floor as well as the furniture. It was obvious that neither Russ nor Edy were inclined towards neatness. If they did have a housekeeper, he or she was lousy at their job or only worked on rare occasions.

My relationship with Russ Meyer ended in 1971 with *The Seven Minutes*—until about three years ago (Sept. '99), when I read in the paper that they were going to screen *Beyond the Valley of the Dolls* at the Egyptian Theater on Hollywood Blvd. The article said that members of the cast as well as Russ himself would be on hand to answer questions after the screening. I went to the theater that evening and, when I introduced myself to the staff, they were thrilled that I had come.

I joined the panel in the question-and-answer segment, and was quite delighted when I was introduced to the audience and received a big hand. I discovered that the fans of the movie thought the songs were fantastic. After the screening, I spent several minutes talking to Russ. He obviously was not well, as he was suffering the early stages of Alzheimer's. We tossed around a few memories and then I left, as I found it difficult watching this once active and vibrant man reduced to this sad condition.

In the last few years, I have been invited to attend some of the Hollywood Collectors conventions. Generally, I can be found sitting with the *Beyond the Valley of the Dolls* contingent. *Dolls* has become a *major* cult film, as have most of Russ Meyer's movies. I feel a bit out of place sitting with Cynthia Myers and Erica Gavin, who were two of the stars of *Dolls*, as well as past *Playboy* Centerfolds. Lynn Carey, who by the way did a *Penthouse* layout as well, in her younger days, was also on hand. Siouxzan Perry was the manager of our little entourage.

It's really amazing to think that many of those *schlock* pictures and TV shows that I worked on are now cult items: *The Monkees*; the four biker-films; *Battlestar Galactica*; two surfing movies and *Dolls*. I'm slowly, but not so surely, becoming a bit proud at having done these films. Alas, I still would prefer being known as the composer who wrote *Schindler's List*.

Things Slow Down

IN 1971, AFTER SCORING *Beyond the Valley of the Dolls* and *The Seven Minutes*, I was reduced to actually trying to drum up some work. The days of people calling me for my services were becoming few and far between. I obviously had not impressed Lionel Newman enough with the two films I had scored at Fox for him to hire me for any additional work. I decided that it might now be the perfect time to try and rejuvenate my dormant record career.

I called Capitol Records and managed to get an appointment with Dave Cavanaugh, now head of A&R. I told him that I thought it might be time to resurrect The Hollyridge Strings. The Beatles were still hot, and there was an abundance of new material for an album. I also suggested an album called *Hits of the '70s*.

Dave presented my suggestions at the next A&R meeting. They gave me the go-ahead, and I enthusiastically threw myself into my favorite kind of arranging and recording. I do believe that I matured on these two albums, and wrote the best arrangements of my career. Unfortunately, neither *Hits of the '70s* nor *George, John, Paul and Ringo* became a chart album. In fact, both albums are now rather rare collectors' items, and worth 10 times more than when they were released—if you can find them.

To further exasperate me, I discovered that in 1971, Enoch Light (remember him, from 1959?) recorded and released an album called *The Beatles Classics*, with arrangements closely resembling mine. Some 22 years after the fact, Enoch Light decided that—now—*my* arrangements were worth copying. Such are the quirks of life in the music business.

The aforementioned two albums did manage to stir some interest around town in my arranging abilities, and I did some writing for Ed Ames, formerly of the Ames Brothers. He is probably best known as the man who, as a guest on Johnny Carson, threw a hatchet at a cardboard cutout of a man and hit him right in the crotch. I also did some arrangements for Roger Williams (famous for his hit records "Autumn Leaves" and "Born Free").

I think that of all the non-singers I have produced, the least talented vocally was Adam West, famous as TV's *Batman*. However, he made up for his lack of singing talent by being one hell of a fun guy. I seem to remember first meeting him in a hospital, where he was recuperating from an injury suffered while filming *Batman*. The record we made, "Miranda," a *Batman* take-off, unfortunately did not take-off on the charts.

Jud and four or five other insignificant independent films filled out the years between '69 and '73. One of the films was titled, *How To Seduce a Woman*, and I hooked up with Arthur Hamilton; the composer of "Cry me a River" and "Shadow Woman," which I had recorded with Karen O'Hara back in 1956. Arthur and I wrote a song for the main title. Just recently, I had lunch with Arthur and gave him a copy of Karen's recording of his song from 45 years ago.

My composing fee for these low budget films was rather meager, and our cash flow was once again beginning to suffer. During these somewhat unproductive years I had time to practice golf and became a much-improved player—though still a hacker. I took up tennis, and was able to find a great deal of time indulging in my favorite hobby, art. I also became something of a carpenter, doing quite a bit of woodwork and home repair—or disrepair. Depends on one's point of view, I guess.

The commercials I was involved in during this period did not earn me a great deal of money, but they turned out to be a lot of fun. Armour Hotdogs in particular was a ball. The ad agency played me a version of the jingle with a chorus of young children singing. They were unhappy with the sound because the voices sounded too professional. They had tried non-singers, but they were so bad it was hard to listen to the commercial. They said that they needed something in-between. "Could I find the right sound for them?" they asked. I said I would give it some thought and get back to them.

After rejecting a few quick fixes, I came up with a concept of hiring non-professional children whose parents were professional musicians or singers. I hoped that, having been exposed to the industry through their parents, the children might have that middle-sound that the client was looking for.

I had Jackie Ward assist me in rounding up some children, ages seven to about 15 (as long as their voices hadn't yet changed). Of course I included my own daughter Toni. The kids were great, and we nailed the sound that the client and agency were looking for. It was a lucky shot-in-the-dark on my part.

After we had turned the tapes over to the agency for dubbing, a slight problem arose with one of the spoken solo voices. They called me frantically one day and said that I had to replace this one line immediately. Fortunately, the recording studio was available, but I needed a child's voice and it was school time. I called my wife, and told her to pick up our daughter Toni after school and bring her directly to the recording studio.

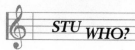

Trouper that she is, Toni did a difficult *punch-in vocal* (not easy, even for a pro) like it was the simplest thing in the world. Dori and I felt proud of our little nine-year-old daughter, and figured some of our show-biz genes might definitely be swimming around in her body. (However, it now appears that Julie, our younger daughter, has the show-biz bug more than Toni.)

The client was so pleased with the commercials we produced, that he used us again for the next series of ad campaigns. Even Julie got on film in one of the commercials. Our versions of the Armour Hotdogs commercial ran for about two years.

Rainbo bread was another commercial endeavor that had a novel twist to it. I was given the existing Rainbo bread jingle and asked to prepare about five or six versions of it. One of the versions was a father-and-son duet. For the demo, I did both vocals imitating a father with a deep voice, and his son with a squeaky little boy's voice. After the client had approved the arrangements, I asked the agency if they had anyone special in mind to perform the vocals. They said that they would leave it up to me—but definitely not to change the vocals on the father-and-son duet. I quickly explained that *I* was the voice for *both* characters. They said that they didn't care who the voices were. That was what the client wanted, and that's what the client was going to get. So I went out and joined SAG and AFTRA. Another unexpected musical field had been added to my career. (I've left singing off my résumé for obvious reasons. I can't sing.)

After a hiatus in Dori's career of about 12 years, I hired her to do the voice of the mother on the other versions. She proved to be the same consummate pro she had always been. Her long layoff did not diminish her professionalism. The entire Phillips' family was now earning residuals from commercials. I do believe the family had some fun together during this period.

After these commercials, the roller-coaster ride I had been on was beginning to slow down. Nine or ten incredible years of success had flown by, and a nervous feeling of anxiety was starting to replace the exultation of my past successes. I constantly worried that I had *shot my load*, to use a rather crude vernacular, and that my career was now on the way down. After all those years in records, film and TV, it now seemed strange that commercials, which I had only dabbled in back in New York, appeared to have become the major part of my career. What next, I wondered?

11 The Last Out... Roger Craig
From Film Composer to Film Maker

WHEN 1973 KICKED OFF, THE IMMEDIATE future was not looking too promising. Even though I had been busy writing films and commercials for the last four years, the money was not even close to what I had been previously earning while in the record business. Our financial situation was definitely not looking as rosy as we would have liked.

In the early part of the year, I became so disheartened that I even investigated the possibility of relocating to Sydney, Australia. The TV and film business there was still in an infant stage, and not yet a major industry. It seemed to me that Australia just might present some good opportunities to get in on the ground floor. My résumé was rather impressive, and I had a feeling that "down-under" I might once more hit a lucky streak. Dori—though not particularly excited about the idea—was willing to support me, if that indeed became my decision. She is one hell of a wonderful person: My best friend, a terrific lover and the world's greatest mother. At this point, "Go west, young man" was beginning to sound good to me.

While still contemplating our possible move to Australia, I searched for something to get my creative juices flowing again. I turned to writing—specifically, a screenplay for a dramatic short film. During my time at the Eastman School of Music, it was required of each student that they take one academic class not associated with music. I decided on creative writing, and enjoyed it enough to feel that someday I might try to make use of what I had learned. This seemed to be the perfect opportunity to experiment.

As a member of the Motion Picture Academy, for several years I had observed that at times, there were very few entries in the Dramatic Short Subject category, occasionally referred to as "two-reelers." Every now and then, not even enough to constitute a full category. This appeared to be the perfect opportunity to perhaps sneak in a nomination, thereby creating the chance of a possible Academy Award. This now became my new goal. I forgot about Australia for the moment, and dove into my new obsession.

The story I created concerned a washed-up minor-league pitcher in his mid-forties, named Luke Walters, who gets one last chance to prove to himself and the fans that he was, and still is, a good pitcher. The time period was the late 1940s, and the title of my little opus was *The Last Out*.

Luke was now playing in a league that was *lower* than the minors. Each team in this league was sponsored by some manufacturing company or retail business. On this particular day, standing in Luke's way was a young 19-year-old phenom. The kid was considered a lock to make it to the major leagues as a great hitter. He also happened to be Luke's estranged son. Will Luke prove his mettle on this particular day? Or will his son, Little Luke, destroy his father's dreams by getting the winning hit off of his old man? This was the basic plot.

As there was to be no dialogue, the 20-minute film was to be narrated by someone like Buddy Ebsen, Will Geer or Ben Johnson. I showed the script to Bob Fisher, a director of commercials that I had worked with several times. He liked it well enough to become my partner in the project. We made a deal to co-produce and co-direct. My next step was to show the script to Igo Kantor and Jim Nelson of Synchro-Film. They both admired the script and offered their services free of charge. Bud Cardos, who owned a fully equipped grip truck, also graciously joined the project. We were on our way. All we needed now were a pair of lead actors.

There were two possible directions we could go in our selection of the father and son. We could look for two actors who could play a little baseball, or locate two baseball players who could act a little. Since there was to

Roger Craig as he looked in 1973.

be no dialogue, we decided to look for two ball players with expressive faces.

I called the LA Dodgers' office, and asked if they could send me a list of some of their retired players. They were very cooperative, and supplied me with quite a good deal of information. On the list that they sent me was a retired pitcher named Roger Craig. He was the right age, and had a marvelously weathered face. It had a wonderfully tired and worn-out look, which seemed perfect for the role.

Roger had had two or three good years out of the many he spent in the major leagues as a pitcher. But unfortunately, he was best remembered for the one horrible year he suffered through with the NY Mets, where he lost 24 games and set a major-league record for the most losses in a season. In his long career, Roger pitched for the Dodgers, Mets, Cardinals, Cincinnati and Philadelphia. On the bright side, Roger's World Series record was seven wins and four losses for three different teams. The dossier said that Roger was currently employed by the LA Dodgers as a minor-league pitching coach and scout. Since the baseball season had yet to start, I located him at his home in Alpine, California, just outside of San Diego.

Over the phone I briefly explained the story. Roger said that he was definitely interested. (Let's face it: Doesn't everyone want to be in the movies?) Bob Fisher and I drove down to Roger's ranch just outside of San Diego. We talked at length about the screenplay while Bob shot a whole roll of stills. Roger then inquired as to who was going to play the role of his son. I said that, with the pictures Bob was taking, we would scout some high school and college baseball teams for a boy who resembled him enough to pass as his son. We were getting ready to leave when Roger asked us to wait a few minutes more. He said that he would like us to meet his son.

When Roger's boy walked in, it was like we were seeing double. Roger Jr. was the image of Roger Sr., only 27 years younger. When Roger saw the excited look on our faces, he smiled and said, "He also plays baseball." Bob quickly got his camera out and started shooting more film of the two of them. As we

Roger and his son Roger Jr.

drove back to LA, we couldn't believe our good fortune. We had found the perfect cast on our first try. We felt this was a good omen and, with great enthusiasm, we proceeded with our plans.

The baseball season was to start a few weeks later, and Roger figured that the most convenient time for he to be available would be in early September. His son would still be out of school and also available. Plus, the

baseball season would be winding down, so he could easily get away for the seven days of shooting. (That is, unless the Dodgers where going to be in the playoffs—which was a long shot.)

What we now needed was a place to shoot the ballgame section of the story. It had to be an old and broken-down stadium. At first we were worried that we might have to go on location too far from Los Angeles to find such a place, and that would for sure wreak havoc with our limited budget.

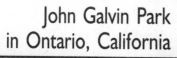

John Galvin Park
in Ontario, California

Checking out the dilapidated locker room. At the right is the stadium sign.

One of the dugouts

A view of the rundown stands

Fate smiled on us again, when I was told about an old stadium built in 1934 that was used occasionally by the USC baseball team for training. John Galvin Park was located in Ontario, California, only about 40 miles east of LA. I took a drive down to the stadium by myself and looked it over. It could not have been better, even if we had had it built for us. I called the city council in Ontario, since it was a city-owned stadium, and made a deal with them for the rental of the ballpark. The price, a mere $30 a day, was more than reasonable, and easily fit into our budget. As a bonus, the care-taker was a rabid baseball fan and little league coach. He promised us that he could fill the stands with kids. I sent the council a deposit and we were now on our way, big-time.

Up to now, I was personally paying all the bills. We had figured the budget at between three to five thousand dollars. Once again, good things were about to happen. I was at a party at a friend's house when I was introduced to a young man, who as it turned out, owned one of the biggest burglar-alarm companies on the West Coast, Morse Burglar Alarms.

His name was Mike Weinstock, and he told me how he had always been fascinated by the movie business, and that someday he would love to be-come a part of it. Quickly I mentioned to him that the opportunity might be sooner than he thought. I then explained the project to Mike, and told him about Roger Craig and the stadium.

Anyone who followed baseball had heard of Roger Craig. Fortunately for us, Mike and his brother were big baseball fans, and their eyes lit up at the thought of meeting Roger Craig personally. Mike practically pleaded with me to let him invest in the movie. I explained that the chance of making money on a short subject like this film was very remote, and that I was making this film primarily to try and win an Academy Award. Mike still wanted in, and I was more than happy to take his money. With his $5,000, I was able to up the budget to $8,500.

Someone had to play the part of the catcher. After all, Roger had been a professional pitcher, and would need a seasoned pro to catch for him. I called Roger and explained the problem. He said, "not to worry," and got his good friend Norm Sherry, who had been his catcher in the big leagues, to come on board. Roger also arranged for a retired umpire to join the movie team, so that everything on film would look professional. Since most of the action centered on extreme close-ups of Roger, his son, the catcher, and the umpire, all the other players were basically just standing around. They simply had to look like pros, but be able to at least throw and catch a little.

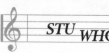

Between myself, my brother-in-law Wynn, Dori's uncle Artie, my brother and several friends—all of whom had played a little ball in their youth—we were able to cover all the shots and angles with a full team of amateurs.

The next step that needed to be solved was acquiring the proper baseball uniforms. The story took place in the late 1940s, and in those days, the player's uniforms were woolen, not polyester as they are now. I needed old uniforms and that seemed to present a problem. I called several costume houses and struck out (pun intended). Then I remembered meeting the head of the costume department at 20th Century-Fox when I was working on *Beyond the Valley of the Dolls*. I called him and explained my dilemma. Again, the movie gods smiled on our project.

When I arrived at Fox, he showed me several racks of old baseball uniforms with no team markings on them. They had been used for *The Pride of the Yankees* (the Lou Gehrig story) and another old baseball film. Not only were the uniforms perfect, but also he was considerate enough to rent them to me for about $150. All I had to do was bring them back dry-cleaned.

Bob and I held auditions for the two remaining parts. We found the perfect girl and young boy (to appear in the flashbacks) to fill the roles. Our luck was still running good.

When August arrived, I started to make final arrangements for the shoot. I had succeeded in finding all my locations (except the ballpark) at no cost to the production. So far my only expenses were a small salary to Roger and his son, a token payment to Norm Sherry and the umpire, the stadium rental and the cost of the film stock and cameras. The one person in the crew we had to pay union scale to was the AD (Assistant Director). We could not find anyone willing to join us just for the glory.

To help enlarge the crowd in the stadium, we called all our friends and invited them to take a drive down to Ontario and participate on Saturday and Sunday in our movie. We managed to get about 30 people who said that they would be there. Next we called the local paper in Ontario, and spoke to the sports editor and asked him if he would print an article explaining about the filming on Saturday and Sunday, and mention that anyone who comes by to watch the filming would become a part of the crowd and receive free hot dogs and Cokes. As an added bonus, Roger Craig and Norm Sherry would be available at the end of filming to sign autographs. The editor agreed to do it, and it appeared we were on our way. Nobody had ever seen pre-production on a film progress as smoothly and trouble free as this.

The shoot was to begin on Sunday, September 8th, at a farmhouse location just around the corner from where I lived. On Friday, Roger and his son showed up at my house for a little rehearsal and costuming. Roger told me that on Saturday night he was to be the bullpen coach for the Dodgers. The following evening I went over the shooting schedule again and again, trying to make sure that as little time as possible would be wasted. My work was interrupted by a phone call.

It was Roger's son. He said that his Dad was in the hospital. Roger's back had gone into spasm when he bent over to pick up a ball in the bullpen. He was in traction and couldn't move. I asked if the doctor was there. He said yes, and that Dr. Jobe would call me as soon as he had made a more complete diagnosis.

I was so shocked at this news, that I just stared at the wall and said nothing. When the phone rang again, it was Dr. Jobe. He informed me that Roger could not possibly pitch a baseball for at least a month. That was it. All the good fortune we had experienced on this film was now nothing but a distant memory.

I immediately had to make calls and cancel as many things as I could. The task at hand now was to save as much money as possible. It was without a doubt the worst day in my life. Failure is bad enough, but I didn't even *get* the opportunity to fail. The project never left the ground. This definitely was *the last out*.

The following morning, Roger personally called me from the hospital and said that he would still like to try and do the film. He said he could stay in his wheel chair until he actually had to pitch. Even though he knew it would be very painful, he still didn't want to let us down.

I started visualizing all the scenes Roger would be in, and how getting him in and out of the wheel chair was going to add so much time to the shooting schedule that there would be no way we could finish on time. I told him to get well, which was certainly more important than the film, and proceeded to cancel the whole project.

We only lost about five or six hundred dollars—but I lost all my ambition to continue with any future projects like this. I never felt so defeated in my entire life. What made it positively revolting was the fact that my birthday was the next day. This birthday was turning out to be even more distressing than my 21st birthday, 24 years previous.

To wrap up this chapter, Roger called me about a month later and said that he now felt well enough to pitch. "Perhaps, we could reschedule the filming?" he asked. I explained that there were now too many obstacles for

us to hurdle. First of all, his son was back in school and not readily available. The people who had offered their services to us for free were now employed on other projects. It also would be too late to qualify for this year's Academy nominations. Again I said thanks and wished him good health and God speed.

Roger went on to become a fairly successful baseball manager in the big leagues. He was the manager of the San Diego Padres and the San Francisco Giants, where he led the Giants to a National League Pennant. Craig retired to his ranch not too long ago, a very successful baseball legend (unlike my screenplay). To my knowledge, I don't believe that Roger Jr. ever continued his baseball career.

My little screenwriting episode took a very unexpected turn. I wrote the baseball script in February of 1973. As you already know, on the basis of the script, many people were willing to work on the project *gratis*. At about the same approximate time, Igo Kantor was in the midst of finalizing a deal with the Peruvian government, who were going to finance three or four films to be shot in Peru, with only a skeleton U.S. crew.

Kantor had the four scripts that he wanted them to film, but was told by the Minister of Culture in Peru to bring at least six or seven for him to read and choose from. Igo, needing some quick scripts to throw into the pile, asked me if I would like to write one. I eagerly accepted and in March 1973 I handed Igo an action/adventure screenplay titled *Pisces*.

I don't know whether or not Igo ever read the script, as it was supposed to be a just a throwaway. Miracle of miracles, guess what? My script was picked as one of the screenplays that Peruvians wanted to film. We were all flabbergasted. This was the most dreadful looking script in the world, full of misspellings, bad punctuation, bad typing, etc. etc.—but obviously an appealing story. Before I could get started on a second draft, the Peruvian government suffered a *coup*, and all bets were off.

It is now 2001, and I have showed that old script of *Pisces* to several people. They all seemed to like it. With a bit of self-prodding I have proceeded with a belated rewrite. Who knows, maybe 29 years after the first draft it might find someone willing to film it. I guess I'll never give up trying to be a jack-of-all-trades.

12 The Glen Larson Years

A New Beginning

A FEW DAYS AFTER THE DEMISE of my movie, as I was contemplating my future and once again considering emigrating to Australia, I received a morning phone call from the office of Glen A. Larson.

During the late 1960s I used to watch a show called *It Takes a Thief*. I noticed that the name Glen A. Larson appeared on the screen as story editor and sometimes as a producer. I always wondered if he was the same Glen Larson of the Four Preps that I had worked with at Capitol Records. It turned out that he was.

Glen gave me a cheerful hello, as though it hadn't been about nine years since we had last seen each other, and asked me what I was up to. Of course I was not going to tell him how deflated I really was from my recent escapade with *The Last Out*, so I lied a bit and said that things were great. He asked me if I might be interested in composing the music for a pilot that he was writing and producing called *The Six Million-Dollar Man*. For the last eight years I had naturally assumed that Glen was not too fond of me, after my having thrown him out of the studio during the dubbing of the Four Preps record. I tried my best to sound blasé—whereas in reality I was thrilled at his offer— and said that the concept seemed to be an interesting project.

Glen was involved in the production of two shows during that approximate time period: *McCloud* and *Alias Smith & Jones*. At the time, he was not particularly enamored with the composers that Harry Garfield (the head of the Music Department) was making available to him, so he asked a music editor for a list of some other composers that he might consider for this pilot.

The music editor, Bob Simard, was my editor on *Beyond the Valley of the Dolls*, and he graciously placed my name on the list. When Glen saw my name, he asked Bob if I was the same Stu Phillips who was once in the

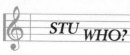

record business. Bob replied that I was, which prompted Glen to place the call to me. He set up a meeting at his office the following day.

For many years, I had frequently called Harry Garfield (the music supervisor at Universal), trying to solicit work, but to no avail. It was a situation similar to my experiences with Lionel Newman at Fox. After receiving Glen's call in the morning, that same afternoon I received a call from Harry Garfield's office. Harry got on the phone, and very excitedly informed me that he finally acquired a composing assignment for me. He said that with a great deal of effort he had convinced Glen Larson to use me on Glen's new pilot. I played along with Harry and didn't mention to him the fact that Larson had already called me. I surmised that I had more to gain by feeding Harry's ego than I did by embarrassing him.

As I drove through the gates of Universal Pictures the following day, little did I imagine that I would be working there for the next eight years. After parking my car, I proceeded to walk to Glen's office in the executive building just opposite the "Black Tower." (The nickname given to the building housing the offices of Lew Wasserman, Sid Scheinberg and all the other "suit-and-tie-guys.") I had a great and exhilarating feeling as I fantasized about the wonderful possibilities that might come my way while working at Universal.

When I gave Glen a run-down of some of my film and TV credits from the previous nine years, I believe that he felt reassured that perhaps he had indeed made a good choice. (He never mentioned the incident at Capitol—nor did I.)

As you read in the last chapter, it's a rarity in the business of film making when things progress without a hitch. This event proved to be no exception. A minor problem arose when Glen was advised that another composer, Gil Mellé, was contractually bound to write the music. Thankfully, Glen went to bat for me, and eventually I got the assignment. The pilot starred Lee Majors, and the story was very much in the James Bond genre. The type of music required was exactly the style I enjoyed writing and, as a result, I was able to compose the score in record time.

Glen had written a song for the pilot and engaged Dusty Springfield to perform it on the soundtrack. It became my job to record and produce the recording. Though I had always admired Dusty's records, she turned out to be not quite the talented singer I had envisioned, and I became somewhat disappointed with her performance—or rather, lack of performance.

It didn't take long for me to learn about Glen's habit of never really finishing the editing of a show prior to the scoring sessions. This was the usual scenario on almost every show of Glen's that I worked on, even if he wasn't directly involved. I had been accustomed to a film being in the final-edit stage when I started scoring the music. Getting used to Glen's constant re-editing was going to take time and patience.

The score for the show, as far as I was aware, was well received and the pilot was picked up as a series. For some reason, which I was never privy to, Glen did not continue on as executive producer of the show. The production was turned over to another producer who had his own choice of composer, and it appeared that my days at Universal were coming to a sudden and unanticipated end.

The only other show that Glen was doing at this particular juncture was *McCloud*. Glen felt badly that, even though I had done a creditable job on the pilot, I now had nothing to show for it. He asked if I would like to work on some *McCloud* episodes. I jumped at the chance. It was the type of action show that called for a great deal of music, and could be very challenging. *McCloud* was a two-hour or sometimes a 90-minute show that aired only once a month. It was part of the *Mystery Movie Series*, which also included *McMillan & Wife* and *Columbo*.

My music editor on *McCloud* was Jerry Teuber, a man that I won't easily forget. Jerry was what one might describe as a *reluctant* editor, and he found that meeting the nearly impossible-but-necessary deadlines associated with working for Glen Larson, not to his liking.

Jerry was one of the nicest men that I ever had the pleasure of working with, but every editing change that Glen made would drive Jerry crazy. To boot, Jerry smoked like a chimney, and the tiny cubicle we laughingly called a room was always filled with smoke.

Larson's presence made Jerry very nervous, and whenever Glen visited the editing room to work with us, Jerry would get nervous and flustered and generally screw things up a bit. Glen was impatient—as his time was at a premium—and constantly asked me to request a different editor: But Jerry and I worked well together, and I stubbornly kept him on. Several years down the line, Jerry retired from music editing and moved to Palm Springs, where he went into the real-estate business.

With my modest success at Universal, I was now able to put the disastrous ending to my September film project, *The Last Out*, behind me. Australia was now relegated to the back burner.

Dennis Weaver

IN MY HUMBLE OPINION, DENNIS WEAVER was quite introverted for an actor. Whereas Robert Wagner, Eddie Albert and Jack Klugman were very candid in their approach when discussing problems with Glen, Dennis sort of hemmed and hawed.

Weaver wanted to have more love scenes with his on-screen girlfriend Diana Muldaur, but Glen felt that Dennis appeared awkward in all the kissing scenes. Whenever Glen needed to shorten a show, the first trims he would make were in Dennis' love scenes. This would generally bring Weaver scurrying up to Glen's office, and the door would remain closed while a heated discussion took place. Glen generally got his way. Larson was Mr. Smooth: So smooth, that when you finished a minor disagreement with him, you always wondered what in the world you were arguing about.

Cowboy Stu is perched on high. Dennis (McCloud) Weaver is on the right. Never did know who the woman was. Circa 1976

One of the episodes of *McCloud* that I worked on featured an actress who was a *Playboy* Centerfold. She also had the distinction of being one of Hugh Hefner's almost-wives. Her name was Barbi Benton, and I had the eye-filling pleasure of spending about a week working closely with her. She was a delightful girl, and was completely different from what one might expect from a *Playboy* Centerfold. (Barbi became the third Centerfold playmate I was fortunate enough to work with.)

In between takes, we would move to some shady spot and talk. To me, it appeared as though Barbi wished that she could momentarily loose the prying eyes of her bodyguard. Being Heffner's woman, it appeared, was a full time job.

Glen, Bruce Belland (of the Four Preps) and myself collaborated on a song called "Ain't That Just the Way" for Barbi to sing in the episode. I wrote an arrangement and produced the session, which eventually was released as a single.

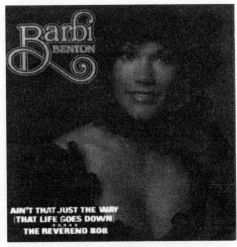

The script called for several scenes to take place at an outdoor theater not unlike the Hollywood Bowl. Barbi was required to sing a couple of songs on stage while accompanied by a rock group. Since it was my job to supervise the music playbacks, and I had to be present at the shoot, I decided to play the part of one of the musicians. It was a lot more interesting than sitting and watching the filming for three days, in a blazing hot California sun.

Barbi Benton (on the extreme right) rehearsing her song in an episode of *McCloud*. If you look carefully to the left of the picture, you will notice a guy in a straw hat and sleeveless shirt. That's me. Don't I look real *rock and roll?*

The music department at Universal Studios was usually teeming with activity, as the two-block-long corridor seemed to be everybody's shortcut to *wherever.* There was no telling whom you might bump into on any given day.

One morning while walking down the corridor outside the long string of music-editing rooms (which closely resembled prison cells), I recognized Elmer Bernstein walking towards me. Elmer was a casual acquaintance of mine at that time. We knew each other mainly from meetings of the

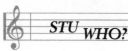
Composers and Lyricists Guild (of which Elmer was the President). As we exchanged handshakes, Elmer inquired as to what I was working on. When I replied that I was writing music for *McCloud*, he said that he would give anything for the opportunity to write some *McCloud* episodes. I quickly countered that I would gladly trade him all of my *McClouds* for one *To Kill a Mockingbird* or *Great Escape*. Elmer never did do a *McCloud*—and I'm still waiting to write an award-winning movie.

In the early days of motion pictures (1930s, '40s and '50s), the studios preferred to have composers do their composing on the studio lot. The studio would generally provide an office for the composer, as Columbia had done for me on the *Diner's Club* movie. This made the composer easily accessible for sudden meetings with producers and directors. By the 1960s, office space on the studio lots (as well as parking spaces) was becoming a rare commodity and, little by little, composers began to work *off* the lot.

Universal provided one composers' office on the lot, that was supposed to be shared by all the currently-active composers. The room had a piano in it and was next door to Sandy de Crescent's office (who was the musician's contractor), and directly across the hall from Hal Mooney's office. (Mooney was the studio's music director, who never seemed to direct much of anything. A nice, congenial man, but seemingly without authority.)

By some means a composer named John Cacavas quietly took over the composer's room as his own. John was scoring the TV show *Kojak*, and the rumor going around was that Telly Savalas had bent a few executive arms to get John the personal use of the office. For all intents and purposes, this was John's office.

Several times when Glen and I needed to work together and required the use of a piano, the office would not be available and Glen would get slightly annoyed. When I explained the situation to him, he said he would to take it up with Sid Scheinberg. Obviously, Glen's clout was not as big as Telly Savalas', since the situation concerning the office did not change. In deference to John Cacavas, who is a friend and a very likable person, he always tried to be very considerate about allowing others to use the office but, somehow, it always felt like we were borrowing John's office.

One of the co-producers and writers of the *McCloud* series was Ron Satlof. Ron was a big fan of my music and we soon became good friends. Later on down the line, he and I were to work together on some projects not connected with Glen Larson. We did about ten episodes of *Spiderman*, as well as a movie of the week called *Waikiki* for Aaron Spelling.

There was an incident that occurred concerning *Waikiki* that bears re-telling. When Ron Satlof told E. Duke Vincent, Aaron Spelling's associate, that he was hiring Stu Phillips to compose the music, Duke was not overly impressed. Ron went to bat for me but was unfortunately losing the battle. However, he did manage to get Duke to at least meet with me.

When I arrived at the Spelling offices, Duke said that he would call Aaron Spelling and get his input. When Aaron heard that I worked for Glen Larson he said, "If he's good enough for Glen Larson, then he's good enough for us." As an afterthought, I must mention that Aaron and Glen were fierce competitors. (They were often appropriating each other's casts, writers, directors, etc.; and constantly trying to top each other. It appears that I might have become an innocent pawn in that scenario.)

Roy Huggins originally, and subsequently Glen Larson's modus operandi in those years, was to adapt and develop hit movies into a television series format. Thus *Coogan's Bluff* became *McCloud*; *To Catch a Thief* became, *It Takes a Thief*; *Butch Cassidy & The Sundance Kid* turned into, *Alias Smith & Jones*; and *The Sting* was converted into, *Switch*.

♫   ♫   ♫

Robert Wagner

SWITCH (WHICH ORIGINALLY AIRED IN 1975), starred Robert Wagner, Eddie Albert and Sharon Gless. It was Glen's next new project after *The Six Million-Dollar Man* pilot. I had obviously impressed Larson enough on the *McCloud* series, and several episodes of *Get Christie Love*, to have him ask me to work on the pilot of *Switch*. Musically, *Switch* was straightforward, standard film/TV writing. A cute little personal incident involving Robert Wagner occurred while I was working on the *Switch* series.

I received a message from Glen's secretary Jan, to come to his office to discuss some music cues. When I walked into the room, I noticed that R.J. (as Robert Wagner's friends affectionately referred to him) was in the room. After a brief discussion with Glen about music, he turned away from me and began to discuss house hunting with R.J. Specifically, one particular property in Toluca Lake. I could not help but eavesdrop, so I casually mentioned that my wife Dori had just received her real-estate license. Glen's eyes lit up and he said, "Call Dori and ask her to meet us and arrange to show us this house in Toluca Lake." With Glen it was always assumed that when he wanted you, you would make yourself available. Most did.

I called Dori and, knowing how important Glen was to my career, she of course agreed to meet us. The ink was barely dry on her real-estate license when she met R.J., Glen and myself at the house. If I remember correctly, the house was once owned by Dick Powell. I don't know if Wagner ever bought the house, but it's a kick to think that Dori's first client was (almost) Robert Wagner.

Quincy, Glen's next show, was co-created by he and Lou Shaw. Shaw and his wife Michele, a very talented opera and musical-comedy singer, became personal friends of Dori and myself, and I worked closely with Lou on many TV projects during the following 10 years. We also played a lot of tennis together on my court, as Lou was my neighbor and lived about 10 houses from me in a home previously owned by Ricky Nelson.

♫   ♫   ♫

Jack Klugman

JACK KLUGMAN WAS THE STAR OF *Quincy* and, though I never considered myself a close friend of his, Jack was aware of who I was and what I did. When we would pass each other on the lot, he always acknowledged me with a friendly hello.

One day as we exchanged greetings, Jack stopped and began a conversation with me. He asked me if I could possibly employ his brother, who was a string player, in my weekly scoring session for *Quincy*. Jack said that he would appreciate any work that I might be able to throw his brother's way. If I remember correctly, I do believe that I hired his brother once or twice. To think that this big star had to solicit work for a relative is mind-boggling—but not uncommon in the film business.

At dailies and first-cut screenings, Jack always seemed to find time to attend. He was very active in giving suggestions to Larson and the film editors, which didn't always sit too well with Glen or the editors. On many occasions, Klugman's suggestions turned into rather animated quarrels.

When Larson was no longer the active executive producer of *Quincy*, I went to Klugman, who was now the producer, and asked if I might continue on as the regular composer. He said that he was pleased with my music, and saw no reason to make a change. I often wonder if hiring his brother had anything to do with his decision? You know—*quid pro quo*.

Of great assistance to me during the nine years that I worked at Universal was Irwin Coster. Irwin was the music librarian and general all-purpose authority on music. Without his calming influence, I really think that I most likely would have gone bonkers. Several times, his firm and fatherly guidance stopped me from making a damn fool of myself with either Harry Garfield or Glen.

I was surprised one day to receive a phone call from Mickey Crofford. Mickey, if you recall, had been my favorite recording engineer in New York City, and was the man responsible for my getting the opportunity to work at Colpix Records. Without his recommendation to Paul Wexler's brother, who knows exactly where I might be at this moment in time? As I wrote at the beginning of this book, there were many little twists of fate shaping my career.

Mickey explained that he had relocated to the West Coast and was soon to start work at Universal as the recording engineer on the scoring stage. It really, truly is a small, small world—making it all the more important to be nice to everybody you meet on the way up the ladder of success. You are bound to run into them on the way down.

Quincy was followed by *The Hardy Boys & Nancy Drew*. *The Hardy Boys* starred Shaun Cassidy and Parker Stevenson. Pamela Sue Martin was the star of *Nancy Drew*. The studio felt that the series had great potential, but somewhere along the way the two shows did not find a big enough audience, and went off the air after a short run. So far, all the shows I worked on with Glen were detective shows, of one sort or another. Though my career was thriving, musically, I was stagnating.

Shaun Cassidy and I shared a common interest. He was a successful recording artist, and my previous successes were in the same field. We talked occasionally about making records together, but because of our busy schedules we never managed to get around to it. At present Shaun and his wife live about four blocks from me, and I often see him strolling by my house. Lately, he has been producing and writing TV shows, the most recent being *The Agency*.

♫　　♫　　♫

All About G.A.L.

ON MANY OCCASIONS WHEN I'M being interviewed, or find myself being questioned by fans, or just plain curious people, the one person I've

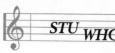

worked with that I am asked about more than any other is Glen Larson. What is Glen Larson *really* like? This seems to be the burning question. As I have stated previously, I've known Glen off and on since 1964. I worked closely with him as a composer for about 15 years, and that's the full extent of my personal relationship.

As I recall, the majority of the time, Glen was soft spoken, rarely used profanity and always seemed composed and in complete control of the daily tribulations of an executive producer. But there were those other times, when he would show no mercy and demand absolute compliance to his demands—which quite often could be a bit unreasonable.

Glen possessed a wry sense of humor that often left you wondering if he was serious, or just kidding. There were many instances when one never did find out.

On the surface, it appeared as though Larson preferred keeping a low profile. You rarely saw any public relations copy on him, and he was not a zealous habitué of wild Hollywood parties—but did entertain quite often at his home(s). What he was, was a very hard and dedicated professional. Even when "on vacation" he would maintain constant communication with his current projects. If Glen asked you to work weekends, you could bet your ass that he was also working. He led by example, and most of us followed. I haven't worked with him for 13 years, but I assume that he is currently still the same old Glen.

Larson loved the excitement and tumult connected with writing and producing TV. He thrived on challenges and impossible situations, that he could solve straightforwardly, or if necessary, deviously. The more chaos there was, the better he flourished. He once told me, confidentially, that when he leaves this world he would like it to be while sitting at his word processor cranking out another script. Glen was an early proponent of 24/7.

He fancied new gadgets and grown-up toys, not unlike Don Kirshner. It was a kick for him to be among first to own a portable cell phone. He had a bowling alley in his home as well as a private jet and a yacht. Glen, had tables permanently held at his favorite lunching spots with "Reserved for Glen Larson" gold plaques placed on the tables. At one point in the 1980s, he simultaneously owned a home in LA, another in Lake Arrowhead, an abode in Palm Springs, and a Hawaiian get-away where Don Ho was a frequent visitor. (Don Ho was also a recurrent guest star on many of Glen's shows.) He also had a house in Malibu, but I'm not quite sure when that was.

Cars were also one of Larson's passions: Especially fast cars. Though he generally traveled around town in a chauffeured-driven limousine, he owned and occasionally drove everything from a Rolls Royce, to Porsche, to Ferrari. He also had an old Cadillac convertible that was his pride and joy. His passionate love of auto racing and speed was one of the reasons for his close friendship with the Smothers Brothers.

I remember one little trip as Glen's passenger while he was piloting his Porsche. He wanted to discuss some music with me, but found that he was needed on the set of the *Hardy Boys* TV show, which was shooting on location at the Burbank Airport. He suggested that I accompany him to the airport and we could talk on the way. Since his wife was using the limo, he decided to drive there in his Porsche.

The airport is approximately four or five miles from Universal Studios. At speeds in excess of 50 miles an hour (on city streets), and a bit of tailgating thrown in, we headed for the airport. At that time I owned an English sports car, and occasionally even I was tempted to do a little adventurous driving. But this ride was ridiculous. I looked down at my knuckles holding on to the door and watched them turn white—just as they had done years earlier during my plane ride in Japan. In his defense, Glen did stop for red lights and managed to miss all the cars and pedestrians on the road.

Among one of Larson's assets was, and probably still is, his loyalty to his staff. If you stood by Glen—on *his* terms—he would show his appreciation by keeping you on as part of his team. Several of his film editors worked for him for over 20 years—which was generally unheard-of. One even came out of retirement to reconnect with Glen. Overall, Larson was a good man to work for—as long as he liked you.

Glen's major forte in TV was his uncanny ability to sell concepts and pilots to the networks. For a period of about 10 to 12 years, he had at least one new show on the air every season. That's a rare talent that very few individuals in the television business possess.

♫   ♫   ♫

Battlestar Galactica

IN 1978, THE GREAT EPIC SAGA of *Battlestar Galactica* was to begin. *Battlestar Galactica* was advertised as being the most expensive television pilot ever made. If I recall, the budget was in the neighborhood of 14 million dollars. Naturally, Universal was considering composers with greater

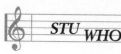

name value than I had, but Glen insisted on me. As I may have mentioned earlier, he was very loyal to those who worked for him—and I was also, in a way, a bit of a lucky charm for him. All the pilots up to now that I was involved in with Larson, were fortunate enough to have become series, and sometimes superstition can be a very strong motivating force. Perhaps that's one of the reasons why Glen often fought like hell for me.

A big-budget epic like this required something sensational regarding the music. Glen asked me what bright ideas I might have. I casually, almost as a joke, suggested hiring a well-known symphony orchestra to perform the score. Glen said, "Why not?" The man's approach to writing and producing, as well as life, was that there wasn't anything or anybody who was ever out of reach. Together, we hurried to Harry Garfield's office (the head of the music department), and presented him with our concept.

As luck would have it, the Los Angeles Philharmonic had just performed the music for a film called *The Turning Point*, a movie concerning the ballet. Harry knew that the orchestra was looking to do more of that same type of work in order to expand its dwindling audience base. Garfield placed a call to Ernest Fleischmann, the Philharmonic's manager, and asked if the orchestra would be interested in performing the score to *Battlestar Galactica*.

Ernest, of course, wanted to know who was composing the music, and who was going to conduct. I had made up my mind that even if I might jeopardize this great fortuitous opportunity, I was not going to accept the assignment unless I was to be the conductor. The conversation went back and forth between Harry, Glen and Ernest, and eventually, to my delight, everyone agreed that I would conduct the orchestra. Glen and Harry were putting their asses on the line for me and I will always be eternally grateful to both of them. As it turned out, I did not let either of them down.

Where to record the score was the next minor obstacle. I had calculated that five days would be needed to do the symphonic part of the score. The synthesized music I could record at other sessions. I discussed it with Harry Garfield and he thought it best to get Ernest Fleischmann involved in the decision. With Ernest on the speakerphone, we tossed around a few possibilities. I personally would have liked Royce Hall where the Philharmonic usually recorded. But there was no film projection available there, which would have meant a remote crew for the film projection—an added expense that the studio was not willing to okay.

Ernest suggested 20th Century-Fox, where the orchestra had recorded the *Turning Point* score. Harry said that unfortunately, that might present a small problem, as 20th was suing Universal over the fact that they felt that *Galactica* was a rip-off of *Star Wars*.

Nevertheless, Harry placed a call to Lionel Newman (still the music director at Fox), and asked if there was any reason why Universal could not rent the scoring stage for *Galactica*. Lionel, in his usual colorful gutter language said, "I don't give a rat's ass about the legal department here, they can go f— themselves. If you want to rent the stage, its yours." All the parts were now in place, and the saga began.

While composing the music for the show, many unforeseen problems were constantly arising. To start with, there were going to be two different versions of the film that had to be scored. There was the American TV movie-of-the-week version, as well as the shorter cut for foreign theatrical release. With neither version in the final-cut stage, the length of every scene was more or less a calculated guess. There were days while working on the score when I wished that we *had* moved to Australia.

Jim Young was originally assigned to me as the music editor, but for some reason, was reassigned to another project and I ended up with Don Woods. Don proved to be an expert at his job, and as a team we worked well together. I asked Nathan Scott (of *Lassie* fame) if he was up to being my assistant on this project, and happily he joined our team. Without Don Woods and Scotty (as Nathan was affectionately known), I would have drowned in a quagmire of editing changes.

To further complicate my upcoming composing efforts, Glen had prepared a rough cut for the network executives to see. He wanted to have music on the soundtrack, and asked me to track the entire film with library music. We are talking about over an hour's worth of music, a major undertaking.

Since my intention was to compose the music in a classical mode, I decided to track the music in the same style. I utilized the music of Stravinsky, Shostakovich, Walton, Honneger, Strauss, Ravel, Phillips and others. The job that Don Woods (my editor), and I did on the score was exemplary. I immodestly state that I thought it was magnificent. The network and studio executives were so delighted with the music that they expressed their desire to have the final score sound similar. Glen, of course, agreed. I'm sure the above-mentioned composers would have been delighted to hear such encouraging news about their work, especially coming from some network *suits*.

Unfortunately, our stellar tracking job came back to haunt me. A great deal of the music I had used for tracking was not in the public domain. Any

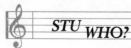

attempt to write something too similar might present problems. In other words, I could be sued for plagiarism. It took a little extra work to make sure that *similar* did not turn out to be *same*.

The *Galactica* script called for a song to be sung by a female trio in the casino on the planet Ovion. I mentioned to Glen that we should get busy writing it, and he spent a few minutes giving me some of his ideas. I worked on the song, but whenever I tried to meet with Glen to finish it up, he was always busy. Then one day he remarked that the song was already written. He, John Tartaglia and Sue Collins had written the song and recorded it. Thanks a lot, Glen.

Needless to say, the composing time generally allowed a composer for a film of this magnitude—especially with the large amount of music to be written—was not granted to me. I was given far less time than I would have liked. When I complained a bit I was given two succinct choices by the powers that be, which were, "Knock it off, just do it," or "We can easily find someone else to do it."

As I composed the music, I kept envisioning some synthesizer sounds mixed in with the orchestra. The Philharmonic did not have a synth player as part of their compliment. I needed to supply my own player and tried to hire my friend Ian Underwood who, in my opinion, was the best around. Ian was not available, as he had decided to go back on the road with Frank Zappa. With a bit of hesitation, since I had never worked with him before, I hired Mike Boddicker. Mike did not let me down and performed admirably.

In August of 1978, I stepped onto the scoring stage of 20th Century-Fox about to complete a journey of about 28 years. The last time that I stood in front of an orchestra of this size was at age 19, when I conducted the symphonic band at my high school. I looked around for familiar faces, or anything else that might help to reduce the tension. Some smiles from a handful of musicians who had worked for me before infused me with resolve.

Finally, I tapped the stand with my baton to get the orchestra's attention, raised my arms in preparation, and… proceeded to give the most important downbeat of my life.

♫   ♫   ♫

13 The Slopes of Everest, But No Summit
Battlestar Galactica

CONDUCTING THE LOS ANGELES PHILHARMONIC in 1978, on the first day of scoring, was at that point in my life the biggest accomplishment of my career. Giving that first downbeat, as I previously stated, was a little on the tentative side. Over the years, I had become accustomed to conducting studio musicians who treated film and television conductors as though they were all Leonard Bernsteins. For studio musicians, being completely cooperative with the composer/conductor was one of the reasons—along with their amazing ability—that would get them recalled for subsequent sessions.

On the other hand, most Symphony Orchestra musicians like to put down any conductor who shows even the slightest lack of control over the orchestra. One little misplaced downbeat or hesitation, and you were up the proverbial *shit creek*. A symphony orchestra is like a finely-trained horse when it senses that its rider (conductor) is a novice and not in complete control, refusing to obey even the most basic commands. The orchestra, like the horse, seems to take delight in making you, the conductor, ill at ease. Musicians can, on occasion, act like real bastards, which in no way undermines their great talent.

As I mentioned earlier, it was fortunate that several members of the Philharmonic had worked with me on many of my TV dates. I was especially grateful to Glen Dickterow, who was the acting concertmaster during the week of recording. After a tenuous and fragile first two hours of recording, Dickterow quietly spoke to the orchestra members and convinced them to give me the respect due a *maestro*. A short time after the completion of the recording, I received a congratulatory letter from Ernest Fleischmann and the orchestra, acknowledging a job well done. (Glen Dickterow, by the way, is currently the concertmaster of the New York Philharmonic.)

Every morning during those five days of recording, my editor Don Woods would present me with Larson's latest editing changes. At times, the changes in the film were so drastic that complete cues were almost unusable. I wrote and re-wrote the music and, occasionally, after lunch I would be presented with even more changes. It was a never-ending battle and quite maddening.

In the afternoon of the first day of recording, I noticed that Lionel Newman and John Williams were in the engineer's booth listening to the music. This seemed odd to me, since *Galactica* was a Universal picture and not a Fox movie. Universal had only rented the studio, so why were they observing my sessions? (Not that it wasn't a kick having John Williams listening to my music!)

I subsequently found out, that John had been requested by Fox's legal department to check out what I had composed, and to make sure that I was not stealing any of his music from *Star Wars*. John was considerate enough to say that my music in no way intentionally tried to copy his, and I was off the hook.

(For the record, I did not intentionally try to copy John's music, nor was I asked to by Glen. Actually, I was simulating Stravinsky, Ravel and Walton, etc.—which was probably what John, had unintentionally done on *Star Wars*. It was/is a common practice used by many film composers—whether they choose to admit it or not. All through the years, film composers have

Who *is* that long-haired weirdo being admired by Glen Larson? Galactica 1978

Conducting the Los Angeles Philharmonic.
Notice the tee shirt advertising *Battlestar Galactica*. 1978

borrowed generously from the great masters: Dimitri Tiomkin, one of filmdom's greatest composers, upon accepting an Academy Award, graciously thanked Brahms, Beethoven and Richard Strauss in his acceptance speech.)

After five days of double-scoring sessions, the recording was completed. Everyone thought that I had done a wonderful job. Glen Larson was happy and, of course, that was my main concern. Glen's being pleased with the score meant that Harry Garfield was also happy. We quickly put together a soundtrack album, and recorded a disco version of the main theme. It became necessary to call the LA Philharmonic back for a day of additional recording when it was discovered that there was some distortion on the tapes from the original session. It proved to be a problem that was 20th Century-Fox's fault, and they were forced to pay for all the additional charges.

Besides the necessity of re-recording some of the music for the soundtrack album, two other problems were to materialize during the preparation for the album's release. Even though I produced the album completely on my own, the producing credit was shared by Sonny Burke and myself. (Sonny was the head of A&R at MCA Records, and it was company policy to credit him on all album releases—unless Sonny agreed to be omitted. In this case, he didn't.) This minor snag did not sit well with me, but there was little that I could do about *company policy*.

I was at home when I received a call that the album was in the process of shipping, even though I had not as yet approved the cover art or the liner notes. This was a key part of my job as producer of the album. Obviously, they had accepted Sonny Burke's approval, which, in my opinion, he had no right to give. I immediately called the record company and insisted that they messenger the items to me. They argued that the album release would be held up because of my demand. Even Glen called me and asked me to forego my approval so that I wouldn't upset the applecart. But I was insistent and within an hour the items were delivered to my home.

The album cover had one glaring omission. Neither my name, nor the Los Angeles Philharmonic's appeared anywhere on the cover. I wasn't sure about the Philharmonic's contract with MCA, but mine definitely included front-cover credits. When I called the record company, they said that all they did was duplicate the Battlestar Galactica "one sheet." This bit of news just exacerbated the problem. Obviously, the one sheet was also incorrect. As an excuse they cited a clerical error, which we all believed to be true—since there seemed to be no rational reason to deny the Philharmonic or myself our proper credits. Clerical error or not, I was pissed. They promised to rectify the error immediately.

A few months later, I discovered that they had inadvertently shipped a great deal of albums without the properly revised credits. I asked that those albums be instantly recalled. The company refused. It took a letter from my attorney (my brother Lee), threatening to sue MCA and Universal before the matter was taken care of. About two years later I received a monetary settlement from MCA in a pleasantly lucrative five-figure range: One more example of nothing going smoothly in the movie and TV business.

The movie was originally broadcast as the pilot episode on TV here in the States, and as a feature film around the rest of the world. Eventually, it was shown as a theatrical feature in the United States.

The soundtrack album was nominated for a Grammy Award. However, it lost to *Close Encounters of the Third Kind*—ironically, a John Williams score. So what else is new? So far I had lost four Grammy Awards: the first to The Tokens; then Jimmy Dean; Henry Mancini, and the last to John Williams. In the words of my dear wife, you can't have everything—but I sure keep wishing and hoping.

Back in the early '50s, when I used to *cruise* the Sunset Strip, I never dreamed that one day my name would be on a billboard in letters big enough for anyone to see for blocks away. Near Laurel Canyon and Sunset Blvd., a giant billboard had been erected advertising *Battlestar Galactica… Music Composed by Stu Phillips Conducting The Los Angeles Philharmonic.*

The bottom of the billboard was a scrolling device that kept running the following: *music composed by Stu Phillips conducting the Los Angeles Philharmonic.*

As I stood there on the sidewalk looking up at the billboard and admiring my achievement, I wished that I could find all the people I knew back in those old days in Hollywood and say, "Guess what, people? I finally made it!" Paradoxically, the billboard was almost directly across the street from where the Garden of Allah (the location of my first cocktail piano job in 1950) used to be; and just above The Black Watch where I also worked. (It was called Derrick's at the time this photo of the billboard was taken.) Such are the ironies of life. Louis Diaz, eat your heart out—and you still owe me a weeks pay from the Chi Chi Club.

Writing the music every week for the *Galactica* TV series was, to paraphrase an old movie, *The Agony and the Ecstasy.* I loved the musical challenge and the chance to write predominately classically-oriented music. But the deadlines were unreal, and on many occasions I was prone to little outbursts of temper while trying to deal with those deadlines. During some of these tempestuous moments, I would refocus on my past life in Hollywood in 1951 and how, back then, I would have given anything to be in this position—and now, here I was. I kept telling myself, "Keep your mouth shut and write. Isn't this what you always dreamed of?"

Similar to the pilot film, editing changes were being made right up until recording time. Every week was a composer's nightmare. Nevertheless, I magically seemed to thrive on the pressure. (Perhaps I caught Glen's work ethic.) I was also fortunate to have Scotty as my assistant, a dear and wonderful man who helped make my job a bit easier. I was proud of the fact that I never missed a deadline. Never missing a deadline also meant never having much family time. Dori and I didn't have an abundant social life during the years from 1978 through 1985, but we made up for it in the 1990s.

In 1983, John Williams, who at that time was the music director of the Boston Pops, said he would like to perform the theme from *Battlestar Galactica* at a Pops concert and asked me to write a special arrangement for him. He also wondered if I would do an arrangement of the theme from

Dori and Stu in Vermont, 1983.
We are considering taking up farming. NOT!

The Twilight Zone. I wrote a *Twilight Zone Theme and Variations* that John liked so much he performed it at several subsequent concerts, and included it, along with *Battlestar Galactica*, on his next Boston Pops CD.

The concert with the Boston Pops where *Galactica* and *The Twilight Zone* were being performed took place during a hiatus in the television season. This time off gave Dori and I a wonderful opportunity to travel to Boston and attend the concert. It was early June and, after the performance, we decided to rent a car and drive to Vermont. I had this annoying itch to visit the farm where my career had had its early beginnings. It was in the parlor of the farmhouse where I had learned the *Rachmaninoff Prelude*, which turned out to be the first step-ping-stone in my modest little career.

When Dori and I arrived in Randolph Center, it took me a little while to get my bearings, but eventually we found the old farm. After 45 years, nothing seemed to have really changed. Unfortunately, the Cooleys no longer lived there, but the new owner said that Mr. Cooley was still alive and living on a farm just a mile or so down the road. We drove there and, sure enough, we found him taking a mid-day siesta in the front seat of an old wrecked car. After a day of reminiscing with him and one of his daughters, I enjoyed a wonderful feeling of fulfillment. I'm not quite sure that Dori found the visit as satisfying as I did, but she put on a good act.

Battlestar Galactica in one form or another has been recorded about 16 or 17 times by different orchestras and groups. I felt very honored when Henry Mancini recorded it and sent me a personally autographed copy of the album.

One recording I'd like to discuss is the one credited to Giorgio Moroder. In actuality it is Harold Faltermeyer who is credited for doing most of the work. The unique feature of the album was that a large portion of the *Galactica* score was done electronically. (All synthesizers.) After listening to the album, I decided to call Giorgio at A&M Records and compliment him on the concept and execution. Mr. Moroder ignored my calls and never got back to me. He becomes one more addition to the list of arrogant and impolite people that I have encountered (and are still encountering), in the recording industry.

Everyone at Universal believed that *Battlestar Galactica* would be a shoo-in for an Emmy Award. However, because of some miscommunica-tion between the studio, Glen and myself—and the added inflexibility of John Leverance at the Academy of Television Arts & Sciences—the music was never even nominated.

To be nominated for an Emmy award in those days, either the studio, the producer, or the composer had to fill out and submit an entry form. The studio thought that Glen was doing it. Glen thought that I was doing it. I assumed that the studio was doing it. It turned out that none of us did it. This little mistake taught me never to *assume* anything in the future.

It was on the day that the entry forms were due at the Academy that I found out that no one had submitted the proper paperwork. I immediately called John Leverance, who was in charge of the Awards division, and in-formed him of the oversight. I asked for an extension of a few hours, so that we could get the entry form to the Academy. John ignored all our entreaties, and refused to grant us any extension.

Another grand opportunity for one of those little gold statues slid by me. It was as much my fault as anyone else's, but John Leverance definitely turned out to be the major villain of this scenario. A little compassion on his behalf would have gone a long way. A nomination and a possible Emmy would have been the *summit* of Everest. Instead, I was left stranded on the slopes. Oh well, I understand from those that have won awards, that all those gold statues do is gather dust. I can live with dust.

The LA Philharmonic recording the music to *Battlestar Galactica*.
That's me conducting... not Andre Previn.

In 1988 I was invited to attend the tenth anniversary reunion of the *Galactica* fan clubs. The event took place at the Sheraton Hotel adjacent to Universal Studios. I never in a million years expected the mania and adoration given to the show, and any and all people who had a hand in its creation. As I entered the hotel, I was pleasantly surprised to see Glen Larson and J.C. (Glen's young wife) present. These *Galactica* conventions may seem a bit outlandish, but they certainly are personal ego boosters.

I had attended two *Monkees* reunions, where I *expected* mania from the people who were present. *The Monkees* after all, was a very successful endeavor, and even though the ex-teenagers who attended were now in their mid-to-late 30s, I could understand their dedication.

But *Galactica* had nowhere near the success or popularity of *The Monkees*, so all this hoopla was rather a big surprise to me. Even so, I somehow managed to revel in the glory. In 1998, *Galactica's* 20th anniversary was celebrated. I was not able to attend, but sent some autographed first pages of the Galactica theme to be auctioned off.

The other day while surfing the Internet on eBay, out of curiosity I punched up *Battlestar Galactica*. No fewer than 2,170 items were listed for sale, including a four-disc CD of the music from the TV series—expertly compiled by Ford Thaxton and Mark Banning—selling for $79. What an unusual and bizarre world we live in.

One of the strangest requests from a fan that I ever received came from two of the participants at the first *Battlestar Galactica* reunion. They told me that they were getting married in about six months, and would like to have the wedding music that I wrote for an episode of *Galactica* (the one in which Jane Seymour gets married), that was played during the nuptials. This piece of music existed only in the TV film and on an audiotape that was my personal copy: Even though it was slightly illegal for me to give them a duplicate of the tape, I did so, and at the next convention they told me all about being married to the *Galactica* music. How about that—Wagner, Mendelssohn, and me!

I recently (1998) traveled to Glasgow, Scotland to re-record the original *Galactica* soundtrack album in digital sound. I was fortunate to have the opportunity to conduct The Royal Scottish National Orchestra, which is a really first-class organization. The CD was released by

Composer John Debney and Robert Townson (at the desk) discussing either music or where to go for lunch, while I listen in. Glasgow, Scotland 1998

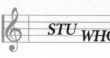

Varése Sarabande records and the recording supervised by Robert Townson.

For the last 20 years there have been many rumors circulating the industry about *Galactica's* return. Richard Hatch was, and still is, trying to get his version off the ground. Glen has also mentioned several times about bringing *Galactica* back as a feature film. Currently *Galactica* is on the drawing board as a series on the USA cable network. To my knowledge, Glen is not directly involved. (Late flash: On March 27, 2001, I had lunch with Tom DeSanto, one of the producers of the potential new *Galactica* TV movie. I was pleased when he told me how much he admired the music to the series. The other producer/director is Bryan Singer. There is a glimmer of hope on the horizon.)

♫   ♫   ♫

Knight Rider… and much more

IN THE LATE '70s AND EARLY '80s, the main hallway in the music building at Universal was being traversed by some of the elite of TV music composers. On any given day you might bump into Mike Post and the late Pete Carpenter; Tom Scott; the aforementioned John Cacavas; Bruce Broughton; Jack Elliott and Allyn Ferguson; Oliver Nelson; Dick Markowitz; Nan Schwartz or Joe Harnell, all of whom were working on Universal shows. And of course, there were always the theatrical film composers who just might wander in and out. It was a diverse group age-wise and in composing ability, but there was one thing we all had in common. We *worked* because some producer liked what we wrote and, as a result, we each carefully safeguarded our particular connections.

Following *Battlestar Galactica*, from 1979 to 1988, my career as a composer was primarily in television. Each show has some little yarn attached to it, but most of the accounts are fairly insignificant in the large scheme of things. I've chosen a few to particularize that you might find interesting.

During *Galactica's* hiatus period, Ron Satloff called to offer me an opportunity to work with him on the *Spiderman* series. I composed a new main title and did six or seven episodes before Ron was replaced by another producer—who of course wanted his own composer and a new theme. (The new composer turned out to be Dana Kaproff, whom I had helped get started in the business during my early *McCloud* days.)

Galactica was succeeded by *Buck Rogers, Knight Rider, B.J. & the Bear, Sheriff Lobo, Benny & Barney* and *Fitz & Bones*, which starred the Smothers Brothers. I was also fortunate to have two movies of the week come my way. First there was a four-hour epic called *Evening in Byzantium*, which was a Glen Larson production. *Byzantium* starred Glen Ford, Erin Gray, Vince Edwards and Shirley Jones. Then in 1981, I scored the remake of *Midnight Lace*, the old Doris Day/Rex Harrison film. This version featured Mary Crosby.

The main theme to *Knight Rider* (starring David Hasselhof) was possibly the first TV theme to be scored almost exclusively for synthesizers. The wonderful synth players that I used were Ian Underwood, Mike Lang, Mike Boddicker (who played on the Galactica session), and Ralph Grierson. All good friends whose talent and expertise was of invaluable help to me. (I cannot mention the above musicians without throwing kudos to Artie Kane, Michel Rubini and Chuck Domanico.)

I was never completely satisfied with the sound of the Knight Rider theme recording, and felt that I could definitely improve it. At the start of every TV season it is necessary to either repay the musicians, or re-record the main and end title music. So at the beginning of the second season, I contacted Universal and asked if I might re-record the main title music.

Even though another composer was writing the show at that time, I offered to redo the recording of the theme gratis. The studio informed me that the network would not sanction any change in the theme music. Even though I reassured them that the changes would only slightly affect the sound and not the musical content, they said absolutely *no*. I had to suffer through five seasons of what I personally considered a mediocre recording.

Any wise person will tell you that you should be thankful for the positives in life and not dwell on the negatives. At the start of the second season of *Knight Rider*, while I was working at Fox, I heard from my spies at Universal that the current producer of *Knight Rider* wanted to replace the main title theme that Glen and I had written. When I informed Glen of this, he was not at all happy, and said he would take care of it immediately. He placed a call to the network brass, and that was the last we heard of any change to the *Knight Rider* theme. That Glen had his name on the theme as co-composer might have given him a strong personal incentive to make sure that the theme was not changed. You think?

While working on *Sheriff Lobo*, I was fortunate to make the acquaintance of Robert Jason, a very multi-talented person. Robert is a wonderful songwriter, as well as a gifted pianist: and as a vocalist has a remarkable ability to mimic other singers. In fact, my first association with Robert was when I needed him to perform a re-creation of Ray Charles' rendition of

"Georgia on My Mind" for the *Sheriff Lobo* main title. For the next few years, Robert and I collaborated on several projects and, even though he now lives in Nashville, to the present day we remain in contact.

Two obviously happy guys...Robert Jason and myself in Denison, Iowa, at the Donna Reed Festival.

In 1979 while toiling away on *Galactica,* I was offered the opportunity to work on a film called *Fast Charlie, The Moonbeam Rider.* The stars of the film were David Carradine and Brenda Vaccaro. The main reason for my being hired was that Universal wanted desperately to save money on the score. Roger Corman had produced the film for $1,200,000. When Universal procured the rights to the film they managed to make a quick deal with one of the TV networks for $1,600,000. That gave Universal a $400,000 profit without lifting a finger. With the picture now a TV movie and no longer a feature film, the music allowance was pared down to TV-budget size. This is where I came in.

Since I was on the scoring stage at least twice a week, they asked if I couldn't take an extra hour or so each session and record some cues to *Fast Charlie.* There was also quite a lot of marching band source music that did not need to be recorded to picture. I agreed with their foxy little scheme, and proceeded to put the wheels in motion. It took me a little over a month to finish recording the score, but the end product was very satisfactory, considering the slightly adverse conditions.

One of the film editors that I was friendly with recommended me to the Universal Studio Tours division. They were putting together a new exhibit, and hired me to write some special music for it. It was the first event that people taking the tour would see, and I got a kick thinking about the millions and millions who would eventually hear my music. About ten years later I checked and found that it was still running. Currently, I have no idea if it is still being utilized.

If it is possible to have pleasant nightmares, then the years 1981-82 were without a doubt, the most heavenly of nightmares I could have ever envisioned. During that season, I was working on three shows at Universal, and the beginning of one at 20th Century-Fox.

Having all of this success should have made me a contented man. But I was not content and wanted more than anything to accomplish the one major achievement that had managed to elude me throughout my career. I wanted desperately to compose the music for a really important, *major* motion picture. (You know the old adage… What you *have*, you don't *really* want—and what you *don't have*, you *must have*.)

I had heard some complimentary things about one composers' agent in particular, which prompted me to call her. I asked her if she would be interested in representing me. Up to this point in my career I had managed to get where I was without the help of an agent or personal manager. (Except for my brief alliance with Al Herman in New York in 1960.) I had always known that having an agent representing you was almost a necessity in my line of work. However, I hated the thought of sharing all my financial gains with someone who had nothing whatsoever to do with getting the assignments that generated my income. As far as making the deals, I had my brother handling the legal end, so basically all my agent would be required to do was *find* the work.

The effort involved in making inroads back into the feature film business is very time consuming. It would have been nearly impossible for me to pursue any leads myself, being as busy as I was fortunate enough to be. This agent showed a great deal of interest in representing me—and why shouldn't she? I'm sure she was well aware of how much money I was earning. I presented her with the following plan that *I* had concocted.

If she were to secure for me an assignment to compose the music for an important, blockbuster film, I would sign with her and give up all my work in TV. I was prepared to give her the usual percentage and also include a percentage of all my BMI residuals in her cut—which, lets face it, was going to amount to a rather large sum in the very near future. Also, if for some reason I were to turn down what she had acquired for me, I offered to pay her a commission on the job regardless of whether or not I accepted it. She basically had nothing to lose, and agreed to the deal and our partnership was underway.

Being as active in the business as I was at that time, I was privy to a great deal of inside information as to who was looking for composers. Whenever I found out some of this early inside info, I would relate it to her. For two years I never even got close to getting any of the assignments involving the leads I gave her. I never even managed to get an interview with a producer or director. However, very curiously and quite suspiciously, several of the pictures that I had called her about ended up being composed by some of her *other* clients. Though I have no concrete proof that anything underhanded was taking place, I sure believed at the time that there might be just one too many coincidences. Obviously, I dropped my association with her ASAP.

Buck Rogers, like *Galactica*, was an enjoyable film to work on. For this picture, Glen decided to handle the theme song all by himself. He wrote a kind of country waltz for the main titles. All I can think of to comment on about the song, is that it certainly was an adventurous and unusual concept. Unfortunately, it was next to impossible for me to integrate this little country waltz into the body of an action score—which left the music a bit on the rambling side, desperately searching for a direction.

After the network viewed a rough dub-down, they informed Glen that they were not happy with the score. They felt that it had no *direction*. (Duh!) Two additional recording sessions were booked and I re-wrote a large number of cues. I composed a new instrumental theme, which I then incorporated into the score. The main-title song remained unchanged. The revised score seemed to make the network execs happy. (Either that, or they ran out of money.) A soundtrack album was put together and quickly released.

The very sexy Erin Gray, co-star of *Buck Rogers*.

Gil Gerard's co-star in *Buck Rogers* was an extremely beautiful actress named Erin Gray. I did not have the privilege of meeting her during the filming of the movie, but at a Hollywood Collector's convention in June of 2001, there she was, signing autographs. I introduced myself and we exchanged autographs. She signed a picture, and I autographed a soundtrack album. It only took 20 years for us to meet.

When the pilot of *Buck Rogers* sold as a series, Glen continued to stay involved with the production for several episodes. I however, was still tied up with *Lobo* and *B.J.* and not available to score *Buck Rogers*. I was surprised one day to discover that Larson was no longer the producer. Either he had decided to turn over the production chores to someone else, or the studio chose to make a change. It was strangely similar to what had happened on *The Six Million Dollar Man* pilot, when Ken Johnson took over producing the series.

During the first season of *Knight Rider*, Glen's association with Universal came to an end, and he moved his operations over to 20ᵗʰ Century-Fox. After two Russ Meyer movies at Fox, I was now back there again, only this time with Glen Larson.

♫   ♫   ♫

The Fortuitous Fox Years

THE FIRST PILOT ON GLEN'S agenda at Fox was *The Fall Guy*. Glen would have liked me to forego writing the shows at Universal but I was living in a state of euphoria which I had no intention of losing. I convinced Glen that, *with a little help from my friends*, I could handle all the work. I had waited all my life to be in such a wondrous state of existence, and there was no way I was going to lose this moment. My work was overwhelming me, which suited me just fine.

Back at Universal—with my able assistant Nathan Scott helping me on *Sheriff Lobo* and *B.J.& the Bear*, and a new second assistant, Bill Broughton, pitching in on *Knight Rider*—I was able to pull off the impossible. With the driving back and forth from Fox to Universal, it was a bit like an old movie title… *If it's Monday it must be Fox… If it's Thursday it's Universal.*

After the first half-season of *Knight Rider*, I had to give up writing the show. The *Fall Guy* pilot had sold, and I now had to make myself completely available for the ensuing series and some of Glen's forthcoming pilots at Fox. The other two Universal shows had not been renewed and I was now down to only one show, and didn't mind a bit.

By 1982, I had finished all of my scoring assignments at Universal, and settled in at 20th Century-Fox. Believe it or not, Lionel Newman was still the man in charge. Every week on the end credits, I was condemned to share the music card with Lionel Newman—who of course had absolutely nothing to do with the supervision of the music on the show. But we eventually did become very close friends, and the Lionel Newman story was finally book-ended. In 1950 he had said no to hiring me. Now, in 1981, he had no choice. I worked for Fox whether or not he approved.

Like previously at Universal, Fox provided no office space to its television or film composers. The only composer with space on the lot was John Williams. John had an office regardless of whether or not the film he was currently working on was a Fox film or some other studios. Lionel treated John as he would his own son. Until Lionel passed away, their relationship was something very special.

Aside from Lionel's colorful use of curse words, there were a few other "Lionel-isms." One of his little quirks was to give nicknames to many of the film composers. His all-time favorite was Lalo *Shit-can* (for Lalo Schifrin). Mine was Stu *Phil-pots*.

Lunch at the music table in the executive dining room at Fox was quite a kick. John and Lionel were the regulars. I had an open invitation whenever I happened to be on the lot, which was generally about twice a week. Also joining the round table occasionally was Herb Spencer (John's orchestrator at the time) and my old friend Arthur Morton (from the *Diner's Club* movie). There may be over 3,000,000 people in Los Angeles, but as you can see, it really is a small town.

While working on the *Fall Guy*, I heard it through the grapevine that Eric Bercovici (the producer of *Shogun*) was about to get underway on a TV series at MGM called *Chicago Story*. I recalled that my friend Jerry London, who was the director of *Evening in Byzantium*, which I had scored, had also been the director of *Shogun*, and it figured that he most likely knew Eric very well. I buzzed Jerry, and he was considerate enough to call Eric and recommend me.

When I met Eric he said that he was pleased to have me on the show, but explained that there was a small problem. The film editor and one of the other producers had already spoken to another composer: one James DiPasquale. James felt that he deserved to do the show because he was originally from Chicago. Logical? Not really!

The compromise solution was that I would write half the shows, and he would write the other half. *Chicago Story* had a wonderful cast of newcomers, including Dennis Franz, Craig T. Nelson and Maud Adams. Although the show only lasted one season, in my opinion it stands as the forerunner of *Law & Order, E.R. and NYPD Blue*. Fortunately for me, MGM was just a stone's throw away from Fox, so I was able to juggle the two shows without too much panic. Also, *Chicago Story* did not call for an abundance of music, which made for a short composing schedule.

Masquerade, an action series starring a young Kirstie Alley, Greg Evigan and Rod Taylor, had a relatively short run of one season. It was a fun show to write music for, since it featured a tourist group working undercover in a different country each week. To be able to write various styles of music each episode is definitely this composer's preference. It kept me reaching for inventive ideas instead of settling for the first thing that came into my head. Various other composers were writing the *Fall Guy* while I was busy working on *Masquerade*.

There was a main-title song in *Masquerade* that was sung over the opening credits of each episode. The recording of this song gave me the opportunity to go to Nashville, renew an old acquaintance, and meet a wonderful country artist named Crystal Gayle. (She of the *long tresses* down to her heels.) Glen sent me to Nashville as an observer, to make sure that the recording of the main-title song met the proper time requirements.

Jimmy Bowen, a very capable and successful record producer, as well as an old golfing buddy from the Music Industry Golf Tournaments, was Crystal Gayle's producer, and in charge of the session. Initially, I felt a little embarrassed about the situation. Jimmy certainly did not need my help producing records. Fortunately, Bowen was very understanding, and I spent most of the day keeping my mouth shut and observing.

The "Nashville Sound." I had heard it on records, but up to now, had never been present when it was being put into practice. Truthfully, to my eyes and ears, a session in Nashville was no different than one in New York, LA, Memphis or London. Instead of reading *notes*, the musicians invented their own secret code. I believe that regardless of the method used in accomplishing the final result, it all comes out sounding like *music*.

Given that I lived only about a mile from Universal Studios, during a rare slow week, I drove to the lot to renew old friendships. Irwin Coster, the librarian, suggested that I get in touch with the then current producer of Buck Rogers. It appeared as though the weekly composing assignments were up for grabs. I met with the producer and subsequently scored three episodes of the show. I utilized my theme from the pilot, which had not

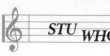

been used by any of the previous composers. It was fun visiting some of my old notes.

♪   ♪   ♪

Peter Guber

AROUND 1983-84, WITH THE SUMMER Olympics about to take place, my brother called to tell me that Peter Guber, a client of his, was planning a musical Olympics album. Peter was looking for someone to help oversee production, and my brother had suggested me. My brother, Peter, and myself were to have our first meeting at a pizza joint in an outdoor mall at the top of Mulholland Drive and Beverly Glen. I will enlighten you that at that time, Peter Guber was "a major player," and a very wealthy man.

As I sat at the pizza joint waiting for Peter, I kept eyeing all the cars driving in. I, of course, was expecting to see him drive up in a Porsche, Rolls, Bentley, etc. Instead, he eventually showed up in a Volkswagen Rabbit. Peter was quite an unusual and interesting man: Definitely, not your average run-of-the-mill VIP.

After explaining his vision of the album, Peter asked me to think about it and present him with some suggestions. I did some preliminary work on the concept and, when I felt I had something concrete to offer, I called him and we set up another meeting. This time he asked me to meet him at the Sports Deli in Century City at about three o'clock.

His secretary met me and said that Peter was running a little late. We waited for quite a long time before he finally showed up. After more discussions about the album, it appeared that if I were to produce this album, it would be necessary for me to travel about the world making deals with international artists and their record and publishing companies. Peter asked if I would have the time, given my current involvement with the *Fall Guy* series. I made a hasty decision on the spot. Peter was a very influential man with major connections in the industry. I reasoned that this might be my best opportunity to finally get that *big* movie I was still coveting.

I told Peter that I might be willing to give up my association with Glen Larson and proceed with the album. Peter was pleased, and said that we would meet again very soon to finalize the plans to go forward.

I went back to Fox and wondered if I should immediately tell Glen, or wait a few days. Then I realized where I was, and what business I was in. This was Hollywood, and I was in show business—where nothing is final until the dotted line is signed. And even then it's not a sure thing. So I decided to wait. It was a very fortunate decision on my part.

Days went by, then weeks, but there was no word from Peter. I finally called his secretary and said that I was patiently waiting to hear from him. She said that she would deliver my message. Weeks turned into months. I called my brother and even he played phone tag with me.

I finally said screw it and tried to forget about the whole mess. The Olympics took place, and one day in a record store I came across the album. The credits read, "produced by Peter Guber." I'll be fair and say that the original ideas that we had discussed were only a part of the concept that constituted the album. Yet, I somehow thought that he at least could have called me and said, *No thanks, I'm going to do it myself.*

If nothing else, I certainly prophesized correctly in thinking that Guber might have been my answer to acquiring that *big* movie. A short time after this episode, Peter Guber and his partner Jon Peters (one of Barbra Streisand's husbands) became the moguls of Sony Pictures. He definitely *would* have been in a position to hire me—so much for that little escapade. I was beginning to accept the ugly fact that *big movies and me* were somehow, not to be.

In total, I composed music for 96 episodes of *The Fall Guy*. There were, all-inclusive, about 112 episodes. Some of those that I didn't score were because of my working on *Masquerade*, and the others were because of Glen's insistence that I jump in and help several other floundering shows. (As though music could *save* any bad show! Cover some bad spots—maybe!)

One of the shows Glen asked me to help revitalize was *Manimal*, a pilot for which I had originally composed the music. The score to *Manimal* was the first time in my career that music I had written was thrown out, and replaced by another composer.

At the outset I was devastated. But my attitude changed when I recalled that no less than Lalo Schifrin, Jerry Goldsmith, Alex North, Michel LeGrand and John Barry (whom *I* once replaced) and other prestigious composers, had seen their scores rejected. Unfortunately, I was in good company.

Among the other shows I worked on during my years at Fox were *Automan*, with Desi Arnaz, Jr; *Rooster*, with Paul Williams and Pat McCormick; *Half Nelson*, with Joe Pesci; and *Highwayman*, with Sam Jones.

The main theme to *Automan* was co-written by Billy Hinsche and myself. Billy, of course, along with Dino and Desi, recorded the songs that David Gates and I wrote for the surfing movie *Follow Me*. Again I reiterate, it's a small town, getting smaller all the time.

Half Nelson was the first show that I scored exclusively with synthesizers. But the circumstances' encompassing the main-title song is what I'd like to comment on first.

Glen was adamant about licensing "I Love LA" by Randy Newman as the opening theme music in the show. Since Lionel Newman was the head of the music department—and also Randy's uncle—Glen assumed that Lionel could get an inexpensive license fee for the song and recording. In this case, studio nepotism did not pay off. The publisher and record company wanted a fee way beyond what 20th Century Fox, or Glen, was willing to pay. As usual, I was asked to replicate "I Love LA."

I called in Robert Jason and he and I proceeded to write the second best song about LA. We called it "LA, You belong to me," and personally, we thought we had written one hell-of-a good song without plagiarizing "I Love LA." In fact, I felt so utterly positive about it that I spent my own money to make a first-class demo—figuring I would eventually be reimbursed by the studio. When we played it for Glen, he was not at all enthusiastic. He asked us to cut out the verse, start with the chorus and expand it. Truthfully, he really didn't seem to like the song at all. We made the revisions and recorded the new version at Fox, and I ate the cost of the demo.

At the dubbing of the show, Glen was still not happy with the song and was constantly thinking of some way to replace it. There was a party at Chasens on the night that the pilot was aired. I arrived not knowing whether or not the song was in or out of the show. Turned out that it was in. I presumed that Glen had run out of options.

During the past 20 years, whoever has heard the original version of the song (with the verse), thinks very highly of it. This has caused me to wonder about Glen's strong dislike of the song. He seemed to be the only person who did not like it. What finally dawned on me is that this was the first time that his name was not included with mine on a theme to one of his TV shows. I had not invited him to join Robert and me in the writing of the original version or, in the re-write. Hmm, I wonder! Nah, it couldn't be—or could it?

Returning to *Half Nelson* and synthesizers, I was discovering that composing is a constant learning experience, and so I began investing in synthesizers and all the electronics that accompany them. As much as I disliked synthesized music (and still do), time marches on, and I needed to keep up with technology.

Back in the late '60s, when I composed the score for *The Name of the Game is—Kill,* I was given a very small budget to work with. I had heard about this new phenomenon called *synthesizers,* and thought that it might be the answer to my budget problem. I was given Paul Beaver's name, and I proceeded to contact him. When it came to synthesizers, Paul was considered the most knowledgeable person in Hollywood at that time.

I went to his studio, which was as big as a warehouse, and looked over his equipment. I'm not exaggerating—it stretched from one wall to the other, at a height of about six feet. There were so many cables plugged in that it looked like a scene out of a bad science-fiction movie. I soon found out that this was an early version of a Moog synthesizer. (That same equipment now measures about 48 inches by 16, and at times even less.)

After recording the score with six electrified cellos, electrified woodwinds, electrified keyboards (harpsichord and piano), I had Paul Beaver come in the following day and set up his equipment in the booth for overdubbing. It was quite a weird scene, which is beyond description. Cables, wires, waveform knobs, white noise gizmos, gates etc. etc. were all over the booth. Suffice it to say, all went reasonably well. (It was like a scene from the film *2001-A Space Odyssey*: Only this wasn't Hal—it was Paul).

In Like Flynn was a challenging show that I got great satisfaction writing. It was a two-part movie of the week that had romance, adventure and lots of action. It bore an amazing similarity to *Romancing the Stone.* It seemed that Glen was back to developing hit movies into television shows.

There is an amusing anecdote concerning the title music for *In Like Flynn.* Glen had me come to his house to discuss the main theme to the show. As I sat at the piano, we talked about the possibility of using an existing classical piece of music. After aimlessly playing through some Bach, Dvorak and Wagner, I segued into a very well known theme from Handel's *Water Music.* He liked it and asked me to modify it so that it would work with the show. Since all of Handel's music is in the public domain, there would be no music-clearance problems. I utilized the theme throughout the film and it seemed to work perfectly.

When the screen credit sheet was delivered to me, I noticed that the theme was credited as being written by Stu Phillips and Glen Larson. There was no mention of George Frideric Handel. When I mentioned this to Glen he became quite annoyed with me. Glen's answer to my request—

that we show that our theme was based on a melody by G.F. Handel—was put very simply: "I don't seem to recall Handel being at my house and taking part in our meeting." At first I thought that he was being funny, his wry sense of humor taking over: But I quickly realized that Glen was dead serious. Enough said.

♪   ♪   ♪

Lee Majors

DURING THE FIVE YEARS I worked on *The Fall Guy*, I had on many occasions met Lee Majors. Stories abound about Lee's private and public life, and I don't believe that it's for me to expand on them. I didn't know him that well. Most of what I heard was second- hand information.

In my brief visits with him I found him to be friendly and considerate. He always waved to me whenever we would see each other on the lot, and overall treated me with professional respect. When the series finally ended, I felt that I wanted to let Lee know how much I valued our relationship. I bought a Ferrari watch and had an inscription engraved on the back. I presented it to Lee one day as he came out of his trailer. I do believe that he was touched by the thought. As far as *I* am personally concerned, he is another one of the *nice guys*.

During my stay at 20th, another one of those wonderful people called *music editors* helped save my sanity. Mark Green was an indispensable part of my life at Fox. After all these years I have newfound admiration for every music editor that I ever worked with. Bless you all. And while I'm in this complimentary frame of mind, a big thanks to Jo Ann Kane, librarian *extraordinaire*; Armin Steiner, recording engineer *par excellence*; Mike Rubin (and his talented and lovely wife, Claudine), and Carol Farhat, who always had and, still has, a smile for everyone.

Mike Rubin, who had been the orchestra contractor at Fox since 1948, passed away in November of 2001. A wonderful memorial service was held for him on the scoring stage of 20th Century Fox in December. My wife and I attended and I renewed many old acquaintances. John Williams was there as well as Carol Farhat, Randy Newman and many others.

Socially during these years, Dori and I spent a great deal of time with Sam Riddle and his wife Adrienne. Sam and I had been casual acquaintances through the years when he was a disc jockey. The exact circumstance of our becoming close friends is locked away in one of my missing brain cells. I got involved in the beginnings of several of Sam's projects, but never seemed to be around at the end of them. However, I was invited to be a judge on *Star Search*. I have a jacket and a letter from Ed McMahon as souvenirs. Whoopee!

The Highwayman series proved to be the last show I would do at Fox. After the initial pilot, Glen again packed up his company and returned to Universal, albeit more of an independent producer than he originally was.

Larson and I were, little by little, losing our once-close relationship. I was accustomed to having a reasonably sized orchestra for scoring, but Glen was now more of an independent producer without studio money to bail out his sometimes excessive over-spending. He was resolute about trying to keep expenditures, especially the music budgets, as low as possible. Several people convinced him that with synthesizers, they could turn out much cheaper and more up-to-date scores. Glen went along with this philosophy, and I found myself not being called to do any more *Highwayman* episodes.

I became a bit disenchanted with the situation at this juncture, so I called Glen and told him that if he wanted synths, I could give him synths. I reminded him of the scores to *Half Nelson* and the theme to Knight Rider, which were *predominately* electronic. He acquiesced and hired me for two more episodes, but it was becoming obvious that my relationship with Glen was on the wane.

Highwayman was soon dropped from the network schedule, and I found myself unemployed for the first time since 1973. It was now 1987 and, since 1959, I had written music for nearly 350 television episodes, pilots and movies of the week. I had produced a large amount of successful records and managed to mix in about 25 feature films. Instead of feeling depressed, which would have been quite natural, I found myself breathing a big sigh of relief. Now I could reintroduce myself to my wife and children.

♫   ♫   ♫

14 Epilogue
It Ain't Over, 'til it Says Fine

AFTER GLEN LARSON HAD LEFT FOX in or about 1987, and moved back to Universal, I received a call from him to do one more TV show. After the *Highwayman* series was cancelled, Glen came up with a story concept dealing with the fighting in the Pacific Theater during World War II. It was a pilot/movie-of-the-week called *Road Raiders* (starring Bruce Boxleitner), which unfortunately, did not make it as a series.

The story called for a great deal of source music, all of it reflecting the years 1941-45. It was quite a lot of fun recreating some of the old big-band records of that period. Especially since a several of the musicians I hired had actually played on some of the original recordings.

Since our last collaboration, Glen and I have met each other a few times since then and there are always warm handshakes and embraces between us. Several times in the last ten years, I called Larson to inform him of some current successes we were having with old projects that we had worked on together. Glen took my calls almost immediately, even when he was at lunch or on the set. I've always admired him for that.

My personal relationship with Larson has remained the same during the 15 years I was actively associated with him. We were friends—sort of. During all the time that I worked for him, we saw each other socially about once a year. That would generally be lunch in the late spring, when the television season was on hiatus. The one really important social event that Dori and I were invited to—along with hundreds of others—was Glen's wedding, when he married his second wife, J.C. (Janet).

Other people who worked for Larson seemed to be closer to him socially than I was, and were often invited on his boat or as guests at one of his many homes. *I* was never invited. Yet, the feeling among Glen's staff was that he and I were very close friends. My phone calls he usually answered, while others he very often disregarded. Our unusual friendship of many years seems to still exist.

Just recently, about three years ago, a song titled, "Ain't That Just the Way," which Glen, Bruce Belland and I wrote back in 1974, which you may recall was sung by Barbi Benton in an episode of *McCloud*, became a big hit all over the world—except in the United States. Unfortunately, it was not the Barbi Benton recording that was a hit, but a new record by a singer named Latrisha McNeal. I am not too fond of her rendition, but I enjoyed the feeling of once again being associated with a hit record.

The *Knight Rider* theme also experienced a rebirth, and was utilized by two different *rap* artists (Busta Rhymes and Timbaland & Magoo), as the underlying music sample on their records. Fortunately, everything old seems to be coming around again.

Television is a medium that seems to breed a distinctive kind of producer. I believe that the *sound of silence* on any television show is a sound that most TV producers cannot tolerate. They appear to have an intrinsic fear that even one brief moment of dead air on the screen will cause the audience to rise from their seats, go directly to the kitchen, bathroom or, heaven forbid, to the bedroom for a little wrestling between the sheets. As a result, we get laugh tracks, sound effects, off-camera dialogue and music that exist for no other apparent reason than to fill a few seconds of silence on the screen.

Glen Larson, along with about 90% of all other television producers, believes in this philosophy. Because of his insistence for more and more music, *I* have earned a great deal of money. The arithmetic is quite simple: the more music in the show, the more money I eventually earn in residuals. Two current successful producers that come to mind, who are the exception to the rule and use a very limited amount of music on their shows, are Dick Wolf (*Law & Order*) and Steven Bochco (*NYPD Blue*).

During the time I was working on *Road Raiders*, I decided once again to try my luck with an agent. My main purpose was to have him get me back into the feature-film business, as I had had enough of car chases and episodic television. Though I had failed ten years earlier with a different agent, I was still searching for that elusive *blockbuster* film to write. I explained to my new agent that my main objective was feature films or a mini-series on television. That's it!

The first thing that he hit me with, was informing me that he wanted to drop all the old credits from my résumé. He said that they made me appear too old. When I replied that, conversely, my long list of credits showed how much *experience* I had, he told me that experience was no longer an essential factor in getting work. I seem to remember that back in 1950, my *lack* of experience was the main reason for Ray Heindorf and Lionel Newman *not* hiring me. What happened to change all this? I think I know the answer, but that's probably an entire book by itself.

That news about my age was a real kick in the head. It was not the kind of thing that I needed to hear in these, my later years. After making countless demo tapes for a bunch of *child* producers, I finally said, enough. Our relationship lasted about two years, at which time this agent procured for me absolutely nada… zip. I have noticed, that lately I don't see or hear his name mentioned anymore when anyone refers to composer's agents. I'd like to think that maybe he also became too old and passé. Revenge can be sweet.

♫　　♫　　♫

Semi-Retirement

IN 1989, MY DEAR WIFE threw a party for my 60th birthday. About 90 people showed up for the gala at The Beverly Wilshire Hotel. Shelley Fabares was there, as well as Paul Petersen and James Darren. I became a little

James Darren, Shelley Fabares, the birthday boy and Paul Petersen.
Do we really look 28 years older? Personally, I think we all look great.

maudlin when I started to recount to the audience my early association with them in 1961. They were so young then. Come to think of it, so was I. Lou Shaw, from *Quincy* was at the party. So were Mark Green and Don Woods, two of my music editors from the Universal and Fox days.

(About ten years later at my daughter Julie's wedding, Jimmy Darren surprised the whole gathering by proceeding unannounced to the bandstand, and extemporaneously singing, "You'll Never Know" to the delight of Dori and myself. This of course, was the song played at our wedding and it is still our favorite song.)

The party was an absolute blast. I wrote some self-deprecating parodies, which my wife and daughters performed. Also my nephews Eric and Derek sang a song. Even some of my non-show-business friends were willing to get up to the mike and make fools of themselves attempting to sing.

The Phillips family and Dori's brother Wynn Farrell.
Bottom three: Sammy Fain, my mother and Dori.
Toni is behind Sammy and I'm behind my mother.
To my left is my nephew Eric, then Wynn, Julie and my sister-in-law Marla.
My brother Lee and my nephew Derek are in the back.

My mother, ham that she was, sang a song for me; accompanied at the piano, of course, by Sammy Fain. Sammy also performed one of his "And then I wrote" medleys. Sadly, this turned out to be his last public performance. Several months later he passed away. Just this year, I donated the video of Sammy's last performance at my party to ASCAP. They were very pleased to receive it and it is now a part of their historical archives.

At the end of the party as I thanked everyone in song (ironically, it was a parody of one of Danny Kaye's songs), the final line of the lyric was " I've just retired." Nobody at the party took it seriously. Nobody, that is, except me.

My decision to retire was based on the fact that I was no longer finding creative fulfillment scoring car chases and doing episodic television. Earning money is always a pleasant endeavor, but it loses its luster when the work that you do does nothing to satisfy the inner you. Coupled with my agent's failure to reach the type of film producers that I eagerly wanted to work for, I decided to devote my time to several of my hobbies.

As I had stated earlier on in this book, I had an innate ability towards art. I saw this as a perfect opportunity to devote more of my time to it, which I subsequently have.

I had now become more serious about my tennis, and wanted very much to improve and reach a higher level of proficiency. I had no excuses for not improving, since I now had an abundance of time in which to practice.

Dori and I were finally able to travel about the world without my having to worry about my being called back to LA on some recording or writing deadline. I also wanted to experiment in the classical field, with some ideas I had been kicking around for years. All in all it appeared that I had many interesting projects to keep me busy.

Lou Shaw, the co-creator of the *Quincy* TV show, who had attended my birthday party, called me about a year later to ask if I might be interested in collaborating with him on a re-write of a musical show he had been working on. For a little over two years, off and on, Lou and I worked on the songs. We wrote a great deal of new material and eventually recorded a demo. To the dismay of Lou and myself, the show did not attract any backers, and as far as I know it is currently in Limbo, wherever that is.

One of the singers I recommended to perform on the demo was Lynn Carey. It had been many years since I had last seen Lynn at the recording of *Beyond the Valley of the Dolls*, and I was delighted to discover that she seemed to have lost none of her great talent. She also hadn't lost any of her problems. Like a bad penny, troubles seem to follow her wherever she goes.

Mort Kasman, my friend from my commercial days back in the 1960s in New York City, also called me about a show that he was trying to put together. It was a period piece and, similar to *Road Raiders*, took place during World War II. It was called *Swingtime Canteen*, and featured music

associated with World War II. I was to be its music supervisor. After four years of trying to get it off the ground as a film or TV show, I do believe the project is now a dead issue. Maybe it's also in Limbo. Limbo may be getting a bit overcrowded. (Just recently, I noticed that the original theater show is once again on tour.)

In retrospect, my decision to retire may have been a tad premature. Several composers, approximately the same age as I am, are currently writing film and TV on a continuous basis. My wife insists that it's not too late for me to re-enter the film-composing field. I personally have had enough of the business. But there are still those occasional days when I find myself once again *wishing and hoping* for the opportunity to do just one more movie. A special one… A big one… A blockbuster! (For *Galactica*, I'll un-retire.)

One of the results of renewing old friendships with Shelley Fabares and Paul Petersen at my birthday party was having them invite me to participate in The Donna Reed Performing Arts Festival in Denison, Iowa. For six years, between 1990 and 1996, every June I would spend eight days in Denison, lecturing on all aspects of the music business to people of all ages. I also assisted in the production of the Musical Theater Workshop, and wrote a few parodies and occasionally performed.

In Denison, I had the extreme pleasure of working alongside some wonderful show-biz troupers. People like Bonnie Franklin (*One Day at a Time*), Karen Morrow (of the Broadway stage), and Eddie Foy Jr. (one of the Seven Little Foys), whom I had worked with during my days at Screen Gems. Jimmy Hawkins (*It's a Wonderful Life* and *The Donna Reed Show*); Gigi Perreau (a child star of the early days of TV); Alan Young (of *Mr. Ed* fame) and Lloyd Schwartz (*Gilligan's Island* and *The Brady Bunch*) were also regular attendees. On several occasions, Lynn Carey showed up.

It wasn't by accident that Lynn was at Denison. After her mother Betty had divorced Macdonald Carey, Betty married Grover Asmus, who had previously been married to Donna Reed—after Donna had divorced Tony Owen. Sounds a bit like a soap opera script, doesn't it? Maybe it's a sitcom idea waiting to be born.

Grover Asmus, along with Shelley Fabares, Paul Petersen, Jimmy Hawkins and Ann McCrea, were the founders of The Donna Reed Festival. It never ceases to amaze me, how my association with Donna Reed would affect my life from 1961 all the way to 1996. And how people I met along the way, some of whom had no direct connection to her, would eventually become a part of my life's continuous merry-go-round.

The group from The Donna Reed Festival in Shelley's home. circa 1964
<u>Seated-left to right</u>: James Byrnes/Ann McCrea/Shelley Fabares/Kathleen Nolan/Andrea Muller.
<u>Middle row:</u> Susan Williams/Jeff Jancarek/???/Patti Petersen/Dawn Nelson/Evelyn Jensen/Barbara Mallory/Norma Connolly.
<u>Across the back</u>: Mike Farrell/???/Jimmy Hawkins/Half of an unidentified face/yours truly/Paul Petersen/???/Lloyd Schwartz/Grover Asmus.

Sharing my experiences in show business with such a varied group of talented people has been very satisfying to me. I really enjoyed those years, and the people in and around Denison. I cherish the flattering letters that I received from many of the young per-formers. I found great satisfaction in recounting many of the episodes you have read about in this book (excluding the sex), to groups of eager listeners. I subse-quently lectured at The College of Santa Fe, New Mexico and at UCLA.

The last year that I lectured at The Donna Reed Festival, I met a very talented young piano prodigy. His name was Jeremie Michael-Pigman. His brilliant keyboard artistry inspired me to complete a project that I had been working on, off and on, for about ten years. I had started writing a piece for piano and orchestra but

Jeremie Pigman and myself at the 1997 recording. Lucas Sound Studios.

had never finished it to my satisfaction, and lost interest in the project. When Jeremy agreed to learn the composition and perform it, I decided to drag it out of the closet and try to complete it.

The work is a theme and variations, not unlike the Rachmaninoff *Variations on a Theme of Paganini*. My piece is a difficult one to perform, for both the pianist and the orchestra. I sent the piano part to Jeremie (he lived just outside of San Francisco), and a few months later he called to say that he was prepared to play a large portion of it for me. I sent him a plane ticket to LA, and he flew down and stayed at my house. When I heard him play the excerpts that he had learned, I was convinced that he could handle the entire piece.

One of the other music projects that I dove into after my retirement was the orchestration of two Beethoven piano sonatas for symphonic orchestra. I decided to take a small gamble and record the *Piano Variations* and one of the Beethoven sonatas, paying for them out my own pocket. I made arrangements to hire a community orchestra in San Francisco led by Urs Steiner, and do the recording at Skywalker Sound in Marin County (George Lucas' studio). In June of 1997 Dori and I drove up to San Francisco for the rehearsal and subsequent recording.

Much to my dismay, the Sinfonietta orchestra that I had hired was not up to the task of performing the music as professionally as I had envisioned. As a result, I squandered a great deal of money on the project. I could be philosophical about all this and say that we all *live and learn*, but at my age it's a little late for that old homily. Jeremie's performance, however, was outstanding. The young teenager proved to be the consummate pro. At least I was right about him. Subsequently, Jeremie informed me that he was accepted into the Juilliard School of Music in New York City. I heard from him just last year and he informed me that besides studying at Juilliard, he was playing cocktail piano at various clubs and hotels in New York.

In late September of 1997, I received a phone call from England, from one Chris Phipps. Chris was an organizer (for lack of a better word), and called to tell me that a Dutch TV production company was making plans to film a special about the Marcels. They were interested in finding any pertinent pictures and documents concerning the Marcels, and thought that I might be able to help.

IDTV Culture (the name of the Dutch company) was producing a series of TV shows called *Single Luck*, having to do with recording artists who basically had only one monster hit, and only minor success thereafter. *Un-*

fortunately, the Marcels fit neatly into that category. When I was told that the Dutch company was travelling to Pittsburgh in October to film the group for three or four days, I offered to go to Pittsburgh and contribute what help I could. Jean Marc van Sambeek (the producer/director) was delighted at my offer, and arranged for me to join them there in late October.

When I met Jean Marc in Pittsburgh, he told me that he had decided to feature me in the show along with the Marcels. The opening scene was to be the reuniting of the Marcels and myself, after not seeing each other for some 33 years. The Marcels' new manager owned a hot dog and hamburger joint, and the following scenario was set up by Jean Marc.

I was to be sitting casually at the counter eating a hot dog, and one by one, at different intervals, each Marcel would enter the place, see me, and then react. The Marcels were not told that I was coming to Pittsburgh. Naturally, the surprise at seeing me was unexpected and real, making the ensuing emotional moments genuine and sincere. It was a very heartwarming experience, and there was a feeling of love and admiration present.

For the next few days, in a steady chilly-fall drizzle, we all traveled around the environs of Pittsburgh filming and reminiscing. A particularly inspiring moment was hearing the group sing a slow *a cappella* version of "Blue Moon," while visiting the grave of Gene Bricker, one of the recently deceased Marcels. The final scene in the TV show is the Marcels singing

S.O.C.
PROUDLY
PRESENTS

THE ORIGINAL MARCELS

OCT 26, 1997

live at an Oldies Doo Wop show. I attended the show, and was acknowledged from the stage by the group. This was a memorable few days, and I must admit that I loved every corny moment of recollection, of a time long past.

To further depict the sometimes-disillusioning quirks of life, I offer the following illustration. Feeling that the time had come for me to thank some people who had, to a degree, a profound influence on my life, I sent a letter to Morton Gould. In the letter I tried to refresh his memory about our meeting in 1947. Then I mentioned some of my successes, and thanked him for his part in making many of my fantasies come true. I never received an answer from him, and soon forgot about it.

Sometime in the late 1980s, at an ASCAP party that Dori and I were invited to by my mother and Sammy Fain, I spotted Morton Gould. I approached him and politely introduced myself. I mentioned the letter I had written and our meeting in 1947. He tried desperately to ignore me—even though I was trying my best to thank him for what he did—and was about as rude as anybody I had come in contact with throughout my career. That helpful, understanding, considerate man that I had idolized for most of my life, turned out to be a *big horse's ass*.

I despise sounding bitter or cynical, but throughout my career there were, unfortunately, a few too many instances of people who fit into the above category of *horse's ass*. Even though I tried as hard as possible to be one of the nice guys in the business, I often wonder how many individuals placed *me* in that inglorious group. Oh well, too late now to worry about it.

During my golfing days, one of my frequent links buddies was Irwin Kostal. Irwin had won Academy Awards

A group of golf nuts from the Music Industry Golf Tournament. <u>Left to right:</u> Irwin Kostal/Nathan (Scotty) Scott/Me, with very long hair/three guys who I don't know and Eddy Manson.

for *West Side Story* and *The Sound of Music,* and was considered one of the premier arrangers in the country. Irwin had two grand pianos in his home, and his wife was prodding him to sell one. Dori and I bought Irwin's Hamburg Steinway grand for a very good price. Like a high-quality piece of art, it has increased in value over the last 20 years by at least 200%.

With my retirement and no more deadlines, Dori and I took up traveling in a big way. We sometimes toured by ourselves, and other times with a group called People to People. It was a tennis group sponsored by the U.S. Department of State. We were, in a way, goodwill ambassadors from the USA. The group traveled to some far-out places, and played tennis with the local residents. Peter and Siggie Davis, a wonderful couple, were our guides. We played tennis in South Africa, Namibia, Denmark, Sweden, The Soviet Union, Indonesia, Australia, New Guinea, China, Taiwan, Malaysia, Morocco, and many other exotic places.

One of these trips took us to Germany, where we spent four days in Berlin. While traveling through Berlin to the tennis club, we passed an odd-shaped building. Dori pointed out the building to me, and thought that it slightly resembled the spaceship on my TV show *Battlestar Galactica.* When I questioned the driver about the building, he replied that it was generally referred to by most Berliners as the "Die Galactica." What a crazy world!

When Dori and I visited Australia, we couldn't help but recall 1972-73, when we were actually considering moving to Sydney. As it turned out, Australia has become a major player in the film business. I just might have been right about the possibilities of furthering my career "down-under." We will never know the answer to that question, but I doubt that it could have turned out much better than my present circumstances.

Lately, I have spent my time trying to break into the classical music field. It's proving to be harder than I thought it would be. It seems to be a completely closed shop. I can't say that I have been rejected. I simply have not had any answers to my letters, E-mails, faxes or phone calls. I have experienced more brush-offs in the last four years, than I did for the last 40. At times I feel like I'm back in Hollywood, circa 1951, trying to get someone, anyone, to pay attention to me. Maybe tomorrow, who knows?

I was fortunate to have several requests from orchestras to perform a suite of music from *Battlestar Galactica,* which I had prepared. Since all of the *Galactica* music is at the Universal Studios lot, I have relied on the expert assistance of Julian Bratolyubov, the current librarian at Universal, to help get me through any and all problems that might arise. And believe me, there have been problems.

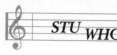

In 1997, I received an invitation to attend the 50-year reunion of my high-school graduating class. Dori and I flew to New York and, personally, I must reluctantly admit that I was looking forward to seeing old friends from the past. What made the trip even more inviting is the fact that Dori was a graduate of The High School of Performing Arts, which, as I mentioned earlier, has now been integrated with Music & Art, and become The LaGuardia School of Performing Arts. Unfortunately, Dori is not into the entire alumni scene. Actually, she doesn't even like discussing it.

The dinner party took place on a Hudson River sightseeing boat. The whole vessel was reserved for the group and, though the entire idea seemed a trifle hackneyed, it turned into a memorable event.

I was able to rekindle my acquaintance with Cy Coleman and James Yannatos, and renewed a friendship with Arthur Lilienstein and his wife Estelle. I had known Arthur only casually during my school days at M&A. The four of us hit it off, and we spent a great deal of time together. A year later on a trip to Florida, we met them for dinner, along with my cousins Iris and Leon Krause and continued our friendship. (When I was in my teens, my slightly older cousin Iris escorted me to my first opera. It was Carmen at the Met, with Rise Stevens. I somehow have never forgotten that night.)

The concert at the school was given in honor of the Class of '47, and we all stood up to enthusiastic applause and took a bow. I presume the reason that we got such a big ovation from a group of teenagers, was that they were surprised that we were still alive. Longevity deserves to be rewarded, especially by those looking ahead to eventually being in the same circumstance.

One enterprising alumnus arranged for Mayor Giuliani of New York and President Clinton to write a personal congratulatory note to each individual graduate. The two letters look very impressive hanging on my dining room wall. All in all, as reunions go, this one wasn't half-bad.

Toni, my oldest daughter, has continually made us proud of her determination in achieving her goals. She has risen from menial jobs to her present employment with one of the most prestigious law firms in LA. She has her own beautiful home, and soon I know she will meet the man of her dreams. She is the best, deserves the best, and should hold out for the best. (Late news flash: Toni has met *the* man. She and Brad Boim will be married this spring... 2002.)

At one time, Toni used to have two dogs. The story of how Dori and I became the owners of Toni's dog Jasper, is quite amazing. Jasper was a runner. Show her an opening in the fence, and she would leave to pay a visit to any and all neighbors. If there were no openings, then she would go over or under the fence. It got so bad that we had our phone number put on Jasper's dog tag. Since Toni worked in Beverly Hills and lived in the Valley, it fell on Dori or I to go and retrieve Jasper.

On the occasion of Jasper's last great escape, Dori took the phone call from the man whose yard Jasper had wandered into. She gave me the address and the man's name, which was Nick Carras. As I drove to his house, I kept thinking that I once knew a fellow named Nick Carras—but that was way back in 1952, and this was 1999. It couldn't possibly be the same person—or could it? Nah.

As I drove up to the address, there was Jasper, sitting in the driveway awaiting her ride home. With her was a very familiar-looking man. As I got out of my car, he walked towards me, extended his hand, and said "Stu, remember me? I'm Nick Carras. We worked together several times back in 1952." Talk about coincidences, of all the driveways in Los Angeles, my daughter's dog picks the driveway of someone I haven't seen for almost half a century. As I've stated many times, this is a small town. Nick and I have re-established our friendship since our meeting two years ago.

In many portions of my story, I have often mentioned Morton Gould and Dave Rose. I have come full circle with Morton Gould. Now meeting with Nick Carras was to complete the Dave Rose segment.

In filling in the empty years between 1952 and the present, Nick said that in the '60s and '70s, he worked for Dave Rose as his assistant and part-time ghostwriter. Now, with that revelation, all the segments of my career were now neatly tied together.

With Jasper's last escapade over, Dori and I suggested to our daughter that we keep the dog for a short time, and allow her to get a bit of rest from the constant anxiety of worrying about Jasper's wanderings. Jasper has decided that she likes our home, since we are here most of the time, and all she was really looking for was *people*-company. Jasper's roaming days are now over.

To write about Jasper and not mention anything about our other two dogs would be criminal. Lucky, a white Hungarian sheep dog arrived at our house one Easter morning in the early 70s. She was an abandoned puppy, left unannounced in our yard by her owner. She died some 15 years later, and during her stay with us brought nothing but good luck to our family. She was aptly named.

Rerun, a ten-pound shih tzu, was also a foundling. She joined our family in 1988 and shared her home with Jasper until March of 2002, when she went to doggie heaven.

Julie, my youngest daughter, got married a few years ago. She chose a wonderful man. Warren Stein is the perfect son-in-law, even though he is from Great Britain (we kid you Warren), and we love him for who and what he is, and for the way he treats Julie.

My brother Lee, who in 1963 started his music-business career at Mitchell, Silberburg & Knupf, is now a managing partner at Manatt, Phelps & Phillips and regarded by those, whose opinions count, as one of the premier attorneys in the music business.

Writing this book has gained me a new friend. As you may have noticed, the editor of this book is Alex Patterson. Alex's kind compliments about my writing ability motivated me to show him about a half-dozen story ideas I had drafted during the last 20 years. His favorable critique of my work has encouraged me to finish one screenplay and write another. Two of my ideas he liked so much, that we are now collaborators on a musical comedy and a TV sitcom. Who knows? With a great deal of good fortune, I might find myself writing—"Stu... Now You *Know* Who, Part Two."

♫　　♫　　♫

15 If There is a Foreword,

Then There Must Be an After-word

IT'S BEEN A LONG AND EXCITING ride. From working as a copyist on *The Milton Berle Show*, to playing in a cocktail lounge on Sunset Blvd. in 1951, to conducting the Los Angeles Philharmonic. I have labored, lived and loved, all with reasonable success. And best of all, I am loved by a wonderful woman—my wife Dori.

It always fascinates me when I revisit my past and find that my most auspicious endeavors came in two areas of music that I had no intention of ever pursuing. I never had aspirations of becoming a record producer, nor did I ever originally desire to be a television or film composer. But, somehow, it's those two careers where I was most successful. Actually, all I ever wanted to be was a first-rate arranger. It was a modest goal.

Well, that's about it. It's now March 2002. September 11th is in the past and the country is, for all intent and purpose, at war. *Battlestar Galactica*, which as I stated earlier, was about to be remade, was at the last moment postponed and put on hold due to the defection of the director, Bryan Singer, to his *X-Men 2* project. Tom DeSanto, the producer, assures me that the project will still go forward. I'll be patient.

I also just found out that *Knight Rider 3000* is about to get underway. I noticed that Glen Larson is credited as Executive Producer. I'm not sure if that is just a contractual thing, or Glen is really involved. I guess I'll have to call him and find out.

Throughout the years, André Previn achieved worldwide fame as one of the world's greatest conductors, won several Academy Awards, was married to a famous movie star and a lyricist named Dory. He is admired as one of the world's musical giants. But I'm not the least bit jealous. I think that after all is said and done, I have definitely *topped* André Previn. You see, *I* have Dori, and *he* hasn't.

So Long…for now

Self-portrait by... Guess who?

ADDENDA

DUE TO THE LONG, DRAWN-OUT process of preparing a book for publication, I find that what were my final reflections concerning "*Stu Who?*" are now a bit antiquated. Between March and June of 2002, there are a few updates as well as several new events I would like to include in this book.

♫   ♫   ♫

IN MY LAST REFERENCE TO *Battlestar Galactica*, I stated that in spite of Bryan Singer's defection to the X-Men 2 project, Tom DeSanto was still highly optimistic about a 21st Century *Galactica* remake. About two months ago I discovered, through the *BSG* fan club that Tom was no longer involved. USA Films and the Sci-Fi Network had assigned three other individuals to it. The *BSG* fan clubs are not happy with the new people in charge; it appears their intentions are rather different from the show's original concept. Not keeping to the initial concept translates into not using most of the original cast, and probably going in a different direction than the large orchestra and classically-oriented music that was a signature of the series. So my anticipated return to once again working on *Galactica* seems to have hit a major snag. There is one slim ray of hope: There are petitions being sent to the "big brass"—signed by thousands of loyal fans—for a return to the *Galactica* of old that, with luck, might dissuade the new team from dumping the old concept. Meanwhile, on another front, Glen Larson is still attempting to get his own competing feature-film version of *BSG* off the ground.

♫   ♫   ♫

DURING THE PROCESS OF SEARCHING out ways to sell and promote this book, I happened upon several groups on Yahoo whose main interest is "easy-listening music." The members of these groups defy the current trend of music appreciation toward the loud and the vulgar; preferring the pleasant and romantic sounds of instrumental music—especially arrangements featuring *strings*. These people even have the guts to call this genre "elevator music." I was flabbergasted to find out that my recordings of The Hollyridge Strings, as well as the Stu Phillips Orchestra releases, are among some of their favorites. Now that they have discovered that I am still alive and kicking, I have been besieged with e-mails from these nice folks. The discovery that my old instrumental arrangements are being compared favorably to those of my past idols–Dave Rose, Morton Gould, Percy Faith, *et al*–has really given me renewed enthusiasm about my career accomplishments.

♫   ♫   ♫

IN CHAPTER X, WHERE I wrote about my experiences at Epic Records, one of the artists that I mentioned very briefly was Nancy Ames. Nancy and I recorded an album entitled *Spiced with Brasil*. It was an LP featuring pop songs, as well as Brazilian melodies, in a *bossa nova* format. The disc, unfortunately, was not a big seller, which may be why I neglected to mention it in the appropriate chapter. While surfing the Internet, I came across a CD of our collaboration recently issued by a Japanese company and immediately ordered it. When it arrived at my home and I looked at the cover, with Nancy Ames pretty face smiling at me, I suddenly felt an urge to find Nancy and see if she was aware of this CD. Bottom line: after a great deal of Internet searching, I located her. Nancy is alive and well and thriving in Texas. I sent her an e-mail and when I received an answer I was elated. Not only did Nancy remember me (we hadn't seen each other or spoken for 33 years), but also she was just as excited as I was to renew an old friendship. I look forward to our getting together in the very near future.

♫   ♫   ♫

ROBERT JASON, WITH WHOM I collaborated on several songs during the early '80s, has once again entered my life. In April of this year, Paul Petersen and a friend of his, Don Blanton, approached me about finding a song to use as theme music for a talk-radio program they were putting together. After weighing all the various possibilities, they opted for a new composition and asked if might be interested in writing it. I called Robert in Nashville and extended to him the opportunity to work on the song with me; he was delighted that we could once again team up. In the following month the song was written without our ever physically meeting. (We utilized the telephone, faxes, mp3 and the US mail.) The final product was well received by Paul and Don, and we are now awaiting word about the show itself. A pleasant result of this renewed friendship with Robert is his sincere interest in helping to promote this book. He has offered to work on my behalf in the Nashville area to publicize and campaign for *"Stu Who?"* Robert and his wife Skye are true friends.

♫   ♫   ♫

HAVING RECENTLY DISCOVERED THAT out there in cyber-space—from the UK to Scandinavia, from Japan to Australia—that I have fans that I never knew about, I must take this opportunity to express my gratitude to them for their continued interest in my music. I am indeed fortunate to have found this out in time to include this heartfelt thank-you as the final words of my story.

♫   ♫   ♫

Fine

FILM CREDITS

"Mad Dog" Coll (1961)   Telly Savalas, Jerry Orbach, John Chandler, Vincent Gardenia

Katie's Private Lot (1961)   Dramatic short subject

Man from the Diner's Club (1963)   Danny Kaye, Telly Savalas, George Kennedy, Martha Hyer Cara Williams

Ride the Wild Surf (1964)   Shelley Fabares, Fabian, Tab Hunter, Barbara Eden, Peter Brown

Good Neighbor Sam (1964)   Jack Lemmon, Romy Schneider, Mike
   (Pre-production music supervisor)   Connors

Dead Heat on a Merry-go-round (1966)   James Coburn, Camilla Sparv, Aldo Ray

Hells Angels on Wheels (1967)   Jack Nicholson, Adam Roarke

Angels from Hell (1968)   Tom Stern, Jack Starrett

Run Angel Run (1968)   Bill Smith

Follow Me (1967-68)   (Surfing semi-documentary)

The Name of the Game is Kill (1969)   Jack Lord, Susan Strasberg, Collin Wilcox, Tisha Sterling

The Gay Deceivers (1969)   Larry Casey, Brooke Bundy

2000 Years Later (1969)   Terry -Thomas, Pat Harrington, Monte Rock, Casey Kasem

The Curious Female (1969)   Angelique Pettyjohn

The Appointment (1969)   Omar Sharif, Anouk Aimee, LotteLenya

The Losers (1970)   Bill Smith, Jack Starrett

Beyond the Valley of the Dolls (1970)   Dolly Read, Cynthia Myers, Edy Williams

Simon, King of the Witches (1971)   Andrew Prine, Brenda Scott

The Seven Minutes (1971)   Marianne McAndrew, Yvonne DeCarlo, Philip Carey

Jud (1971)   Claudia Jennings, Joseph Kaufman

A Time to Every Purpose (1972) (AKA: Pickup on 101)   Martin Sheen, Lesley Ann Warren, Jack Albertson

Macon County Line (1974)   Max Baer, Jr., Alan Vint, Jesse Vint

How to Seduce a Woman (1974)   Angus Duncan, Heidi Bruhl

The Meal (1974)   Dina Merrill, Carl Betz

Throw out the Anchor (1974)   Dina Merrill, Richard Egan

Fast Charlie, the Moonbeam Rider (1978)   David Carradine, Brenda Vaccaro

♫   ♫   ♫

TELEVISION CREDITS

The Donna Reed Show (1962-66)   Donna Reed, Carl Betz, Shelley Fabares, Paul Petersen

Gidget (1966)   Sally Field

Rock-a-bye the Infantry (Pilot 60s)   William Bendix, Bobby Rydell

The Monkees (1966-68)   Davy Jones, Mike Nesmith, Peter Tork, Mickey Dolenz

The Barbara Rush Show (Pilot)   Barbara Rush

From Here to Eternity (1st Pilot)   William Devane

Then Came Bronson (1970)   Michael Parks

Medical Center (early '70s)   Chad Everett

The Six Million Dollar Man (Pilot)(1973)   Lee Majors, Britt Ekland, Richard Anderson

McCloud (1974-78)   Dennis Weaver

Switch (1975)   Robert Wagner, Eddie Albert, Sharon Gless

Quincy (1976)	Jack Klugman
Get Christie Love (1974)	Teresa Graves, Harry Guardino
Windows and Doors (Pilot)	Bill Dana (Producer/Writer)
Hardy Boys and Nancy Drew (1977-78)	Shaun Cassidy, Parker Stevenson, Pamela Sue Martin
Benny & Barney (Pilot) (1977)	Terry Kiser, Tim Thomerson, Jane Seymour
Battlestar Galactica (1978-80)	Lorne Green, Dirk Benedict, Richard Hatch
Spiderman (1978)	Nicholas Hammond
Buck Rogers (1979)	Gil Gerard, Erin Gray
BJ and the Bear (1980)	Greg Evigan
Sheriff Lobo (1980)	Claude Akins
Fitz and Bones (1981)	Smothers Brothers
Knight Rider (1981)	David Hasselhoff
The Fall Guy (1981-86)	Lee Majors, Heather Thomas
Chicago Story (1982)	Maud Adams, Dennis Franz,
Masquerade (1984)	Greg Evigan, Kirstie Alley, Rod Taylor
Automan (1984)	Desi Arnaz, Jr.
Manimal (1984)	Simon MacCorkindale,
Half Nelson (1985-86)	Joe Pesci
The Highwayman (1987-88)	Sam Jones
Harry's Girls (Main Title Song) (1963)	Larry Blyden

♪   ♪   ♪

MOVIES OF THE WEEK AND TV SPECIALS

Bell & Howell Close-up	1960	(ABC)	Documentary
Do Not Enter	1960	(ABC)	Documentary
Small World	1960	(ABC)	Documentary

The John Glenn Special	1961	(ABC)	Documentary
Evening in Byzantium	1978		Glenn Ford, Erin Gray, Vince Edwards, Shirley Jones
Midnight Lace	1979		Mary Crosby
Waikiki	1980		Dack Rambo, Donna Mills
Rooster	1982		Paul Williams, Pat McCormick, Jill St. John, J.D.Cannon
In Like Flynn	1986		Jenny Seagrove, Robert Weber
Road Raiders	1988		Bruce Boxleitner, Susan Diol

LETTERS, TELEGRAMS, & STUFF

THE WHITE HOUSE

WASHINGTON

May 22, 1997

Stu Phillips

Greetings to the members of the High School of Music and Art's Class of January 1947 as you gather to celebrate the fiftieth anniversary of your graduation.

The Class of January 1947 has contributed so much to America during some of the most dramatic and historic times in our nation's history. Each of you can take pride in being part of a generation that has enhanced our nation and added to the legacy of the High School of Music and Art. I know you will enjoy your time together as you reflect on the enduring bonds you share.

Best wishes for a memorable celebration.

Bill Clinton

THE CITY OF NEW YORK
OFFICE OF THE MAYOR
NEW YORK, N.Y. 10007

Stu Phillips

June 8, 1997

Dear Friends:

As you gather for the 50th reunion of the graduating class of The High School of Music and Art, please accept my warmest greetings. This is a special occasion as the graduating class of January, 1947 gathers together to reminisce and recount their experiences and accomplishments over the last 50 years.

On behalf of the residents of New York City I congratulate all those attending this reunion for their achievements during the past five decades. I would also like to take this opportunity to express my appreciation to those associated with this reunion for their contributions to the High School of Music and Art and to the community. I wish you the very best, and hope that you will have health and happiness for many years to come.

Please accept my best wishes for an enjoyable and successful reunion.

Sincerely,

Rudolph W. Giuliani
Mayor

LOS ANGELES PHILHARMONIC ASSOCIATION

AT THE MUSIC CENTER
AND HOLLYWOOD BOWL

ZUBIN MEHTA
Music Director

ROCCO C. SICILIANO
President

EDWARD W. CARTER
Chairman of the Board

ERNEST FLEISCHMANN
Executive Director

July 5, 1978

Mr. Stu Phillips
3293 Fryman Road
Studio City, Ca. 91604

Dear Mr. Phillips:

Thank you so much for your very kind letter of June 26. It was prominently
displayed on the Orchestra's bulletin board, and everyone was most touched
to read it.

Good luck with Galactica, and we all hope that we may collaborate with you
on other ventures.

Sincerely,

Ernest Fleischmann

EF/p

135 NORTH GRAND AVENUE, LOS ANGELES, CALIFORNIA 90012. 213 972-7300, CABLE: LAPHILORCH LOS ANGELES

TWENTIETH CENTURY-FOX FILM CORPORATION

P. O. BOX 900, BEVERLY HILLS, CALIFORNIA   90213

PHONE: (213) 277-2211   CABLE ADDRESS: CENTFOX, LOS ANGELES - TELEX: 6-74875

December 3, 1970

Mr. Stu Phillips
3293 Fryman Road
Studio City, Calif. 91604

Dear Stu:

I enclose herewith two (2) letters, one
from Ed Shanaphy (together with a disc) and
another from Tim Johnson with accompanying
sheet music. You might give it a once-over,
whatever it is worth. I enclose carbon
copies of their correspondence and enclosures.

I think "Love Train" is the greatest you have
produced. It's a great comfort to have you
on THE SEVEN MINUTES.

Sincerely,

Russ Meyer

P.S. I enjoyed the letter from Jim Wnoroski.

DIVISION OF METRO-GOLDWYN-MAYER INC., Metro-Goldwyn-Mayer Studios, Culver City, California 90230

MGM
TELEVISION

November 17, 1969

Mr. Stuart Phillips
3293 Fryman Road
Studio City, Calif   91604

Dear Stu:

That sure was a beautiful score you did for us. I am
sorry I had to leave so early, but I have heard the
answer print and I am immensely pleased.

Thank you again for lending us the use of your talent.

Sincerely,

Bob

Bob Justman

RJ/DM

Entr'acte Recording Society Inc. • P.O. Box 2319 • Chicago, Illinois 60690

22 August, 1978

Mr. Stuart Phillips
3293 Fryman Road
Studio City, CA 91604

Dear Mr. Phillips:

I'm not one given to writing letters based on first
impressions; this, however, is an exception.

I can only tell you that in my opinion your score for
<u>Battlestar Galactica</u> is without question the finest score
yet written for a television production. And it comes
pretty damn close to the best written by Friedhofer,
Herrmann, Waxman and Rozsa for the cinema.

And it's light-years (even eons!) ahead of <u>Star Wars</u> in
originality, brilliance, and sheer musicianship. Words
alone are not enough to explain my admiration for your
accomplishment.

Hopefully I can tell you more over the phone when I am
next in L.A. the week of the 26th of October (I am
mastering the original score of Hugo's <u>Best Years of Our
Lives</u>, which Emil Newman and I will record the previous
week with the London Philharmonic).

You tell Harry Garfield that whatever he paid you for
<u>BSG</u> should be doubled!

Cordially yours,

John Steven Lasher
President

JSL/ah

TONY OWEN
9601 WILSHIRE BOULEVARD
BEVERLY HILLS

December 29, 1965

Mr. Stu Phillips
3354 Wrightview Place
Studio City, California

Dear Stu:

The gold Rolls Royce key is sensational. I sure appreciate it!

Hope you, Dori and little Toni
will have a Happy, Healthy and Prosperous
New Year.

See you soon - and many thanks
again!

Love and kisses -

TONY OWEN

COLUMBIA PICTURES CORPORATION
1438 NO. GOWER STREET
HOLLYWOOD 28, CALIFORNIA

OFFICE OF
JONIE TAPS

STUDIO EXECUTIVE

March 23, 1961

Stu Phillips
Colpix
New York Office

Dear Stu:

I finally got a chance to listen
to your cues from MAD DOG COLL. Your
musical approach to the various moods
is excellent particularly the jazz
approach. I would like very much to
hear more of your legitimate type of
writing but from what I've already
heard I would say that you have an
excellent overall musical background.
It would be very interesting to hear
the music with the picture as it is
rather difficult to judge anyone's
dramatic approach just from listening
to the music alone.

Kindest personal regards.

Cordially,

JONIE TAPS

JT:aw
cc: Paul Wexler

AMERICAN SOCIETY OF CINEMATOGRAPHERS

1782 NORTH ORANGE DRIVE • HOLLYWOOD, CALIFORNIA 90028 • (213) 876-5080

OFFICERS

HARRY WOLF
PRESIDENT

LEONARD SOUTH
VICE PRESIDENT

HOWARD SCHWARTZ
VICE PRESIDENT

CHARLES WHEELER
VICE PRESIDENT

ALFRED KELLER
SECRETARY

JOSEPH WESTHEIMER
TREASURER

JACK COOPERMAN
SERGEANT-AT-ARMS

**BOARD OF
GOVERNORS**

HOWARD ANDERSON
JOSEPH BIROC
JACK COOPERMAN
STANLEY CORTEZ
LINWOOD G. DUNN
WILLIAM A. FRAKER
MILTON KRASNER
PHILIP LATHROP
HOWARD SCHWARTZ
LESTER SHORR
LEONARD SOUTH
TED VOIGTLANDER
JOSEPH WESTHEIMER
CHARLES WHEELER
HARRY WOLF

KEMP NIVER
MUSEUM CURATOR

DAVID FLEMING
LEGAL COUNSEL

March 23, 1987

Mr. Stu Phillips
3293 Fryman Road
Studio City, 91604

Dear Stu,

On behalf of the Awards Committee of the American
Society of Cinematographers, we would like to take
this opportunity to thank you for your participation
in making our historic First Annual Awards for
Excellence in Cinematography dinner such a successful and rewarding event.

Your help was greatly appreciated. Thank you.

Most Sincerely,

Michael Margulies
Chairman, Awards Committee

Harry Wolf
President

:275:

WESTERN UNION
TELEGRAM
W. P. MARSHALL, PRESIDENT

CLASS OF SERVICE
This is a fast message unless its deferred character is indicated by the proper symbol.

SYMBOLS
DL = Day Letter
NL = Night Letter
LT = International Letter Telegram

SF-1201 (4-60)

The filing time shown in the date line on domestic telegrams is LOCAL TIME at point of origin. Time of receipt is LOCAL TIME at point of destination

KLA241 NC486

PD NEW YORK NY 27 524P EDT

STU PHILLIPS, COLPIX RECORDS

711 FITH AVE NYK

VERY HAPPY JIMMY DARRIN IS A SMASH. HOPE THIS IS THE BEGINNING

OF A SUCCEFFUL ASSOCIATION

AL NEVINS AND DON KIRSHNER.

WESTERN UNION
TELEGRAM
W. P. MARSHALL, PRESIDENT

CLASS OF SERVICE
This is a fast message unless its deferred character is indicated by the proper symbol.

SYMBOLS
DL = Day Letter
NL = Night Letter
LT = International Letter Telegram

SF-1201 (4-60)

The filing time shown in the date line on domestic telegrams is LOCAL TIME at point of origin. Time of receipt is LOCAL TIME at point of destination

1251P PDT APR 29 64 LA213

SSE097 L NHA068 (B KLBO181) PD KL NEW YORK NY 29 232P EDT

STU PHILLIPS

3354 WRIGHTWOOD DR STUDIO CITY CALIF

HAPPY YOU'RE ON THE TEAM. I'M SURE THIS TIME OUR ASSOCIATION

WILL NOT ONLY BE SWINGING, BUT A HAPPY ONE WITHOUT ANY PETTY

OBSTACLES IN OUR WAY. I'M SURE WITH THE COMBINATION OF ALL OUR

TALENT, WE CAN MAKE THIS ONE OF THE BIGGEST COMPANIES AROUND.

REGARDS TO JONIE AND YOUR FAMILY. LOVE YA

DONNIE (KIRSHNER

(41).

WESTERN UNION
TELEGRAM

NIA114 DEB272

DE IDB399 PD INDIANAPOLIS IND 7 352P EST

1963 Mar 7 PM 4 07

STU PHILLIPS

  11 RIVERSIDE DRIVE NYK

CONGRATULATIONS TO YOU BOTH ON THE NEW ARRIVAL TONI

  BRUNO SARDI AND PAUL PETERSEN

(04).

WESTERN UNION
TELEGRAM

NN787 OA583

O LWA095 NL PD LOSANGELES CALIF 9

1962 MAR 9 PM 10 59

STU PHILLIPS

  COLPIX RECORDS 711 5 VE NYK

DEAR STU JUST WANT YOU TO KNOW MY FRIEND QUOTE JOHNNY ANGEL
UNQUOTE AND I WILL BE ETERNALLY GRATEFUL TO YOU, HONESTLY WITHOUT
YOU STU, NONE OF THIS WOULD EVER HAVE BEEN POSSIBLE. I'M LOOKING
FORWARD TO SEEING YOU AGAIN SO VERY SOON. LOTS OF LOVE

SHELLEY

WESTERN UNION
TELEGRAM
W. P. MARSHALL, PRESIDENT

CLASS OF SERVICE
This is a fast message unless its deferred character is indicated by the proper symbol.

SF-1201 (4-60)

SYMBOLS
DL = Day Letter
NL = Night Letter
LT = International Letter Telegram

The filing time shown in the date line on domestic telegrams is LOCAL TIME at point of origin. Time of receipt is LOCAL TIME at point of destination

108P PDT JUN 28 63 LB142
SA183 BA398 B AHD077 PD FAX NEW YORK NY 28 333P EDT
STU PHILLIPS, CARE SIDNEY GOLDSTEIN, EDWIN H MORRIS & CO INC
   1777 NORTH VINE ST HOLLYWOOD CALIF
DEAR STU: WE JUST HEARD YOUR GREAT "BIRDIE" ALBUM. IT IS ABSOLUTELY
MARBELOUS. THANKS FOR DOING SUCH AN AFFECTIONATE JOB
   CHARLES STROUSE AND LEE ADAMS
(40).

WESTERN UNION
TELEGRAM
W. P. MARSHALL, PRESIDENT

CLASS OF SERVICE
This is a fast message unless its deferred character is indicated by the proper symbol.

SF-1201 (4-60)

SYMBOLS
DL = Day Letter
NL = Night Letter
LT = International Letter Telegram

The filing time shown in the date line on domestic telegrams is LOCAL TIME at point of origin. Time of receipt is LOCAL TIME at point of destination

KLA076 SYG132
SY PGA165 CGN PD PITTSBURGH PENN 8 1119A EST
STU PHILLIPS, COLPIX RECORDS   1961 Mar 8
   711 FIFTH AVE NYK
DEAR STU OUR SINCERE CONGRATULATIONS ON YOUR PROMOTION AS MUSICAL
DIRECTOR WE ARE BOTH PLEASED AND PROUD TO BE ASSOCIATED WITH
YOU AND COLPIX MAY THE FUTURE BRING YOU CONTINUED AND EVEN
GREATER SUCCESS WARMEST REGARDS
   THE SKYLINERS AND JOE.

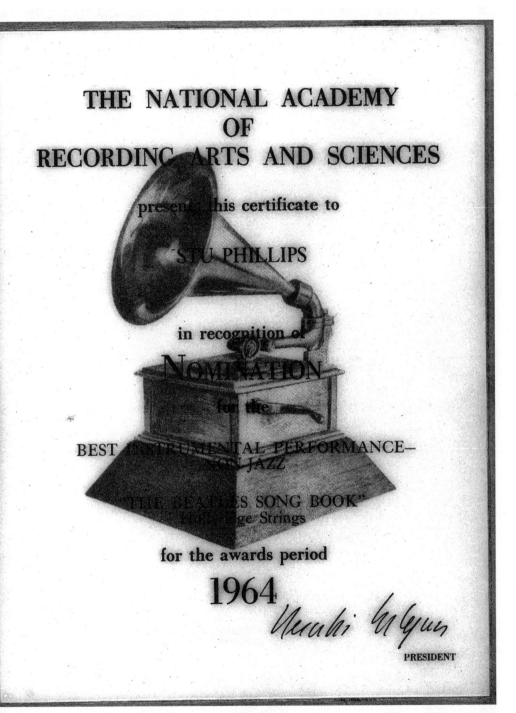

THE NATIONAL ACADEMY
OF
RECORDING ARTS AND SCIENCES

presents this certificate to

STU PHILLIPS

in recognition of

NOMINATION

for the

BEST INSTRUMENTAL PERFORMANCE—
NON-JAZZ

"THE BEATLES SONG BOOK"
Hollyridge Strings

for the awards period

1964

PRESIDENT

Your Grammy Nomination

STU PHILLIPS, Composer

Has been nominated in the Twenty-First Annual Grammy Awards for:

"BATTLESTAR GALACTICA"

In the category of:

BEST ORIGINAL SCORE WRITTEN FOR A MOTION PICTURE
OR TELEVISION SPECIAL

Co-Nominees: JOHN TARTAGLIA, GLEN LARSON and
               SUE COLLINS, Co-Composers

The National Academy of Recording Arts & Sciences
January 1979

INDEX

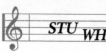 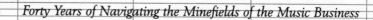

PLACES INDEX

PHOTO CREDITS

Unless otherwise noted, photos are from the personal collection of Stu Phillips.

Pg. 121	James Darren (Courtesy James Darren)	1961
Pg. 126	Shelley Fabares (Courtesy Shelley Fabares)	1961
Pg. 127	The Donna Reed Show cast (Courtesy Donna Reed Festival)	1959
Pg. 128	Paul Petersen (Courtesy Paul Petersen)	1961
Pg. 130	Darren, Fabares & Petersen	1963
Pg. 131	Jorge Bolet and me	1963
Pg. 133	Donna Reed (Courtesy Donna Reed Festival)	N/A
Pg. 134	Donna Reed and Dori Phillips	1963
Pg. 137	Danny Kaye (unknown source)	circa 1950
Pg. 137	One Sheet/*Man from the Diner's Club* (Collectable)	1963
Pg. 151	Variety ad for the Hollyridge Strings	1964
Pg. 152	Karl Engemann, Tom Morgan & me (Capitol Records) (Cashbox)	1964
Pg. 156	Vince Edwards (Dr. Ben Casey)	1964
Pg. 157	Bronislaw Caper, Charley Albertine and me	1964
Pg. 160	The all star band for the film *Good Neighbor Sam*	1964
Pg. 161	Rainbow Room newspaper ad	1963
Pg. 162	Hollyridge Strings gag photo	1964
Pg. 163	David Jones and Toni Phillips	1967
Pg. 167	Bob Crane and me	1968
Pg. 168	Bobby Vinton, Bob Morgan and me (Las Vegas) (Cashbox)	1968
Pg. 170	Screen credit cel from *Hells Angels on Wheels* (Courtesy Fanfare Films)	1969
Pg. 173	*Tammy's Greatest Hits* album cover (Tammy Wynette, courtesy of Epic Records)	1969

GLOSSARY

"WE WANT CANTOR," CHANGES: Back in the old days ('40s & '50s), and even currently, a particular progression of harmonies (chords), which was very often employed by many songwriters, were sometimes called the "We Want Cantor changes." It derived its name from the notes used in the bass-line, which happened to be the same notes sung when the expression "We Want Cantor" was chanted on the Eddie Cantor radio show. "Blue Moon" and "Heart and Soul" are two such examples of songs utilizing these changes.

A SCORE: The actual notes on paper from which the individual musician's parts are extracted. Scoring a movie is synonymous with composing music for a film. Since the early 1970's the words SONG SCORE are also used to describe a group of songs used in the film as background music.

A&R/A&R MAN: The letters stand for "Artist & Repertoire." It originally was a term used to designate the person responsible for discovering and signing an artist, and then acquiring the songs for them to perform. The term is now all-encompassing, covering all of the above and includes the actual producing and recording of the artist and material.

ARRANGEMENT/ARRANGER: Musical arrangers contribute to an existing piece of music what an interior decorator might contribute to a home; decorate it. Arrangers may make changes in the harmonies, the tempo, rhythms and on occasion, even make slight changes to the melody. The result of their labor is called an ARRANGEMENT.

CLICK TRACK: A conductor's aid in keeping in sync with the picture. It is akin to a metronome. In the early years (1930s to 1960s), the click was produced by punching holes in the film, which made the most irritating sound imaginable. Currently, it is done electronically.

DUBBING-DOWN: In records or film, the term refers to the process of combining all the elements involved in the project. In a film dub-down, it would include: dialogue, sound effects, music etc. In the mix-down of a record, vocal and orchestra (band) are the usual ingredients.

FREE TIME: In the context of film scoring, it designates conducting the music without the aid of a click track. (See CLICK TRACK.) Free time utilizes only markings placed on the film as an aid to the conductor.

JINGLE: In the years in question 1959-1975, any piece of music, whether vocal or instrumental, serious or comic, written to be played on radio or TV during the advertisement of a product, was referred to as a "jingle." It's possible that the term is still in vogue.

LIP-SYNC: When you view a singer performing a song in a movie or TV show, you are seeing what is generally referred to as a "lip-sync." This a process whereby the vocal and musical accompaniment are recorded before hand. The singer then mimes the vocal as the recording is played. On occasion, the singer will sing live to a pre-recorded track. Rarely, the singer and band will record and film live.

MUSIC EDITOR: A person of invaluable assistance to a composer. He/she will break down the scene to be scored to a tenth of a second if needed. They will write scene descriptions, and during the recording double check all the important film "hits." After the session they will make whatever cuts are necessary to help the music fit the picture.

ONE SHEET: An advertising poster for a film. It is generally exhibited in the lobby or outside the theater. Through the years, they have become collectibles and some are worth a great deal of money.

ORCHESTRATION/ORCHESTRATOR: Unlike an arranger, an orchestrator makes almost no major changes in the music given to him by a composer or arranger. He simply transfers to score paper the notes and ideas presented to him. About the only addition an orchestrator may sometimes make, is expanding the instrument range of the composition to better utilize the full orchestra. (Note: Some composers, who have worked with the same orchestrator for a long time, may very often rely on him/her to add a great deal more to the score then is the norm.)

PUBLIC DOMAIN: A piece of music that has outlasted the life of its copyright protection. Even though a composer is still credited as the writer, he/she has no rights to the music. (The most obvious examples of P.D. would be Bach, Mozart, Beethoven, etc.)

SCORE/SCORING/TO SCORE: The process of recording music for a theatrical film or television show or any other similar medium.

SCORE: Not to be confused with the above definition. This score refers to the act of having sex.

SCORING WILD: The process of recording music to film without the actual film being utilized (projected) as an aid in the procedure. The composer will usually use click tracks and a clock as his/her only aids.

SESSION: Means about the same in any context. In music, it refers to a gathering of musicians in a recording studio to record music.

SKETCH: An abbreviated score. Sometimes extremely brief, consisting of just the bare essentials. (Sort of like jotting down some ideas before you write a letter.) At other times, it can be so complete that almost nothing needs to be added when orchestrating the sketch.

STREAMER: A mark placed on the film to aid the conductor in keeping the music in sync with the action. The streamer runs diagonally across the screen from left to right, and at the end, the film is punched (a hole is made) so that a quick flash of white light fills the screen. The length of the streamer is generally determined by the tempo of the piece of music.

TIN PAN ALLEY: A mythical section of NYC, honored as the home of the great songwriters from the turn of the century to the mid-1900s. In reality, it was an area in midtown Manhattan where the bulk of the music publishers' offices were located.

TRACK/TRACKING: To track a film, is to use pre-existing music instead of newly-composed music, as the musical score of the movie. This has been in practice since the very early days of filmdom. Mainly, it was used in the print that was shown to preview audiences. Soon, some low- budget independent filmmakers began tracking final-release prints. It is a device currently used for demonstration purposes.

WILD: See **Scoring wild.**

Give the Gift of

"Stu Who?"

to Your Friends and Colleagues

CHECK YOUR LEADING BOOKSTORE OR ORDER HERE

❑ **YES**, I want _____ copies of *"Stu Who?" Forty Years of Navigating the Minefields of the Music Business* at $29.95 each, plus $4.95 shipping per book (California residents please add $2.47 sales tax per book). Canadian orders must be accompanied by a postal money order in U.S. funds. Allow 15 days for delivery.

My check or money order for $_____ is enclosed.

Name _____

Organization _____

Address _____

City/State/Zip _____

Phone_____ E-mail _____

Please make your check payable and return to:

cisum press
12400 Ventura Blvd., Box 663
Studio City, CA 91604

or order online at
cisumpress.com